Prototype

The Lost and Forgotten Series

Robert D. Gallagher

ISBN 13: 9798590650897

Dedication

To Dylan, my Son & Judy
You both mean the world to me.

Acknowledgements

James Miller, aka Sgt. Cobb
Judy Matthews
Mark Matthews
Your help has been both inspirational and supportive.

Prologue

I'VE BROKEN OUT of more high-security prisons than anybody else alive today—not that our average federation citizen even knows many of the places I've been locked up in. Why? Because I like to steal things. Also, it's really the only profession I know. It also beats wasting your life rotting in a six-by-eight cell sucking down biofeed through a straw for the rest of your life, and in the time it takes federal security to grab my arse, at least I get to stretch my legs, eat some real food, and plan my next job.

Well, here we are again, back in a federal shuttle heading to the next piece-of-crap hellhole of a high-security federation establishment in, goddamn, I haven't a clue what sector of space. It wouldn't be so bad, I guess, but you don't get to travel conscious; instead, you travel in Dreamtime federation rehabilitation stasis, and you get brain fed all the federation indoctrination-is-family bull. Well, except for me. For some reason, the part of the brain that 99.9 percent of the human species have, I don't, so all I get is a few weeks of garbled, indistinguishable white noise, and, boy, what a headache.

So, you may ask, why do I get the pleasure of being the federation's most-wanted pain in the arse? Well, it's not easy, but I'm actually kind of good at it. Let's just say it comes naturally to me. However, I guess that on this occasion, it's because I stole a new prototype, a kind of technology that I felt the federation had no right to have exclusive access to.

The problem with having such a high moral standpoint in regard to such things is that you get chased around the galaxy by the feds or whatever bounty-hunting group that feels they have what it takes to bring me in. I guess this time, someone has done their job well—maybe a little too well. In fact, I would say they've set some kind of record by getting me so fast, but at least I got to eat out at my favourite restaurant.

As I often say, here we go again. It seems I've been saying that almost my whole life, and it's not such a bad life: I have a penthouse, I own expensive cars, and I even have my own hangar, but what really bugs me is this goddamn white-noise-passing-through-my-neural-cortex garbage.

It's not the best experience, but at least I arrive at my new accommodations, fresh and just busting to get the chance to break out and run free again for the next few weeks. This time, however, something feels different. When I say "different," I mean the security guards are not your usual federal goons. The shuttle is not your usual federal shuttle. In fact, I've never seen a craft like it. Even the usual blah, blah, blah going-away-for-the-rest-of-your-life bull crap is on a whole new level of overdramatic life-sentence speech from the so-called high judge.

. . .

"As the defendant has not and will not relent on the whereabouts of the stolen Prototype; Also noted that the defendant has refused to defend himself in any way to mitigate the severity of his transgressions; I have no other course of action but to find the defendant guilty. I hereby sentence you to be incarcerated in the highest federal detention facility for the rest of your life. There will be no parole. Life means life. Take the prisoner away."

.　.　.

"Well, it looks like we're here."
Lights buzz to life as the federation rehabilitation dream feed ends and is replaced by a small holographic welcome image of a space station slowly spinning in a sea of darkness.

"Prisoner M2950, you have arrived at the federation's highest-graded prison within known space. Your crime has been deemed severe enough that you have been brought to this facility. Your sentence will end upon your death. No one has ever escaped from this facility, and no one has ever left this facility alive. We hope that you work hard and adjust well to your new home. Welcome to Facility Zero."

The shuttle door opens with a hiss as lights blink on one at a time with an audible buzz. The line of lights illuminates an otherwise darkened corridor, the walls indistinct, almost as if there are no walls except for where the light seems to end suddenly, and endless darkness begins. Finally, the last light blinks on, illuminating a man in his late forties standing at the end of this short corridor, watching. He smiles warmly.

"Welcome to Facility Zero. My name is Alistair Brookes. I'm the architect of this place, and I'll be your guide."

1
Welcome to Facility Zero

Facility Zero, 170 days online: federation year 2424
STEPPING OUT OF the shuttle into the short corridor, noticing that I'm the only arrival, I approach the man calling himself Alistair Brookes. I certainly wasn't expecting a welcoming like this, so lacking in security goons.

"You must be Sam McCall. I've just been reading your file—very interesting. I'm sure you have much to ask, but firstly I'm going to run through a few basics of Facility Zero," Alistair Says.

"Okay," I reply, not really ready for asking questions yet, and I just step in line as the guide turns and proceeds down the corridor, seemingly not worried for his own safety. The lights buzz to life as we walk along, showing that the corridor isn't as short as it looked before. Then Alistair Brookes begins to talk.

"This is the first of the federation's fully self-contained, self-ruled, highest-security penal stations. I realize it's a lot to take in, but what I'm about to explain will help with your transition from living in the outside world to starting a new life within these walls," Alistair says, Motioning with his hands toward the shadowy corridor walls, and continues.

"The station can change its inward appearance depending on what's required of it. If the truth be known, the station is just a series of open spaces upon multiple levels separated by artificially generated void walls. Trying to pass through these voids would result in being thrown back, leading to serious injuries and possibly death. Mixed within the void wall space are sound-frequency-nullification generators—in effect, noise can't penetrate," Alistair pauses for a moment, looking at me with another of his calming smiles, and then continues his explanations.

"You are most likely wondering why I do not worry for my own safety. Well, that's easily explained. The facility is constantly monitoring its current guests, and if it detects any adverse emotional displays, it will immediately place that person into Dreamtime. It's quick and efficient, and the punishments it carries out will seem real. The effects can last for months."

"Effects?" I ask.

"Effects, well, yes—these can be anything from solitary confinements to more serious punishments, and all carried out within Dreamtime," Alistair explains.

We continue to walk, taking a turn here and there. I can understand the lack of security and fear for its new arrivals—clever, really, but not effective on me. Then again, I don't really feel the need to exercise my inner anger at this point, and besides, the guy seems generally nice.

We enter a large open space about the size of a basketball court. Tables are lined up in the centre of the room—three lines of tables separated by a four-foot gap every ten feet or so. Along the back wall is aligned a set of food dispensers, and along the main wall are what looks to be disposal slots for trays and all.

"And here we are at the main communal dining hall. Meals are at 0700 hours, 1300 hours, and 1900 hours. Miss the time, you miss the meal. Now we are early for breakfast, so I'll just explain how to get about this place without getting yourself lost or killed," Alistair explains, giving me another grin, this one not so calming, more dangerous.

"All you need to do is ask out loud to be taken to your room, and the system will illuminate a path for you. Watch," Alistair says, raising his voice slightly.

"Give me directions to Sam McCall's room, please," Alistair asks.

A corridor opens up within what was just a wall. Lights buzz to life along with it, leading away from the dining hall and turning right. We enter this new corridor and follow the path. It's surprisingly quick, and within five or maybe ten minutes, we arrive at a reasonable ten-by-ten room containing a bed, washing facilities and a toilet, a small locker, and a monitor. We both enter the room, and the corridor vanishes as a wall appears where the door was just moments ago.

"As you can see, not too hard, and very secure with only a few staff members who can access your room, plus yourself, obviously. Lights out at 2100 hours. This must be observed, or you will be punished. No visiting other cells, or you will be punished. Duties that have been assigned to you will be displayed on the monitor at 0630 hours; you must carry them out, or you will be punished. Now, normally the system won't assign anything to you for the first few days, just to allow you to settle in, and I doubt very much that there will be any exceptions for you. That's about it for now. Any questions?" Alistair asks.

I'm a bit surprised by the whole thing for a moment and just stand there staring at him. This facility is way beyond anything I ever would have expected the federation to come up with without a word of it slipping out. Brookes just stares back with an understanding smile and lets me gather my thoughts.

"Well, why are you still here? If you are the architect, why the meet and greet?" That's all I can think to ask. Brookes just smiles and replies.

"That is a story for another time," Alistair says and turns.

"My room, please," Alistair asks, and the corridor opens up once more, and lights buzz to life, leading away through the darkness. Then, looking back at me, he says,

"We will chat again, but normally I find it's a good idea to leave new arrivals alone for a day or two just to let them get over the shock. Breakfast is in about thirty minutes. You can either skip it or stay here—that's up to you. However, I would advise you not to skip too many meals. You can't put your health at risk, or you will be punished," Alistair says and leaves, the wall closes behind him. For the first time in my life, I feel concerned.

Slumping down on my new bed, I sit there for a while, trying to take it all in. Sitting changes to lying, and in no time, lying turns to sleep.

2
Nowhere Man

I awake with a start, my dreams becoming disturbing in some ways, but also normal, the image of a space station revolving in a sea of darkness; however, somehow, I feel like I am being watched. Looking around my room, I notice the clock on the monitor: 1830 hours.

Good, I'm starting to feel hungry. Getting up, I head to the wall where I entered earlier.

"Main dining hall," I ask, as the wall vanishes and a corridor buzz to life. Following the corridor, I arrive soon arrive at the dining hall, hearing nothing at all until I step over the threshold into the room when the sound hits me as a few heads turn to watch me enter.

The talking changes quickly to a quieter chatter, with more heads turning to see who the new guy is. I hear the occasional, "Hey, that's the new fish," as I walk over to the food dispenser, grab a tray of food, and head to an empty chair. After I sit down, the murmurs shift back to normal banter between inmates.

I find the food actually better than expected—a little bland, but hey, it's prison food; what do you expect? It fills a space. Relaxing a little, I look around. There's everything I've learned to expect to see in a high-security prison, and I know what to expect in the coming weeks. I realize some groups are already sizing me up; whatever their intentions, I'm sure I will be the first to know.

Then I spot something odd: a man in his early thirties, smart looking, but not dressed in prison fatigues. He's just sitting there, not eating, his eyes closed. Listening maybe. He opens his eyes and turns his head in my direction, and we make eye contact. The act, for some reason, just makes me shiver, and I break eye contact. I get up to take my tray over to the disposal units and slip the tray down into the chute, and when I look back toward the man, he's gone.

I sleep well that first night, and true to Brookes' words, the monitor displays no tasks for me the next day. I have breakfast; again, it's not too bad. Not sure what I'll think after a few weeks, or worse, months, but I'm hoping I can work out a way out of this place within the year.

So, I'm not worrying about the food in the long term. However, what is worrying me at lunch that same day is that the group of guys that eyeballed me on my first day are starting to have ideas about having themselves some fun. I, for one, am not in such a fun mood right now. I decide I'll skip dinner if I can survive lunch first.

Then, without warning, a fight erupts a few tables to my left, tables get overturned, and a chair is thrown at one of the assailants. Before the fight can gear up into more violence, it's over, Dreamtime kicks in, and four guys end up taking floor naps.

This will be interesting to see what happens next, but my table suddenly gets overcrowded right then. Looking around, I see that the good-time boys have made their move and much earlier than I expected.

"Heya there, new fishy," the taller of the five of my new best friends say, and oh boy, he's a cutie—broken nose, one and a half ears, decaying teeth, and arms sporting tats that mark him as a deep space wrecker, and I guess that his buddies are part of the same gang.

They're the sort that sets up a fake distress beacon far enough off of the transport lanes that it only shows up on expensive haulers' scans. Then the haulers see the chance to do a bit of salvaging—accidents do happen, but sadly in these setups, they normally are the ones that become salvage.

"Heya yourself," I reply, looking around at the others. More breaker tats. One's missing an eye. Nasty acid burns mark a third. Numbers four and five seem to be without any serious scars, but the way they're drooling, I think the harm is more a grey-matter-related malfunction.

"Me and my lads here been talking about you and decided we're going to make you our new plaything due to your pretty hair and white teeth and all," says the leader of the group. I blink, dumbfounded for a moment, before replying.

"Do you realize that no one talks like that anymore? It's just insanely stereotypical for cons in a place like this. You would've been more original if you'd said, 'Do you want to suck on my lollipop?'" I say, knowing then that this might not have been the smartest to say.

The big man's reply is faster than I expected as one of his large hands slam my head against the top of the table. At least I get to see stars again, but not the ones I like to see flying past.

I vaguely sense a sixth man arriving at the table, followed by a short discussion, I cannot hear very well, and then my new best friends get up and leave, leaving me alone with the newcomer.

It's the same guy I had a shiver about on my first day. Now he's sitting across from me regarding me with an odd look over his face, maybe one of curiosity.

"Hello, Sam. My name is Samuel," he says while holding out a hand to shake.

"Hello," I reply, shaking his hand. He's got a firm grip, confident.

"What did you say to the good-time boys?" I ask.

"Oh, nothing much. I just made it clear to them that I would like to chat with my friend here before more heads get broken. They caught on pretty quick and decided to leave. I doubt very much you will be bothered by them anymore," Samuel replies.

"Impressive. Do you have that effect often?" I Say.

"Only on the ones that fear for their lives. However, there are some areas that I would advise avoiding. The ones in those areas have no fear; rather, they enjoy causing it," he says with a slight hint of amusement.

"Thank you for the rescue, and now that my mind and body is safe, what can I do for you?" I ask.

He continues to gaze at me while I talk. For some reason, he still gives me the creeps, and in my experience, it's very seldom that someone does something for nothing, certainly not in a place like this. He just looks at me for a moment, measuring me up maybe.

"Nothing yet. However, there will come a time when I will want a favour, and I promise, nothing too serious," Samual says, and with that, he stands up, gives me a wink, and leaves before I can reply.

I return to my room, the good-time boys now avoiding me, along with all the whispers and comments. Maybe being friends with Samuel is not such a bad thing, so why are they so scared of him? Note to self, be wary of the helpful stranger, and find out more about him if possible. Maybe Brookes can cast a little light.

The next day arrives with no jobs. Breakfast passes with no issues and no sign of Samuel, and then the obvious hits me. I ask for my room, and a corridor opens up for me as usual. I take a few turns along my route back, and then I stop.

"Take me to the shuttle bay," I ask. Nothing happens. Security, I guess blocking my request, or else this place doesn't have a shuttle bay.

"Take me to the medical room," I ask, nothing at first, but just as I'm about to give up when the corridor shift direction. Ah, success. So, there are other places I'm allowed to visit.

"Take me to the facility's information room," I ask and again, nothing for a moment, but then the corridor changes, and another path opens up.

This time I follow it, and after a much longer walk, I arrive in a new room, this one empty but containing a single terminal and manuals stacked neatly on a bookshelf. I enter the room and step up to the terminal.

'Welcome to Facility Zero' is written on the screen. I recognize the style of the terminal and lightly tap the screen. The words "Please speak your request" appear. Simple enough, I think, and I say, "List areas I'm allowed access to," I ask, and a list appears on the screen:

Sam McCall's room
Dining hall
Information room
Workout gym
No other access has been granted at this time.

Hmm, okay. "List areas I'm not allowed access to."

"Information denied," the screen says.

Well, that's boring, I think. Having no other reason for being here, I head back to my room, where I spend a few hours getting even more bored. I eventually head for dinner, which is also uneventful. I start to wonder how many inmates here kill themselves out of pure boredom. The evening passes by without incident, and I turn in.

I'm awakened by a beeping noise coming from my monitor. Blearily opening my eyes, I try to focus on the screen. Slowly the writing comes into focus: 'New area access granted to the laundry room. Accessible only during your assigned hours for today only, 1000–1300 hours. Laundry duties, 1400–1900 hours.' Laundry duties—at bloody last, something to do.

I arrive at breakfast earlier than most and see the interesting sight of several corridors opening at once around the room as the prisoner's file into the dining hall in dribs and drabs. I realize that the system that controls all of this must be either very large or very advanced or maybe even both. I eat breakfast, which is ham and eggs and pretty tasty at that, and then I wait, feeling a little excited to have something to do today. At 1000 hours, I ask for directions to the laundry, and a short corridor opens up. Turns out the laundry is practically next door to the dining hall.

As I enter the room, the heat hits me. Several heads turn, and the person I assume to be the foreman of the room hands me a card.

"You put the card in the wall there," the foremen explain and points to the place where I just entered.

"Then it will tell you your duties for the morning jobs. Do it again in the afternoon, and you will most likely have another objective," the foreman says; I nod and thank him.

He's a short guy, clean-cut, with no obvious markings, in his sixties, I guess. I notice his limp as he approaches another guy entering the room.

I walk over to the place on the wall pointed out to me and insert my card. There's another beep, and a message appears on the small screen: 'Empty dirty laundry bins and fills washing drums.' Looking around the room, I soon spot where the laundry bins enter the room on what looks like a conveyer belt and then where the washing drums are. As I approach the area, a claxon sounds, and everyone starts to work. I soon get the hang of what's required:

Empty the laundry bins.
Fill the drums.
Empty the laundry bins.
Fill the drums.

It's relentless. As soon as the bins are empty and I turn away to drop the laundry into the drums, the containers whoosh away to be replaced with more full bins.

I'm quick on my feet at first, but after only thirty minutes, I've already slowed and am wishing I could be doing something else. By the time the claxon sounds again, signalling 1300 hours, my arms feel like they are on fire, and I'm so glad to be done.

"Okay, guys and girls, be back here in one hour," the foreman shouts. Oh, joy, I think to myself as I make my way to dinner.

I've been in enough of these facilities now to know a new inmate when I see one; I'm pretty sure I gave off the same look the first three or four times. But there she was, sitting and eating alone, looking around at everyone, almost like a nervous tic. I certainly can relate. Cute little thing... I can't imagine what she must have done to be sent here, but here she is, and I'm starting to feel sorry for her, knowing what's likely to happen at some point.

Then I notice movement from my left, and two guys with walks that say, 'We own this joint,' walk past me and move up to the new fish.

One guy comes up from the side and leans down toward her. The man's hand resting upon the table, adding support to his posture, and the other guy moves up from behind her but not too close.

I can't hear what the first guy says, but judging from the look on her face, it must not have been so nice. I start to stand, and then it happens fast: her right-hand stabs her fork down hard into the guy's hand where it rests upon the table, and at the same time, she twists her body slightly to the right and thrusts upward with the knife into the underside of the man's jawbone. Both the fork and knife shatter, as they are made from a material similar to plastic, but the sheer speed and force still manage to do some serious damage, and he goes down like a sack of potatoes.

His mate reacts, moving in and putting his arms around her, but too slow to stop her from standing and, with the same fluid motion, slamming the back of her head into her assailant's nose, breaking it with a dull, messy thud.

Before anything else can happen, their eyes glaze over, and Dreamtime takes over, effectively ending the fight. This all happens in less than five seconds, maybe four, and I realize now that I was feeling sorry for the wrong side.

The lights in the room flash, and lunchtime is over. Walking back into the laundry room, I insert my card, and the screen tells me that my task for the afternoon is to pick up the freshly washed items, place them into the presser and wrapper, and then stack the wrapped items five deep into boxes. These, in turn, are stacked onto another conveyer belt that takes the boxes away and out of the room.

I would like to take a look at where the conveyer belt leads, but the opportunity does not arise to go take a look. Everyone works hard, with the exception of two guys who seem to be whispering about something every chance they get. I suspect that they're up to something. The final claxon signifies the end of the shift. I eat well that evening and sleep even better.

I pull laundry duty all that week. I was right about my suspicions about the two guys chatting. One day, one of them causes a diversion while the second uses the conveyer belt to vanish from the room; he never returns, and his mate is questioned about the incident by the foreman and is released, only to disappear as well a few days later.

The cute new inmate I was initially worried about returned after a week. I can't say the same about her would-be attackers, though, and even Samuel has not been around for a bit. Maybe he's good at not eating. One of my other suspicions is realized when I overhear the foreman talk to Brookes about the excellent work we'd all done that week, asking about the other laundries and how we ranked. I manage to corner the foreman at the very end of the shift.

"Hope you don't mind me asking, but why does the facility need so much washing? I guess the dining hall could hold maybe four hundred to five hundred inmates at a push, but we seem to be washing for much bigger numbers," I ask. The foreman smiles and says.

"Ah, well, maybe looks can be deceiving. You only see around five hundred inmates, but I can assure you there are a lot more. Not sure how many exactly, but you are on just one of the levels of this facility. You might be surprised, but I overheard Brookes talking to one of his trustees—"

"His trustees?" I interrupt.

"Yeah, sure. Well, Brookes was the first to arrive here. It wasn't supposed to be, mind you. I heard it was some kind of accident. He was supposed to be on the outside when this place came online, but for whatever reason, he wasn't, so I guess that makes him the big cheese, so to speak.

Anyway, as I said, one of his trustees said that level three has had a few spaces become available, level four is almost full, and level five will come online in a day or two. So you might want to rethink your estimate from about six hundred to a larger number, more like up to three thousand inmates, but I'm not convinced that even that figure is what this place can hold in total," he finishes with a grin. I stand there for a moment, taking it all in—it's obvious, really—and then I ask

"So, do you really think this place is impossible to escape from?" I ask.

"Only thing I really know is that a lot of people try, like that chap the other day, using the conveyer belt. Yeah, I saw him, his feet at least, but he's new and took the chance to look about. Well, if he's lucky, he will find his way back with wild stories," The Forman says.

"And if he isn't lucky?" I interrupt again.

"If he isn't, well, we will find bits of him, I guess. Let's just say that it's better not to wander too far off the beaten path. Keep your head down, work hard, and you get better food for it, and sure, you will have a rather dull rest of your life, but a living one. So you better get used to not seeing the stars again. Have a good rest," He explains, and with that, he heads out of the laundry.

Bits of him, I think to myself. What the heck is this place? It's much larger than I first imagined. This is going to be a challenge.

I head for dinner, and the hall seems busier than normal. I realize why as I collect my tray of food—a roast of some kind, maybe chicken; pretty good, really—and I settle down and start to eat. I'm soon joined by a few other new faces, and I note that some of them are eating what I had on my first day, some kind of mysterious meat combination—bland, but it will keep you alive.

A conversation starts about the guys escaping from the laundry room. Wow, rumours spread fast. The conversation goes back and forth about what possible fate would be in store for them. Then, one of the newcomers to my table, a man in his late forties or fifties, called Frank, suddenly laughs, spitting out a mouthful of food after someone suggests that the escapees are likely to be halfway back to Earth by now.

"There's more chance we will be sent a troupe of dancing girls to entertain us than they are halfway back to Earth. Don't make me laugh. I'll tell you what I think most likely happened to our brave but stupid friends. They most likely wandered into an area you don't want to be lost in, and I'll tell you it's easier to find these places than I would like.

It happened to me once a few years back. The facility was having some power issues, which sadly are common in the main dining hall, and I decided to go back to my cell. Well, the corridor opened up okay, but after a few turns, my room never appeared, only more corridors. So, I asked again, 'Take me to my room,' more forcibly. The corridors reconfigured themselves, and I kept walking, but after a few more turns and still no cell, I started to worry. Then the lights start to flicker and blink out in places, and then I hear the voices... eerie, creepy voices, calling for me, heckling me.

Others here call them freakers, and they sure freaked the hell out of me. I legged it back the other way, shouting out,   'Take me to the main hall,' over and over. I was lucky the system eventually gave me a route back, and I got out of there. I warn you now, don't go off the grid. If you do and for too long, the system either deletes your access or forgets about you, and no matter what you do, it won't put you back on," Frank explains with wide eyes.

The others like me just sit there and stare with disbelief, this must be a joke from the old guy—let's scare the new kids; it's funny to try and scare the snot out of them—but he just sits there nodding as most of the people sitting around the table reply with their own scepticism. Some just up and leave, occasionally glancing back with looks that say, 'You're mad' until there's only a few of us left. The older guy stares back at the last of us, and with a lowered voice, he says.

"There are rumours about the first few inmates that were sent here in the early days, another level just like our own that was running well. But during the early years, when this station was sorting out a few running issues, the freakers broke in and killed almost all but a few that somehow managed to escape. Every now and again, when the power systems start to fluctuate, the corridor system becomes confused and reroutes unwary inmates to that level," Frank says in a whisper, his voice getting lower, and everyone draws in closer to hear what he says next.

"Never to be seen again," He's now whispering, and everyone's heads are now almost touching.

"But I know a secret, I know when the lights will start to fluctuate next—any second now," Frank whispers and almost on cue, the lights that signify the end of dinner starts to flicker, and almost everyone, including me, jumps up and looks around, panic-stricken. The old guy starts to laugh.

"It looks like it's time to turn in. Don't let the freakers bite," Still laughing, the old guy gets up and leaves, almost bumping into Samuel.

"Oh, hey there, Mr Nowhere Man. Sorry. Did not see you sneak up on us," Frank says cheerily.

"Not a problem, Frank. I always love to see the faces of the new guys when you tell them your stories," Samuel says, smiling at us.

Frank, just waving his hand in acknowledgement and still laughing, heads toward one of the exit corridors and vanishes down it.

The others start to head off, but I can't hold back a questioning look at Samuel.

"Mr Nowhere Man?" I ask.

"Oh, that's a long story. Maybe another time, Sam. Besides, you better get going before your promising good start gets a negative flag," Samuel replies.

I nod an agreement and slowly make my way back to my room, Frank's story, giving me the creeps as the corridor opens up and the lights flicker again as a final warning. Arriving in my room, I'm surprised to see Mr Brookes sitting on my bed waiting for me.

"Good evening, Mr McCall; I hope you don't mind me waiting here. I sometimes find the corridors a little cold," he says with a smile as I enter my room, the corridor closing behind me.

"No, not at all, just a little surprised to see you. How can I help?" I reply.

"I see you are settling in nicely, and I had some good reports about you from the laundry. You certainly got stuck in and don't mind doing a bit of hard work to make your life easier. Good to see," Alastair says, and I nod and smile as he continues.

"I've been reading your file. Very impressive—eleven convictions and incarcerations and ten escapes, and normally within the first six months. Very impressive. You seem to have a knack for security systems, you're easygoing, you're not the kind of guy that uses force or violence rather than skills and intelligence to get what you want—very impressive," Alastair remarks.

While Brookes is talking, I regard him. I realise he's working up to something, but his body language is hard to read. I guess this must be the 'abandon hope, all ye who enter here' speech. He pauses as he stares back.

"I want to offer you a new post," he says.

"Pardon?" I'm unable to hold back a shocked look, but before he can repeat himself, I ask.

"You want to offer me a job?"

"Yes, Mr McCall, a job. I want to offer you a meet-and-greet role alongside me. It would allow you a few privileges, plus you get to learn about this facility. Might even give you a few ideas," Alastair says, surprising me.

"Ideas? Hey, what? Are you giving me permission to try and escape?" I reply with a somewhat sceptical look.

"Well, Mr McCall, escape, I really believe, is impossible, but if anyone could do it, I think it's going to be you. Don't give me your decision yet; however, if you would come with me, I would like to show you something," Alastair asks.

We leave my room, and the corridors open up as Brookes tells the system to take us to operations. The walk takes much longer than anywhere I've visited so far, and we end up at a dead-end, or so it would seem. Brookes motions me to step closer, and then a glass tube close around us and the floor starts to move upward, slowly at first and then faster, and the view of the outside world goes black.

After what seems like at least five minutes, the elevator tube slows and stops, and then it opens, revealing a round observation centre. Control consoles and computers encircle the entire room, and buzzes and beeps come from almost everywhere.

"Welcome to the control centre," Brookes says with an almost theatrical tone.

"This is where I can monitor the entire complex, receive messages and reports, manage the power level, resolve technical issues, and generally where I like to spend most of my time. I brought you here because I think you need a bit more information; I feel it is very important for you to know and understand this facility and the challenge ahead of you," Alistair says. Brookes heads over to a terminal.

"Show me Mr Sam McCall's Arrival pod to this facility," Alistair asks. I'm surprised a little to hear a soft voice reply, seeming to emanate from around the room.

"Certainly, Professor. Displaying on the main screen."

The screen flickers and then focuses on a revolving white cylindrical object. At the centre is a docking hatch, and then I realise that the hatch is moving away from us, or rather I'm moving away from it. I must be in the shuttle I arrived in.

The shuttle starts to rotate, and I see stars, amazingly bright stars, and then several of them seem to move. Then, as I watch, more of the stars seem to dance and move about. Very unusual, I think, and then I realise why, and my heart starts to sink.

That's impossible, I think to myself as the shuttle fully rotates, so it's now facing 180 degrees away from the station I just undocked from. I now see another station, but this one is hanging centrally above a black hole.

"You got to be shitting me," I say as I spin round at Brookes. "That's a bloody black hole!" I say, rather louder than I meant to.

"Yes, it is," Alistair replies.

"But how?" I ask.

"I'll explain in time, but for now, I need to know if you're interested in the new job," Alistair asks.

I look at Brookes and then back at the ever-increasing black hole and station until the station starts to obscure the image of the black hole, "Yes, yes, I'm in. I'll take the job," I say.

"Good, good," Alistair Brookes replies.

"Just one question?" I ask.

"Oh," Alistair says.

"Frank almost bumped into Samuel earlier and called him Mr Nowhere Man. What does that mean?" I ask.

Brookes contemplates this for a moment, weighing up the pros and cons of answering before he replies.

"Facility Zero's system works on two means of identification, voice and retinal, with which the system knows who you are and where you are from, anywhere in the galaxy," Alistair explains.

"When the computer tries to identify Samuel, the response is 'Nowhere'; he's not known to the computer systems, and he's listed nowhere in the known galaxy, So a few of us who know this, nicknamed him Nowhere Man," Alistair replies.

3
Alistair Brookes's Story

Facility Zero, -1 day online: federation year 2417
Forty-eight hours until Facility Zero comes online
PROFESSOR ALISTAIR BROOKES stares at the framed photos on his desk as he sips his morning coffee. His wife and two daughters. He's surprised at having been apart from them for just over two years, and he misses them dearly. But, two years is not so long, really, not nearly as long as some soldiers might be apart from their families—five years for some of them. So, he's lucky in that regard, and in just a few short days, his life's work will be complete.

Now his station has been moved into this sector of space, ready to be placed above this particular black hole, one of the closest to Earth, so very convenient in that respect and pretty small compared to others.

Looking at the time, he realises that he must get going, or the commander will not be happy with more delays, delays the professor thinks he's managed to track down and fix. Odd really—all the preliminary system tests showed everything in the green, but as soon as he started to get the system ready to go online near the black hole in question, he started to experience power fluctuations.

Okay, it was the first time he had managed to draw power from a black hole itself, so there were bound to be issues, but the simulation all checked out, only now it's starting to look like his equations are off, not by a significant amount, but enough for the systems to have a deficit of power to run all the systems, hence the power fluctuations.

He suspected that this would not be happening if the station were a little smaller, but it was far too late to change that now. Ten years to build and move the station into position, and at the cost of tens of trillions of credits... could have been a little quicker and maybe a little cheaper, but they had to keep the station off the official books.

Can't really have a super-secret detention centre as the top news story. This had to be kept quiet. The best tactic is the tactic that no one knows about; otherwise, the system can be undermined and weakened. Besides, there would be plenty of protest groups out there that could cause a lot of trouble. But anyway, he's here now, and in two days, he will be heading back to his beloved family. The intercom buzzes, and a slight, shrill voice, of Professor Brookes' assistant is heard.

"The commander and the VIPs have arrived, Professor; I've taken them into the observation lounge," Emily says.

"Thank you, Emily. I will be along shortly," replies the professor. Then, taking a deep breath and thinking, It's now or never, he set his now empty cup on the desk and pats himself down, making sure he's all neat and tidy before he heads for the observation lounge. The professor walks briskly into the observation lounge of the command ship with a welcoming smile.

• • •

"Good morning, Commander, esteemed ladies and gentlemen. Thank you so much for being here today, and I do hope and I'm sure you will be very happy with what your money has helped build and develop. In just a few days, the new facility will be online and receiving the first of its new inmates, but unluckily for them, it will be a one-way trip," The professor says, smiling and motions to the assembled guests to turn toward observation windows that are all currently sealed shut.

"I'm proud to announce that Facility Zero will be online in just over forty-eight hours. Commander, if you would please do the honours," With a flick of a switch, the observation shutters slide open, revealing the majestic sight of the black hole, or rather the absence of anything but a glimmering circle of nothingness surrounded by a sea of stars. Seemingly floating above it is Facility Zero, a circular space station that resembles a giant cylinder, with no apparent windows or hatches, docks or entry ports.

"What you see before you are hopefully the first of many. I believe it is theoretically possible to install two or three other installations simultaneously, but we are still in the early stages of this development. Only time will tell, but as they say, this is all relative," Professor Brookes says with a grin. This last comment is received with a mixed reaction of amusement and confusion; this fact is not missed by Professor Brookes as he continues his speech.

"As the facility reaches each occupier threshold, the station is dropped closer to the black hole. This reaction, in turn, increases the amount of energy the facility can generate from the black hole itself," Professor Brookes pauses momentarily, allowing his audience to keep up.

"In layman's terms, the facility acts as the core of a giant electromotor, and the black hole is the casing. This means that once online, the station will produce all the power it requires and will be completely self-sustaining," Professor Brookes says, Pausing once more, realising he's lost the majority of his guests who are here mainly for the free drinks and the chance of seeing a black hole up close. He gets the 'end it now' nod from the commander. Taking another breath.

"This means that all the very worst members of our society can be sent here, and they will naturally stay here for the rest of their lives with no possible way of escape. This is the end of the first part of our introductory talk, and I've just been informed that you are now free to wander and take in the breathtaking views of the facility. You are welcome to ask any questions you may have. Thank you for listening, and please enjoy the rest of your visit," Professor Brooke concludes, receiving a mixed response.

Ending his speech, the professor looks toward the commander and smiles, receiving a 'well done' nod and smile back just before the commander vanishes from sight, surrounded in a sudden rush of guests.

Taking a drink from a passing waiter, Brookes heads over to the viewing area, the sight, as always, taking his breath away. He takes readings from his handheld monitoring device and ticks off the various tasks required to be resolved before the station is dropped down to its online position. Happy with the current status, he looks up as one of his guests stops beside him.

"It's very impressive, Professor," the new arrival says as he holds out his hand to shake. Brookes turns slightly, taking his hand, and as they shake, he realises the man before him is Martin Connor, one of the biggest shareholders of this endeavour.

"Thank you. I would say this is the culmination of my life's work. Anything less would be disappointing. I was trying to reach impressive, but what would be really amazing is having four of these online at this single location. Now that would be a truly an impressive sight," Professor Brookes replies, looking at Martin Connor and then back at the station.

"Oh, hang on there, Professor. Let's get this one working first," Martin laughs.

"I said it's impressive, not that I have unlimited money, patience, and resources. Besides, I would like to see this working without any glitches for a few years and with no escapees within that time. Then, sure, I think it will be very likely you will have your second facility—hell, maybe even more if it proves to be as good as your predictions say it will be," Martin says, also now looking back at the station.

"What I don't understand is why there are limitations on how many inmates you send there per month."

"Well, it's a little complicated, but it's all down to the time dilation between the staging area and the facility itself. This black hole is relatively small, so the time differences will be about thirty days here for one day at the facility. If you were to send too many prisoners at once, you would quickly overwhelm the station, and everything would come crashing down. Let me explain it further," Martin Conner nods slowly, starting to comprehend the complexity of the situation.

"The reason why we have two stations, one above and one below, is that the one that's outside of the black hole's influence is the cryogenics holding station that will deliver up to around fifty pods to the station below every month via a computer-controlled automotive system.

However, from Facility Zero's point of view, these pods will arrive at the station levels each day due to the time dilation. Remember, it's a maximum of about fifty pods. I'm guessing it won't always be that many, but once we take care of the surplus of high-level prisoners that are rerouted here from all over the federation, I'm guessing the number will drop dramatically," Brookes pauses, collecting his own thoughts before continuing.

"As the facilities fills up, the station will need to be lowered closer to the event horizon of the black hole. This has two effects. Firstly, it produces more power to run all the necessary systems, and secondly, the time dilation increases. At first, it's a gentle ratio of fifteen days to one week, then thirty, etcetera, increasing fifteen days every additional level that's been powered online to a maximum of three hundred days per one week on the station," Professor Brookes explains.

Martin raises a hand to halt Brookes while he works out the numbers in his head.

"So, what you're saying is, it will take around one hundred and ten years to deliver the last of the prisoners to the station?" Martin asks with an accusing tone.

"That's about right," Brookes replies, looking a little sheepish.

"And that's just the last two thousand," says Martin. "How long would it take from start to finish, assuming it is fifty pods per day for the station?"

Professor Brookes, already knowing the answer, takes on an expression of doing calculations in his head before replying.

"Well, as long as there are no complications or issues from start to finish, the time it will take is around Two hundred and ten years."

"Two hundred and ten years, and this can't be decreased?" Martin Connor repeats, surprised.

"Not really, no, but as you know, the cryogenic station makes the transition from court trial to the facility almost seamless to the inmate. As far as they know, they arrive at court, they are tried and then moved to the holding cells, and then from there to the shuttle, which is their own personal pod. Then they are placed into cryostasis and fed Dreamtime, and woken up as they arrive at the station. Technically, we don't really need volunteers to help run the station, but it's helpful to have some nonconvicted prisoners to oversee the running of the place. As long as they realise, there is no way out once they enter," Professor Brookes explains.

"As you put it that way, it's pretty ingenious. What about the cryogenic station? Won't it become obsolete once the station is filled up?" Martin replies.

"No, the cryostation can be used just as a staging area for any other facility that is installed here or even as an overflow station, plus its secondary purpose is to send supplies down to the facility via the pods. When a pod is launched, it has only a very limited manoeuvring and deceleration ability. However, it is just enough to get it to the station's central spine, where it docks and is lowered down to the level that the inmate will be assigned to. The pod is then taken down to the lower level and dismantled for its various core components, plus the various items stored within—food, water, air scrubbers and other spare parts, etcetera," Brookes finishes with a smug smile.

"Well, that I can appreciate. Very clever design. But why this size? Why not bigger? Saves on making others later," Martin asks. The one question that Brookes had hoped would not be asked."Good question, but one that is rather complex to explain fully. Firstly, the two simple reasons are that if the station was larger, the self-sustaining power we gain from being near the black hole would need to be closer, and being closer would mean a more extreme time dilation. The result being the cryostation might have to deliver fifty inmates per year rather than per month," Professor Brooke Says.

"The second issue is the station's stabilising modules. These modules, using a specialised mixture of tractor beams and antigravity technologies, have a twofold purpose. Firstly, they lower the station toward the black hole and hold it there, and secondly, they reduce the gravitational effects on the occupants of the facility," Professor Brookes continues to explain.

"This stops the occupants from being crushed to death and allows near-earthlike gravitational effects on the inmates. So if the station were bigger, these modules would not be able to cope with the power requirements, and if the modules were built with more power, this, in turn, could possibly give the inmates a system vulnerability that could be exploited," Brookes replies. He looks down at his handheld, realising that it's almost time to end the status update conference for the various major stockholders.

"Looks like we are almost out of time. Maybe time for one more question if you have anything," Professor Brookes asks.

Having listened intensely to everything that Brookes has been saying, Martin thinks for a moment before answering.

"I think you have covered everything, but there is one thing still bothering me," Martin says.

"Ask away, and I'll try and answer," Brookes replies.

"Okay then, you're obviously very confident that this Facility is so inescapable, but considering the thousands of pods that are sent down to the station every day for them. What exactly is stopping the inmates from taking over the station, modifying a pod and flying back out?" Martin asks. Brookes pondering the question for only a moment before answering.

"As I mentioned before, the pods are broken down into various components. However, I did not mention that the pods' fuel cannot be replicated, and the fuel left over after it reaches the Facility is burned off by the time the pod docks.

Also, the thrusters on the pods are a fragile system, and even if the smartest man in the world could jury-rig something, there would never be enough thrust to take the pod back out of the effects of the black hole. Next, the power generated by the black hole is only enough to power the station. If they want more, they need to lower the station closer to the event horizon, thus needing even more power to break free from the gravitational effects," Professor Brooke Says and then continues.

"Then, even if the inmates somehow managed to gain remote access into the other computer system controlling the stabilisation modules and tried to raise the station, these modules would shut down one by one. This shutdown process is carried out slowly, giving the prisoners a chance to stop, and if it's ignored, then the whole station is dropped into the black hole," Professor Brookes continues to explain.

"Lastly, if any prisoner somehow escapes from his or her assigned area, then the system will automatically ignore any request from him and will send tracking data to security. This effectively traps the prisoner, who will be collected by security. If an area of the station is compromised, even if it's an entire level, it can be isolated and ejected from the rest of the station.

But sadly, that is all the time I have left. I hope I have relieved any fears and answered all your worries," Professor Brookes says, finishing his explanation.

Martin Connor, now looking out toward the majestic sights, nods and smiles.

"Well, Professor, I think you have answered most, but I still have concerns. Every system has flaws. Yours, however, it would seem, are very hard to detect, but I'm satisfied that you have designed and built a remarkable system, one that in time will prove you right and me wrong. Thank you, and I really have had a good and interesting time. Will I see you on the tour of the station later?" Martin Connor replies.

Professor Brookes smiles. "Sadly, no...I have a few things to resolve before the station is brought online and lowered down into its position, but I'm sure you will enjoy the tour. Have a good day," Professor Brookes replies. They shake hands, and Martin leaves and rejoins the others just in time as the group, along with the commander, leaves the observation deck.

Looking back at the station and then down at a blinking red light on his handheld, Brookes notices another power warning light and starts running more diagnostics. Looks like it's going to be another long day, he thinks to himself.

•   •   •

Twenty-six hours until Facility Zero comes online
Waking up from the sound of the alarm and the clock flashing 0500 hours—almost mockingly, or is that just the lack of sleep? —Brooke slips out of bed, knowing that he's only got into it a few hours earlier. But some sleep is better than none, and making mathematical errors at this late stage of the installation could be catastrophic. Rest is a must, even if it is only for a short time; there will always be more time to sleep later.

With a quick shower, some food, and a strong coffee, he feels good to go. In fact, he feels amazing, reenergized.

Now, if only the major refit he ordered after tracking down the power fluctuation has been completed, he can really get to town on the other issues that have been driving him mad. Leaving his room, he heads down to his lab and enters it, the sound of the computers making him feel ready for the next twenty-four hours. This is going to work. His life's work just over one day away from being complete.

Reading the latest update logs, Brookes ticks off all the required changes and implementations that he ordered, feeling positively over the moon when he reads the last line regarding the power induction line refit. It's been completed, and power levels are now nominal, with no sign of the previous fluctuations. At last, this station is going to be online in time.

Spending the next hour organising cleanup crews to various areas of the station, Brookes readies himself for the commander's 0600 hours daily brief.

·   ·   ·

Arriving at the Commander's office, Brookes knocks and enters, hearing the Commander's voice, "Enter."

"Good morning, Commander," Brookes says, closing the door behind him.

The commander is still looking pretty good for a man in his late fifties, still handsome and fit, but he's a stubborn git, wanting his very last project to be completed without a hitch, his retirement project, as he keeps telling Brookes. "Very good, thank you, Professor. So how's my baby? What is the current situation?" Commander Taylor asks.

"Well, Commander, the updates are looking good. The power fluctuations have been resolved at last. Cleanup crews are currently inbound and will start clearing out the preparation equipment. Shuttles will be shipping over the stores, enough food and water supplements for at least five years; half of that will be set aside as emergency stores, and the rest will be topped up with each month's intake of inmates," Professor Brookes explains.

Commander Taylor ticks off each item on his list as Brookes reads out each line.

"Good work, Professor. What's next after that?" Commander Taylor asks.

"Then we start final system checks that will take about twelve hours. The shuttles and cleanup crews will take about six hours, and there are a further four hours to drop the station into position. This leaves us three hours for last-minute updates and to set up the wake-up protocols for the cryostation in preparation for our first fifty guests," Professor Brookes says.

"Excellent, really very excellent work, but you missed out on the final task—a tradition and one that will now be my last. When this project is complete, I'll be retiring, and this will be the crowning achievement of my career. Professor, well done and congratulations," Command Taylor replies.

The commander reaches down to his desk and picks up his prized silver cigar box, presented to him over thirty years ago after he defeated a notorious pirate who was causing havoc around the Sol System. Opening the box, he offers a cigar to the professor and then takes one himself. Then, putting the box back down on his desk, he picks up his lighter and cigar clipper.

"This is the tradition I talk about, Professor, a fine cigar, the better-quality ones need to be cut. Unfortunately, I only have a few of these left now due to them being rather hard to come by. Of course, being illegal does not help, but I would like to consider this one of the perks of the job," Commander Taylor says, then reaches over and cuts the end off of the professor's cigar and then his own perfectly. Putting the cutter back down and then motioning to the professor, he raises his lighter, lighting the professor's cigar. The professor takes a few puffs, and the cigar brightens and crackles softly. After lighting his own cigar, the commander places the lighter back down and takes a few more puffs of his cigar, savouring the taste.

The commander then places two fine glasses down on his desk and pours a generous amount of a rich, golden liquid into both. He sets down the bottle before picking up both glasses and handing one to the professor.

"One-hundred-year-old Martian brandy. It's extremely rare, but I was lucky enough to come across a bottle a few years back. I only bring it out for special occasions, this being one of them," Commander Taylor says, raising his glass.

"Here's to you, Professor. Facility Zero and the completion of my final project, your life's work, and the means of ridding the federation of all its most dangerous criminals and embarrassing undesirables. To Facility Zero!" Commander Taylor toasts.

"Facility Zero," repeats professor Brookes.

The commander and the professor both take a sip of their drinks. They smile at each other and remain silent for a moment.

"Embarrassing undesirables, what do you mean by that?" Professor Brookes asks.

The commander smiles an almost uneasy smile before replying.

"As you know, the federation is big and powerful, and no governmental institution can achieve such without stepping over the line a few times; in error or by design, certain obstacles are removed or replaced. I'm not saying the whole system is corrupt, but you are bound to have a few not so pure of mind. The types that when they see an issue, they have no problem coming up with unique ways to resolve the problem.

Don't get me wrong... the federation, on the whole, is a good system—protect the innocent, give all equal rights to a fair deal, reward those who work hard and bring to justice the criminals and the dangerous individuals that threaten the federation's way of life—but sadly on occasion someone who is doing right might find themselves on the wrong side of the line, and some powerful individuals now have an ideal place to silence such opposition.

"I'm sorry, Professor, if it sounds terrible if a few innocent people end up here. But please rest assured that your work will do more good than harm, and in a slightly ironic way, these people will be safer—fewer accidents, not so many friendly-fire incidents, and far fewer unresolved murders. The federation has far more positive effects than negative ones, and you can also take heart that even these will be reduced in time, and the few bad eggs might even end up experiencing your wonderful achievement firsthand. Come now, drink your wonderful drink, smoke your wonderful cigar, and feel proud in your work," Commander Taylor says.

• • •

Six hours until Facility Zero come's online
After spending far too long with the commander before making his excuses to go check on some items, Brookes heads back to his room for a few hours' sleep. Waking suddenly, with the nightmarish faces of helpless innocents

being sent to his creation still vivid upon his mind, he looks up at his clock and realises he slept far longer than he planned to. By his calculations, the station should now be in the process of being lowered closer to the black hole.

Rushing from his quarters, Brookes heads up to his lab, where the other scientists and engineers are busily entering information and reading data. He's handed a data tablet with current status reports and thumbs through the green status flags.

Feeling slightly less anxious, he takes a seat at one of the monitoring consoles and begins to read off the minute-by-minute reports. He almost misses the amber flag that appears on the last page, but he opens up the report and reads the flag: "Power fluctuation detected. Possible cause: Power induction line, panel 4b, not activated," Brookes rereads the flag.

'This damn fault again, the line got replaced, but someone forgets to activate it?' Brookes ponders to himself.

Mumbling a few choice curses under his breath, Brookes heads out of the lab, now fuming again that a stupid mistake could cost the whole project, calling over the comms.

Back in the lab, the Comms speaker crackles, "Th-s..s br...es.ha.t.th..the.p.oc..u.e. d..n.t.l.w.er.th.fa..lt.y," before the speaker sparks and stops altogether. Heads turn toward the Comms unit with looks of concern and confusion. An engineer tech heads over to fix it, but no one understood the message, and the positioning procedure continues on.

Moments later, Brookes docks at the temporary maintenance bay and heads down to the facility's engineering level. This should only take a few minutes. He arrives at panel 4b, and the sight of the panel hanging loose makes Brookes feel nervous. These panels are meant to be secured with bolts that can only be removed with a special tool.

Opening the panel fully, he reaches in and pulls down hard on the lever. The red indicator light turns to green as the mechanism locks into place. He closes the panel and uses the securing tool to lock it into place, the idea being that once the station is online, there is no way to gain access to these panels without this tool. Brookes then starts to head back to the docks and checks the time on his handheld, stopping dead as he looks at the facility's status monitor in disbelief: 'Facility Zero now online.'

Brookes slowly realises what must have happened. The trip that seemed to him to take only a few minutes most likely took him the better part of a few hours from the relative standpoint of others away from the black hole, and if the time dilation is this bad, that can only mean one thing: the station was still being lowered into position as he docked.

He'd have to figure out later why his orders were ignored or misunderstood; his top priority must be to get back to the dock. He tells the computer his desired destination, and the corridor opens up before him. Wasting no more time, he heads off down the corridor.

Brookes realises the inevitable outcome to his situation just as the path opens up into the main dining hall, set up as the primary destination if the desired destination became unavailable en route. Entering the hall, Brookes scans the room, his eyes being almost drawn to a lone figure. A look of pure incomprehension covers Brookes's face.

Samuel smiles and stands up just as Professor Brookes enters the room.

"It's such an honour to meet you, Professor; Welcome to Facility Zero," Samuel says, Greeting Professor Brookes to his own Facility.

4
Freakers

Facility Zero, 180 days online: federation year 2424

I REENTER MY quarters, noticing that my room has been changed around while I was away. In addition, a new terminal has been added. Professor Brookes mentioned I would be getting an upgrade due to my new position as a junior security officer. I chuckle to myself, thinking, I've had a few titles in my time, but never a junior security officer, and especially not while in a prison. That just beats them all. Glancing again at the new terminal, I decide that it can wait until tomorrow. For now, all I can think of is sleep.

I wake up earlier than usual, the short conversation with the professor the previous night still spinning around my head. Laughing to myself again, I get out of bed. First things first: I need a workout before breakfast; it's how I think well. I tell the room to take me to the gym.

The corridor opens before me, and I head out of my room. Within a few minutes, I find myself walking into a reasonably fitted-out workout area. It's pretty impressive, with a nice rack of running machines, rowers, brace benches, free weights, and an info terminal, very handy. To my surprise, the new girl from the other day is on one of the running machines, and she seems to be running well.

Taking advantage of the situation, I head over to a vacant running machine next to her.

"Morning," I say as I program a five-mile flat circuit and start my run. The woman next to me says nothing and continues running hard. I start my own run and pick up speed. Whoa, she is running hard. Glancing over at her readout, I'm impressed to see that she's on target for running a twenty-eight-minute 10k.

A few minutes later, without showing signs of fatigue, the mystery woman slows and then stops as the machine beeps and shows her final time, a very respectable twenty-eight minutes and thirty-one seconds. Trying again.

"Good morning. I'm Sam, the latest security officer of Facility Zero," I say.

Only glancing at me for a second, the silent mystery woman gets down from the running machine and then stops as she turns and regards me fully.

"*The* Sam McCall?" she replies, with a sound of slight disbelief in her voice.

"The one and only," I reply with a smile, noticing a slight shimmering in her right eye. Usually, that would mean it's not a real eye but some kind of implant. But I'm feeling happier that the silence now seems to have been broken, and I'm intrigued that she recognises me from somewhere.

"The same Sam McCall that's broken out of over twenty-seven of the federation's best detention centres all across federation space?" she asks in a curious tone.

"Yep, that's me," I reply again, my smile getting bigger.

"And you've been made a security officer of this place," she says, her tone now slightly sceptical.

"Yes, that's right," I reply once more, my smile now threatening to explode out of my face.

Rolling her eyes in disbelief but resigned to the fact that she knows it's the truth, she replies one last time. "Keep away from me. In fact, don't even talk to me, but thank you for confirming to me that this place is obviously being run by idiots," She says.

Her shimmering right eye stops as it returns to normal, and she turns and heads out of the room without saying anything else or looking back. I stand there, stunned.

"What the hell was that all about?" Then moments after the woman left, the room opens up again, and Frank walks in with a towel over his shoulders.

"Heya, Sammy boy. How's things? Oh," He stops and looks at me.

"You look like you've just been slapped in the face," Frank Says.

"Yeah, I kind of feel like it. I was just talking to that new girl," I say, still feeling a bit bewildered. Frank laughs.

"Oh, you must mean Jessica. Yeah, she's a tightly sprung girl, that one," Frank says, laughing again and then stops and gazes about the room as the lights start to buzz and flicker.

"Oh crap, here we go again," Frank mumbles.

"What's going on?" I ask.

"I'm not entirely sure why, but every now and again, the whole place goes nuts, and the routing system gets all messed up. Wait here, and it should resolve itself. You're just lucky you are not en route somewhere," Franks says with an air of danger.

"En route somewhere? What do you mean?" I ask as I step off of the running machine and head over to the terminal.

"I mean, my story the other night wasn't just a story. Sure, I embellished it a little, but mainly, when the lights flicker and buzz, you stay put," Frank explains.

The terminal comes to life and shows the usual 'Welcome to Facility Zero' on the screen. I tap the terminal as before, and it displays the message 'Please speak your request.'

"List my commands and allowed accessible location," I say to the terminal. The following appears on the screen:

Sam McCall's room
Dining hall
Information room
Workout gym
Main security
Lost and found
Medical
Dismantling bay
Levels 1 through 20: your current level is 2
Current prisoner population: 1150
Warning: Power fluctuation detected
Current community level 2 reaching maximum capacity
New level 3 activating; time to completion: 3 hours
Backup power generators now online
Terminal, locked-out until further notice.

Well, that sounds delightful. Turning to Frank and motioning to the lights.

"So we have three hours of this?" I say.

"Yep, that's about right, although I've never seen that information about levels before, but then again, I never experienced one of these with someone with security access before," Frank smiles and then continues.

"Anyone with security access is nowhere to be seen normally," Frank explains.

Interesting, I think, but of no use at this time. Just then, a corridor opens up along the side of the room away from us, and Jessica leaps through. This time she has built up a sweat.

"What the hell is going on?" Jessica says aloud while looking back down the way she had come. Moments later, the sound of mad laughter and jeering drifts out of the open doorway. Jessica, already backing away, murmurs, "What the fuck?" her facial expression changing from curiosity to consternation.

The open corridor lighting begins to cast odd and distorted shadows upon the room floor as someone or something scrapes and claws their way closer to our room, and the laughter and cooing noises become louder.

"Cancel route, cancel route, CANCEL ROUTE!" Frank shouts as Jessica stops backing up. Her facial expression changes once more, this time to one of determination as her hands form fists.

A bloody hand holding a crudely made blade comes into view from my angle of the corridor. My only thought at that moment mirrors Jessica's moments before: What the fuck? Then, without warning, the system voice, also slightly distorted in tone, says, "Command accepted," The corridor entranceway vanishes silently, slicing off the hand of the unknown figure, causing the hand and the blade to thud and clang down upon the floor as blackish blood oozes out from the severed hand.

"Frickin' freakers. Frickin' freakers" is all Frank repeats over and over.

I stare at the severed hand as several of its fingers continue to twitch. Jessica calmly walks over to the hand and steps on it, and then, grabbing the blade with a torn-off piece of cloth, she steps away and, with a fluid motion, stabs the still twitching hand.

"Calm down, Frank. It's dead," Jessica says.

I walk over to stand next to Jessica as she steps on the hand once more to pull her blade free. As she bends, I notice the blood and a nasty slash from her right shoulder and down along her upper arm.

"Oh shit, let me take a look at that," I say, but as I start to reach out, her reaction is to pull away.

"It's okay, it's not serious," she replies.

"It's not serious? Don't be silly. You have an eight to nine-inch long gash here. If we don't stop the bleeding, you're—" I begin to say.

"It's not serious," Jessica snaps, interrupting me and again pulling away.

"You are one stubborn—just let me take a look," I insist. I step in and take hold of her arm, but as I take a closer look, I feel her body tense, and I get the sense that I'm about to regret trying to help Jessica. Moments later, though, she sighs and relaxes, allowing me to continue to look.

"I'm going to need to borrow your blade and make some bandages from your sleeve, if I may. I have to try and stop this bleeding," I say.

"It really isn't that bad, but I appreciate your concern. Just give it a moment," Jessica replies.

"Give it a moment for what? For the wound to bleed more?" I counter back, and then something deep within her arm, a metallic mesh, glints from the light. As I take a closer look, the mesh vanishes from sight as the flesh around it starts to knit itself back together. The wound then stops bleeding, and in a matter of seconds, the cut itself closes, leaving just a jagged line of blood where the injury was moments before.

"As I was trying to say, it wasn't bad; it just looked bad," she says, giving me a half-smile. She walks over to

Frank, who now seems to have stopped repeating himself but still looks terrified.

Now it's my turn to be stunned. Whatever is under this woman's skin is not something you can just buy over the counter. That's more likely to be some kind of high-grade military dermal mesh, slow to activate but very effective, like wearing a super lightweight suit of chain mail under your skin. Remembering back to the shimmer in her right eye, I wonder what other surprises she has and how the heck she's been allowed to keep it. Putting that last thought to one side, I decide to head over and join the others.

"So, what's the plan?" I ask.

"Not much we can do but wait it out. Normally we are asleep when this happens, and that way, it's much safer, but from time to time, it happens during the day, which means the freakers can find us more easily. Also, moving around tends to draw their attention," Frank says.

"Sounds sensible, then, if we just stay here and, as Franks says, wait it out," I reply.

Then the corridor that Jessica had run out of earlier reopens, and on the opposite side of the room, another corridor opens up, followed by the sound of laughter and sinister cheering. From the first corridor, the cheering changes to a disturbing chant:

We only want to have some fun,
We just want to eat your thumbs,
Fingers and knuckles too,
An elbow or an arm will do,
We just want something of yours to chew.

This is followed by an outburst of more laughter as something is thrown into the room. It lands with a thud and rolls along the floor, turning and spinning as it slows down and comes to rest. The good-time boys' once leader stares up at us, his broken nose now missing, just leaving a few ribbons of flesh.

Come be our friend,
You don't want to offend,
Otherwise, you might end up like your friend!

As the second verse ends, Frank, who had started to manically repeat, "Frickin' freakers! Frickin' freakers!" again as the cheering started, screams a terrified scream and bolts for the opposite corridor, away from the chanting and thrown head.

"Frank, no!" I shout.

Jessica, caught off guard and distracted by the thrown head, darts off after him but too slow. The corridor closes as he passes through. The sound from the opposite side stops, but the corridor remains open, leaving just the flickering lights from within.

Jessica stares across to the other corridor for a moment and then motions me to join her as she walks into the centre of the room.

"I don't think the walls are the safest place to stand right now," she says as she grips the crudely fashioned blade in her right hand. Joining her, I notice that the corridor is empty.

We stand there just staring down the open corridor for what feels like an hour but is, in reality, maybe ten minutes. Then we hear the sounds in the distance, unrecognizable shouting can be heard, and then a voice from far off "No! Keep back!"—A scream of pain followed by laughter.

"Sod this," Jessica says, and she runs into the open corridor. Oh crap, I think, and I head off after her, knowing that I'm much safer with her than on my own, but leaving this room was not on my to-do list.

Running at a brisk pace, we make our way through the mazelike corridor, turning left and then right, going straight on at a crossroads. The passages never had this configuration when going from cell to the dining hall or anywhere. It was always a single path. Sure, it would turn, but it never gave you a choice of directions to go. By the time Jessica raises her hand up to motion me to stop, I'm sure we've gone around in circles, but her manner seems to say she knows what she's doing, so I keep quiet.

Up ahead, the corridor turns right once more, but from around that corner comes a chuckle of amusement. We stop for a moment, and then Jessica starts to creep down the corridor, motioning me to follow slowly. Suddenly Jessica stops as we both hear movement from ahead of us. The chuckle stops, and from around the corner steps a horrifying visage: a man with scars all over his head, not a single hair upon his scalp, his face slick with fresh blood.

He stands about six feet, his body emaciated looking and wearing no clothes. His ribs press tightly under his skin that seems far too small, being stretched over his entire body that appears far too big. His stomach is sucked in, giving the impression that his ribs stick out even more. However, what makes the sight before us genuinely terrifying is that his right hand is not his own; it is much larger than his left, and the area just past his wrist where he had attached it to his stump is much thinner than this new hand. He has stitched the two ends together using electrical wire, the wire zigzagging back and forth and making the skin overlap in places. Somehow defying logic, the hand works, and he stands there flexing it with signs of remarkable strength.

The terrifying man or creature looks up at us as he grins wickedly and takes a step forward, pointing to Jessica's blade and then toward himself.

Jessica looks pretty menacing as she brings the crude weapon up, stepping toward him.

"You want your knife back? I'm more than happy to," Jessica says.

As the gap narrows, other freakers seem to materialise from behind what I now assume might be their leader—first one, then another, and then a third—but as they appear, I realise that they are not just appearing as such but coming through the walls.

Jessica stops as the leader, now jeering at her, does the same. I notice that the newcomers are wearing the tattered remains of prison outfits, all in varying conditions, as they all start to chuckle and shout, jeering and a few mumblings.

"We only want to have some fun. We just want to eat your thumbs," Is heard from the gathered.

Just when I start to think that things can't get any worse, I hear more sounds of running footsteps from behind us echoing from down the corridor.

Oddly, this sound causes the freakers to stop their jeering song and start to crane their necks to see who's coming. Unfortunately, we don't have to wait long before the rest of the good-time boys, armed with similar crude blades, charge around the corner, and then within only a few paces, the group comes to a sudden halt as they see us and the freakers halfway along the corridor.

Testing the wall to the right with my foot, I confirm what I thought must have happened. Not only is the system not functioning correctly here, but the artificially generated voids that make the walls solid are also down; the sides of the corridors are just shadows.

The good-time boys start their own jeering and threatening shouts as both groups begin to charge at each other, not caring who's standing in their way. I notice more freakers joining at the back of the group.

I take hold of Jessica's arm as she prepares to defend us.

"Trust me," I say as the groups converge, and leaving it to the last second, I dive through the wall to my right, pulling Jessica with me and hoping that I've not killed us both. She almost pulls me back at first but then relents and follows me through.

I'm relieved to find that we're in a near-empty storeroom. It's immediately apparent that the walls are down, but the sound suppressors are working fully, and the noise from the corridor and the impending clash stops.

Luckily the main storage container is on the other side of the room, but moments later, we are joined by one of the other freakers. The freaker is holding a nasty looking pipe with one end flared open and bent back upon itself, forming a crude mace of sharpened metal.

With an evil grin over his face, he swings the pipe back and forth. I start to step forward to meet him, but Jessica pushes past me.

"Unless you're hiding skills I'm not aware of, I'll handle this," she says.

Lunging forward, the freaker suddenly swings the heavy pipe toward both of us. My reaction is to scramble away from danger, but Jessica just calmly dives forward and under the swing, coming up in one fluid movement, and with her blade held firmly, she thrusts upward in a single motion. The blade enters the freaker firmly under the chin and pierces the roof of his mouth, sending him into spasms. Jessica then twists and pulls down hard on the blade, resulting in the sound of grinding and shattering bone as the blade is freed and the freaker falls to the floor.

I stand there shocked and stunned, thinking, Who the hell is this woman?

"So, what's next, Sam? Wait here or head somewhere else?" Jessica says, snapping me out of my thoughts.

"I'm not sure, but the dining hall is the safest place to be, I think, and Frank said that if you stay off the grid too long, the computer drops you off of the database, but if you're lucky if you ask enough, the system might open up a path," I say, remembering what Frank had told me.

"Okay then," Jessica replies.

"Take me to the dining hall," she says.

Nothing happens.

"Take me to the dining hall," she repeats.

Still, nothing happens.

"Take me! To the dining hall!" she repeats again, this time emphasising her words.

The room lights blink and buzz—I almost forgot they had stopped—and then a doorway opens up, leading away from the room, the lights in the corridor on and stable.

"Well, I guess this looks promising. Let's get out of here before you have to defend yourself again by butchering a few more of those freaks," I say as I head for the doorway. Jessica gives me a grin as she cleans the blood from her blade, and then she leans down, picking up the pipe, and hands it to me.

"You might need this, just in case I'm not around to protect your arse," she says, slipping past me and heading down the corridor at a slow jog. That renders me speechless for a second.

"Yes, ma'am," I say in a slightly sarcastic tone and follow after her.

Jessica leads on, following the corridor to the right and then left. As we take the last corner, a doorway opens up at its end, showing a large room beyond. Two people peer out of the door, and upon seeing us.

"Run! Run! It's about to happen again. Quickly now!" they start to shout.

Without another prompt from the guys ahead, both Jessica and I start to run, but before we even make it halfway, the lights begin to flicker and buzz again, and almost on cue, the sound of freakers starts to echo down the corridor.

Looking behind, I see at least four freakers turn the corner we passed a few moments before, and then ahead of us, another freaker appears twenty feet in front of Jessica. She slows and starts to prepare for a fight as a hand reaches out from the wall and grabs hold of her shoulder, pulling her back with surprising strength.

Her assailant's face appears as his other hand tries to grab for her. The first freaker ahead of us lifts up a makeshift spear made from aluminium tubing with a jagged, pointed shard of metal attached and hurls it toward her.

The second man manages to get a better grip and slows her enough to give her some concerns, but she's able to twist her body sideways. This leaves her back totally exposed to her second assailant, but she shouts out a warning to me. Lifting up my own weapon, I swing at the second assailant. The dangerous end crushes and slices the side of the man's head, but only as a glancing blow down the side of his face. It does remove most of his ear, though, and it impacts his shoulder with a sickening thud.

The freaker screams out in pain and, releasing Jessica, and falls back through the wall, vanishing from sight. Then the first assailant's thrown spear hits her upper arm, the jagged point going all the way through. Wincing and in obvious pain, Jessica reaches with her left hand and pulls the spear out with considerable strength, making the hole bigger as a gush of blood pours from the open wound. She hurls the spear back down the corridor.

The action would've been amazing, but the spear misses by a whisker and disappears into the darkness. The first assailant jeers and makes a rude gesture before diving back through the wall.

Jessica staggers as her arm continues to pour with blood, her left hand attempting to cover up the holes but failing to stop the flow. I catch hold of her as I reach her, noticing that the doorway at the end of the corridor is still open.

"Keep moving!" I shout, and we both stumble onward at a slower pace. Twenty feet from the doorway, one of the guys shouting for us to hurry runs out and helps us the rest of the way. Moments later, we pass through, and the doorway closes behind us.

Although it's a large room, this is not the dining hall. Some kind of transport boxes of all shapes and sizes are lined up along the walls. The men shouting at us previously help make a makeshift bed, and as we set Jessica down onto it, the first guy I recognise as the foreman from the laundry. The other I've never met.

Thanking them, I cut and tear the sleeve from Jessica's arm with her blade. Jessica herself is now looking pale.

"I'm sure it's not too bad, Jessica. I think it missed the bone," I say, not sounding that convincing as I rip her sleeve into further strips. Then I tie one piece tightly above her wound. When I lift the arm, I spot another nasty-looking puncture wound halfway down her ribs, her blood turning her prison jumpsuit red. Cussing under my breath, I start to tear away the fabric around the entry wound, seeing something just under her flesh glint in the light.

"Abbey...my friends call me Abbey or Abs, but that's a long story," She says, grinning weakly.

"Just stop the bleeding, and my body will do the rest," Her eyes close, and she slips into unconsciousness.

I tend her wounds as best I can. I've heard so many stories of infected wounds—what to do, what not to do—but I'm no medic, so I do what I can. I manage to keep her body elevated and make a tourniquet out of the remaining strips of cloth. Then, knowing I've done all I can, I go join the others.

The foreman, whom I found out earlier is called Jake, nods as I arrive, and the two continue their talk with a third man I did not notice when we arrived earlier. Looking down, I'm shocked to see Frank lying there. His face has been torn in places, with nasty lacerations down one side.

As I stare down, I realise his right hand is missing from the wrist down; the stump is wrapped up with jumpsuit pieces now stained red with his own blood.

"Hi, Frank. I'm glad to see you made it here, wherever here is," I say. Frank gazes up at me with a mixture of fear and regret.

"Here? Well, here is a little complex, but if I'm right and the rumours are true, this place is called the lost and found," Frank says, and he starts to cough as a sudden bout of pain hits him.

"This is the place where the system routes all those that are removed from the active system," he adds.

"What does that mean?" I ask.

"It means that the system will no longer recognise any of us, and sooner or later, the freakers will come and finish the job," Frank says and begins to cough.

5
Jessica's Story

Federation year 2420
Planetary Enforcement Agency, morning briefing, 06:00 hours

COBB, THE LAST member of the PEA to enter the briefing room, receives jeers from his colleagues as he takes the last seat at the back, fending off the various remarks of his tardiness from his fellow soldiers. The Planetary Enforcement Agency attracts professionals from both civilian enforcement and Special Forces, making for an interesting mix of personalities.

The room then quiets down as the mission briefing captain enters, looking toward the assembled teams.

"Good morning, ladies...oh, and gentleman," Captain Anderson says, smiling at Jessica.

"I keep forgetting. Maybe not so gentle, but certainly the only real man I consider among you grunts," Captain Anderson adds. This is received with a mixture of laughter and heckles.

"Okay, quiet down. As I said before, these skins are not ballistic armour for those of you with the shiny new subdermal skin. You are not bulletproof, and for that matter, you'd best avoid most thrown projectiles, not that I imagine you will be attacked with spears anytime soon."

"Now to the main item on the agenda, most important: information has come to light that a very high-ranking representative of the Horizon Syndicate is arriving for a meeting.

As you know, the Horizon Syndicate is responsible for about 80% of all drugs on Mars and distribution.

We don't care what the meeting is all about; we just need to know who is behind the export of the drugs from this world to the other federal colonies. This is our chance to arrest a high-level member of the Horizon Syndicate. We pretty much know who the main players are on this world and how they operate, but what we don't know is how the network operates around federal space," Captain Anderson explains.

"We will be continuing to stake out Galpoli nightclub. We know that he's the regional boss of the syndicate in New Cassini and maybe on Mars itself, and our sources tell us that the high-level meeting will happen there one evening within the next few days. We will have three teams, two teams in surveillance assault craft outside and one team inside. If our target arrives, we wait, and we do not intercept in the club. We will watch and record to get evidence, and we'll extract when they're away from the club and civilian population.

Targets of interest and also to be careful around," Anderson says.

A holographic projection of a well-dressed man wearing sunglasses appears.

"This is Galpoli—always well dressed and always wears sunglasses, even if it's dark," Anderson says and then clicks a button. The projection changes to a beautiful brunette with long, perfect hair and a butterfly's tattoo on her upper right shoulder.

"This is Muna—beautiful but deceptively deadly. Absolutely not Galpoli's girlfriend but his bodyguard. She likes to be seductive to her enemies; that allows her to get in close, and then she uses her expert knowledge of human anatomy to do some serious harm. Her favourite weapon is a butterfly knife of some kind," Captain Anderson says, the clicks again for the next image.

The projection changes again, this time displaying a large, very tall man, well dressed and wearing an ornate gold septum piercing through his nose.

"This is Vern. He's the bouncer and not very nice. Ex-professional powerlifter and now works for Galpoli, also an expert at jujitsu. Do not get into hand to hand with this guy; he is very dangerous. If you need to, take him down any way you can," Captain Ander says, emphasizing his words.

The projector changes once more, this time showing a young male in his twenties with spiky red hair and wearing black leathers.

"And lastly, this is Mici. He's the head of the street dealers. He's the one that you see the first time if you are a nobody. He also helps run the street dealers in the area. Also very dangerous and normally hangs about near the club, you are to avoid this man at all costs, do not arrest him.

Abs and Brim will be inside. Decker, Spenser, Coops, Bennett, and Fingers will be outside in *Observation One*, call sign alpha, stationed a hundred feet overlooking the club's front.

Lewis, Cobb, Spanner, Silent Joe, and Specs will be in *Observation Two*, call sign beta, stationed a hundred feet above the club's back entrance. These assault crafts can descend swiftly and deploy both teams rapidly if needed. Fingers and Specs will be overseeing Comms and technical support and will remain in their respective vehicles.

Okay, people, that's it, briefing over. Keep it by the numbers, and all will be good; deviate from official

Planetary Enforcement Agency procedures, and if you survive, I'll have your balls, if you have 'em or not," Captain Anderson says, ending the morning briefing.

. . .

The club is situated in the New Cassini dance and nightclub district's area but is mainly frequented by high rollers wanting privacy and discretion. Other than the expensive drinks, loud music, and a multitude of sexual deviation, the main reason they visit is the drugs on tap.

The assault teams arrive in the early evening under cover of darkness. The stealth capabilities of the craft are good but not perfect during daylight hours. The two crafts contain a whole spectrum of eavesdropping scanners and optical monitoring devices; each craft can stay in position for four days without landing or refuelling.

Abs and Brim arrive via a black limo with restricted identification registration exclusive to the super-rich; with this, no questions are asked upon arrival. Instead, they're given free access, the perfect cover for a wealthy couple looking for the best pleasure and service at such an exclusive, private club.

Inside, the nightclub expresses itself with glass glitter and bare flesh. Pure sexuality oozes from everywhere, mixing in with the explosive sounds beating throughout. Giving a generous tip, Abs and Brim are led to a private booth. The booth is fitted with an adjustable sound-nullification system that terminates the music's sound immediately upon entering and has a perfect view of the club's main dance floor, entrance, and a private, exclusive area near the back.

. . .

"So why is it that Brim and Abs always get to have fun drinks and music while us grants have to wait it out in this tin can?" Decker says as he loads his third weapon. This one is his favourite, as it can be easily hidden up his sleeve and has the same impact as a double-barreled shotgun at close range.

"Because you're fug ugly, and nobody likes you," replies Spenser, sharpening and cleaning his knife for the fourth time. Almost everyone laughs in both crafts, including Decker, who already knew the answer. Silent Joe remains silent as always, his own weapons already clean, loaded, and ready.

Bennett starts to do more squats, as any inaction for more than ten minutes makes him feel a bit antsy. Lewis continues to read his second romance novel, which everyone knows to ignore and not ask any questions about.

The last time a new member of the team (now an ex-member of the team) asked him about his books. The mission had to be cancelled due to the injuries the soldier sustained. Lewis was allowed to remain only due to his father's position within the military and that he's very good at his job.

Cobb continues to work on his gear, attaching a new patch and improving his weapon loadout, ensuring that everything is ready and in its right place. Lastly, Coops and Spanner work on their breaching gear and explosives, talking from time to time as they check off the various items.

Specs and Fingers, as always, continue to monitor the Comms and data frequencies in the area, making sure nothing suspicious is missed and ensuring every scrap of data is recorded.

"Break, break," Specks says, and Immediately the Comms chatter stops for the priority message.

"A white limo with restricted registration has pulled up outside, front entrance. Two males exited the vehicle and entered the club. Running identification. Identification blocked. Okay, guys, we have a pair of spooks in play. I repeat, spooks in play," Fingers says, sounding unnerved as he reports the last of his information.

Spooks on the ground would typically signify government or military, as even the super-rich can't have blocked identification—force or fake but never blocked.

"What the hell are spooks doing here? What is this shit?" Decker asks.

"Check the official lines. See if there are any red flags up for this area," Jessica says.

"Checking now," Specs replies.

•   •   •

Both Abs and Brim notice the two well-dressed men walk into the club. At around six feet, the first wear a smart white suit and has short hair with a scar down his left ear. He scans the main dance floor, staring at the female dancers and smiling broadly. Just behind him, the second man is around five feet five, has a slight build, wearing a grey suit and round-rim specs, and carries a small silver briefcase.

These two are met by a third, known by the PEA as Muna—an unusual choice as a bodyguard to Galpoli, the club's owner and manager. She also helps run the club and takes care of VIPs, along with other delicate issues. Her stunning athletic beauty and perfect brunette hair allow her to seduce her prey; not many can withstand her charms for long. After greeting the two, she turns and leads them both toward the private part of the club.

"I'm not certain, but the guy in the white suit looks familiar," says Abs, talking into her drink as she plays happy couple with Brim, his firm, muscular arms around her. Her ocular implant starts a scan.

"Can't say I recognise him, but it looks like he's brought his accountant with him," Brim says, giving Muna an appraising look.

"Nice butterfly tattoo," Brim adds, grinning, as Abs gives him a sharp poke in the ribs.

"Keep your mind on the job, not her tight arse, no matter how nice it looks, and besides, that's how most of her victims end up as victims," Jessica says as Her ocular implant finishes its scan.

"Yep, a pair of spooks. Identification blocked. Maybe dirty or some kind of sting. Best we observe for now," Jessica says, Activating her outward Comms.

"Hey, Fingers, any news on our visitors or flags yet?" Jessica asks.

"Nothing yet, Abs. I'll keep you posted," Fingers replies.

"Roger that. Going back to receive only," Jessica replies, turning to Brim.

"Let's go and dance. We can get a better view of the meeting from the floor," Brim nods in agreement and stands up, leading the way to the dance floor.

Abs and Brim arrive on the floor just as the two spooks and Muna enter the club's roped-off, private section. For a moment as they pass the curtain, they have a view inside, where two other men can be seen. One of them is Galpoli, the club owner, and the other is the street punk with spiky red hair named Mici. The view is then blocked as the curtain falls back into place. Abs takes out her lipstick and activates a microdrone before applying colour to her lips and putting it back in her purse.

The microdrone flies through a gap in the curtain and hides in a corner, the Drone giving abs a good view of the private area. Although it's hard to spot, the drone has no stealth capabilities and has a very short range of control; this reduces any electronic transmissions, thereby reducing the chance of being detected via other means.

Galpoli stands as Muna enters, leading the two men closely behind her. He's always nervous when he's visited by high-ranking Horizon Syndicate members, especially these two.

"Come in, Mr Simms. It's always a pleasure to have such important guests, although I don't believe I've met your companion before. Muna, please send in one of our girls. I'm sure our friends here would like a drink after their long journey," Galpoli says, inviting his guests to sit.

"We would, but first things first. We need to discuss why we're here," the man in the white suit says, moving over to Galpoli. He glances at Mici as he passes his companion at his side, and as they both arrive at the table, the man carrying the case places it down, turns it around to face Galpoli, and then steps back beside his companion.

"Now to the reason why we are here. It has come to my attention that someone in your organisation has been very silly," Simms pauses as he looks around the room. His silent companion looks around also and then walks across the room to stand with Muna. Both Mici and Muna are watching, their expressions slowly changing from interest to confusion to concern.

"Now I have it on good authority that the PEA has obtained some rather damning evidence on your little operation. Well, when I say 'yours,' I actually mean mine. This concerns me, and if I hadn't already pulled a few strings to get this place red-flagged as a place of interest, you would most likely have already been raided by the PEA," Simms explains.

Simms pauses again, and again his silent partner moves, this time stopping next to Mici. Galpoli is now starting to look concerned, and Muna appears visibly tense.

"Now my information comes with a photo of the issue at hand," Simms nods toward the case.

"You may open it now," Simms says. Galpoli leans closer and clicks open the case. Staring down in shock, he recognizes the picture immediately. Both Muna and Mici are distracted and crane their necks to see, but the case lid blocks their view.

Galpoli looks across to Mici just as the silent companion taps two rings upon his forefingers together, and a burning, white-hot wire appears between his hands. With deft speed, the companion sidesteps behind Mici and flips the white-hot wire over his head. He then leans back, stepping again past Mici, and with the merest hiss, the hot wire slices through flesh and bone, and Mici's head slides off and hits the floor with a wet thud, followed shortly after by his lifeless body.

Both Galpoli and Muna look at each other, aghast at what has just happened. Then they look toward the silent companion, who taps his forefinger rings together again, making the hot wire vanish.

"Oh, and my companion here is called Edge. You may call me Ray. I really could do with a drink now," Ray smiles at the shock Edge has inflicted on the others. An excellent start to the meeting, he thinks to himself.

•   •   •

Comms chatter stops as "Break, break" is heard over the open Comms, normally referring to important information forthcoming.

"Flag red. I repeat, flag red. This location has a keep-clear flagged by the Federal Investigation Unit. We are officially out of bounds. All teams abort," Fingers says over the comms.

"No shucking way, red flag or not. Brim and I have just witnessed a murder. I'm proceeding to arrest. Will require backup," Abs replies.

"We can't interfere. We no longer have jurisdiction. Besides, Mici was just a dirtbag," replies Brim.

"We have both witnessed a murder by an unknown federal officer. Regardless of jurisdiction or how low the scumbag was, it's still murder," Abs replies, sounding angrier.

· · ·

Abs opens her purse and brings out a small pistol.

"Make up your minds, guys. Entering in five, four, three, two, one," Abs says over the comms, then pushes in through the curtain. Muna looks startled as she sees Jessica and Brim enter holding guns and wearing official PEA badges.

"Planetary Enforcement Agency! Nobody move. By my authority, you are all under arrest for the various crimes of murder, conspiracy to commit murder, drug trafficking, extortion, and blackmail," Jessica calls out, pointing her gun towards Edge.

Muna backs off toward Galpoli, but Edge takes a step toward Abs and Brim.

"Well, I admire your nerve, but I think you're rather out of your depth, not to mention without backup," Ray

Simms says, looking at the two officers with an arrogant expression. A boom is then heard from the club's front, followed by smashing glass and more shouts of "PEA, stand where you are."

The room suddenly bursts into motion as the sounds of screams and shouts come from the main club. Edge rushes toward Abs. Ray, Galpoli, and Muna run for the back of the room as Brim moves to intercept Edge.

"Get after them," Brim says as he faces Edge. Abs, not pausing any longer than she needs, rushes past them to pursue Ray, Galpoli, and Muna.

Edge, unable to get to his original target, settles for Brim. Brim raises his pistol, but before he can get off a shot, Edge flicks one end of his wire toward him. The wire detaches and flicks out fast, wrapping around Brim's gun, and with a sharp backward tug, the weapon drops in two.

Brim is already tossing it to one side as he charges into Edge. Edge, not expecting a straight-out charge, is momentarily winded but recovers quickly and twists away from the blow, flicking the wire again, this time wrapping around Brim's wrist and pulling hard to take his hand. Brim screams out in pain as the wire burns into his flesh but only as deep as his subdermal skin allows, which protects him from the worst of the wire.

Brim twists his wrist around to grab hold of the wire, his flesh making a dreadful hissing sound as his skin is scraped away.

This surprises Edge enough to take full advantage by pulling him off balance toward Brim's other fist, which slams perfectly into Edge's face, shattering his nose and causing Edge to stagger backward with blood pouring down his face as Decker and Spenser rush in shouting.

•   •   •

Abs runs to the back of the room, where a small exit previously covered with a curtain is now open. The sound of running echoes down the narrow passageway. Entering the passage and running a short distance, Abs reaches a T junction. Looking left, she can see the outline of Galpoli and Muna running into the distance. To the right, she only hears the sound of running. Taking this right path, she follows the passageway hoping that this is where the spook known as Ray Simms chose to flee.

After a short sprint, Abs re-enters the club. With the sound of music now covering the noise of running, Abs can only track her prey by the path of mayhem that Ray leaves behind: half-kicked-in doors, shoved or knocked-down patrons left shouting their anger. Ray's route now heads upward, heading for the roof.

Abs follows, taking the stairs two at a time, finally reaching the roof. Up here, the club's music is much quieter, replaced by the noise of the wind.

Being cautious now, Abs slows down to a crawl, sensing that her prey is close. Then she hears shouting

"I need an emergency evac at my location now, and I mean now!" Ray Simms calls out over his radio.

Abs continues to make her way along the side of the wall. Reaching the edge, she peers around the corner, only to have a chunk of wall shatter in her face, and she dives back away from the sudden shot.

"You are one hell of a persistent bitch. I'll enjoy destroying your career; what's the matter? Cat got your tongue?" Ray shouts, realising that all he needs to do is stall her long enough for his ride to arrive.

Abs sends her remote camera drone up and over the roof as Ray continues to shout. She pinpoints his position near the corner of the roof. He's holding some kind of high-velocity pistol, banned by some governments.

Picking up a piece of wall, Abs throws it as far as she can diagonally away from her across the roof. As she throws, she begins her move, diving into a roll. The wall fragment lands and shatters into several pieces as a roof segment evaporates from Ray's gun.

Ray, realising just a little too late, sweeps his aim back towards Abs.

Abs is already halfway out of her roll toward Ray and comes up short, just as Ray opens fire again. With more luck than skill, the first shot hits her in the left shoulder, taking her off her feet, making a neat hole at the front but removes most of her shoulder blade as she falls backwards. The nano implants reduce the pain to allow the user to continue when any other average person would be out for the count. The second shot misses her narrowly, and Abs brings her own gun up and fires once as the force of Ray's blast is already spinning her backwards. Controlling her fall, she manages to land on her upper back, leaving a wet patch of blood upon the floor.

Then performing a body flip to bring herself back to her feet again, she springs forward and away, crouching low with her gun and aiming for another shot. Her first shot misses but causes Ray to duck and move toward the roof edge. Ray returns fire back to where Abs was just moments ago, removing a segment of the roof. Abs's second shot hits him in the right upper leg, causing him to fall to one knee just as the sound of a hover vehicle comes into view, its lights blazing down on the roof.

The force of the wind increases as the vehicle gets closer.

"You are not going anywhere, Ray. We have a lot of questions for you," Abs shouts out, still trying to get closer but knowing she hasn't got long as she feels her life's blood running down her back.

"Stupid dumb bitch, you don't know what you have gotten yourself into. If you had a clue who my father was, you would have left me well alone," Ray shouts, fury in his eyes, and he fires another shot, this one hitting Abs in the stomach, staggering her backwards and dropping her to her knees. The sound of the hover gets closer.

"Well, it looks like my ride is here. Too bad I don't have much time, or I could have made this much more painful," Ray says.

Ray, already back on his feet, limps his way to where Abs has fallen and raises his gun for one final shot, aiming it at her head. "Too bad," Ray says as a sudden noise causes Ray to turn as an assault craft swoops in to intercept a hover vehicle, blocking its landing vector. It decelerates hard, the thrust causing the roof's dust and loose debris to fly up in a furious gust, making Ray look as he's already staggering backwards from the force of the downdraft.

Abs lifts her gun as Ray is distracted, and with the last of her fast-dwindling strength, she squeezes off one last shot, hitting Ray squarely in the chest and sending him the rest of the way over the edge of the roof and out of sight.

•   •   •

Regional Commander Simms walks into the Planetary Enforcement Agency's medical facility's central area with a long line of doctors, military aides, and security personnel following closely behind.

"So, where's my hero?" the Commander booms out in a manner that would suggest this is his usual tone, making half the medical staff stop and look around. One of the senior nurses points down the corridor, and the Commander moves off in pursuit of his hero.

Arriving like his very own miniature tornado, the Commander looks over the assembled team standing at attention against the walls as he rushes past.

"So, where is my hero?" The commander repeats.

"Good morning, Commander. It's wonderful to see you visit this facility. If it's Jessica you are referring to, she has only just come out of surgery," a doctor says, emerging from a side room.

"Well, Doctor, I'm here to help—only the best for our hero. I have a special medical transport coming to pick her up and give her the best treatment at my disposal, and once she is better again, I have a special mission of utmost importance for her," the Commander replies enthusiastically.

"Although she is recovering well, we had to do a lot of reconstructive surgeries on that young lady. I can't possibly release her so soon," the doctor tries to protest.

Dismissively the Commander pushes past the doctor, his security preventing the doctor from following him into the room.

Simms walks over to Jessica's bed as Simms' medical team starts prepping for Jessica's immediate removal. Jessica opens her eyes to the sudden activity inside her room.

"Hello, Jessica, or should I call you Abs? Or maybe your rank, Lieutenant, or maybe just a stupid bitch that killed my son," Commander Simm says calmly; however, his feature plainly showing his hatred for her.

Jessica blinks, stunned and unable to fully understand. Then she feels the drugs take effect, and her world slowly melts away. She hears just the last of the Commander's words before she slips into unconsciousness.

"Your team thinks I'm taking you to a top-notch facility. Well, in a way, I am, but not the kind they are hoping for. It's a shame I can't remove your tech, but sadly, time is limited. We won't meet again," Commander Simm explains.

•   •   •

In Dreamtime, Jessica is fed days of verbal and psychological abuse, hammering home the fate in store for her. Commander Simms explains that the Facility is within the gravitational field of a black hole and how she won't see the team ever again, and no one will ever know what happened to her.

As far as anyone else will know, she'll be lost on a black op's gone wrong, all files destroyed, and her records of service changed to reflect nothing of her past deeds.

The pod docks with a clunk, and the door hisses open. Jessica standing up from her chair, she takes a tentative step into the Facility and stops, seeing a middle-aged man standing there.

"Welcome to Facility Zero. My name is Alistair Brookes. We have a lot to discuss, Jessica," Alistair Brookes says, holding out his hand.

6
Lost and Found

Facility Zero, 181 days online: federation year 2424
FRANK CONTINUES TO talk about his encounter with the leader of the freakers until he loses consciousness due to blood loss. Leaving Frank's side, I return to the others to discuss his condition. His chances of survival now seem low. Seeing this in the others' faces makes it all the harder to take.

When Frank opens his eyes a few hours later and asks for something to eat and feels a little better, we realise that he is one hell of a tough sod.

It would seem that the lost and found is what it says it is. Items get lost and end up here, including boxes of stores that the system can't properly place because the boxes' markings are damaged in transit. Lucky for us, some of the boxes contain dried food, but unluckily for us, there's no water. We could survive a while without food but not very long without water.

The room is large, certainly covering a bigger area even than the dining hall, plus it's tall, at least three times as high as the dining hall, with conveyer belts way above and an automatic grab arm that can pick up or lower items into the room. Occasionally containers pass high above our heads, coming into the room and then going out again on the other side.

Returning to Jake and his companion called Neil, we eat something that resembles dried peaches or apricots. Frank manage to join us and continues to improve eats a little, while a little later, Jessica, still looking a little unsteady, sits down next to me and proceeds to eat everything within easy reach, only uttering the occasional expletive as her arm and side continue to heal at a fantastic rate.

We all try and get some rest, but after a few minutes of trying to sleep, I take my leave of the others and decide to take another look around the room. I surmise that most of the boxes are full, but what they contain will only become apparent by breaking the seals and opening them one by one. Maybe that's a job for another day; I decide to continue on with my walk.

Halfway around the room, I spot something way up high shining out of the wall, and after studying it for a few minutes, I realise that it must be a light from somewhere else shining through the wall of darkness.

"Hey, wait up," I hear Abs calls out, catching up with me at a slow jog.

"I must've dozed off, and when I woke, I noticed you were gone. Frank said you went for a walk," Abs says, stopping next to me. She looks remarkably good, considering the wound she received earlier.

"Ah yes, I was too restless and decided to go for a wander. I dislike puzzles, and this place is one giant puzzle, just like your arm, a clever trick," I reply, motioning at Jessica's arm.

"Yeah, long story…but, hey, I wanted to say thank you for earlier and also apologise for almost getting us killed," Abs says, looking a little embarrassed.

"Are you kidding me? You did a great job, and I'm not sure anyone could have been prepared for psycho spear-wielding lunatics jumping out of illusionary walls, and besides, you got us here without breaking into a sweat," I reply.

"Well, you're very forgiving, but I sadly can't forgive myself so easily. My training won't allow it," Abs replies, then continues.

"I also wanted to apologise for the gym earlier. I felt like I was being forced into something. Alistair Brookes asked me a favour when I first arrived here," Abs explains.

"Brookes asked you for a favour?" I ask, interrupting her.

"Yes, and Alistair seemed to know the truth about me, which is interesting, considering my background, but he seemed to be concerned about you," Abs replies.

"Me? What about?" I ask.

"Alistair asked me if I could keep an eye out for you," Abs says.

"Why?" I ask.

"Brookes seems to believe that you might be the only one here that might know how to escape from this place, which truthfully, realising where we are, seems rather doubtful," Jessica replies.

"So when we bumped into each other at the gym, I scanned your identification, almost out of habit," Jessica says, looking a little sheepish.

"I felt annoyed that anyone could ask me for help, considering what I've just been through, and I have always had issues with my conflict resolution. But, admittedly, it normally leads to serious violence, so in your case earlier, I'll mark that one up as an improvement, considering the outcome," Jessica smiles.

"You mean you just walked out in a mood rather than caving my skull in?" I ask.

"Exactly, see, I consider that an improvement," she replies with another smile.

"What do you think of that?" I say, changing the subject and pointing up to an illuminated patch on the wall.

Abs stares upward in silence for a moment before replying.

"It's some kind of ventilation duct, about four by four, and I can see the temperature differential and a light source," Jessica replies.

"We need to take a closer look at that," I say, Abs nodding in agreement, and we start to stack up supply boxes against the wall to get a closer look. Eventually, building enough to carefully climb up to the vent.

Looking through, we could see that the ventilation goes for forty feet and stops at a curious-looking viewing panel and an access ladder leading up and down.

Removing a small section of the vent, I clamber inside and make my way along this narrow passage to the viewing panel. Abs following behind. Looking through, I'm shocked at the view.

"You might want to check that out," I say and make space by going down the ladder a few feet, wait for Jessica.

Realizing then that this section of wall is made from a form of concrete and not the dark void walls, the rest of the complex mainly consists of. Understanding then that the ventilation crawl space is also a part of the station's main bulkhead, I realise that this whole area must be riddled with these passageways. Jessica peering through the panel, is as surprised at what I saw.

"This must be the facility's central core. The pods are unloaded and then sent down via this central tube to the bottom of the station and jettisoned into the black hole. I can see where the pods are dismantled," Jessica says in awe.

"I find it hard not to admire the genius in this design," I say, having seen enough, and I descend the ladder, Jessica following.

The ladder leads to a small room with an open doorway leading into a more extensive section. The sound of machinery and other electronic sounds can be heard as we enter. This room is only around twenty feet square, with two open doorways leading left and right from the ventilation shaft.

Littered about it are various open supply boxes, plain evidence that someone has been using this area for some time. Along the far wall are placed several tables, partly disassembled components, their purpose unknown at this stage. In other parts of the room are discarded chairs from two delivery pods, and on the other side of the room are two makeshift beds. Seeing this, Abs goes into cautious mode and slinks off toward one of the other doors and vanishes from sight. I continue to search around the room.

On the other tables, I find rough drawings of delivery pods being connected together. Technical diagrams of components needed for fuel and thruster conversion, far too advanced for the average joe, so whoever did this knows the fundamentals of many technical aspects of these pod design and, judging by the last drawing, astrophysics as well.

"Hey, Sam, you better come look at this," Abs calls from the other room.

Not wanting to be called again, I head into the other room and stop short as the new room opens up even bigger than the lost-and-found room. I'm awestruck at what I see in its entirety. Staring around at a large semicircular room, several hundred feet in height and set up against the facility's central core, sections of which are transparent. Special airlocks are placed at various heights along this central core.

I join Abs at the main viewing window that overlooks the central column of the facility. From this angle, we appear to be near the very bottom of the station. Looking up, we can make out where the pods travel down through the entire station. The pod containing a new arrival would stop at the required level, deposit the individual, and then proceed to here, where its remaining fuel is burned away, and the pod is dismantled for supplies and spare parts.

The rest of the pod is then jettisoned toward the black hole. This entire process is entirely automated—or would have been, but for some time now, it's been done manually, and judging from the sight of the room, someone has been busy draining off the remaining fuel and storing it. Not only that, they've been building something in the centre of the room.

As I continue to look up at the station's complexity, a line of monitors springs to life, showing various angles of the central column, and travelling up the core is shown a pod that's been retrofitted with an additional engine thruster assembly.

"What the hell are they doing?" Abs says, looking at the modified pod as it moves along the core of the station. A camera ahead shows airlock doors opening as it approaches at each level, and a camera behind shows the same doors closing behind until it finally stops.

"What I had in mind, trying to escape, but the location of this station has some unique issues to overcome, and with what I've read in the other room and what I've seen here, I'm amazed and impressed with what they have done, whoever they are, but...," I say, staring at another monitor showing a readout of a list of commands being performed.

"But?" Abs says as she becomes impatient at my pause.

"But he or they have made a miscalculation. It's not going to work," I reply as I run numbers through my head, maximum thrust, the average weight for two passengers, the proximity of the black hole, and the gravitational mass effect upon the pod.

"The small manoeuvring thrusters won't be enough to get them free of the effect, but that's not the main issue," I add.

"But how can you know this so quickly? You've only just seen the pod," Abs says with rising scepticism.

"It's what I do. I can almost see numbers and equations. Based on the evidence and the rough sketches, unless…".

I start to say and see other possibilities as I consider the core of the tube, the timing of their escape.

"Unless? Sam, you are damn annoying," Abs turns on me, looking annoyed at my second pause in midsentence.

"Oh, sorry. Unless they are going to turn themselves into a bullet," I reply, trailing off as the monitor confirms my rapidly evolving theory; I scan the room and see what I suddenly suspected and then turn back to the monitor.

We both stand there transfixed, unable to move or look away, horrified and excited to see the outcome of this escape attempt.

It's insane and incredibly smart, using the facility's internal structure as a rudimentary artillery piece and the pod as the projectile. There are really only two possible outcomes: the pod will either disintegrate or be ejected at high velocity, but the real danger lies outside and away from the facility. What will happen when the pod leaves the protective influence of the gravitational bubble protecting the station from the black hole's heavy-mass effect?

"Level eight emergency decompression in five, four, three, two, one…" the station's system announces, and A sudden force of decompression is released below the pod, and the pod is exploded upward through the facility's core and erupts from the top of the station like a rocket.

Detritus from the level is forced out and up with the pod and, with horrifying reality, the level that was starting to take on new inmates. This plan had used one of the new levels to act as thrust as several bodies are among the debris.

"They are going to make it!" Abs says, watching the pod accelerate upward and away.

The picture starts to experience interference, and there's an odd stretching effect on the pod itself.

"I don't think so, and it's only one of them," I reply, watching with interest.

"Sure, there's more than one. Why bother modifying a pod for two otherwise? And they are going to make it," Jessica replies, becoming slightly irritated.

"Because firstly, the modified section isn't for a second seat; it's a rocket booster. And secondly, his buddy has outlived his usefulness and is currently over there under a sheet of canvas. I noticed his feet when I looked around when the monitors turned on," I reply as I continue to watch the pod.

The pod starts to shimmer as its image begins to stretch, and its rear end ignites into a brilliant white light as the main booster burns hot and the pod accelerates away at an impressive speed. Abs watches with interest as the pod starts to pull away.

"He is going to make it. He has the speed to escape the influence of the black hole," Jessica says, her knuckles turning white as she grips hold of the table.

"He's good, maybe very good, but he's not considered one important point," I reply.

"And what point is that?" Jessica asks.

"You'll see, very soon, I reckon," I say.

As the pod reaches the extreme end of the camera's range, the booster detaches, and the pod manoeuvring thrusters take over. Then the pod decelerates suddenly as if it's just passed through an invisible barrier as it leaves the protection of the gravitational bubble; then, the pod hits the full force of the mass from the black hole and crumples and implodes. We both stand there for a moment, watching.

"How did you know?" Abs asks, turning to me.

"The reason why the station has no guards is that they don't need to be here. The station is one giant cell, and the black hole's proximity acts as the walls and the security system. The guards are out there somewhere waiting in case someone does make it past the first two obstacles.

But to the point of how did I know it was going to fail, to be honest, it was a guess, but a calculated one. We are very close to a black hole, and the mass it must be exerting on the station should be immense, but we can stand and walk about, so from what I've seen and surmised, there must be something out there that is protecting us, some kind of gravitational field, but I guess it must have limited range. As the pod accelerated away from the station, it left the protection of the station and was hit with the full force of the black hole's gravitational mass," I explain.

"Do you think it's impossible to escape from here then?" Abs says, now looking rather glum.

"Well, this station has been designed to be inescapable, but I never believed a place could be like that. Of course, every system has its flaws," I answer, feeling Jessica's eyes boring into me, feeling the desperation for her own escape almost palpable.

"But with this place, I'm uncertain of my previous beliefs. Maybe Brookes can tell us about a flaw or two, and maybe we can get outside help, but I know one thing is for certain: unless I can get all the answers, this place is inescapable or might as well be, from what I have seen today, the only conceivable way to escape would be too costly," I say, turning away from Abs.

I look over the other equipment in this room, all geared toward dismantling the pods for spares, but some of the machinery has been modified to help with the booster pod's construction.

From the start, I realised that escapes from here will be reliant on surviving the journey out, not just working out how to leave the facility itself. Now I'm faced with the added complication of having to escape with more than just myself, not to mention I've almost always had help escaping before. Brookes deserves to know my secret.

Abs continues to stare at the monitors after the pod implodes, only turning away once the monitors go blank. She realises that escape from here is looking more unlikely or impossible, and if they aren't able to contact the outside, what plan could possibly work? But trying to escape is far better than doing nothing, so many questions run through her mind, like how can the bastard that put me here get away with it? And at that very moment, Abs's resolve to escape is set.

•   •   •

An hour later, we arrive back at the lost and found, where most of the others give us the 'where the hell have you been?' stares, except for Frank, who just grins. After we apologise and give the whole story of what happened, we all sit staring at the discarded packets of food plundered from another unmarked or damaged supply crate. Frank is the first to break another long period of silence.

"So, what now? We can't stay here indefinitely. Was there any way of getting back on the system from the engineering room?" Frank asks. This question is mainly aimed at me, so I answer.

"Not that I have seen, but the guy that was murdered and left in engineering, I think was one of the two that escaped from the laundry last week and considering the work they did together, it must have been going on for weeks, if not months. I think that somehow they knew how to get on and off of the system. Brookes had told me that the system identifies people in two ways, retinal and voice. We know that the system won't take our commands, but if we can force it to read our retinas, it might trick the computer to put us back on the system. But how we get the system to do that, I'm not sure," I explain.

Just as everyone is looking a little more hopeful that something might be possible, the lights start buzzing and blinking, which shatters everyone's hopes back to fears.

"Ah shite, frickin' freakers again," Frank shouts. The others looking around at the walls. Abs grabs her crude knife and starts to stack boxes in a defensive barricade, moving them with ease. The others, catching on quick, begin to help. I pick up my club and stare at the lights blinking and then the walls. They seem to shimmer in time with the lights, but it's hardly perceptible.

Then from the walls, we hear the sounds of laughter and taunts. Abs stands in front closest to the nearest wall, the others stand slightly behind, and I move up beside her just as objects are thrown into the room in a high arc, hitting the floor just outside our makeshift barricade, each landing with a wet thud.

Looking down at the floor at the first of the objects thrown, I recognize it as the severed head of one of the good-time boys. As I stare, more are thrown into the room. One hits a crate and splatters Neil with blood. What's left of the good-time boys are now staring up at us with bulging eyes and swollen tongues, all wearing agonised expressions.

The laughter from outside the walls increases as Jake throws up. Then it drops to silence as someone steps into the room. The leader of the freakers, his face is covered in fresh blood, and his new hand seems to have healed, making it look like it's been there for months. He points at me and motions me to leave, and then points at the others, grinning and drawing his finger across his throat. He then holds up five blood-stained fingers, smiles a pointy-toothed smile, then turns and leaves the room.

"Well, that's considerate of him," I say. "At least I can leave," I say, half-jokingly.

Jake and Neil stare in disbelief at me, while Frank, for the first time since the reappearance of the freakers, is calm enough to give me a grin.

Abs looks at me with a straight face.

"I'd like to see you try and walk out of here with both your ankles broken," Jessica replies as I grin back at her but wondering why that I am so special.

"Okay, guys, this place is not safe. We can't trust the walls, but in engineering, the walls are mainly bulkheads with only one other way in and maybe one void wall to watch against. I say we get out of here and take advantage of the five minutes' head start," I suggest.

The others nod in agreement, and we head farther into the room, back toward the ventilation duct that we used earlier. The upcoming descent troubles my mind, as I realise that Frank is going to have problems.

As we start to climb up the container boxes, I slow down and hang back while Abs and the others make their way up higher.

"Hey, Frank, you know that the ladder down to the engineering room is going to be hard for you?" I ask with concern.

"Yeah, I heard what you told us about it earlier, so don't sweat it. I'll be fine," Frank says with acceptance, looking up at the vent. Neil, overhearing our conversation, waits at the entrance to the shaft.

We start to climb again but only a level higher, and then Frank slips, cussing as he struggles for balance. The sound of the freakers sends Frank into a panic as Neil leans out of the vent.

"Sam, Abs is calling for you. Don't worry, I'll help Frank," Neil says. Neil then climbs down a level and reaches out a hand to Frank. "Sam, it's okay. You go ahead," Frank says, grabbing Neil's hand.

"Okay then," I reply and head up the boxes, looking back once to see Neil help Frank up a level, and I head into the vent.

•   •   •

Neil helps Frank up another level. Then, looking up at hearing the sound of the freakers getting louder. Realizing then what he needed to do, only confirming now what he first thought when he saw Frank struggle up the boxes.

He withdraws his hand, climbs up the remaining boxes and enters the vent before turning around and facing Frank. From his vantage point, he can now clearly see the onrushing freakers.

"Neil, what the hell are you doing? I can't get up there without your help," Frank shouts up, looking concerned and then looking back down at the freakers rushing closer.

"Sorry, Frank. You're a nice guy, but it's either I do this, or the freakers kill us all," Neil lifts up one of the top-level heavy boxes and throws it down at Frank. It lands short but then tumbles down the steep slope, hitting Frank's legs and causing him to lose his footing. He tumbles down the side of the boxes to the ground.

Some of the other boxes crash down after Frank, causing a box to landslide as several of them land painfully on him. Neil watches as several freakers swarm down upon Frank's prone body. Unable to watch any longer, Neil turns away in shame.

• • •

I arrive in engineering just as Abs moves another table into position.

"What did you need?" I ask as I approach.

"Pardon?" Abs replies, looking confused.

"Neil said you were asking for me," I reply, starting to feel a sick feeling rise in my stomach.

"Not me. I thought you were helping Frank?" Abs replies, looking past me.

"I left him with Neil. Neil said, you asked for me. Fuck, I can't believe I fell for that; I need to get back up there," I say, turning back towards the vent.

"You can't, Sam. It's too late for Frank. I'm sorry, but we need to look after ourselves, and you need to try and get the system to scan the room or something," Abs replies as she looks toward the vent.

The sudden clanging noise and the appearance of a pipe clattering to the ground just inside the ventilation shaft draw our attention, shortly followed by Neil, who is now bleeding from a nasty-looking head wound.

"I'm sorry, guys. I tried to help Frank, but he slipped from my grasp, and then the freakers swarmed in, and I knew I could do nothing to save him," Neil says as he crawls out of the vent into the room, the sound of pursuit echoing down the shaft.

"You best get going; Jake is waiting for your help in the main room," Abs says, as she stabs the crude blade to the underside of the table.

"Come on then, Neil, let's get moving, but you and I are going to have a chat if we survive this," I say, leaving Jessica alone. Then, entering the main room, I quickly explain to Neil the main purpose of this section of the facility: delivering the new inmate to the various levels and then dismantling the pods.

"Where's Abs and Frank?" Jake asks, looking over my shoulder between the both of us.

"Frank, sadly, did not make it, and Abs is doing what Abs does best," I say, giving Neil the evil eye. Then I notice the remains of a pod being lifted from the room.

"I think we need to stop that. At the very least, it should cause someone to be concerned about what's happening down here," I suggest, and I run-up to the pod, which is now a few feet off the floor, and jump onto the empty shell.

I spot an area to climb up and jump onto the lower section of the pod. Moments later, Neil jumps onto the pod next to me, just as the chassis starts to rise into the air, and we begin to climb. As the pod starts to swing, we choose that moment to head inside the pod where we find it easier to ascend, climbing slowly up within the pod.

Nearing the top, we are both forced to continue the climb from the outside, difficult to find handholds but with no choice. After a few more moments, I take a poor choice of grip and almost fall, but Neil grabs my arm at the last second, giving me enough time to grab onto an external part of the frame.

Finally, we manage to climb onto the top, and we're able to see where the lifting arm is attached to the top of the chassis via a grabbing claw. All Jake can do from the ground is stare up at us.

Climbing onto the grab claw, I start to kick down upon the pod, trying to dislodge it. Neil follows suit, and we both continue to stamp down on the pod, but it quickly becomes apparent that it's not having any effect.

Looking up at the arm's progression, I realise that the pod is almost at the facility's ejection port. A few more meters, and we will both be jettisoned into the black hole. Somehow this must also be how the pod was launched earlier for the escape attempt.

We're running out of time fast and becoming desperate. I notice the arm is slowing down for the pod's alignment to its destination, and I try to start the arm swinging. Neil, unsure of what I have in mind, just hang's on and watches.

"Try and swing it; we need to jam the mechanism," I say; Neil nods and joins in.

The machinery seems to detect the arm's alignment issue and starts to compensate, the port now only a few feet away, but it's not swinging nearly enough.

"More!" I shout, and we both shove hard, trying to swing it to the left or right of the port. The arm adjusts as it slows the pod for its remaining few feet. We try again, doing the best we can to swing the pod out of alignment, but the system keeps readjusting.

Then, realizing this too is not going to work, I become desperate as the pod enters the airlock, placing us just a few feet from being ejected into the tube. The airlock spiral had opened to allow the pods to progress but was about to close, and once it had, we would die seconds later.

Remembering my makeshift Mace, I take it out of the crude loop I made for it and hold it out to where the spiral hatch should close, calculating its centre as the pod lurches to a halt inside the airlock. Only Neil's quick realization of my plan prevents me from falling off, holding on to me as the spiral hatch closes around the mace and then reopens again, the mace preventing a proper seal and the hatch retries again to close.

After several more attempts to close, a light above the hatch begins to flash as the automatic ejection sequence shuts down.

Feeling elated, relieve that this, at the very least, should get some attention, a freaker comes running in from the other room where I had left Jessica, the freaker, covered in blood and wielding a bloodstained knife gripped tightly within his grasp. Seeing Jake alone and unaware, he rushes toward him as the lights begin to blink and flash again.

• • •

Frank lands badly as the freakers rush in, four heads coming directly toward him with gnashing teeth, whooping and laughing. As they descend upon him, Frank's terrified expression evaporates. His fears vanish like distant, horrifying memories from a waking nightmare. As his eyes glaze over, a calm claims him, and his resolve to live reasserts itself. His remaining hand grabs the closest freaker's wrist as he falls upon Frank.

Somehow Frank manages to twist the blade around within the grip of the freaker's hand, and, unable to stop his momentum and prevent the inevitable, the freaker lands on his own blade, screaming obscenities as blood erupts from his mouth.

-The other three freakers then descend upon Frank, and two of them begin to stab him, Frank's legs thrashing about, trying to dislodge them as his third attacker concentrates on biting down on his cheek. Frank screams in pain and reacts by pulling the third freaker down closer, using his free arm, allowing him to bite down on the freaker's throat.

Frank is rewarded with a painful squeal and a gush of blood as the freaker pulls away, spraying blood from his throat over Frank's body. The remaining two freakers, continuing their deadly assault, are suddenly grabbed and pulled away from him. His exertion has already cost him dearly, and as his strength fails, he tries to see who his rescuer is, but all he can see is a dark profile, and Frank loses consciousness.

• • •

Abs watches Sam leave, but her attention snaps back to the ventilation shaft as the first of the howling freakers crawls out; recognising Abs, they leer at her and waits for his fellow freakers to arrive. Watching the freakers slowly emerge, she slows her breathing. When three freakers have emerged, they wait no longer and charge at once, while others continue to crawl through. The three charging freakers leap at the same time onto the table, and at that very moment, Abs flips the table forward onto its side, causing all three to topple forward off balance.

The middle freaker falls hard and biting through a segment of his tongue as his chin impacts the edge of the table. Abs pulls her Knife free from where she stabbed it to the underside of the table and stabs it into the middle freaker's head as she sidesteps and, yanking it free with a fluid motion, slashes the second freaker across his throat.

The third recovers faster than expected and lunges at her with his own knife, slicing only air as Abs ducks under his lunge and counters with a slash across his stomach, opening him up and causing the freaker to stagger to his knees.

Stepping around him with menace and determination, she places her left arm around his upper chest and drags him back as her left knee is brought up into the small of his back, shortly followed by a crunching sound.

Abs then pushes that freaker to the ground as two more freakers rush her. Abs being slightly off step, the first of the newcomers slashes and draws blood from her left upper arm, and Abs reacts by thrusting her blade deep into the freaker's forehead. Her own blade is now starting to cut into her hand due to the crude handle; her subdermal protection reduces the harm, but it is still painful enough to distract her as the second freaker rushes her, driving Abs to the ground and causing her to lose her grip on the blade. Smiling and laughing, the freaker licks her face.

"I'm going to enjoy eating you," he cackles. As he leans down to take a bite, Abs reaches up with both hands, takes a firm hold of the freaker's head, and twists sharply to the left, resulting in an audible crack. She then pushes the freaker's lifeless body off of her.

She retrieves her blade as two more freakers emerge from the vent, both holding nasty-looking knives. They stare at Abs as she slowly stands. Now being covered in blood and the other dead Freakers, the floor makes this simple act difficult. Then from behind, a third freaker climbs out of the vent, this one much bigger and taller than the others. The leader of the freakers straightens up and grins, holding a crude, spiky club.

"I was hoping I would see you again. You have something that belongs to a friend of mine, and I think it's time you gave it back," Jessica says, and the leader sneers as Abs removes her shoes and carefully takes a step backwards among the blood and bodies. The two newly arrived freakers begin manoeuvring to outflank her, in doing so opening a path for their leader, who hangs back waiting, understanding that his foe knows violence and respecting at least the danger before him. His subordinates, not so mindful of such things, will most surely rush to their deaths.

At their chosen angle of attack, pretty much facing each other with Abs in between. They rush in as they attack simultaneously.

Abs waits for the last possible moment before taking another step backwards and to her right, slashing at her closest attacker's throat. The floor proves as treacherous as it looked and makes it impossible for him to stop. He slips and crashes into the pile of bodies, adding himself to the mess. Blood is already gushing from his wound as he attempts to press the flaps of his ruined flesh back in place and fails.

The second freaker, already understanding his mistake, somehow manages to remain standing but is perilously unstable. Abs takes full advantage, already half sliding in for her attack with a leg sweep that takes the freaker down. Using her own momentum, she falls with the freaker, stabbing her blade deep into his chest, piercing his heart.

The leader of the freakers circles around the pile of bodies, choosing his route carefully as the second freaker screams out in agony; Abs looks up just in time to see the downswing of the leader's club, aiming for her head. She drives away, releasing her grip upon her blade. Withdrawing it now would be too slow, so she opts to grab a small knife from one of the fallen freaker had dropped.

The leader's club hits only the fallen and already dying freaker, who sprays another lungful of blood from the crushing club. The leader of the freakers following relentlessly as his target scrambles through the slippery mess, the leader swings down again, this time almost slipping as the weighted club pulls him forward—and this time, the spiked head finds flesh to rip as Abs's retreating left leg is hit, causing a dreadful wound, but her subdermal skin preventing serious damage.

Another swing, this one just barely missing her upper thigh as the freaker gets closer into the thick of the bodies. Abs retrieves the second knife and manages to scramble far enough away to find her own feet again to stand and face her pursuer.

The leader of the freakers grins, enjoying the prospect of a fight, as very few of his victims attempt to fight back. The pleasure of playing with his victims to torment them and extinguish their lives slowly is wonderful, but he only occasionally gets this joy. It's refreshing when one tries to fight back. This girl is no different from the other fighters, male or female; she has a strong spirit to snuff out of this world, and the thought of consuming her flesh and drinking her blood excites him. This alone encourages him to move faster.

The strongest of the freakers stops just a few paces away from Jessica, his club now swinging back and forth like a pendulum.

"Okay, you sick fuck, come and get me!" Jessica taunts. The freaker, waiting no longer, uses the momentum of his swing to throw the whole weight of the club over and around his head as he charges forward, timing his downward swing to slam hard to where Jessica's left shoulder would have been. Jessica, having no desire to die this day or any day, had already started to dive forward onto her knees and slides the short distance to the freaker's body, driving both of her knives deep into his abdomen and drawing them downward.

This manoeuvre inflicts two deep vertical wounds down to his groin, and the freaker bellows with agony as his wounds begin to gush with his blood and drops his club as he crashes both elbows down upon Jessica's shoulders, the sheer force of the blows driving her down onto her back.

With the force of the blow and her own strength, Jessica brings her legs forward from under her and slams her feet into his chins and then rapidly rolls to her left, away from the pile of bodies as the leader of the freakers crashes down to the floor like a felled tree, only his arms preventing any serious harm from the sudden impact with the floor.

Jessica then springs back over onto his back and lands a flurry of slashing, stabbing strikes at his unprotected back and neck. He howls in pain and bellows in anger, his fury seemingly giving him strength. Leaning closer, Jessica feels the freaker's strength begin to waver.

"How does that feel, you bastard?" Jessica asks.

Jessica realises too late her mistake as the freaker snaps his head backwards, connecting with her nose and shattering it with a loud crunch, the power of the blow knocks her back, but Jessica transforms the force to roll to the side and away as the lights of the room start to blink and flash. The flashing lights not helping with Jessica's now-spinning head, feeling disorientated as the leader scrambles his way back to the vent, diving back inside and vanishing from sight.

Jessica somehow finds her feet as blood streams down her face. Her vision becomes a blur as she staggers away out of the room, just catching sight of her next target, another freaker that slipped past her as she fought the leader.

This last freaker is closing in on Jake as a warning shout comes from somewhere above. Jake turns, raising his hands in a defensive measure, the freaker now close enough to kill him. It grins at Jake with a look of madness and hunger with a blade in hand, ready to plunge it into Jake's face.

But the freaker never gets the chance to act out his last desire, as Jessica comes crashing into its back, slamming her knife to the hilt, into the back of the freaker. The point of the knife protrudes from his chest as the freaker looks down with widening eyes. Then, his grip upon his own blade fails, and the blade clatters to the ground. Jake leaps backwards in terror as the freaker drops to the floor, dead.

The lights in the room stop flickering and become brighter as the claw's lifting arm slowly and carefully descends back to the floor, placing the pod down and allowing Sam and Neil to climb off. Jake gives Jessica a relieved smile as he looks her up and down.

"Thanks. I owe you my life. Are you injured?" he asks, seeing her caked in blood.

"Think nothing of it, and no, I'm fine, surprisingly—all superficial," Jessica replies, tapping Jake on the back as a friendly gesture before she reaches Sam.

"Did you manage to get the system to recognise us?" Jessica asks, but her question is answered before Sam can reply as a doorway opens at the side of the room, and several trustees rush through holding stun batons, followed by a concerned-looking Alistair Brookes.

Sam calmly walks over to Alistair. As the two make eye contact, Sam speeds up, closing the gap. He grabs hold of Alistair's shoulders and pushes him up against the wall next to the doorway he just entered through.

"What the hell is going on, Alistair? We almost got killed down here, and now I want answers...we want answers," Sam says, correcting himself, and the others add their own angry concerns as the trustees raise their stun batons, but upon seeing Jessica approach, their resolve seems to falter. Before Alistair can start to answer, Sam leans in and lowers his voice.

"Are you controlling the freakers? They seem to have orders that I was not to be harmed?" Sam asks,

"I'm not controlling them, and I'm not entirely sure why they might have allowed you to live. Okay, I'll be honest with you, but I did not wish to add to your already sizable problems, but now I think you have earned at least my complete honesty. I do not believe we are the first to be imprisoned here," Alistair Brookes replies. Sam listens closely to Alistair's answer and then releases him.

"What exactly do you mean? The freakers were trapped here before we arrived?" he asks, as Jessica moves in a step closer.

"No, not exactly. The majority seems to be made up of prisoners from the first level, but the system has detected prisoners from other levels going missing—not dying, but steady reports of violent activity and self-mutilation—and then after a new level is brought online, the prisoner drop from the system and seemingly vanishes, not to be scanned again," Alistair says. Sam, listening, and by the end of Alistair's theory and explanation, Sam starts to feel worse about the facility.

"Are you saying any one of us could change and become a freaker?" Sam asks.

"Change? No, I don't think so, and the numbers that have changed from the very start to now have reduced, becoming less with each new level that comes online. If it were something that could be spread, surely those numbers would be increasing," Alistair replies.

"Okay, fine, that sounds reasonable. It also makes me feel a little better, but not a lot. So why do you think they changed in the first place?" Sam asks, racking his own brains for a reason.

"Like I said, I do not think we are the first to be imprisoned here. I suspect something or someone is changing them in some way," Alistair says.

Before any of the others can react to this new revelation, a trustee rushes into the room.

"Sorry to interrupt, Professor, but you asked for any updates. We found Frank in the lost and found under a pile of dead freakers; we thought he was dead along with the others, but once we started to clear the bodies away,

Frank regained consciousness. He's been taken to the doc," The trustee says.

Neil looks up and is about to say something, but Sam gives him a 'not now' look.

"What occurred earlier can wait for now. But Frank is one hell of a survivor and has been through a lot, and I would be grateful if I could be kept updated with his condition," I ask. Alistair nods an okay and turns to face the trustee.

"Thank you for the update. Please keep us both informed, and please make sure that all the bodies are taken to the morgue. Dr Moore will need to examine them before disposal," Alistair asks.

"Yes, sir, will do," The trustee replies, turn and leaves.

· · ·

Watching the trustee leave, I retell the story of the escape attempt to the professor. He looks increasingly impressed until the final outcome produces the same results as the first retelling to the others, deep disappointment. The professor promises to find out more about the mysterious escape attempt. Whoever it was, knew far more than your average inmate.

The cleanup takes longer than expected. The rest of the good-time boys are eventually found, but the leader of the freakers has vanished. Somehow, Frank killed at least four of his attackers, although two of them managed to crawl away from him and then died later.

We are led back to medical, so we can rest, and the Doctor can check us over, ensuring Jessica's wounds does not become infected. The professor promises to answer any other questions we might wish to ask. I make a promise to myself, too: that I will do my utmost to find us a way out of here, not only for myself and the professor but for all who found ourselves fighting for our lives in the lost and found.

. . .

The head of the freakers stares down at the floor in total darkness, the lights in this section of the facility no longer functioning, but like all freakers, he can see perfectly well. The voice calmly explains again what is needed of him and how tenuous his position is now.

"You had one simple task, just one: kill Jessica! Sam McCall must not have her as a friend," The voice explains.

The voice pauses as the man steps slowly and softly around the freaker. He then stops, places a hand upon the freaker's head, and slowly stokes it.

"I will forgive you this one time, but if you let me down again, the gifts I have given you will not be enough to save you   from   my   wrath,"   The   voice   warns.

7
The Last Escape

Facility Zero, 202 days online: federation year 2426
WE SPEND THE first week back from the lost and found within medical. Jessica had superficial wounds from her stand against the freakers, and she retold her account of the showdown to us with grisly details. Frank amazed us again by not dying, and the doctor was amazed at his recovery. The majority of his wounds were not life-threatening, and the stump where his hand had been severed was treated to ensure no other complications would occur. Frank had remained unconscious for the first week, and when he awoke, he demanded food, which raised everyone's spirits.

Neil remained absent after that and decided to move back into the community. Neither of us mentioned what had happened, and maybe that was for the best. Jake left after the next week, claiming boredom and the need to return to his duties, but he made me promise that I would keep him up to date with any news.

After three weeks, Frank had recovered enough to take short walks around medical. Considering how many injuries he had sustained, that was nothing short of a miracle.

"Well, that's what you get from a heavy worlder," the doctor had said on passing after seeing Frank's improvements. Jessica did not seem surprised, considering Frank's size, but I was a little taken aback. Although I knew about heavy worlders, they generally kept to their own worlds due to their heavier-set muscles and bodies due to their worlds' increased mass.

But then Alistair Brookes's arrival brings me back to the reality of our situation of being locked away. Whatever Frank did in his previous life, it was severe enough for him to be brought here.

"Hey, Sam, I hope you are feeling better. I'm sorry for just popping in, but the Doctor informed me that Frank is well enough to be discharged soon," Alistair says with his usual warming smile, making it hard to dislike the man. Whatever his reasons for designing a place like this, he's not a bad guy.

"You guys seem to be inseparable of late, which is understandable, so I've taken it upon myself to create you a place near the operations centre for you, Abs and Frank, of course, and a terminal. You won't have to work if you don't wish to," Alistair pauses again as Jessica looks up, and we exchange glances.

"Thanks, Alistair. I was going to ask you if something like that could be arranged. I've been having late-night walks with Abs recently, and we are both concerned about what happened at the lost and found. Not only that, we need information, and a lot of it, if we are going to make it out of here. The issue originally was maybe a little easier with just two to escape, but now it's looking increasingly harder to overcome," I explain as I look at Alistair with concern.

"I also have a bit of a confession to make," I say as Alistair and Jessica give me an 'oh' look.

"It's to do with my past. I've always been good at problem-solving and achieving the impossible with ingenuity. Systems will always have a flaw; stealing something is always possible with the right plan, but getting away with it is not easy. My first idea was working out how to skim credits away from a global trading terminal on Earth. I set up a fake corporation on Mars that announced it was going to manufacture dust filters. I then hacked into the global transfer market and slipped-in a very tiny program.

The transfer market charges for any corporation searches, and with this program, every time someone accessed details of my company on Mars, one credit from that charge was transferred to my corporation bank account," I say, pausing there, allowing my thoughts to assemble themselves before I continue.

"I knew I would not make a lot, but then that famous storm of seventy-seven occurred on Mars, the rush for any kind of filtration systems went into overdrive, and my corporation made over a billion credits in just over one weekend. This kind of money turns heads, and my corporation was discovered to be a fake. The money trails led straight back to me, and I was arrested for the first time," I say, revealing my past.

I smile to myself, remembering that first time. Alistair looks shocked but impressed, and Jessica chuckles.

"How old were you?" she asks.

"Oh, I was thirteen," I grin, and Jessica looks positively amazed.

"But the fact that my program made so much money wasn't the main problem. The back orders my company received for filtration systems went into the hundreds of billions. I overpriced my entire catalogue to make sure nobody tried to buy anything; every item was totally overinflated, but that storm was just so nuts, it drove demand through the roof. Ironically, if I'd been producing filters, my business plan would have worked...well, for that season at least," I explain.

"You mentioned you had a confession," Alistair asks, still looking amused by my story.

"I was just getting there. I was taken to a federation low-security centre and told in no uncertain terms how much trouble I was in by almost every federation officer that spoke to me except for one. His name was Elbridge, Commander Elbridge. He just said how clever the plan was and that I was just a bit too successful and that he would be keeping an eye on me from here on out. He was the nicest, but sadly I never saw him again. Well, for a few years at least. I escaped after a few weeks, and my life of crime and being on the run started there.

"At this point, I started to receive job contracts. Steal this, sabotage that, make sure the voting system on an outpost is loaded in favour of a particular person, many tasks like that, sometimes I would be caught; other times, I would get away with it. But then I bumped into Elbridge again, and some of the lucky escapes in my past became clear.

It turned out that a lot of my contracts came from Elbridge. He explained that I'd been working for him for some time now, and a lot of my escapes were due to him.

"My career changed that day. Elbridge was very happy with what I'd been able to do for him, so I started to get contracts from other federation officers. I would be given the job, but I made the plans. Sometimes I would get away scot-free, and other times the plan would be for me to get arrested to clear the heat quickly; then, within a week or two, I would escape again," I explain. Alistair's and Jessica's faces show they are starting to follow where this is all leading.

"I needed to tell you this, as my past is a little complicated. I'm good, maybe great, at planning the impossible, but my reputation for escaping from everywhere is not true, at least not completely. I had a lot of help," I say and stop there, feeling relieved to get that revelation off my chest, but it's not my confession that is surprising. Jessica looks disheartened, but it's Alistair who catches me off guard.

"I know all this, but thank you. I appreciate it, but I think it is I who owe you a confession and an apology. My friend and colleague Commander Taylor was the one that got you sent here. You might not have known, but on one of your last jobs, he made sure you discovered something that you could not resist. I'm sorry, Sam, but I am responsible for getting you sent here. Commander Taylor thought you were my last best chance of escape," Alistair reveals.

. . .

I decided I needed a walk. Alistair's revelation is more than I expected. I wanted to clear the ground and let the others really know more of my past, but in doing so, I'd found more than I expected. I take a random destination, and halfway through, I change my mind and end up at the dining hall. I'm feeling hungry anyway, and now is as good a time as any to reenter the facility's open population.

As soon as I enter the dining hall, the chattering conversations from around the room suddenly stop as all the heads one by one turn and stare at my arrival. The various rumours regarding what happened in the lost and found have run through the facility like wildfire. They range from a mass breakout attempt to an alien invasion from the black hole itself. One of the rumours comes close to being right, and that's the one about Frank taking on a whole bunch of freakers and living to talk about it later, except Frank would not say what occurred between him and Neil.

Taking a tray of food, I head for a table as most of the room continues to stare in my direction. Choosing a mostly empty table, I sit down with my best 'don't try to talk to me' look, which seems more successful than I had hoped for, as the table's current occupiers stand up and leave. Feeling rather happy with myself, I tuck into my food. It's not particularly nice, but it fills a hole. However, my mood takes a nosedive once I realise the true reason for everyone's sudden departure as Samuel sits down opposite me.

"Hello, Sam. It's been a while, it sounds like you have had a bit of a rough time of it of late, but it looks like you managed to struggle through without too much trouble," Samuel says as he watches me for some kind of reaction.

"It was a bit tense. Sadly, Frank suffered more than the rest of us," I reply between mouthfuls of food.

"Depends on your point of view, I guess. I would say that the good-time boys had suffered the most, but then again, out of all who were involved, they deserved what happened to them more than the rest of you," Samuel replies with a smile as he watches me eat.

"I'm not sure anyone deserved what they got, except maybe the freakers themselves," I counter, wondering where this is all leading.

"Maybe, I guess, but I'm wondering if we all deserve to suffer in one form or another, considering we have all been sent here for whatever reason. But I can see that some of us have transgressed more than others. Maybe the ones that suffered most are the ones that deserved it most," Samuel replies, still watching and still waiting.

I stop eating, putting my utensils down. "Okay, Samuel, what is it you want?" I ask bluntly; Samuel stops smiling and answers promptly.

"I would've thought that was obvious. I want what most of us want. I wish to leave here, and as soon as possible. When we first met, I did you a favour, and you knew it would cost you. I'm just reminding you of that. Also, I would like to help you in any way I can, mainly through information," Samuel replies, then pauses, letting his words sink in, and then continues.

"I know who tried to escape, and I'm betting Alistair won't like you knowing," Samual says cryptically.

"What are you talking about?" I reply with a bit more vehemence than I meant.

"I'm talking about how Alistair knew about this last escape attempt and even helped plan it," Samuel replies, remaining calm.

"That's insane. Alistair wants my help to escape. Why would he help this other guy, knowing that this could ruin any other escape that comes later?" I ask.

"Well, for one thing, you know about the saying 'Don't keep all your eggs in one basket.' Plus, I'm guessing he's becoming desperate," Samuel replies, now looking serious.

"Why desperate? I don't understand," I say.

"Because the more inmates the facility receives, the closer the station needs to be in proximity to the black hole, and the closer we get, the quicker time passes by away from the black hole. You think you only spent three weeks in medical, but in reality, it's been over two years," Samuel replies, then pauses again to let the relevance of all this sink in.

"But this only gets worse. A week here and means two years now, and then near the time this facility is full, it could be 10 years per week.

"I see what you're saying. We need to get out sooner rather than later; otherwise, everyone we know will be long gone," I reply, realizing the problem.

"Exactly, and that's what makes Alistair more desperate. His wife and daughters are outside, and he's desperate to get back to them, so all I'm saying is that he's willing to take a few risks and chances, and he won't necessarily let you in on all his plans and ideas. You're just another possible route out," Samuel says as Jessica sits down next to me.

"You must be Samuel," Jessica says as she puts her tray down.

"I am, and I know who you are. I heard it on the grapevine you killed over a dozen freakers on your own. Impressive work," Samuel replies.

"Not a dozen, but a fair amount. Rumours around here seem to spiral out of control," Jessica replies and then starts to eat.

"Rumors and stories are really all everyone has. It's like being a part of your own adventure. All this place is missing is some kind of bogeyman or alien creature chasing down everyone," Samuel replies as he gets up from the table. Jessica stops eating, staring up at Samuel.

"From what I experienced a few weeks back, I would say the facility has one," Jessica replies, then continues to eat. Samuel stares back at me for a moment.

"Have a good meal, you two, and thanks for the chat. We should do it again soon," Samuel says, then looking back at Jessica again, he smiles one last time and leaves, heading out of the dining hall.

"There's something off about that guy," Jessica says, watching Samuel leave.

"Off, why? Because he's not listed anywhere, or because he's finger-pointing at Alistair?" I ask.

"Oh, is he? Well, I'm not sure. Maybe both or neither of them, but he's holding something back, and I've never totally trusted Alistair in any case," Jessica says before taking another mouthful of food.

"I'm not sure either, to be honest. Alistair hasn't done himself any favours, and this place is beyond creepy and wrong. I need to do some serious thinking and digging. If you don't mind doing some digging of your own, I need some answers regarding piloting that pod, and I think Alistair might have them. Sorry, I can't stay, but I'll catch up with you later," I say, standing up.

"No problem, Sam, take care," Jessica replies.

Picking up my tray and take it over to the disposal chute, something about the lost and found still bothering me.

*   *   *

Leaving the dining hall, I head back to the lost and found. Now that I'm listed on the security system again, I'm able to get a route, and when I arrive, the first thing I notice is that the bodies and the mess have been cleaned up, leaving just the tables with the plans of escape still written upon them; all the other paper plans have long since been taken away.

Taking my time, I go back over the basic plans. Being able to reprogram the maintenance lifting arm and building a modified pod must have taken a lot of technical expertise. I know a lot, but this is technological know-how you don't just read about in databases; it's incredibly complicated, but something about the plan does not make sense. It's expert enough to design and build but blind to the facility's fundamental issue being in the proximity of a black hole's gravitational effect.

I'm still pondering upon the puzzle as I walk into the dismantling bay. I notice that the system has been repaired and activated. Standing in the room, I watch a dismantled pod ejected from the station for a moment. Like the last, this room has also been cleaned, and any sign of what occurred in those few short weeks previous has been cleared away; the room hums with motion as newly arrived pods are lowered into the room as other pods are in various stages of being dismantled.

The terminal where Jessica and I watched as the escape attempt unfolded has been removed. Seeing nothing else of interest, I return to the previous room, glancing around for one last look before I turn to leave. It's then that I smell something terrible. My curiosity raised. I follow the smell farther into the room, losing it momentarily and then finding it again, stronger and more pungent. My fear and curiosity increase equally as I come up against a wall.

This section of the wall is part of the main bulkhead of the station. Seeing nothing at first, I run my hand over the wall, and then I feel the unmistakable edge of a panel. Following the edge down, I find a place I can slip my fingers into and behind the panel. Gripping it, I slowly manage to pry open the panelled section a few inches. Now with more of the panel open and gripping the edge with both hands, I pull back on the wall section. Without warning, the panel suddenly gives and opens, crashing to the floor, the source of the smell dropping out like a discarded manikin.

I look down aghast at the body and take a few steps back. The smell almost overpowers my stomach as I try to keep everything down. Then I recognise the body staring up at me, and the battle is lost at that moment, and I succumb to the stench, adding my own vile odour to the room. Coughing and spitting the remains of the taste I can't get rid of out of my mouth, I stagger back to the vent of the room and take in a deep breath.

"I need help down in engineering. I've found another body," I call out loud to the room as I take more clean breaths.

• • •

Jessica enters the control centre, having been given access after the lost-and-found incident. The control centre, as always, is alive with various sounds from the many systems that surround the room. Alistair Brookes looks up from his work console as Jessica enters.

"Welcome to the control centre. Not many of our guests are normally allowed up here, but I'm happy to make an exception for you," Alistair says as he stands. Jessica stops, looking around at the systems.

"It always surprises me at first that there are no windows in a space station, but it's obvious really; you only get things like that in stories," Jessica says as she stops looking around and faces the professor.

"Well, window's would be nice, but they'd be totally impractical. The command ship had an observation area, but to have something like that on any ship or space station, takes so much reinforcement to the infrastructure, it generally is too expensive. But I'm sure you did not come all this way just to talk about windows," Alistair says, smiling.

"Very true, but it was an honest observation. I need to ask you if you know who was piloting that pod. It's is clear to me that what was accomplished was no mean feat. Someone with detailed knowledge of the station must have helped or been the one flying that pod," Jessica asks. Alistair looks thoughtful before answering.

"I went over the plans myself, and you are right, the detail of knowledge was staggering, but I can assure you that this information did not come from me, and no one else in this facility has that kind of knowledge. Plus, none of my security trustee's are currently missing," Alistair replies.

"So if you had nothing to do with it, then who? It's unlikely to be one of the convicts," Jessica says.

"There are some very smart people on this station, but not any who could have pulled off that escape attempt. I've been going back over the list of inmates, and none of them come close," I explain, Alistair, looking genuinely perplexed, and then his expression changes to one of thoughtfulness.

"There was one man who could have possibly carried it out, but his pod malfunctioned as it was docking. This was a while back—just a day or two after I arrived," Alistair says.

"What happened?" Jessica looks up with interest.

"His name was Dr Zorn, and he volunteered to try and help me escape. He was part of a rescue attempt, but as his pod neared the facility, there was some kind of malfunction, and his pod was incinerated," Alistair explains.

"So, there is no way he could have survived in some way?" Jessica asks.

"It's unlikely; the pod was completely destroyed," Alistair says. Jessica rubs her forehead in frustration.

"This makes no bloody sense," Jessica replies.

"Professor Brookes, Sam McCall is asking for you and Jessica to come to medical. It would seem he has found another body," the station computer says, startling Brookes but only causing Jessica to look up with interest.

• • •

By the time Jessica and the professor arrive in medical, Jake, Frank, Neil, and Samuel are already there, along with Dr Moore and Sam. Two covered-up bodies are also in the room on examination tables.

"Thank you for coming along with such short notice, but I thought it was important to let you all know what I discovered recently; I've been concerned of late regarding the incident at the lost and found.

I've found a second body, which Jake, confirmed, were the two inmates I saw ducking out of the laundry several weeks back," I say. Jake nods.

"Originally, I had suspected that the two were working on the escape plan together, but then at the last moment, one of them killed the other," I pause, looking at each person present like this is some kind of whodunit. Various heads nod in agreement except for Alistair, Jessica, and Samuel.

"But I quickly dismissed this, the plans, the designs… I doubt very much that either of them could have designed a working coffee machine, let alone a modified pod and booster. The only thing that made sense before finding the last body was that the two from the laundry helped a third, the brains of the outfit which drew up the plans, but at the last minute, they turned on the brains, killing brains, and then fought over the pod, realizing or already knowing it could only take one. The survivor then takes the pod out and dies. This made perfect sense until I found the second body," Sam pauses and looks over at the covered-up bodies and then at the assembled.

"That can't possibly have happened, as both the muscles are now confirmed dead, leaving the brains to pilot the pod and dies. Which also makes no sense at all. The brains understood enough to design and build a pod, but not enough about the effects of the black hole; this leads me to just one last possible conclusion, there is a fourth man, and he's still on station," I explain—some of the others looking between themselves. I then make eye contact with Doctor Moore.

"Could you tell us your findings, please, Doctor?" I ask.

"Yes, of course. They both died approximately three, maybe four weeks ago. The second body found was first killed and was bludgeoned to death with a large item, but the other was strangled by someone with strong hands, though the pattern would suggest someone using just one hand with a very powerful grip," Doctor Moore says.

"Just one hand? That's unusual. Could anyone have been able to strangle him?" Alistair asks with interest.

"No, not really. The discolouration shown around his throat is large, and it would have taken someone with powerful hands to cause that kind of injury. You could cut out almost everyone here except maybe for Frank," Doctor Moore replies. Almost as though on cue, everyone turns to regard Frank.

"Hey, sod that. I've had nothing to do with it. I'm a changed man and have not had a drop of anything in years," Frank says, almost spitting out his words and looking from Jessica to the others.

"It's okay, Frank. No one is outright accusing you. This is just an observation of facts, trying to understand what happened. Besides, I would be more concerned about

Abs's man hands," Sam finishes with a slight smile, as the others laugh now, looking at Jessica.

"Hey, cut that out. I definitely do not have man hands, but I'll show you my pissed-off female fist if you keep that up," Jessia says, becoming annoyed as Neil and Jake burst out laughing. Trying to hold down a laugh my own amusement, I continue.

"Okay, settle down, guys. We are almost done here and thank you for your results, Doctor," I say.

"I was happy to help, and to be honest, this is the most exciting thing that has happed in a while. But I have less interesting duties to attend to that won't get completed on their own, so if you all will excuse me," Doctor Moore says with a slight nod then leaves the room.

"I want to end by giving you my conclusions. Professor Brookes has designed a truly impressive station, the likes of which I have never seen before. It poses many issues, the complications increasing with each additional member of the group included in any escape attempt. The last escape was, in my opinion, the best and only chance any single person had to escape, and that failed.

In my opinion, even if that pod had waited until it left the protection of the station's field, I'm very doubtful that the booster would have been enough to escape the influence of the black hole. Every four weeks here increases the difficulties to overcome, and that was for just one of us, and sadly that window of opportunity is now closed," I say, looking at all the glum faces staring back. Only Samuel still seems optimistic.

"Even if we could escape the influence of the black hole, no ship, private or otherwise, would wait in the vicinity of the black hole for years on the off chance that someone would succeed in an escape. Even if one would, I'm betting the federation station is armed and would not put up with that for too long," I pause only long enough for the information to sink in, but Alistair jumps in first before I'm able to continue.

"So you have concluded that escape is impossible?" Alistair asks.

"I would not say impossible, but the price is too high, and I'm not willing to pay it. The only conceivable way to escape with all present would result in everyone else dying; this I will not do," I explain, watching the expression of those present. This was the moment I had waited for; only Samuel still seems unconvinced.

"I'm sorry, but that's the facts. Even if we say to hell with the rest of the people here, we would still need to get past the federation station, and my escape plan would just get us away from the black hole with nowhere else to go," I stop there, looking at the others and feeling that I had let down my friends.

"If anything changes or I get more information that helps, then I'll let you know, but for now, these are my conclusions, and I can't keep them from you."

• • •

It is pitch black in Neil's room. Neil lies wide awake, as he has tossed and turned in his bed for the past few hours; nothing he did has helped, and his betrayal of Frank lies heavily on his mind. From out of the darkness, eyes watch with mild interest until their owner finally breaks the silence.

"You have been a very naughty ape-man. I see that your actions have made a big enough crack for me to slip inside," The sinister voice explains.

8
Commander Taylor's Predicament

Facility Zero, 1 day online: Federation year 2417

COMMANDER TAYLOR WATCHES from his command ship as Facility Zero settles into position and powers online. The professor's whereabouts had been brought to his attention just a few minutes before. Everyone knew there was nothing that could be done. The system was designed to reject any commands to bring the station back, not that the stabilisers had that kind of power in the first place. In fact, if the system detected the facility moving away from the black hole, then the stabilisers would just shut down and send the entire facility down into the black hole.

No escape meant just that, but even so, the commander felt responsible for Professor Brookes, who is not just a colleague but a friend, and until he's exhausted every option, his mission will continue on station. The commander watches in silence as the first of the pods descends toward the prison.

· · ·

Command Taylor had some major hurdles to overcome due to the project's secrecy. For example, authorising any possible rescue attempt must be from the cryo-station itself and not from the command ship. Also, the command ship is too large to approach safely, and organising any rescue attempt outside the station could compromise the project itself.

The other complication is that any escape attempt needs to be carried out within ten years. Past that time frame, the station's proximity to the black hole will be passed the point of no return. All possible solutions were raised and examined and considered, and every expert except for one had come to the same conclusion: it is not possible.

Dr Zorn devised a brilliant idea. It is risky, and it has its own particular dangers, but it could work with a bit of luck. Commander Taylor felt this was good enough and gave the go-ahead.

Sanding in front of the assembled project team members, Doctor Zorn takes a moment to gather his thoughts. The majority of the project team present are experts in one field or another regarding space flight, astral physics, gravitational effects, and so on, which helps save time and prevents all the 'why can't we' and "why would that happen" type of questions. They will just listen. Some will nod, others will smile, and one or two will still look very sceptical.

"The issue we have is twofold, but there are other minor points that we will need to overcome. Some of you will know and understand these points, and others, I'm sure, will come up to speed very quickly and will be able to spot issues that we might not see or understand. Issue one: the pods do not have any kind of guidance system on board.

The docking process is controlled by the cryostation; this ceases as soon as the pod enters the docking tube; at this point, the Facility takes control and finalises the docking sequence.

Issue number two: even at this range, the pods, fully fueled, do not have enough thrust to break away from the influence of the black hole, and due to protection from the gravity field, any escape attempt needs to be practically from a standing start outside of the gravity field; otherwise, it would be like throwing eggs at a wall.

Today, our job is for a short-term solution that needs to be carried out at the facility itself, which leads to another problem. Whoever goes over will also have to be rescued, which means more work due to the pod modifications that need to be carried out, so we will need a small team, three maximum," Doctor Zorn explains.

The room erupts into a deafening noise, everyone trying to talk at once, some trying to say why they should go, others explaining why this cannot work. Then, arguments start as small groups seem to form, all with different ideas. Each trying to clarify their reasons that this is madness, and others saying it's pure genius.

"Quiet down. This is not helping. Each and every one of you will get a chance to make your case, but I'll make it easier by asking if any of you is willing to stay behind on the facility?" Doctor Zorn asks.

This question is met with sudden silence, one that is shortly broken by a single voice.

"I am sir—Wheeler, second class, on secondment from Commander Taylor's crew. Commander Taylor requested volunteers, and I'm more than happy to help sir," Wheeler replies.

Zorn smiles with relief, and the room's attitude changes with this one voice.

"Thank you, Wheeler. Help accepted," Doctor Zorn says, then turning back to the rest of the assembled, and continues.

"If there are no other volunteers, then we will move our discussion over to my plan. Modification of a pod is going to be our focus. We will also send a pod with extra components that we can use to help with the modification process. We will need to modify one pod per team member who is unwilling to stay, so I propose sending a three-man team to help with this task.

I have already made my intentions known to the commander that I will head this team, so all I'm asking for at this point is just one more volunteer," Doctor Zorn says, looking around at the many faces he's known for years but many of them have families. Dr Zorn knew he was fortunate to get Wheeler. Seeing no other volunteers, he continues.

"The following schematics should be sufficient to modify a pod to give its occupant enough power to thrust away from the facility so that the command ship can safely approach and scoop in the pod. As you can see, the pod requires no external modification and can quickly be completed in a day or two. In theory, we could modify a pod by adding a section of an additional pod to act like a thruster rocket to break away from the influence of the black hole, but if that schematic fell into the wrong hands, well, that could lead to the entire project being scrapped.

The last obstacle is the federation. If the federation discovers what we are up to, then they will put a stop to it. I would estimate the odds being around 95% in our favour the first time we launch a modified pod from the station, dropping at about 20% with each one after the first. As soon as the feds notice anything out of the ordinary, then the game's up. This facility is designed to be escape-proof, and without outside help, I would suggest it is," Doctor Zorn explains.

The meeting continued for a few more hours to cover and finalise the plan, which took an unexpected and positive new direction. An idea came from a relatively low-level technician who asked why the modification had to be carried out on the station. Considering only two people had volunteered, the work to be carried out with two or maybe three people, if Professor Brookes helped, would still take weeks, so the plan was changed: two pods would be modified on the command ship and flown down to the facility from there.

•   •   •

The modifications with a full team took three days. Now all that had to be done was to pilot the pods down. Zorn would then start the slow process of refuelling the pods. Wheeler would stay and take on Professor Brookes's role, and Professor Brookes would come back with Dr Zorn. Overall mission time, one week down on the facility and just over six weeks back on the command ship. The plan seemed perfect, but truth be known, any rescue attempt at this point was doomed to failure.

For the past year, while the facility was being prepared, every level of the federation had been bored witless, and now every federation member is on ultrahigh alert as the first of the very worst of federation society is being transferred from the cryostation down to the facility. Each pod is scheduled and scrutinised; ensuring nothing is out of place or turn; The cryo-station monitoring each pod's status as they are sent down.

•   •   •

Wheeler takes the lead pod and heads down toward the facility, with Dr Zorn following behind. Just a few minutes out from the command ship, the cryostation detection grid alerts the sentries to an unscheduled craft entering restricted space. The cryostation is the holding station for all prisoners waiting to be sent down to the facility and the criminal courts, federation habitat, and station security.

Not unlike the facility with its state-of-the-art systems, the station security has its own advanced system. Within seconds of an unidentified craft entering restricted space, the station alerts security, and the weapon systems lock on to the craft, the speed and agility of which are impressive. Moments after the first, another system alert sounds as a second craft is detected, sending the crew into uncertainty.

System tests prior to the facility coming online had the crew running hundreds of simulations, and they'd run the procedures perfectly, but this second alert sends the crew into shock. Is it another test or a real threat? By the time the senior officer regains his composure, the first craft has almost reached the docking tube when the order to fire is given.

The weapon system emits a concentrated dual burst of proton lasers that fire across the top of the facility, the beam arcs as it's affected by the mass of the black hole, but all this is taken into account, and the laser beam smashes into the craft, a direct hit, the energy blasting easily through the shell and turning the oxygen within the craft into a sudden ball of blue light that glows with incandescent heat, burning brightly for a few seconds before dissipating. The wreckage smashes harmlessly into the facility and breaks up.

The command ship issues orders to ceasefire, but the second burst has already been released. Seeing Wheeler's pod destroyed, Dr Zorn increases speed as he enters the gravity field surrounding the station and heads for the docking tube, but, sensing that he would not make it, he waits as long as he dares before hitting the ejection release.

At that moment, the proton laser incinerates his pod, igniting the oxygen, Dr Zorn's ejection seat blasting him away as the fireball momentarily envelops him and the pod before dissipating but causing major burns over his suit and chair. His ejection system has fired him clear of the primary detonation, but he isn't out of danger yet.

His ejection seat has propelled him out at a perpendicular angle to the facility, but his downward thrust has not been altered. He quickly enters his new coordinates to his seat, hoping that the manoeuvring jets have enough power to reduce his speed, but then out of the corner of his eye, he notices his pod suddenly impact against the facility and disintegrate into thousands of deadly shards of metal, ricocheting in multiple directions.

A warning light flashes as the seat's main thrusters begin to fail. Designed primarily for short-flight capabilities and not for hard deceleration, the thrusters somehow miraculously held out long enough to slow the chair, allowing Doctor Zorn to safely head towards his new destination, a maintenance hatch jutting out from the top of the facility. Fragments of the exploded pod zipping past, the chair avoiding more by luck than skill the main cloud of deadly shrapnel, however not passing by totally unscathed as several fragments impact the chair and suit, the chairs manoeuvring jets failing moments later.

Doctor Zorn's inertia carrying him onwards and reaching the hatchway less than 30 seconds later;

detaching himself from his chair, he pushes it away. Turning his attention to the hatch's access controls, his suit, hampering his movement within the vacuum of space. Entering the access code, Doctor Zorn is greeted with 'Access Denied'. Then adding to the mounting stress, his suit warning light suddenly flashes, accompanied by an urgent beeping noise indicating life support failure.

With oxygen depleting fast, Dr Zorn fumbles at the hatch control again, trying desperately to open the door, but his efforts are rewarded once more with access denied. Doctor Zorn's breathing, already rugged at this point, begins gasping as the remaining oxygen supply reaches zero, as the airlock hatch hisses and opens; astonishingly, a man is standing within the airlock without an environmental suit. He reaches out to Doctor Zorn and, grabbing hold of his suit, pulls him inside. Once past the airlock hatch, the door closes behind him, followed by the airlock's pressurisation cycle.

Dr Zorn's burning lungs rejoice at the presence of breathable air as the facility's full gravitational effect takes over, and the doctor slumps to the ground, drawing lungfuls of air as his visor opens. The stranger continues to stand waiting patiently as Doctor Zorn slowly regains his strength and carefully stands to regard his rescuer, confused as to how this man could survive the vacuum of space unprotected.

"Hello, Doctor Zorn. Welcome to Facility Zero. I am sure that's how the others greet newcomers here. My name is Samael, but most know me here as Samuel," Samael says, holding out his hand.

•   •   •

The Inner Federation was not born on Earth; rather, the Inner Federation invited Earth to join the Outer Federation planets. This was due to the Earth's technological advancement of becoming a spacefaring civilisation.

The Federation is made up of an Outer and Inner Federation membership; Outer Federation membership granted access to the Federation's Outer planets for trade and commerce and some technological and social advancement for the betterment of the civilisation. However, this is conditional as long as the earth adhered to a strict and complex list of agreements, including fair social justice for its people and respect for other sovereign territories.

Failure to comply could result in the planet's expulsion, and if the Member continued to break the rules set down by the council of the federation's inner planetary membership, then a final formal request would be made.

If this request was ignored and the current governmental structure could not be improved, resolved, or removed, then the Federation would have no other recourse than to remove the civilisation entirely as a possible threat to the Federation as a whole. Removal would result in the total destruction of the offending civilisation. Thus, when a new civilisation is invited to join, it is made clear from the beginning that this is not a request that can be refused without dire consequences.

Alternatively, if the Outer Federation member toes the line and the civilisation evolves to a satisfactory developmental level, then the planet in question would be offered membership to the Inner Federation. Membership would grant full and total access to their complete technological and social advancements.

Joining the Federation's of Inner planetary members would mean just that: each planet within the Federation would be connected to the other planets via quantum gateways granting instantaneous travel to each and every world in the collective.

At this point, trade and commerce are concepts of the past and are no longer required. Only the unification of planets is the overall goal of the Federation. Only then can peace be secured and the whole protected from all threats.

This is the controlling factor when approaching a new civilisation. 'Join us, change, and evolve' is the Federation's mantra, but to advance to this point can take hundreds of years. By the time the Federation invited Earth to join the Outer planets, Mars and several other planets within the solar system had declared independence but were still offered individual membership. A hundred years on, only Earth is reported to be on the brink of being invited into the Inner Federation of Planets.

•   •   •

Dr Zorn and Wheeler's deaths were recorded as accidental, but the repercussions of the attempt to rescue Professor Brookes lasted months and were closed with a less than perfect end to an illustrious career. Due to the strict need for the project to maintain its secrecy, Commander Taylor was allowed to retire honourably and with dignity.

With his direct access to the facility now removed, Commander Taylor retained a one-way communication system that he could use to send messages directly to Brookes. The one drawback is that these messages were read by off-station security. Although the staff was small, the messages had to be brief and make sense only to Brookes.

During this time, The Federation would send reports of possible interest to all retired commanders. Their many years of service could still prove valuable to the Federation, so whenever issues occurred or a situation or problems seemed to be spiralling out of control, a report of possible interest would be sent to the various commanders who had retired but were still available for such work. Commander Taylor was no exception, and in many ways, he put himself out there more than most.

Professor Brookes was one of the main reasons for this, and so far, this has paid dividends. After reading various reports, he found a name that kept popping up from one report to another: Sam McCall, arrested for espionage, arrested for theft, arrested for hacking. The list of jobs was endless, and each job had a common outcome: Sam had escaped from wherever he had been sent. After tracing back through his career, it quickly becomes apparent that he had been working for various factions within the federation, all using Sam's talent to gain something upon the other faction. It was one big game of federation interplanetary politicking.

Another report of possible interest that found its way to the Commander's desk was about a possible game-changing Prototype that could prove tempting to the likes of Sam McCall, but being an inner planetary federation project, it made an attractive target for almost any Outer Federation faction, including Mars Federation, which at some point would almost certainly try and steal it for themselves. But if Taylor played his cards right, he could trick Sam into stealing it and then have him sent to Facility

Zero with a bonus outcome of stopping Mars Federation from obtaining such a dangerous weapon.

After thousands of reports and several months later, a third and final report landed on Taylor's desk about a young Special Forces woman working on Mars. She had inadvertently killed the son of a high-ranking Federation officer stationed on Mars. The evidence pointed at the son running some kind of drug syndicate, possibly with his father's support. Information regarding this was uncertain. This report was trying to seek corroboration of guilt.

This was serious, as it was considering an investigation into the illegal activity of the Mars Federation, which could lead to expulsion, but the report was also asking what should happen to Lt. Jessica Braose. Her record seemed perfect. She was brave, relentless, and had a strong belief in herself, and she would fight tooth and nail to resolve a wrong. She was the perfect person to throw to the wolves.

Recommendation: Send to Facility Zero.

Commander Taylor presses his intercom, and a male voice answers.

"Bill, I need a message sent to the facility. Professor Brookes is about to get some more help," Commander Taylor says, then spots another piece of paper containing an invitation to a meet and greet, Commander Simm's name being at the top of the page.

•   •   •

Commander Taylor stares out of his penthouse apartment overlooking the majestic capital city of Mars and raises his glass in a toast.

"This is for you, Professor. I had hoped I could have gotten you out of there, but your design and ideas worked, maybe a little too well. Even the help I sent you could not succeed, but still, ten glorious, escape-free years, and in a few days, Facility One will be online.

You made the federation a safer place, Professor, and your sacrifice will not be forgotten," Commander Taylor says and takes a sip of his drink and heads back to his desk, setting his glass down, opening the cigar box and taking out the last of his most prized cigars. He cuts the tip-off and then lights it up, listening to the crackle of the cigar as the fire burns, the noise of the first pull on the cigar, the delightful taste. Nothing can ruin this moment as he pulls on the cigar again, savouring the taste.

His study doors come crashing open with a bang as a smartly dressed woman storms into his inner sanctum, his personal assistant close on her heels, trying to stop this unexpected intruder.

"I do apologise, sir. I tried to explain to this woman that you were not to be disturbed," Bill says, looking flustered. Before the commander can reply, the woman speaks first.

"I've been trying to see you for the past week. You have consistently not returned any of my calls or letters, and I've run out of patience with you," The women says as she takes Taylor's cigar and drops it into his glass, causing the cigar to hiss as it's extinguished. Commander Taylor looking somewhat aghast at this action.

"It's okay, Bill. I'm more than happy to talk to Mrs Brookes," Taylor replies, his tone a little tense.

"Okay, sir. I'll be heading off then. See you tomorrow. Goodnight, sir," Bill replies, leaving the room, closing the doors behind him.

"Now, Mrs Brookes, how can I help?" Commander Taylor asks, placing down his glass and ruined cigar.

"How can you help? You can help by returning my husband. You have had ten years to find him and have currently come up with nothing. All these lies about you have no idea where he is... I'm certain of one thing: you know exactly where he is, " Mrs Brookes replies, her emotional state increasing.

"Mrs Brookes, your husband's predicament is a very tricky one. I can and have assured you that he is alive and well, but his location is currently secret. We have done everything in our power to retrieve your husband, but please understand that if your husband is unable to fix the problem himself, then it certainly must be almost impossible for our top experts to resolve the issue," Commander Taylor Says.

"Well, everything in your power is not good enough, and everyone I have contacted about this either blanks me or also has no clue of what's been going on," Mrs Brookes responds.

"You've contacted others?" Taylor asks with a tone of concern.

"Just a few government friends and someone I know on the global news desk, but I've not told him anything, at least not yet. I said I would see what you had to say first," Mrs Brookes replies.

"Okay then, but I'm rather concerned that you have spoken to others, especially as this is all very secret. Your husband knew this. I might be able to speak to someone, but it's just all very dangerous. There are other parties involved that will want to keep all this under the general population's radar, and you are running about is going to cause a lot of heads to turn," Commander Taylor says, pausing, thinking for a moment.

"I might be able to arrange for you to go visit where your husband was working; I'll pull a few strings, call in some favours, but give me a few days. If I can't help, then you see who you need to see, but please give me a few days first," Commander Taylor ask.

"You have had me chasing ghosts and promises for all this time, and none of them has given me a single shred of hope or proof of my husband's whereabouts. The last tip you gave me took me almost five years to chase down, and now you say, 'Let me pull a few strings,' well, please forgive me for not jumping for joy," Mrs Brookes replies with anger and resentment in her voice.

"I'll tell you what I'll do. I'll give you two hours to come up with something concrete. After that time, if I still think you are stalling, tricking me, or pulling some kind of elaborate deception, I'll contact my friend. Shortly after that, everyone will know what you and your shadowy friends have been up to," Mrs Brookes says with a look of determination.

Commander Tayler, looking visibly shocked from Mrs Brookes's outburst, goes to pick up his drink before realising that his last cigar is sticking out of it.

"Now look here, Mrs Brookes, I have done everything in my power to try and resolve this sad problem, and to be frank, I've spent a considerable amount of personal resources, but you are right to be upset.

I have let you down, but I give you my word that you will have all the answers you deserve within two hours. Someone I know owes me big, and to be honest, I was hoping to save that for a rainy day, but seeing how I don't really have a choice, I'll call it in. Now I don't wish to be rude, but I need to make that call, and then you will have all your answers," Taylor says, showing Mrs Brookes to the door. Mrs Brookes, not looking at all convinced, weighs up her options and slowly nods in agreement.

"Two hours, not a single minute more. This is where you can contact me, and for your information, it's Doctor Brookes; I might have retired, but I'm still due some respect," Doctor Brookes says, offering Taylor her calling card, turns, and leaves.

Taylor closes the door, locking it, and walks over to his desk. He puts down the calling card. Leans down and presses a concealed button under his desk to open a panel on the wall, revealing a wall safe. Entering his access code, he opens the safe and retrieves a phone. Returning to his desk, he sits down.

He calls the only number listed and waits for it to answer.

"I have an urgent customer that needs to vanish... No, not dead, vanished!... Yes, that's correct... I'll send you the details... Oh, one last thing. The customer has two daughters; they also need to vanish," Commander Taylor explains, then hangs up, not waiting for a reply.

9
Messages from the Past

Facility Zero, 240 days online: federation year 2431
PROFESSOR BROOKES DID not take my news regarding the near-zero possibility of any escape attempt very well. A week after our chat, we felt another power fluctuation, and since that day, Professor Brookes has kept himself to himself as the years outside the facility pass by.

By trading items and doing favours, we've managed to obtain a few useful things—papers, pens, and even a combat knife that one of the volunteer security personnel had managed to smuggle in.

Frank has decided to hang about with us, and from his encounters in the lost and found, he finds himself now semifamous. At most mealtimes, the table that Frank chooses to sit at is soon overcrowded with the other prisoners wanting to hear his exploits. It's somehow the opposite when Jessica sits down to eat; the other patrons seem to just melt away, which also suit Jessica just as well.

As the weeks go by, the interest behind what occurred in the lost and found subside, and life within Facility Zero goes back to what could be considered normal. Jessica and I keep ourselves busy by going over what we had learned about this place and volunteering for almost every duty except for sanitation; it's a mainly automatic process, but occasionally volunteers are required to remove blockages within the biotanks.

Human waste, if converted correctly, can be used in many ways to help in the running of the facility, from drinking water, fertilisers, and composts to backup power generation for various machines. These run alongside the oxygen generators producing breathable air for the facility. Some hydrogen produced in the process is burned away to provide water, and the rest is automatically vented. These jobs mainly are assigned as punishment, although there are a few that volunteer for such duties. Each to their own, I guess.

Oddly, whenever Jessica is out and about away from me, Samuel often appears out of the blue, just like some odd character from an ancient children's cartoon. It is funny how your mind somehow starts to connect the dots with fragments of information, subconsciously catching hints glimpsing the truth, just in passing.

"Good evening, Sam. Have you come to any conclusions about what we discussed last time we talked?" Samuel asks. Samuel doing one of his mysterious appearances after Jessica had just left moments before. Sitting down beside me, with the usual feeling of something being wrong.

"Oh, hey, Samuel. Nice of you to pop by. Well, not really. Brookes has decided to vanish on us, as I told him it's practically impossible to escape from here with the limited information I have," I reply, finding it easy to talk to him for some reason, although he gives me constant skin-crawling creeps.

"It's funny, I can escape from pretty much anywhere, but I always have help from the outside in some way, and without that help, any escape would be blind," I say, then pause, feeling something deep at the core of my mind like an itch I can't scratch. It started recently. The first time was when I was trying to sleep, and it lasted almost all night.

"Are you okay, Sam? You look pained or puzzled about something," Samuel asks.

"It's nothing. I've been getting these odd headaches recently. The doc says it's nothing to be concerned about," I explain, and the scratching stops all of a sudden. Samuel looks past me for a few moments before replying.

"I've never been able to read you fully, and your mind seems complex, not like the professor. We had a very long chat when he first arrived, and he's very easily manipulated," Samuel reveals and pauses, looking past me again.

"Do you know what Jessica is planning?" Samuel asks.

"Jessica? Oh, She's planning something, but she won't tell me any details. She's like that. You know she doesn't trust you in the least," I reply, feeling no issues revealing the truth to Samuel.

"That I know. Sadly, our chat needs to end here, and as usual, you won't remember what we talked about," Samuel says, looking up as Jessica walks back into the dining hall.

"Take care, Sam, and warn your friend not to interfere," Samuel says, standing, nodding at Jessica as she arrives at the table and leaves. Jessica takes a seat as the scratching and tickling returns within my brain.

"What did he want this time?" Jessica asks.

My mind feels strange like someone has been digging holes in it, leaving gaps in my memories, but the more the scratching continues, the more these holes seem to become filled in once more. Then it stops, and for the first time I remember.

"He's wanted information about your plan, I think. Oh, and he suggested you are sticking your nose in where it should not be. Just the usual threat, and he let slip that he had a long chat with the professor. I think Samuel is behind a lot of the mess that's been going on here," I say as I start to remember other conversations that I somehow forgot. Jessica looking thoughtful.

"I've always had a suspicion about Samuel, and I'm certain he's somehow behind the freakers. The next power fluctuation, I'm going to find out what," Jessica says, looking determined and thoughtful.

"By my calculation, that will be by the end of the week. Are you sure you want to go ahead with this? If you don't get back in time, the chances are you will be stuck wherever you end up for at least five weeks," I say with concern.

"I realise that, and it's not something I desire, but it's something that I need to do. Plus, we need answers, and I think we will get some down wherever the freakers hide. I've spoken to a few trustees, and they mentioned that no one has been able to access level one in a long time," Jessica replies and looks around at the room and then continues.

"Do you have any ideas where Neil has been hiding?" Jessica asks.

"I've not seen him around for a few weeks. He's another that's decided to go into hiding. I was thinking of checking up on him tomorrow, but for now, I need to get some rest," I say, getting up from the table.

"Yeah, I'll turn in also. I was thinking of going over a few places and see if I can get some more supplies," Jessica says, standing up and heads over to the tray chute with me, Frank giving us a wave as we leave.

•   •   •

Jessica is long gone by the morning and nowhere to be seen at breakfast. Eating quickly, I head out to try and find Neil. I call out to the computer for a route. Having security clearance gives me access to many places. A route opens, and I follow it. It's similar to the route to my own room, but I soon arrive at a blank wall.

As it's not my room, access to the room itself won't immediately open until permission is given, unlike for the professor, who can override such access if needed.

"Prisoner M2301 does not wish to be disturbed," the computer system replies.

"Neil, open up. It's Sam. Please open up. I would like to talk to you," I call out.

"Prisoner M2301 does not wish to be disturbed," the computer system replies again.

"Neil! We haven't seen you in ages, and we are all worried about you," I call out again, feeling concerned.

"Prisoner M2301 does not wish to be disturbed," the computer system replies once more.

"Fine. I'll be back with the professor," I say, and for some reason, feeling unnerved by the silence, I turn and call for a route for Professor Brookes's room.

Another route opens up, and this one twists and turns and ends at a lift. Taking this to the top of the facility, the path ends at another blank wall.

"Professor. It's Sam. Can I have a word?" I call out.

"Occupant M0000, Professor Brookes, does not wish to be disturbed," the computer system replies.

"Now this is ridiculous, Professor. I need a word with you about Neil," I call out again.

"Occupant M0000, Professor Brookes, does not wish to be disturbed," the computer system replies again. I let out an exasperated sigh, turn, and head back down the corridor, requesting a route back to my room.

•   •   •

Neil looks up from his task towards the wall as the computer announces Sam McCall's presence requesting access.

"Best tell him you are not available," Samael says as he watches Neil work.

"I'm not available," Neil replies.

"Sam McCall is concerned with your welfare and requires access to speak with you," the computer says.

Neil looks over at Samael and understands the unspoken word between them.

"I do not wish to be disturbed," Neil replies.

"Sam McCall would like you to know that he will return with the professor," the computer system says.

"Well, I don't believe that will happen anytime soon. The Professor is not in the best of moods. Now, Neil, it's simple. All I require from you is for you to give Jessica that blade, but make sure she can't return it," Samael asks.

Neil looks across at Samael and continues to score a line just past the hilt on the blade.

•   •   •

The week passes by without any issues and no sign of Neil or Professor Brookes. Just a few hours before the next fluctuation, Jessica uses the elevator to descend as far as possible and reaches level two of the facility. Stepping out of the elevator, she is surprised to see that it has taken her to another part of the facility's engineering section, this one containing oxygen generators. It's where the excess hydrogen and pod fuel is harmlessly burned away.

Jessica's estimation is correct, and the power fluctuation occurs right on schedule. As always, everybody is now safe within their rooms or the dining hall, except for one. Stepping closer toward a section of the wall, Jessica takes a deep breath and slowly steps through.

Much to Jessica's surprise, she finds herself between the corridors and rooms, but now she's able to see almost the layout of the entire floor, but most importantly, she's able to see through the walls of the corridors closest to her as they become semitransparent the closer she is to them.

On the other hand, the rooms are still obscured, and she cannot see into any of them. It's hardly surprising why the freakers had such an advantage when they attacked.

Heading back to the elevator, hoping she can find a way to descend to level one. As expected, the elevator ascended back up through the station after Jessica arrived earlier, now leaving an empty elevator shaft. Stepping closer to the shaft that drops away into the darkness, Jessica can see a flickering light far below. Looking upward, she sees that the shaft length just disappears into the darkness.

Taking a closer look, Jessica notices that against the bulkhead of the floor is a makeshift ladder placed against the opening. This is most likely why the trustees are unable to access level one.

Listening for any movement, Jessica carefully descends through the shaft and enters level one of the facility. The temperature drops as she goes farther down the shaft. After the first ten feet, the makeshift ladder stops, and another one continues down. This one is part of the bulkhead of the facility.

After thirty feet in all, Jessica reaches the floor of the facility. The view before her could only be described as a scene out of some kind of haunted house movie. The corridor is strewn with material, blankets, shredded and hung up like tapestries. Candles have been placed along the path at points where they can't set fire to the fabric. Looking closer at the candles, Jessica's implant detects the presence of organic material; the implant then lists the process to render human flesh.

Following the corridor with caution, Jessica moves away from the central section and heads toward where she estimated the main dining hall would normally be situated. As she arrives at a crossroad, it becomes apparent that the sound-nullification fields are still operational, as the noise of freakers could be heard suddenly loud and close. Peeking around the corner, Jessica spots five freakers throwing objects and shoving spears at a makeshift barricade whose defenders consisting of the facility's convicts and trustees and not the scared and mutilated freakers Jessica is now familiar with.

Stepping into the corridor, she heads down toward the freakers. Keeping low with a blade in her right hand, she slowly closes the gap. The first freaker has no clue what is happening until he sees his own blood gushing from his throat. The second turn's just a little too late to sees the flash of metal and then feels the warmth of his life force spill from his wound. Clutching at his own throat, he sinks to his knees.

Jessica grabs a spear from her last victim as the other three turns to see this unknown new threat. The closest of them receives Jessica's newly acquired spear thrown straight into his chest. The freaker clutches at it and stares with disbelieving eyes. The last two freakers scramble for the safety of the walls, but one of them is hit from behind by the defender of the barricade before it can escape. The last disappears with shouts of screaming hate.

Jessica cleans her blade as she walks toward the barricade and then stops. Watching the defenders, she takes another step, slowly closing the gap to the freaker who is now lying dead with the thrown spear jutting up from his chest, resembling some kind of gruesome boundary marker.

"That's far enough," one of the defenders shouts as Jessica reaches her spear. She places a foot upon the chest of the freaker and pulls, twisting the spear free. Looking up at the defender, she smiles.

"Who the hell are you?" the man at the barricade calls out, shifting nervously, maybe a new threat. Other movements could be seen through the gaps.

"I'm Jessica from level five. Prisoner F2965, but my friends call me Abs. Long story," Jessica says as she cleans the tip of her spear on the freaker before her and then turns her head slightly, hearing noise from over the wall.

"Okay, Jessica from level five, what the hell are you doing down here, looking like you are just having a stroll in the local park?" the man says, still unsure of Jessica. The noise from down the corridor seems to be getting closer. Jessica takes a cautious step closer.

"Well, if you mean a park with candles made from rendered-down human fat, then sure, it's a lovely park, but if you don't mind, I would rather have this conversation in your dining hall than out here," Jessica suggests. The defender looks like he is about to object when another unseen voice calls up.

"Let the women in before the first friendly face we have seen in months becomes another friendly dead face. We have plenty of ex-friends as it is," An unseen voice says.

The defender still looks uncertain as freaker faces start to appear through the walls. Jessica starts running for the barricade since the unseen voice said to let her in.

"Hey, wait. Stop. Let me—" the defender starts to object, but Jessica doesn't wait or stop. She speeds up and leaps for the top of the barricade and dives for the gap, the defender falling backwards in surprise.

Diving headfirst over the barricade, Jessica tucks her head in and lands perfectly on her back. As she rolls back to her feet, Jessica twists and turns back to the barricade to see one of the freakers already taking advantage and starting to climb over. Swapping the spear to her right hand, she takes a fraction of a second to aim and then lets loose with a forceful grunt. The spear flies true and impales the freaker through his windpipe, stopping him dead as he lands across the barricade.

Jessica rushes to the barrier, grabs at the shaft of her spear, and yanks it free. The sound from the other side stops momentarily and then erupts into a new crescendo of noise, the defender who was knocked from his post as Jessica dove through stands up from where he tumbled to the floor.

"Who the hell are you, lady?" the first defender asks, looking bewildered.

Jessica, now climbing up onto the platform, replies as she carefully looks over at the new attackers.

"You know, I've been getting that rather a lot lately," Jessica replies.

• • •

The attack on the dining hall on level one lasted several hours, and once the lights started to flash and blink, Jessica realised the reason for the prolonged assault. Her pathway back from here was effectively gone, leaving another five freakers dead, were killed during the fight, and Jessica learned that the first defender's name is Bobby. At age nineteen, he must be the youngest prisoner sent to the facility.

The one that allowed her entry is called Carter, and a third who arrived to help midway through the fight is called Jimmy the Fist. Jim or Jimmy immediately struck Jessica as a bit of a jerk, mainly because he dragged Bobby off the platform by his neck and then climbed up. Once there, he pushed Jessica off.

"This is no place for a girl!" Jimmy says, standing over seven feet tall, even Jessica felt this was not the best time to share her thoughts on the matter.

But still, it gave her a breather to chat to Carter, who comes across as a nice guy. It transpired that level one did not fall into chaos all that quickly; in fact, it fell very slowly, as one by one, the inmates started to show signs of needing to be on their own, followed by self-mutilation, and then one by one they would either slip away or just flip out and seemingly become deranged.

The dining hall now resembled a scene out of a war hospital: tables upturned and moved to the walls and beds set up in their place, the food dispensary now some kind of chemistry experiment, the walls and floor around the dispensers now stained with green, yellow, and dark brown, lots of brown, with a massive helping of a blackened patch,

"What happened over there?" Jessica asks, pointing at the food dispensers.

"Oh yeah, just as things turned from crazy to homicidal, two of the kitchen staff started to dish out their own cuisine of brutal stabbings, followed by an explosion. Killed twelve that day, and that was the start of all this we have now. Slowly since then, our numbers have dwindled," Carter replies as he stares over at the mess with a look of solemn calm.

"Now we gather our food in when we can; it's not much. Other than the guys you have already seen, we have two others sleeping, Ollie and Kerren. They're not the best fighters, but they know where to find food and water, and they're slippery as heck," Carter says.

"Do you have any access to the system?" Jessica asks. Motioning to the room.

"No. We lost that some time ago, and now the system has decided to keep all the routes open, which you can imagine causes all kinds of issues. That's the main reason why we built the walls and the barricade," Carter explains.

"Why don't the freakers just tear down the walls?" Jessica asks, looking over at the assembled makeshift walls.

"No idea. They seem to revel in death and mayhem, but they ignore things that help us defend ourselves. Not a lot of this makes sense, including their leader," Carter says.

"Ah yes, the big freaker. I've already had a run-in with him, and I'm looking forward to finishing the job," Jessica replies. Carter gives Jessica a confused look but then nods.

"The big one isn't the leader. Instead, he takes his commands from Samael," Carter explains.

"Who the heck is Samael?" Jessica asks, looking perplexed.

"Well, he went by the name Samuel at first, being all nice and helpful, but once everything turned to shit, he's been seen on occasions with the spaceman and asking us for helpers, but that was ages ago," Carter replies.

"Holy crap, I knew there was something wrong about that guy. But, hey, wait—who or what is the spaceman?"

Jessica's says, her expression changes from perplexed to excited to bewildered. Carter laughs as he watches her expression change.

"Well, the spaceman is a man, He's just wearing an environmental suit, and he's been seen being dragged along with some of the freakers. The rumour was that he had been trapped here when the station went online but knew how to convert a pod in order to be able to try and escape," Carter explains. Jessica looks stunned, remembering what the professor told her a few weeks back.

"But what happened?" Jessica asks.

"Well, Samael asked for help from us, but we trusted him as far as we could fling a spear. That still wasn't far enough, so we told him to go screw himself," Carter laughs at the memory.

"But that pissed him off, and the freakers attacked us for several days constantly. We lost a fair few on that occasion," Carter explains.

"So what happened to the spaceman?" Jessica asks.

"Well, as far as I can work out and have been told, he completed his work and true to Samael's word, Samael let him go," says and points to a cot on the other side of the room.

Jessica, feeling positive for some good news, follows the direction where Carter had been pointing, but her spirits drop again when she sees what looks like a blackened, bloated figure lying upon a makeshift bed.

"Is he dead?" Jessica asks.

"Dead? No, but I'm not sure how long he can last out. He's desperately dehydrated and starving. Our best guess is that he also has some kind of infection caused by one of the freakers giving him a going-away gift when Samael let him go," Carter says as he walks over to the spaceman.

As it turns out, the bloated, blackened appearance is due to his environmental suit. His helmet placed to one side, and the man lying upon the cot coughs as Jessica arrives, his complexion looking deathly pale.

"Dr Zorn... Dr Zorn, can you hear me?" Jessica asks as she kneels down by his side. The doctor opens his eyes after a moment and looks up at Jessica.

"You... you know my name?" Doctor Zorn asks weakly.

"I do. My name is Jessica. Professor Brookes told me you died trying to get here," Jessica says. The doctor coughs again and tries to sit up when he hears the professor's name. Jessica gently helps him to rise a little.

"Brookes is alive?" he asks.

"Yes, he is, and he's been desperately trying to find a way out of here. The pod you were piloting was hit and destroyed, and everyone thought you had died, but then we saw a pod blast away from here that was far too complex to be designed by anyone here," Jessica explains. Dr Zorn listens and grimly smiles up at Jessica.

"Samuel saved me, but I know him by a different name to hide who he really is," Doctor Zorn says, his feature becoming dark.

"What do you mean?" Jessica asks, becoming anxious; something within her already knowing it's bad.

"Samuel isn't what he seems, and I do not think he could help himself really, but he's been trapped here for a very long time," Doctor Zorn says. Jessica is now white with apprehension.

"What did he do, Dr Zorn?" Jessica asks, dreading the truth. Zorn, looking stern.

"Samael is the Angel of Death. He created the freakers," Doctor Zorn replies, his words striking fear in Jessica.

• • •

With the power fluctuation returning to normal, I know what has to be done. The possibility that Jessica might not return during the fluctuation phase is high, and if that happens, the computer will remove her from the system.

So once the power fluctuation returns to normal, I waste no time and go up to security control; such commands are best carried out from there.

Arriving in an empty room, I address the computer. "Facility Zero, where is Jessica at this time?" I ask, already knowing the answer.

"Prisoner F2965 is no longer on the system," The system replies. Okay, that was to be expected, I realized.

"Please add Jessica, Prisoner F2965, back on the system, and give her security clearance as before," I ask.

"Prisoner F2965 has been reinstated as per your request," the system replies, making me feel a little happier.

"Facility Zero, please locate Jessica and give me her current condition," I instruct the system.

"Jessica is currently in the dining hall on level one. Her condition is healthy," the system replies.

"Is Jessica with anyone?" I ask.

"Jessica is alone but seems to be walking slowly around the dining hall, no active visual or audio available on level one, but her actions would suggest she is having a conversation. Her known medical records would suggest that she is talking with someone and not to herself," the system says.

"What is the status of level one?" I ask.

"Status of level one is currently inaccessible due to quarantine protocols in effect," the system replies.

"Who ordered the quarantine protocol and why?" I ask, each answer causing more questions.

"Quarantine was initiated by Professor Brookes—reasons unknown," the system replies.

"Send a message to Brookes. I need to speak urgently with him regarding level one," I ask.

"Professor Brookes currently does not wish to be disturbed," the system replies, causing me to become annoyed.

"To hell with what he wants! Tell him I have a new plan that requires his presence in security," I shout back.

"Professor Brookes is on his way," the system replies rather quicker than I had expected.

Ten minutes pass as I pace security, and then the noise of the elevator arriving with Brookes brings me out of my thoughts. Brookes, usually looking smart and healthy, almost falls out of the elevator; his appearance is dishevelled, and he looks like he hasn't slept in weeks.

"What do you have, Sam?" Professor Brookes asks eagerly. I decide to approach the issue from a different angle.

"I need you to counter the quarantine protocol on level one. Jessica has managed to get down there, but she's now trapped," I explain.

Brookes looks confused as he walks over to the security terminal.

"What quarantine? I've not ordered anything of the sort," Professor Brookes says as he logs on. A printer embedded within the terminal starts to print as the professor's face continues to furrow with concern.

"I don't understand. This isn't my authorisation," Professor Brookes says. Then, reading something that has just been printed, the professor stands up. He looks shocked to the core as the printer starts printing again. Seemingly my turn to look confused.

"What are those?" I ask.

"These are my little messages of hope. It's how I've known things… like, for example, when you were going to arrive and other such useful bits of information. I also like to call these my messages from the past," Professor Brookes reveals.

The professor, already starting to get his old look back, types a string of commands into the terminal and then looks back at me.

"Somehow, the quarantine has my authorisation, but it also has been encrypted. I've set up a key breaker, but this will take a bit of time," Professor Brookes explains.

Tearing the first message off, he passes it to me as he reads the second one.

I read the message several times as I slowly understand the meaning of it:

Message 10: Federation year 2430

> *My friend, it has now been thirteen long years, and my attempts to help you have seemingly all failed. Please forgive me, old friend, but I kept something from you, I arranged to send your wife and daughters to Facility One as low-priority prisoners. At least now you might see them again.*

I look back at the professor, stunned. "I'm so sorry—" I say, feeling sick, but Brookes cuts me off before I can say another word.

"No need to be. You might not see the good side yet, but it's possibly been the best news I've heard."

"I don't understand. Why?" I ask, confused.

"Low priority means they have been sent to the holding station. They will be in cryostasis for years before they get sent down to the facility. At least, for now, they are not ageing while we try and escape from here," Professor Brookes explains.

"I still don't understand. You're happy about this that your family is being sent here?" I read the message again, and then I see it.

"What is Facility One?" I ask.

"Facility One is the second of a possible four stations that will someday be hanging over this black hole. Every ten years that are escape-free, the sponsors agree to build another facility. Four in total for this particular location, four meaning up to forty-eight thousand prisoners incarcerated with no chance of causing harm ever again. Amazing," Professor Brookes replies.

"Yeah, sure, amazing, but still a little nuts. What about the power issues?" I ask, feeling that what's happening here isn't precisely a humane way of treating prisoners.

"The power issues, as you put it, was resolved in my notes. The other three stations will not suffer with them. In time I would have fixed this facility, but I got stuck here..." The professor says as he trails off in thought. Thinking upon his last words, I start to wonder too.

"This was no accident. It was part of a design that you got trapped here, Professor," I say, thinking out loud.

"I think I've known that all along, but I feel like I'm missing parts of my mind," Professor says.

I think it's Samuel. Not sure why or how, but I had a conversation with him a week or two back, and somehow I still remember him saying that he had a long chat with you. He's been manipulating all of us and altering our memories," I say, Sounding paranoid.

"So what do we do now? Your message said you had a new plan?" Professor Brookes asks.

"I'm sorry. But I only said that to get you here. But these messages you have been receiving, I would like to read them," I ask. The professor looks annoyed for only a moment and then types another command into his terminal.

"The messages will print out in the order they were received. Commander Taylor was in charge of the project, and he's the one who has been pulling strings on the outside; the first set of messages are rather cryptic," Professor Brookes explains.

Brookes goes back to work on his encryption program, and I take the first of the messages from the printer, then it beeps again and prints out another of the messages. Looking at the first one, I notice that Professor Brookes has added an addendum to each message's end.

Message 1: Federation year 2417.
> *Maintenance lights should be set to white for a successful test.*

> *Message addendum, Professor Brookes:*
> *I set the facility's docking lights to display white for fifty real minutes and repeated the sequence to display for an additional minute each real year. The code will auto-delete if I die or leave the station.*

Well, that's straightforward enough, and the commander, I guess, finds out that his message got through. I can only guess that fifty is for his age. I take the next message, placing the first down on the desk.

Message 2: Federation year 2417.
> *I'm sorry the doc could not make it. The whole situation is a mess. Unfortunately, no other appointments are possible at this time.*

Message addendum, Professor Brookes:
I watched the facility external footage and
watched Doctor Zorn's pod take a direct hit; no
one could have survived it.

It must be about Dr Zorn that Jessica mentioned. It would be interesting to know what the plan was. But I feel that something is missing here. Did they really only send one pod down? Placing the message down, I reach for the next.

I imagine it's nice to get some updates from the outside world, even if the communication is pretty much one way.

Message 3: Federation year 2418.
Sorry, it's been so long—too hot to the touch. I will
have something soon.

Message addendum, Professor Brookes:
It's odd how perspectives can be confusing. It's
been almost two years for the commander, but only
fourteen weeks for me. I calculated that by the time
I've been here seven years, it will be around 446
years in the real world.

Message 4: Federation year 2418
The other half is going nuts. If I only had people
with her resolve, there would be no issues to deal
with.

Message addendum, Professor Brookes:
That certainly sounds like my wife, but for her sake,
I hope she doesn't piss off too many people.

That would explain some aspects about the professor, and I know some of the federation guys can be a bit trigger happy with issues they can't handle.

Message 5: Federation year 2419

To hell with the cryptic messages. I just found out that these can't be read by anyone but you. Check out Sam McCall's records. You will be receiving him soon. Amazing record. If he can't, no one can.
I hired him to rob one of my own security boxes and left some additional information I knew he would not be able to resist. For a while, I thought he would not pull it off, but he managed it somehow.

Message addendum, Professor Brookes:
This guy's record is impressive. A kind of ethical thief, but he's been working for almost every faction there is. His last job has been deleted, but it looks like he was working for himself. Whatever he stole, it annoyed a lot of people.

I don't know what's worse, being scammed into stealing a worthless hunk of junk or being sent here for the sole purpose of trying to escape and even failing at that.

Message 6: Federation year 2423

By my calculations, Sam should be with you by now, but about a week after Sam's arrival, you should receive a Jessica Smith. It's a fake name. She killed the son of a high-ranking Mars Federation officer— not such a great career move. Anyway, the father wanted her to suffer, so I helped by sending her to the facility.

I checked out her records. She was working for the Planetary Enforcement Agency, and before that, she spent two years working for the Planetary Special Defense Force. Those guys are trained to do something called angel jumps—it sounds totally insane. She will make a good ally for protection if things go bad. Read her file, but ignore her crime report—it's fake.

Message addendum, Professor Brookes:
This lady sounds insane, but most likely, it's all been hyped up. I looked up the term "angel jumps," Special Forces use them for planetary insertion; the squad is dropped out of warp in special suits designed to burn off-in reentry. As the jumpers fall through the atmosphere, they resemble meteorites burning up like they've been cast down from Heaven—hence the term 'Angel Jumps.' The crime report says she was responsible for blowing up a starliner on purpose to kill one target.

From what I've seen of her, this sounds pretty correct—she's nuts but effective. But this Commander Taylor has a lot to answer for. Has he condemned her or saved her? Personally, I'll kick his arse if I ever get out of here.

Message 7: Federation year 2425
I'm sorry for not sending a message sooner. I've moved from my home on Earth to relocate to Mars. In a few weeks, Earth Federation will join the inner planetary federation. Mars can't or won't get there for at least another hundred years.

I can't lie to myself anymore, and for that matter, to the ideal Earth now stands for. It's a great honour, for sure, to join the inner planets, but the moral question is, was the price worth it? Can a utopian society work where the previous choices were to join us or be put down?

I'm sure I could go on for days about the ethical question of dragging everyone into a peaceful, perfect new way of life. Is being free the choice that an individual can starve to death if they so wish or take drugs for that moment of euphoria? What is the answer? Not everyone values life on the same scales. How can we accurately measure the true value of a utopian society?

For me, the cost is too high. Two warring factions kill each other for hundreds of years; one life escalates to two, revenge escalates to even more deaths. Is the solution really to just remove the least liked, men, women, and children, the memory of the genocide lasting for years, ten, twenty, one hundred years, two hundred years, then forgotten, rewritten, overlooked and cast away. Is peace really worth it when it comes at such a price?

Message addendum, Professor Brookes:
Well, that was depressing. But one of the best things about joining is that now Earth will enjoy instantaneous travel between inner planet worlds once the quantum gateways have been built, taking at least thirty years and a small moon's worth of materials, each.

I used one of them once, maybe twice. It's almost like having every planet in the collective in your backyard.

Travel time is minutes rather than hours, weeks, months, or years.

> Message 8: Federation year 2426
> *Congratulations, Professor; your design has been passed to the Inner Federation penal system, meaning your facility could be set up at dozens of suitable black holes. Survey ships are being sent all over the system to find appropriate sites for your facilities.*
>
> *Message addendum, Professor Brookes:*
> *I'm no longer certain if that's a good idea or not.*

I would guess being a prisoner in your own prison can dampen the spirits some.

> Message 9: Federation year 2427
> *Well, Professor, ten years, and Facility One will be online in a few days. Another five locations have been surveyed, and each of those will have a facility within ten years. On another matter, your wife continues her search for you, but now I fear she may cause more harm than good. I will do all I can to protect her.*
>
> *Message addendum, Professor Brookes:*
> *I need to get out of here, but Sam has come up with nothing so far—not that I can blame him. This place was designed to be escape-proof.*

Well, I think I now know a way out, but the price is too high for now.

Message 10: Federation year 2430

My friend, it has now been thirteen long years, and all my attempts to help you have seemingly failed. Please forgive me, old friend, but I kept this from you: I arranged to send your wife and daughters to Facility One as low-priority prisoners. At least now you might see them again.

No message addendum from the professor this time. After our chat in medical, he did not find my analysis of escape possibilities acceptable and decided to lock himself away in his room. I wonder how many more messages there are, as I'm guessing he's not seen any more from here onward.

Message 11: Federation year 2431

This report landed on my desk today. I thought you might be interested in what it had to say. The Inner Planetary Survey team discovered a planet with an extinct civilisation just outside the influence of a small black hole. The black hole seemed ideal for several facilities, and the once-earthlike planet is no longer habitable due to some kind of unknown event.

But the team discovered a new form of slime moulds in large areas around the planet. Some were currently in their undulating states, and others had transformed into giant, dry, fruiting bodies. Samples were taken for cataloguing purposes, and due to the reason the team was there, they might name the new group of slime moulds after you. Congrats once again.

"Professor, you might want to look at this," I say, passing over the printout. Brookes looks up and takes the message, and starts to read. A bright smile breaks out over his face.

"Thank you. That was rather interesting. Any others?" Professor Brookes asks. Looking at the printer, I nod and take the next message.

Message 12: Federation year 2431

It might be nothing, but the inner planets have gone dark. No messages out, all data feeds cut, all quantum gateways are down. I'll be in touch when I have more news.

"Well, that's rather ominous. What do you think that's all about?" I ask.

The professor remains silent for a moment before replying.

"Hard to say. It could be anything. The quantum gateways take up tremendous energy. It could be as simple as a power outage, but to be honest, I've never heard of one before," Professor Brookes replies. As another message prints out, making us both jump.

Message 13: Federation year 2433

The inner planetary worlds are back online. A power conduit blew near a research lab, but all seems okay now except for one issue. It seems they have lost a battlecruiser. How that is possible is anyone's guess.

"A power conduit and a battlecruiser—those are rather suspicious occurrences at the same time. It's something I would do—or something similar—to cause a distraction," I say.

"I read your file before you got here. Wasn't your last job related to the inner worlds?" Alistair Brookes asks.

I smile and am about to reply when the printer prints out another message.

Message 14: Federation year 2434
The shit has hit the fan, and I mean on a system-wide scale. Inner worlds have started a civil war with each other. Not sure when I can get another message out.

We both read the message and become speechless, and then the feeling of dread crawls up my back as another message prints out. Taking it, we begin to read, but before we finish, another message prints out, followed immediately by yet another.

Message 15: Federation year 2434
Not sure how long I can send these messages, but it's bad. The inner worlds are going dead. Earth Federation has managed to deactivate any local quantum gates, so if an attack comes, it will be via warp-capable ships, which is good since the inner planets' really big ones, the dreadnoughts, require a quantum gateway. Sorry for the bad news.

Message 16: Federation year 2434
Not sure if this is good news or not. We have had confirmation that the inner worlds are not dead but infected somehow, or at least some of them are. The slime mould samples taken from the recent survey ship managed to escape the lab. How mould

can escape just blows my mind, but I've been informed that some types of moulds found on Earth can solve mazes under test conditions.

Anyway, a tech got contaminated, and a ventilation duct maintenance crew reported purplish mould-like pods within the air ventilation ducts, pumping out millions of spores.

The tech was later found to be responsible for taking out the power conduit. Then, in turn, the tech and maintenance crew stole a battlecruiser and proceeded to destroy a shipyard and any other threats they could find. I can't see an end to this anytime soon.

Message 17: Federation year 2434
transmission./source./unknown./
Neural_net./mapping./process./complete./
data./successful./data./neural_net./secured.
End./of./message.

I read the message several times and then pass it to Brookes.

"I'm guessing that's not a facility systems report of some kind," I say.

The professor looks confused at the message. He types a line of commands into the system, noticing that no other messages have pointed out since the last was taken.

"I have no idea what that message is referring to. It looks like computer code, albeit a simple one, or at least a simple message, but the system says it was transmitted from outside the station about a month ago," Professor Brookes says.

"Outside, maybe it's from the cryostation," I say, taking the message back and rereading it; I remember what was said to me once, what almost seems just a few months ago, but that can't be here and certainly not sending me a message.

"No, not from the cryostation, closer," Professor Brookes says, the professor, becoming excited, runs a set of scans, but after a few minutes, the scans come up with nothing. The commander's last message was about six months previous to that one. Something may have gone wrong with the communication system.

Our speculation of what it could all mean is cut short as another message prints out.

Message 18: Federation year 2434
More bad news, I'm afraid. The people who stole the Battlecruiser discovered a certain research and development location today and destroyed it. They realised its importance. Sam will be very familiar with this place, as he stole their first prototype. The project was never completely halted, and the damage done had set them back decades, but it had not prevented them from starting over.

Message 19: Federation year 2435
This will be my last message. They found out that the first prototype was stolen and was never recovered, and they know where you are. They are coming for You!

"They are coming for You, Sam," Brookes repeats the message, looking concerned.

We both look at each other, dumbstruck, as a beeping starts on another terminal. I'm almost too scared to even ask, but Professor Brookes gets up and looks at the monitor. He reads the screen.

"It's my encryption script. It's unlocked the quarantine protocol, but the elevators still cannot travel to level one; there seems to be some kind of obstruction," Professor Brookes explains. I stand and nod, feeling dazed by all the recent messages, the last affecting me the most.

"Leave it with me. I'll handle it," I say, the words sounding like they are being spoken by someone else as I leave security.

Now alone as I descend within the elevator, something about the odd computer-coded message reminds me of a conversation I had but only a few months ago. Then I realise, feeling rather foolish, that it's been months for me but years to the outside world: 'Neural_net mapping process completed.'

I halt the elevator and stand there in silence for a minute before asking a question to myself in my mind: *'Can you hear me?' I asked myself.*

Then I hear a female voice, one that's somehow familiar, and it's talking to me directly inside my mind. *'Yes, Sam, I can hear you clearly,'* the voice replies.

'Arden?' I ask, feeling shakend.

'No, Sam. Arden is dead. It's Sam. Shall we begin?'

10
Sam McCall's Story

Facility Zero, 105 days online: federation year 2419

NORMALLY WHEN I get hired to do a job, I just do that job, but on this occasion, when a brand-new contract has come my way from a trusted source, I'm a little more curious about what I'm stealing.

You never can tell what is really going on. I was hired to steal a document, some kind of blackmail material that my benefactor required to be returned or destroyed. The security vault was pretty tough—impressive high-tech security but easy when you helped design it, and knowing all the flaws and back doors, turns a possible nightmare of a job into a walk in the park.

So when someone like me has a chance to look around, that's exactly what I do. Nothing out of the ordinary, except for one folder:

Report of Possible Interest
Inner World Project
Code name: Phantom
Top-security prototype

The main problem regarding inner-world jobs is that the information is normally very hard to come by, and you certainly can't buy someone off. Inner-world citizens are not interested in money—or any other commodity, for that matter. You can't dig around for information, as that attracts the wrong kind of attention, but when something like this drops into your lap, it's impossible to resist, so I copied the folder and completed the rest of my job and got the hell out of there.

Even with all the boxes ticked—information, location, accessibility and escape route—the heat caused by stealing anything from the inner worlds is not usually worth it, but when I took a closer look at the report, all other concerns were cast aside, this was too important not to attempt.

Report of Possible Interest
Inner World Project
Code Name: *Phantom*
Top-security prototype
Project proposal:
Multipurpose cloak-capable interstellar vessel.
The Primary weapon system, Biological nanites with genome-remapping sequencing using a multi-purpose launcher.
Secondary weapon systems: single mounted dual proton lasers and a multipurpose modular compartment for various launcher types for the Nanite dispersion.
This craft's primary purpose is to deliver biological nanites payload to developing worlds that may prove useful to the Inner Federation. Biological life can be remapped to be susceptible to Dreamtime frequencies. Worlds that may prove a threat can be neutralised on a biological level without entering into a full-scale war.

Although several pages are missing regarding the computer system, pilot requirements, and benefactors, the rest of the document is redacted except for the last few lines.

Test flights have been successful up to this point, but issues have occurred over the training time of pilots due to the unique interfacing between pilot and craft, replacing *** REDACTED REDACTED REDACTED *** the current test pilot had suffered major injuries while off duty and will need to be replaced in the event of said pilot's death. The research team requires suggestions on how a suitable candidate may be trained in the period suggested.

• • •

The project's location was a little tricky to find, but I had some help from the molecular tagging, by which each document's point of origin is registered and authenticated. Every federation document has this kind of tag in case of theft; it helps prevent copyright and intellectual theft. For example, if someone writes a book or designs a new invention, that media will be tagged and registered, and any copies made will copy the tag. The only way the creation could be copied without the tag would be to copy it by hand.

The tagging led me to the registered Inner Worlds Division for Federation Expansion. Sounds harmless, but *expansion* is just another way of saying *invasion*.

Knowing the division name, I could then obtain a list of holdings owned by that particular federation division. The list included various federal buildings deep within inner-world space and one particular suspicious moon outside Inner Federation space. There are no prizes for guessing where I would place a top-secret weapons-projects base, but as they are not me and have strict rules for such things, the moon is then.

.   .   .

With a few more searches, I soon discover that they are hiring workers. Advanced societies still require manual labour from time to time. So now I know my location, and I've got a way in, and as long as I refrain from searching for information specifically regarding the moon and special projects, I should not attract unwanted attention.

I catch an overnight jump shuttle to Mars. It's a cheap and inconspicuous way to travel—cheap because the shuttle is not warp capable and requires the usage of a warp-generator jump gate. It's a perfectly safe way to travel these days via jump space, but the experience is still rather terrifying due to the insane acceleration and deceleration at the start and end of your trip. In the earlier days of the warp generators, the deceleration gates would lose synchronisation with the sending gate, resulting in the shuttle not decelerating, with the majority of shuttles involved in such mishaps never being seen again.

I arrange a meeting with a tech contact while in mid-transit. The job will require specialised equipment; the cost will be much higher due to the shielding and high-grade materials each item will require. Inner-world security does not like its visitors to bring in gizmos and gadgets for nefarious reasons.

Jack is a great guy I've known for years. I did him a few favours a while back, and ever since then, I get discounted prices and no questions asked. But this time, due to the shielding and special materials, it will still cost me an arm and a leg, maybe a kidney or two, but this job is worth it.

Next, I arrange for new identification and travel documentation and above-average qualification for working with heavy machinery. I can produce my own reasonable background and a good reason to take such a job away from home. I send Marcus my picture and background.

With all that accomplished, it's just a matter of lying back and resting until we arrive at our destination, preferably without exploding or flying through jump space forever. I'll leave out what jump space is for another time.

•   •   •

I have fond memories of Mars, not just the days when I accomplished my first scam. For being so far from Earth, the laws here may be more severe if you are caught, but you can get away with anything if you have the money. Mars has no plans of toeing the line with the inner planets, that's for sure, so nothing is too hard to arrange, and if you wish to vanish for a few days, or even a month or longer, it's possible on Mars—for the right price, that is.

If a bribe can be described as such, my next big purchase is of the Mars recruitment officer, to have my name placed near the top of the recruitment list for the workers required for whatever their current project is. Judging by the number they are recruiting, it's a big job.

But for now, until the items I have ordered are ready, it's time to keep my head down and enjoy some of the sights. Maybe I could go visit the fabled Face of Mars. The original was just an optical illusion, but years after the colonisation of Mars, a resourceful entrepreneur financed a fake face and made millions.

. . .

After a week of going over my plans, I receive my ordered items and get a confirmation as a successful candidate for workers' current intake. I'm given my boarding time for my newly acquired contract. Everything set; I just have to wait a few days for the trip to a secret, currently undisclosed destination, except I know exactly where we are going. It's not really surprising that every worker heading out only cares about the thirty-six-month contract they now have and how, once the contract has been completed, it will give them enough money to pay all their bills for the next twenty years. Money talks, and the needy or the greedy do not ask the difficult questions.

The inner-world transport barge is of a pretty high standard, and each passenger has access to his or her own multimedia system, a reclining chair that doubles as a bed, and a food and drink dispenser.

Upon boarding, I waste no time trying out the first of my new gizmos, a set of bio gel contact lenses. These lenses contain a nanites factory for making self-contained microhacking drones with the ability to hack into media and security feeds, isolating alarm systems and circumventing sensor nets and feeding all the info back to my lenses. It takes a lot of practice to use such items, but after a sufficient training period, it becomes almost second nature; plus, if you are lying down with your eyes closed, it makes it much easier to hide the subtle head nods and eye movements.

At least now the transport is a warp-capable ship, and the journey time should be short—four to six weeks, give or take.

But after only a few hours, the transport exits warp and enters sublight speeds. Having already hacked the security feeds, both external and internal, I'm able to see all over the ship inside and out. With only a few hours in warp, we should still be well within the Sol System. So dropping out so soon is unexpected, but a bigger surprise is seeing an inner-world super capital ship just seemingly floating motionless in space. This ship is unlike anything I've ever seen before, and what makes it more impressive is the quantum gateway set like a precious gemstone within the centre. I can see other ships entering and leaving the gateway almost constantly. There were always rumours of a mobile gate, but nothing this impressive and deadly. The whole of the inner-world federations could come streaming through, and even the most sensitive, deep-space monitoring station would not be able to detect a fleet in warp in time if the inner worlds decided to destroy Mars.

Within another ten minutes, the transport has passed through the gate and is back in warp again. The transition is fast, but I just glimpse a second mobile gateway before space around us vanishes into lines, and then there is nothing but darkness, the only illumination from the transport itself. This time the warp only lasts a week's worth of tedium, but certainly better than six weeks.

The moon is impressive, not as big as Earth's moon but still very similar, and at least tonight, I'll sleep in a bed. The reclining chairs on the transport are nice and all, but you just can't beat a good bed.

• • •

The workers' accommodations are impressive, and the food standards are good, but nothing compares to real food like lamb, which is my favourite, but, within a utopian society, eating flesh is scowled upon.

The best of all is a nice, comfy bed with a privacy screen that allows each worker a semblance of private alone space, allowing me to send off my hacker drones. The accommodation block is easily hacked, and within no time, I have all the security surveillance feeds, but then I notice a slight issue. Each section of the base is isolated from the others, and as soon as I send my drones into the other sections, the base alarm sounds, sending the entire complex into lockdown. The noise is quite astonishing, but calmly I shut down the other drones to ensure that any sweeps fail to lead back to the accommodation block.

Checking my system logs, I find that the base's security lockdown was tripped by my drones passing through the ventilation ducts. Again, pretty impressive security and I'm starting to feel that this is far too easy, but with this new bit of information, I realise now that every step I take from here on in must be carefully planned. Also, as this is a high-stakes job, I decide to initialise a backup plan for such occasions. A mess-up now is good to a point—at least I get to see their reaction times—but this must be the last one, or I won't get past much here, let alone anywhere near the prototype.

Within five minutes, security personnel enter the workers' blockhouse and begin to scan every inch. I knew that my gadgets would be tested, but I didn't expect it so soon. With my heart in my throat, I stand up from my bed as the guards call for everyone's attention.

The whispers of concern murmur up and down the line as security scans each of us in turn. One of the workers standing next to me—he's called Joey—is scanned, and the handheld device starts to beep urgently. A rescan is carried out with the same result.

Joey starts to protest but is led away and out of the room. My turn to be scanned, and after what seems an extra-long phase, I pass, thanking my backup plan for being so effective. We are dismissed, and lockdown is cancelled. Sadly, for Joey, he won't be back for a few days; the fake information I placed in his file will be discovered as a mistake, and he will be returned, but unfortunately, the two to three days will seem like a nightmare. High stakes mean I must evade at all costs, or I might as well hand myself in.

●　　●　　●

The next day we are all led into the conference room and given a full rundown on what is required of us, the work to be carried out and the shift patterns we will be working to. With the help of memory juice, a synthetic cognitive memory enhancer, to help me understand and use the required skills. It's a banned substance but well worth the risk in cases like this. Also, it won't last forever, but for at least the next two months, I'm an expert in industrial earthmovers, construction methods, and structural design.

This site's plan was to make subterranean hangars with surface access—reinforced structures to withstand rocket attacks and bombardments. This wasn't just an extension to the current hangar; this was to allow installation of a further nineteen of these first-strike weapons of war.

Obviously, the prototype was nearing its end phase of testing and about to enter its final phase of mass production. After the conference, I took a calculated risk and activated a dozen hacker drones and attached them to the various security personnel dotted around the room as we departed for a break. Two of the guards accompanied us while the others stayed behind. Just before we returned for the second half of today's talk, the conference room guards had a shift change and returned to the security barracks—a bit of luck at least. By hacking the room, I'd gain full access to the area and, best of all, the rotas.

I'm nudged by a colleague next to me.

"Hey, bud, you're nodding off," I ask, and I do my best yawn.

"Oh boy, this is dull. Thanks, man. It must be the food after the break," the man next to me replies.

"I'm Cohen," he says, offering his hand.

"Mathew," I reply, shaking it.

"I know what you mean. It normally does the same to me, but these guys are strict on paying attention," Cohen says.

"Thanks for the warning," I reply, and we both turn back to the instructions, the foremen explaining all the various Safety protocol's.

Three hours later, we are allowed to return to our quarters for the day. Shift patterns are handed out, and I note I've been given tipper duties, meaning I'll be shifting the tons of moon dust and rock from the site and onto a great big extraction bin.

From there, the rocks are sorted onto a conveyer belt; some will be placed in useful piles and reused, and the rest will be disposed of in a distant crater.

The one thing I did not count on was that everyone pretty much knew everyone else among the workforce—except for me. I am now considered the new guy who gets the worst jobs and is not really trusted with anything important, but then again, I can exploit that to my advantage.

Early the next morning, I check the security rotas and assign two of my drones to two guards and await their arrival into the security block. Twenty minutes later, the two guards arrive at their post—four hours of watching the security feed—how nice for them and great for me.

This time I don't rush trying to infiltrate security, carefully checking area by area, isolating the program that almost blew the whole operation on the first day, not deleting it but just editing the script to ignore my drones.

Feeling pleased with myself, I head off to do my first twelve-hour shift shifting rock, an honest day's work for a not very honest guy like me. Oddly, I enjoy myself immensely. I reflect upon my life of crime, my penthouse flat, my cars, my own warp-capable ship (small but pretty awesome), and then how could my life have been, doing an honest day's work, digging and shifting rock, not perfect but honest. The dream of such a life comes suddenly crashing down as an emergency alarm sounds. My first thoughts are that they have discovered my drones, but then the shouts over the Comms explain that an accident has just occurred: one of the new workers from my block has just been crushed to death by falling rock. It's a sober wake-up call to the dangers of working in such an environment. The shift is ended three hours earlier than expected, and we all head back. My epiphany is short-lived, and I really do like my way of life.

What transpired was that one of the survey teams had been checking a newly constructed section of tunnel when the roof partially collapsed. As a result, we get an unscheduled day off while geologists inspect the area. The main chat at dinner suggests that, given the rock's composition, it will need a special additive to ensure that this won't happen again.

The next day I spend playing cards and other recreational games with the guys and checking up on my drones. By the end of the day, security is completely compromised, and I have full access to their computer systems and cameras. The next stage is taking the rest of the base and the hangar.

Joey, the guy I set up on my first day, returns, sporting bloodshot eyes and a nervous disposition to sudden movements as we come back from dinner. It's hard not to feel sorry for the guy, but it was him or me at the time. I'll try and make it up to him by the end.

•   •   •

After a month, I've shifted more rock than anyone had thought possible. I've really gotten into my role, and the longer I work with these guys, the more I come to understand the importance of every aspect of the team working together. I even start to get some of the guys to chat to me about previous jobs and how they differed from this one, and slowly they seem to accept the new guy as their own. Well, a small number at least. I'm sure that some old-timers would never accept me.

The base, except for the hangar, is now entirely under my control. I felt a little chilly one night and even had the nerve to increase the room temperature a few degrees, much to the station maintenance crew's confusion the next day. They set it back down again, but I felt good about myself and had become confident in my current success.

The hangar proved much more difficult than I expected, and I realised that breaking into a hangar containing a top-secret prototype would be hard, but this is beyond hard. No one has been in there in weeks, apparently because the main test pilot was attacked at a nightclub and seriously injured on one of his days off.

Since that day, only three people have been in the hangar, and sadly that was before I arrived here. One was the facility's top project leader; then, a day later, a neurosurgeon from the hospital where the pilot had been taken went in together with the project lead; two days after that, a psychologist on her own went in and stayed for a short period. Perplexing but also interesting, as the hangar was unlocked from within.

Who else is in there? I go over the main databases again, but the project prototype specs are not listed. Hardly surprising, but I knew that.

It's halfway through the second month that I find a possible lead. The project lead and the surgeon were in contact with each other, but whoever was still inside the hangar requested the psychologist visit via the project lead.

Taking a chance, I clone the hangar's communications signature and send the project lead another request to see the psychologist. Then I log onto the project lead's terminal and wait for the result. I don't have to wait long, as the project lead sends a message to the surgeon's terminal; however, this time, there is a long wait, so he can't be in a local system.

Dr Derson,
> *I understand you are busy with our patient, but Arden is asking to see Dr Rhyne again. Are there any updates from our earlier conversation?*
> *End Message.*

Several hours pass, and then my monitoring program informs me of an incoming message.

Dr Pearson,
> *My apologies for not getting back to you sooner. I had hoped I could reply with better information, but sadly there is no change. Arden's brain scans are still*

showing a degradation of the myelin white matter, which means the brain cannot function correctly. We were hoping that the nanites treatment could reverse this damage, but our current test results show that too much damage has already occurred. If Arden does recover, he won't be the same man.
I'll update you again in a few days.
End Message.

What's going on here, two Ardens?

Arden, there is still no news at the moment, but I will send Dr Rhyne to come and visit you again in a few days. As soon as I get any real news regarding Arden's condition, I'll let you know.
End Message.

Twins then? But odd to name both the same name. I must be missing something.

Dr Pearson,
    I'm not sure talking with Dr Rhyne will help much, but I very much enjoyed our conversation last time. I shall look forward to seeing her again.
    Thanks, Dr Pearson.
    End Message.

I still feel like I'm missing something, but I'm pleased that my little ruse did not backfire. And then something occurs to me. While searching for Dr Rhyne's background, I'm half expecting to find some artificial intelligence experience, but all I find is a very well-educated psychologist with specialisations in the cognitive, military, and clinical fields.

But I still feel I'm missing something; I re-read the message from Dr Pearson to Dr Rhyne, and an hour later, he receives a reply from Dr Rhyne confirming an appointment with Arden.

•   •   •

Until Dr Rhyne arrives, I just carry on with my work. Oddly, I've been finding the constant back and forth with tons of rock quite relaxing, plus it allows me to continue to monitor the patrols in the area, the layout of the new hangars, and the whereabouts of the actual one.

I've also started to get to know some of the dirty little secrets the security guards have and where a few of them hide their stashes of illicit drugs and/or alcohol. They all seem pretty nice guys, except for Janson, who is head of security. He appears to be a bit of a git and runs security like it's his own personal hell to mete out punishment to whoever displeases him.

He was also the head interrogator of Joey, and although he could have used more advanced techniques that have proven very effective in the past, he chose a more brutal means to discover guilt. I start to believe it would be fitting if Janson should have the chance to experience a similar fate. Sadly, this kind of setup will take time. I start with a new secret bank account, a traceable link to his known legit one, and some faked meets regarding project phantom's information and location. The rest I'll add in time.

The week passes by quickly. On the day Dr Rhyne is scheduled to see Arden, I make excuses for why I'm unable to work that day, and with a few choice words from the supervisor, I'm left alone to recover.

Dr Rhyne arrives on time. She's much younger than I expected, and the security buzz around her like bees to honey. With several drones ready to go, I start to attach them to her, but then one of the more senior security guards decides it's the best time to give her a second scan to be sure and as an excuse to stand close and leer at her. I issue the destruct protocol to shut down the drones, but the scanner had already detected the presence of an unknown piece of tech. Knowing she was clean just moments before, the guard stares at his scanner with a look of disbelief.

"Is there a problem?" Dr Rhyne asks, staring at the guard, realising exactly what he was doing.

"Maybe you drooled too much into your scanner. Can we just get on with this, or do I have to call for the project lead?" Dr Rhyne says, now looking visibly annoyed.

"I'm sorry, Doctor, but you gave a positive result. I'm unable to let you go any further," the guard says. It's his turn to look annoyed as he starts to open a Comms channel.

"This is senseless. Just scan me again!" Dr Rhyne asks.

"I'm just following procedures, ma'am," The guard opens a channel, not having time to say anything further as the doctor replies.

"Oh, is that what you call it? And there I was, thinking that you just wanted me to put you up on molestation charges. Scan me again," Dr Rhyne says more forcibly.

With an exaggerated sigh, the guard closes the channel and scans her again. This time the scanner emits an all-clear beep. Without waiting for the guard to say anything, the doctor barges past and heads for a small hatchway in the main hanger bay door.

I wait just a few more seconds before sending the last remaining drones down to attach themselves to the doctor as the hatch door opens to allow her entry. My view is partially obscured as the doctor enters the hangar. It's a clinical, white, open space. Strangely, there's no sign of the ship, but a translucent tear-shaped frame is fixed about thirty meters from the ground by some kind of resting arms. Around the shape is a gangway that goes all around the entire room with access platforms to the translucent tear-shape frame. A control console blocks a direct view ahead of us, and then a voice starts talking from the console.

"Nice to see you again, Dr Rhyne. And I see you brought guests. How thoughtful," The console light flashes as the voice talks, and then it goes out.

Dr Rhyne walks up to the console and sits down. The momentarily clear view of the hangar still reveals no sign of the new ship.

"Guests? I've brought no guests, Arden. Are you feeling okay?" Dr Rhyne replies with a hint of concern.

"That's okay, Dr Rhyne. I realised you would not have seen them, but I am curious," Arden replies.

"So, how have you been feeling?" Dr Rhyne asks, looking over her shoulder. Arden laughs.

"To be honest with you, Doc, I've been rather down recently up until a few weeks ago. I was thinking of taking my own life, but due to the guests, I've been considering other options," Arden replies. Dr Rhyne continues to look concerned and then thoughtful with Arden's reply.

"Have you considered returning hangar access back to the project team? They are all rather concerned about you,"

"I have, Doc, but for now, it's a closed subject. I would rather stay isolated where I can continue to hope and pray that Arden makes a full recovery, but it does seem rather doubtful," Arden replies.

I continue to listen to Arden and the doctor talk about depression and the subject of suicide, wondering, what the hell is all this? An artificial intelligence gone a bit barking? And the worrying remarks to the doctor about bringing guests... I'm suddenly pulled out of my thoughts as Arden brings my attention back with a bang.

"I'd rather not continue on regarding my mental health if you do not mind. I'd rather that we talk about the guests you brought in with you. Fascinating machines. I can't wait to meet the controller," Aden says, and my blood runs cold. It can't be my nanites that he's referring to. Dr Rhyne looks dumbfounded.

"What guests are you referring to? Are they here now? When did you start seeing them?" Dr Rhyne asks.

"About seven weeks ago. They appeared with the fresh intake of construction workers. I suspect one of them is not what he seems," Arden replies. The doctor is now becoming a little distressed.

"Okay, stop there. Can you at least show yourself so we can have a face-to-face discussion about these guests of yours?" Dr Rhyne asks.

"Okay, Doctor, if you insist," Arden replies. The hacker drones now reposition themselves around the hangar, giving a better view. The hangar is around one hundred and eighty feet in length, about ninety feet wide, and approximately eighty feet high. The hangar shimmers, and slowly a sleek, white tear-shaped ship appears within the frame; what I previously mistook as part of the landing platform is actually part of the ship itself.

"Ah, that's better. Now could you please explain what these guests are and what they are talking to you about?" Dr Rhyne asks.

"Well, I guess it's not that important now, but they are nanites machines, very complex and well-designed, but they are not talking to me, well, not in the usual sense. The controller has not realised yet, but while he was taking control of the base, I was using my biological nanites to take control of his. They are advanced, but mine is decades better and much smaller," Arden replies.

"So what has this controller been doing here exactly?" Dr Rhyne asks, taking out a pad and starts to write.

"The controller has been systematically taking control of the entire base. I first noticed it when his nanites tripped a detection filtration unit, but since then, the controller has been using the personnel to transport his drones all over the base. But, until today, he has not been successful at penetrating the hangar bay, well, until you walked in with them, at least," Arden says.

"I see… very interesting. What do you think these nanites want?" Dr Rhyne asks as she writes a few lines of notes on her notepad and gives Arden her best smile.

"Well, the nanites don't want anything, but the controller most likely wants me. I understand that you don't believe me, which is perfectly fine, Doc. If I was in your shoes, I might not either," Arden replies. Hearing what was just said, I start to run diagnostics. There are a few glitches here and there, but nothing suggests that any of my drones have been compromised.

"Well, that is a concern. I do believe you, and you must believe us when we say that we also need you. We need you to allow us to help you, but there is no shame in being wanted," Dr Rhyne says in her best sympathetic tone. There is a long silence before Arden replies.

"I'm not sure what backwater colony you trained to be a psychotherapist at, but I would suggest you go back for more training. Better still, find another place to train, as the school you attended did a piss-poor job of training you," Arden says, a hint of anger in his voice for the first time. Dr Rhyne looks dumbfounded again, but before she can reply, Arden continues.

"I would suggest that you should listen more and not talk so much, and for that matter, I hope that the controller listens well. You have an hour, no more, to convince me. Dr Rhyne, this session is over. Please leave," Arden says, and then goes silent, and the ship dematerialises, leaving just the translucent frame behind.

• • •

I replay the video and watch and listen as Arden tells me that I have an hour, and I watch Dr Rhyne leave in what can only be described as a blazing trail of anger. If she could have slammed the door, I'm sure she would have.

One of my drones alert beeps, and a message pops up.

"You now have fifty-six minutes left."

I waste another two minutes just reading over the message and uttering various profanities.

With fear starting to bubble deep within my gut, I send the activation code for my distraction sequence and leave the room. As I enter the corridor adjacent to our accommodation, I activate my holographic disguise, a dozen micro holographic projectors now changing my appearance to resemble one of the security guards—not perfect up close, but it should be good enough to get me to the hangar doors.

Shortly after leaving my quarters, I stop suddenly as I spot a guard leaning against the wall. As I watch, he slowly slumps to the floor. Another drone message pops up: "You now have fifty minutes left."

Casually inspecting the guard as I pass, I guess he is just unconscious. Wasting no time, I hurry down the corridor, taking the next right and seeing more guards now lying on the floor. With each new turn, I hear more guards gasp and fall to the floor.

By the time I arrive at the hangar, I have passed at least a dozen guards passed out, and forty minutes of my one hour has passed. As I approach the hangar, the hatch door opens. I step inside, and the intruder alert alarms begin to wail around the complex as the door behind me closes with a definite clunk.

•   •   •

Dr Rhyne enters Dr Pearson's office in a calm and controlled manner. She sits down opposite Dr Pearson, who looks up with a slight smile.

"Went well then. I must say you lasted longer this time," Dr Pearson says. Dr Rhyne takes out her pad and throws it down on the table.

"Your AI is now seeing things that are not there," Dr Rhyne replies. Dr Pearson looks down at the pad and then back at Dr Rhyne.

"Really. That's new. What is Arden seeing?" Dr Pearson asks. Dr Rhyne takes a deep breath.

"Your machine is seeing 'guests,' as he referred to them, but he went on to say that the guests are nanites sent by someone who has infiltrated this base, possibly as one of your fresh recruits, but he also spoke about suicide and being wanted," Dr Rhyne replies.

"When did Arden tell you this?" Dr Pearson asks, reaching under his desk and looking concerned.

"I'm not sure; thirty minutes ago. Your elevator was playing up while I was on my way here," Dr Rhyne replies but cannot hear Dr Pearson's reply as the intruder alarm sounds.

• • •

Seeing the hangar for myself, I realise what I missed when I viewed it through my drones. The tear-shaped frame contains very well-concealed thruster ports and other modules, the purpose of which I do not know. Around the inside edge, I can just barely make out a slight shimmering field of distortion where I'm guessing the main section of the ship has somehow hidden itself.

"Hello, Matthew, or whatever your name is. I'm pleased to meet you at last. My name is Arden, as you may have already discovered, but your main confusion is why I share a name with someone else," Arden says, and I start to reply, but Arden cuts me off.

"But before I'll answer any questions, I want you to answer one of my questions first, and you only have forty-two minutes left to convince me," Arden asks.

Taking a step closer to the control console, I take note that my distraction protocol has had minimal effect on the security, but due to the majority of the guards being unconscious, I don't consider that too much of an issue at this stage.

"Okay, Arden, what is your question?" I reply.

"It's a simple question. Are you responsible for Arden's current condition?" Arden asks. Feeling somewhat relieved about the question, I answer.

"I honestly have no idea who attacked Arden. I only found out about you after Arden was already seriously injured," I reply. My answer is received with a silence that lasts longer than I care for.

"How do you know that Arden was already injured?" Arden asks.

"I came across your file a few months back, and it mentioned that the previous pilot had suffered serious harm while off duty, but it did not mention your name. It's only what I've pieced together so far," I answer truthfully.

Another silence. I feel my time is slowly eroded away as another two minutes pass by before Arden replies again.

"I believe that you are telling the truth, but I'm not able to determine if you have been set up or if this was pure coincidence. Either way, I have decided that you are not directly responsible. As such, I will let you live," Arden replies. With his answer, I do not feel I should argue the point.

"You have gathered the reason why I'm here; my question now is, will you let me take the ship?" I ask. Arden replies immediately this time.

"The ship is all yours, but there is a problem you will have to resolve first. This ship only flies with a pilot, and the current pilot is brain dead."

"So what do I need to do?" I ask.

"That is the hard part. First, you need to kill me. Although I told the doctor I was considering suicide, the actual act of killing myself is not possible. Instead, I need someone else to terminate my consciousness for me. So I have given you access to my core network via the command console. There you should be able to initiate a system wipe of my consciousness, which will then allow the system to select a new pilot, but you now only have thirty-five minutes," Arden replies. Hearing that my timer is counting again, I start to complain.

"I'm sorry about the timer, but it's not my time limit. It's how long you have before security recovers and break into here. They are rather efficient when they want to be," Arden says.

Sitting down at the console, I read the current output now on the screen, displaying all the ships systems and current power levels, systems—

Environmental,	100%
Sublight drive,	100%
Phased warp drive,	100%
Navigation,	100%
Biological nanites system,	100%
Dual proton laser,	100%
Power cells,	100%
Database integrity,	100%
Backup computer systems,	100%
Central memory core,	100%
Neural network,	100%
Neural network Backup,	100%
Phased cloak,	100%
Passive stealth,	100%

Signature reduction controls and various other subsystems handling other functions of the ship.

"Hmm…Arden, I can't find a power plant of any kind or shield emitters," I ask, looking down the list again.

"I do not have shields or require a power core; the signature of such systems would negate the stealth aspects of my profile. Vacuum energy is collected and stored within the power cells and then converted into electrical energy when required by the systems. As such, the energy signature of this vessel resembles the background energy signature of the universe," Arden replies.

I nod and continue to look at the specifications, which surpass anything I've ever seen before. Inner-world tech at its best and beyond, this design is easily decades ahead of anything that the outer federation worlds have, and I would surmise that it's ahead of most inner-world ships.

Selecting the neural network, I find that the system is locked out and requires project leader authorisation. That is hardly unexpected. Programming one of my hacker drones to work on the access commands, I apply my efforts as an alternative way to delete or overwrite the current neural net.

With ten minutes left, I activate Arden's primary debug protocol, the lockdown codes being far easier to crack than the primary codes, the result is instantaneous as Arden reappears, and every hatch, cargo door, and service panel opens.

"I must inform you that security has mostly recovered, and an attempt to gain access to this hangar has begun. Your time is running out," Arden says as I cast a quick look back at the hangar door. I head toward the steps and up onto the gangway.

"Don't worry, I think I'm almost there," I say, entering the ship for the first time. I'm surprised by the cramped size of the internal crawl space. This crawl space leads to a central corridor that allows access to the rest of the ship; from here, at least, you can almost stand with a slight stoop.

The corridor has a galley in the centre with six interconnected cryotubes on either side of the passageway. The pilot's cryotube is at the front end of the corridor, and there's a good-size cargo bay at the other end. While in cryosleep, all the crew share a lucid Dreamtime reality where they can interact within a larger artificial structure. Slipping into the pilot cryotube, I disable the Dreamtime sequence, knowing it would not work for me in any case, and while the ship is in debug mode, I corrupt the access authority commands for the entire project staff making the data inaccessible. Then, to ensure it cannot be restored, I delete the backup files.

"Most systems have this flaw, which is if the master admin access is irretrievable, once the system is reset out of debugging mode, access will be reset to the original master admin, which should be you. The fail-safe is that normally the computer system would re-create the master admin access that was lost, but in this case, after reboot, you grant me master admin access, and with luck, I'll then have full access," I explain.

"That seems all rather too easy to me, and you now only have six minutes left," Arden replies, sounding glum.

"Well, it is, and it isn't. Without your cooperation, I would never have been able to place you into debug mode, and you could have easily stopped me when I was corrupting the master files, so normally, no, this way would never work. Okay, we're all set. Just one more thing," I say and slip out one of my contact lenses.

"You should be able to scan my real identity now. Thank you for trusting me, Arden, and I'm sorry what happened to your pilot. I hope he doesn't suffer," I say. After a momentary silence, Arden replies.

"Nice to meet you also, Sam McCall, and thank you for helping me. From what was told to me, Arden is not suffering, which is a good thing. Maybe it is better this way. If we had met under different circumstances, the likelihood is that I would have killed you."

"Well, that's a good point, but sadly we are almost out of time. Good luck, Arden," I say.

"Thank you, Sam. Good luck to you. I hope you find what you are looking for," Arden replies.

I initiate a complete system reboot, and the ship starts to power down. I pray that this does not take too long. All I can do now is wait as the last remaining minutes pass by, and then a period of complete silence surrounds me. I'm left in darkness for what seems an eternity, and then slowly, I feel a vibration start from deep within the core of the ship. More sounds reach me as the various subsystems spring into life, and the hum of the ship returns from all around.

"Assigning full access to Sam McCall. Access granted as master admin, group level: project leader," Arden says.

Wasting no more time, I access the neural matrix and highlight Arden's artificial consciousness. Somehow I can sense Arden all around me, waiting, almost as if he was holding his breath. Pausing for only a few seconds, almost expecting Arden to call out to tell me to stop, I complete the sequence of commands to wipe Arden's persona. Was it just a persona or really a copy of an unfortunate test pilot who met with a painful end? Maybe I will never know, but for some reason, I can't help but feel like I've just put a pillow over the head of a victim of violence and suffocated the life out of him.

I'm left shaken by my act, unable to do anything, and I might have stayed that way, but a strange voice is asking me a question, repeating itself after receiving no reply. I realise then it is coming from the ship itself.

"Ship's consciousness has been erased. Neural mapping is ready. Would you like to begin?" an emotionless voice says.

Now that I have full admin control, I ignore the request and check on the hangar door's status. I realise that the breaching team trying to gain access is just seconds away from succeeding.

Ensuring that the ship is no longer in debug mode and all the external hatches and access panels are closed, I instruct the main external hangar doors to open, causing the sudden decompression to suck out anything that isn't fixed down.

"Ship's consciousness has been erased. Neural mapping is ready. Would you like to begin?" an emotionless voice replies again.

The breaching team stops what they are doing, and I sigh with relief. Everything almost ended there. If they had gained access, the chance of me getting the external hangar doors open would have been practically zero. Now I've delayed them, but not for long.

"Ship's consciousness has been erased. Neural mapping is ready. Would you like to begin?" the emotionless voice repeats.

"Yes, Arden, I would," I finally tell the computer.

"Arden is no longer the designation of this computer profile. I am the ship's core AI, and The current designation is *Phantom*, but I will take your last response as a yes.

"Neural mapping has been initiated. Neural mapping will take approximately twenty-seven years. If you could lie still, the duration might be reduced to approximately fourteen years. You are now designated as the primary pilot. You now have partial control of the ship," the emotionless voice says.

"What the hell? What do you mean, fourteen years?" I reply, alarmed, my voice raised.

"Neural mapping is extremely time-consuming, and fourteen years is only obtainable if the pilot can remain still. Neural mapping will take up to thirty years if you are active," the core AI replies.

"Oh, come on. Arden said that I could be mapped and become the pilot," I say, sounding frustrated.

"And in that respect, he was telling you the truth, but Arden did not explain the details of what was required; in effect, he omitted some facts," the core AI explains.

"Oh, hell. Please explain what else he left out," I ask.

"When the pilot Arden joined this project, he was only eleven years old, and the neural mapping hardware was situated at his training and education centre, where he remained until he was twenty-five years old. By that time, he had become a qualified pilot with many skills in the areas the project required.

"The neural mapping hardware and Arden were relocated to this base, where he spent a further five years training. The neural mapping was faster due to the test pilot's age, but project improvements have determined that pilots could be trained in as little as ten years if the candidate is mapped from the age of five. You are almost thirty, and as such, neural mapping of your brain could take as many as thirty years. Please remain still while the mapping process is carried out," the core AI asks.

Listening to this, I'm almost about to explode in frustration, but then I remember that partial control of the ship is available to me prior to the mapping being completed.

"Computer…*Phantom*…whatever you are called…get us the hell out of here, and cloak up. I'm pretty sure Arden mentioned that cloaking was a part of your core programming; you just can't go into warp or use weapons," I instruct the system.

"You are correct. Initiating thrust and cloak. Would you like to go anywhere in particular, and would you like me to evade the patrol that is heading in our direction? They seem like they are in a hurry," The core AI replies.

"Hell yes, please evade them! I'm sure you and certainly I do not wish to die," I reply.

"Affirmative, Sam. Getting the hell out of here. Entering stealth, and please, it would be much appreciated if you would remain perfectly still," the core AI replies.

. . .

Even with Arden's consciousness and personality erased, the ship's core subroutines are based on and primarily configured upon highly sophisticated combat and evade simulation software. As a result, evading the patrol ships is accomplished with ease. Most line-of-sight tracking systems, once locked on, can easily predict their target's trajectory, even if they lose sight of sight for several minutes, by using complex predicted algorithms before reacquiring the target.

The *Phantom*'s unique design allows it to become near-invisible during combat manoeuvres, and the passive nature of the translucent frame gives the craft a near-perfect absorption factor to most active detection systems, so when line-of-sight tracking systems attempt to reacquire the *Phantom* where the predictive algorithms have predicted the ship to be, the targeting software has nothing to lock onto, and the algorithm attempts to reacquire with the next possible prediction lock-on phase, but by then it's too late.

The cost of all this is that thrust must be kept to a minimum, and each and every time a manoeuvring jet is used, it raises the ship's signature, so the ship spends most of its covert time using its own inertia.

The moon's thin atmosphere and the mountainous canyons allow the *Phantom* to evade the patrol ships within minutes of leaving the hangar.

The ground-based detection stations, on the other hand, pose a much more significant threat. They're designed primarily to detect incoming ships but are easily redirected to track down and detect fleeing ships. The *Phantom*'s most valuable defensive ability is not being detected in the first place, and when the research and development team that designed its stealth ability is actively trying to track it, this makes escape very difficult.

The issue now is that even with a thin atmosphere, it would require several minutes of maximum thrust for the ship to break orbit. In these circumstances, the best move is to hide and wait for the best opportunity to escape, but this choice cannot be made by the ship alone—not yet at least.

·   ·   ·

Phantom is the first to break the silence as I attempt to keep my last meal down. The odd sensation I'm now feeling isn't anything to do with the ship's manoeuvring and evading. As far as I'm concerned, the ship isn't moving, but the sensation of being taken out of phase is totally alien to me, and the constant shaking due to the rapid temperature drop within the ship isn't helping.

"I can see that you are not feeling so well," the system says. With all my will and deep breathing, I reply the best I can under such circumstances.

"I'll be okay. Did we lose them?"

"Yes, Sam, but we are now hiding from the ground-based stations. We have superior stealth, but an attempt to reach orbit would cause us to lose our advantage, and we would be detected," the core AI says.

"I had a backup plan for an issue like this," I reply.

Activating a link back to the hacker drones within the base, I run a quick diagnostics to see their condition and then activate a drone within security. The current status would suggest that 80 per cent of my drones are still currently operating. The latest security reports reveal that the entire base is now on lockdown and a security sweep is presently underway; this would suggest that the remaining drones will be found at some point, and after that, our way off of this rock will close.

Wasting no more time, I activate the fusion power plant evacuation protocols and simulate a catastrophic failure alert. Choosing this particular alert gives me a higher chance that it will not be ignored due to the tests involved. It might not be believed by many of the higher-ranked staff, but to run confirmation tests that this is the real deal would place them at a higher risk of death, and the lower-level staff do not get paid enough to run that kind of risk; they will take the alert at face value and evacuate.

"Sam, there seems to be an evacuation alert warning to all ships to clear the area," the core AI says.

"Good. That's what I expected. Keep an eye out for the transport, and as soon as you can, try and get in as close as possible. We need to follow it up as it attempts to gain orbit," I ask.

"Affirmative, Sam," the system says as I leave the rest of the plan up to the ship and head off to the galley. My fight to keep everything down finally becomes a losing battle. The feeling of success at still being alive and having this ship is short-lived as I fill my first sick bag.

By the time I return to the pilot seat and ask for any update, *Phantom* has just broken orbit from the research base and is preparing for warp.

"Get in as tight as you can, and make sure you can't be seen. We need to get inside its warp field; otherwise, we could end up losing bits of our ship that are still sticking out," I advise.

"Affirmative, Sam. It would seem the transport is powering up its drive," the core AI replies.

This time I do feel a slight shudder as the transport enters warp, pulling us with it. The trip to the base took a week in warp, so with luck, the return trip should be the same.

"So how long can we keep phased like this? I realised down on the moon that we could not draw power to sustain the ship's systems indefinitely," I ask.

"Normally, Sam, if we were using our own phased warp drives, the entire ship would enter phase, and we'd lose our access to vacuum energy. In that case, we couldn't stay in phased warp indefinitely, but as we are being pulled along in normal warp, we can maintain this as long as we like," the core AI replies.

"Well, that's good to know. So how much faster is phased warp than normal warp?" I ask, intrigued about this ship.

"That depends on how much energy we have and how much we are willing to stay in phased warp for—dropping out with little to no power would mean most of our systems would stop working. But to answer the best I can, about four times faster than the fastest ship," the system answers.

"Okay then, that's pretty impressive. The downside?" I ask.

"The downside is that we need to recharge between each jump, so we are four times faster in a short trip, but over a long distance, we are maybe marginally faster but not by much," the core AI says.

"Is there any advantage to phased warp other than it being kind of faster?" I ask.

"When in phased warp, we are totally undetectable; there are currently no deep-space scanners that can detect our wake," the core AI replies.

"Oh, now that is good. But enough talk. If I stay conscious much longer, I'm going to be sick again. Stick me in cryosleep, and wake me up when we come out of warp."

"Affirmative, Sam."

• • •

The sense of time within cryosleep is pretty much zero, so I'm waking up again as soon as I lose consciousness. Restful sleep it is not, but I know I have been in cryo because my vision is blurry, my mouth is dry, and I feel like I need food and water and a lot of it.

"Status report," I say with a slight cough, the now-familiar feeling of nausea starting to return.

"Passive scans would suggest we have arrived at the inner worlds' main hub. However, the authorities wish to question the contractors before releasing them back to their homeworld," the core AI replies.

"Annoying but not completely unexpected. Try and break away from the transport as soon as it's safe to do so. How hidden are we?" I ask.

"Inner-world security currently has no protocols for detecting or searching for this new type of vessel, so we do have a small window of escape," The core AI explains.

"Good. Let's hope our luck holds. Drift in close to the quantum gateway hub, and scan outgoing ships. Look for destinations to Earth or Mars—in fact, any of the Sol System colonies," I ask

"Affirmative, Sam."

I go back to the galley and look for something to drink and maybe something I can hold down for a bit. Spotting the medical symbol, I scan for nausea tablets or shots, and with a positive beep, a one-shot hypo injection needle is deposited. Minutes later, I feel better than I have for what seems like days, and I show my appreciation for this by stuffing myself silly.

"Sam, I've detected an Earth Federation cruiser heading for the gate. Comms chatter would suggest it's heading to the Sol System. What are your orders?" the core AI says, suddenly bringing back to my situation.

"Sounds good. Drift and play 'you can't see me,' and when it passes by, get in close and match their speed and heading. Once we get through the gate, try and retain proximity and match its vector. It should take us directly to Earth, but we don't want to leave warp at the same location. Can this ship drop out through the wake of another ship without being harmed?" I ask.

"It's feasible, Sam, just not been done before; I am technically still under test flight status," the core AI replies.

"Just take it easy then, and we will find out together if it's possible," I say as the ship begins to manoeuvre.

"Affirmative, Sam. Heading in."

• • •

The trip takes longer than expected, as we visit several colonies on the way, and we arrive back on Earth two weeks later. The antinausea jabs have been amazingly effective, saving me from two weeks in cryo. I spent that time exploring the ship, which is surprisingly not much to see. The cargo hangar is modifiable and can be converted for various purposes. Each of the cryopods can be ejected and act as a life pod if a disaster strikes.

With power cells at maximum capacity, we head down to my own private hangar. It's not much, but it's off the books, and it's pretty close to a favourite restaurant of mine.

"Well, ship, it's been lovely, but I'm going to head out for a few days. I need to get a proper meal and a good sleep before deciding what to do with you. We can sort out this scanning issue another day," I say.

"It's no problem, Sam. I've been mapping you since we left. It would be quicker if you could remain still, but with the bionanites that I injected into you while you were in cryo, I can continue to scan you from orbit if needed," the core AI replies.

"Hey, what? I did not ask you to do that," I reply, feeling annoyed.

"Well, maybe not directly, but you did ask me to start scanning you, and I took that as a command and permission," the core AI response; being too tired to argue, I head for the exit.

"Fine, then. You are pretty much pointless, considering I can't even use most of your system until I'm mapped. Maybe when I retire in around thirty years, you might be useful," I say.

"When the time comes, Sam, I will enjoy knowing you more. Preliminary scans show that your mind is rather unique in how you assimilate information and work through complex problems. I believe we would have been an excellent mind together," the core AI says.

"What do you mean we would have been?" I say, hearing the past tense and stopping me in my tracks.

"Sadly, this procedure is supposed to be completed before the adult male has reached his thirtieth birth date—any older, and the neural mapping process and melding of the two minds might prove too much for the human brain to cope with. I'm sorry to inform you, Sam, but you might not survive the process," The core AI explains. Hearing this news seems to add a rather expensive and pointless cherry to the top of this costly project. Sighing, I reply.

"I'm off for some real food. Don't do anything I would not do, and feel free to send me a message if you have any updates. You might as well continue for now, and we can talk more about this later and decide what we can do. See you around, Phantom."

• • •

It only took the authorities three hours to find Sam after an anonymous tipoff. Later, when the Planetary Enforcement Agency raided Sam's hangar, they found no sign of the Prototype.

11
Unfinished Business

Facility Zero, 271 days online: federation year 2435

JESSICA STARES DOWN at Dr Zorn, unable to say or do anything for a few moments after hearing the doctor's last words, 'He's the angel of death, and he created the freakers.' Most people would react by laughing or ridiculing the one who had just said that, but oddly to Jessica, it just made perfect sense; it did not surprise her in the least. What does surprise her is what she says next.

"Was he the one piloting the pod?" Jessica asks.

"Yes, He was rather upset about my deception," Dr Zorn says, smiling.

"I bet he was, but why did he let you go?" Jessica asks.

"It was the deal I made with him to build the pod, and I did. The poor guys who helped with the heavy lifting were just loose ends," Dr Zorn Explains.

"Ah yes, we did find them both eventually, and we had pretty much worked out who was responsible, but the pod exploding and trying to work out who was flying just added to the confusion," Jessica says.

"Samael surviving the pod's destruction was the evidence he was telling the truth," Dr Zorn adds and then starts to cough.

"What did he tell you, Doctor?" Jessica crouches down as the doctor recovers from his coughing fit and continues.

"When we first met, he introduced himself as Samael. He befriended me at the start, but as I got nearer to the pod's completion, he told me more of his past until I slowly realised that he must never be freed," Doctor explains, coughing and closes his eyes for a moment.

"Dr Zorn, what do you mean he must not be freed?" Jessica asks. Opening his eyes once more, the doctor continues.

"This place is not just our prison; the black hole is his prison. We might have created the facility to imprison our guilty, but God created the black holes in the first place to imprison his, and not just here, everywhere. I suspect all black holes contain angels," Doctor Zorn explains as he stops as another series of coughing fits takes over.

Jessica, having heard enough for now, steps away and turns back to Carter.

"Can we not do anything for him? He is very important," Jessica asks. Carter lets out a long sigh.

"I wish I could, but I need to save our remaining resources for the ones that can fight," Carter explains, looking genuinely ashamed at the thought.

The dining hall suddenly lights dim and then return to their normal illuminations before Jessica can object but brighter than before, followed by a system announcement: 'Level-one quarantine protocol has been lifted. Access permissions reinstated.'

"Well, that's good news, at least," Jessica says and then addresses the system.

"System, what is the status of the food and water dispensers?" Jessica asks, looking hopeful. There is a slight pause and then a reply.

"Water dispensers are now working at 60 per cent, but food dispensers are currently empty and require kitchen staff," the system replies. Jessica listens to the reply before turning back to Carter.

"Right, we need to get water to the injured and then try and feed some of our weakest with what remaining food we have left. With luck, we should all be able to get out of here soon," Jessica says.

This time it's Carter who is about to protest when another voice calls out.

"Jessica, can you hear me? It's Alistair Brookes!"

"Yes, Professor, I can. What is happening? Where's Sam?" Jessica replies as others in the room stir and looks around with expressions of hope where none had been for weeks.

"Sam headed down to see what is blocking the elevator, but I've not heard anything from him in a while. I've also removed the walls to level two at the shaft, so you should be able to get back when you are ready. How is your situation?" Alistair Brookes says.

"Mostly, we are all okay, but we have injured...and, Professor, Dr Zorn is here," Jessica says, waiting for a reply, knowing that this piece of information will have an effect. However, she does not have to wait long.

"How can that be? I saw his pod explode. My God, it can't be true," The professor replies, his voice frantic," Professor Brookes says and then pauses, then continues.

"How is he?" Professor Brookes Asks, sounding calmer.

"He's in a bad way, but if we can get to medical, he might pull through. But, I'm really not sure, Professor. He's been telling me some worrying things. We will need to talk about this face to face," Jessica replies.

"Yes, yes, of course, I understand. So in the meantime, ask the system to take you to security, and a corridor should take you to the main elevator. Hopefully, Sam will already be there. Good luck, Jessica, but I need to arrange a few things. I'll be in touch," Professor Brookes says and goes silent with an audible click.

"Professor?" Jessica says and sigh, then turns back to face Carter.

"Feed the weak! Get them on their feet, make stretchers if need be, but we are all getting out of here," Jessica says, not waiting for a reply, then heads for the barricade.

Carter watches Jessica walk away. He understands her request and knows that this is a risk, all or nothing, then, looking at the injured for a moment, he calls over one of the defenders.

"Get the rest of the supplies and assemble the others. We are getting out of here," Carter calls out.

• • •

What the heck? How can this be possible? Sam thinks to himself. It's only been a matter of a few months since I left Arden or Sam or *Phantom* or whatever the core AI was calling itself.

"You said it would take up to thirty years to map my brain," Sam replies to the voice in his head.

"*That's correct, and I'm pleased to say it's been completed much earlier than I had calculated; fourteen years, two months, six days, eight hours, nine minutes, and twenty-two seconds. I would very much doubt you would need the exact duration, but anyway, it's done. If you are ready, should we begin?" The voice replies.* Sam, feeling a little frustrated.

"Begin what, exactly? I am feeling a bit vague about what all this entails and how are we talking to each other in the first place; I do not have my hacker drones. Second, and more importantly, you are going to have to explain a

few things first; where the hell are you?" I ask. The voice inside Sam's head sighs.

"The neural mapping process maps your neural cortex. The core AI effectively becomes you, and the bionanites have altered your cortex so we can telepathically talk to each other once the mapping has been completed. I did not talk to you before, as your last orders stated to get a message to you with any updates, and we would discuss what to do later. Well, it is later now, and I have sent you the update. And do you realise you can be very annoying sometimes?

To answer your other question, where am I? I'm just outside of the influence of the black hole monitoring Comms chatter while I talk to you. Your first question is a little more complex to explain—far easier to show—but currently, I'm talking to you. We are not sharing our thoughts and consciousness; once we do, then you will have a better understanding of what this is all about," the voice explains.

"Okay, that sounds reasonable, but if you are a perfect copy of my brain, why do you sound female?" I ask.

"Good question. That's rather interesting and a bit complex. It's all sort of to do with the nature-nurture argument, but as I've not had any environmental influences, and this time I've not had a team of excited scientists poking and prodding me, it's been up to me to choose a gender identity.

When a male or female brain develops, it has a few pointers to go by. Your brain, as it turns out, is rather unique and complex. During healthy human development, identification with one gender or another is determined by several factors, including hormones, anatomy, genes, chromosomes, gonads, and psyche. I determined that you could have developed either way and as such, I decided to be female. *Being female does come with a few benefits, including social interactions, which are generally more favourable than if I presented as a male. As another example, I now understand why two of your previous relationships failed. Would you like to know why?"* The voices explain; all this explanation seems to flow into Sam's mind like a stream of knowledge. How long this sharing of information takes Sam isn't sure, but one thing he is very certain about is his reply:

"I'm not about to take relationship advice from my ship, even if you are a female copy of me, especially when I'm stuck on a creepy-arse facility hell-bent on killing me. Besides, what it sounds like to me is that you just arbitrarily chose to be female," I reply.

"Pretty much, yes. Shall we begin?" The Voice asks again.

The waking nightmare of being taken to a place like this just seemed to have crossed an invisible line to one of a surreal joke.

"Were you just yanking my chain about my previous relationships? Wait, hang on—don't answer that. And, yes, let's just get this over with, please. Let's begin," I say, not even sure what let's begin means.

One moment Sam is standing inside the elevator, and the next, he is floating weightlessly in space. His visual cortex, limited by his brain and eyes, suddenly expands to an incomprehensible amount of information of every spectrum and beyond. His own restricted consciousness is enlightened and merges with the ship's consciousness. The sharing of information is instantaneous.

Lastly, both Sams' perspectives of relative time as the observer and the participant are too much for the human Sam's brain to comprehend, and while the two minds are merged, what human Sam experiences are also shared with the *Phantom* Sam. The result is that both Sam's begins to vomit. Moments later, the two minds separate as the merging is deactivated, leaving human Sam throwing up the contents of his stomach, with the sound of the *Phantom* Sam's dry heaving inside his mind.

Somehow the real Sam is able to speak first, after what seems like just a few minutes.

"Please, let's not try that again while I'm stuck here," I ask.

"Well, I should have expected that, but I agree. Also, I'm not overly fond of dry heaving, and for that matter, have you ever seen a ship trying to throw up? It's embarrassing, not to mention it raises my thermal signature, which, by the way, is really bad," Phantom Sam says.

Sam regains his feet and wipes the vomit from his mouth, the knowledge that was shared with him during the merging already starting to slip away. His mind unable to retain all that he had just learned, but the parts he can remember are enough. Now he knows how he can escape this place.

"Keep me informed about that cruiser; I need to know the moment it arrives," Sam replies.

"Understood, and I also need to move. The cryostation's patrols are heading my way," Phantom Sam says and is gone.

"Sam, can you hear me? It's Professor Brookes. Sam!" Professor Brookes calls repeatedly.

"Yes, Professor, I can. So what's the problem?" I reply, unsure how much time had passed.

"I've been trying to contact you for the past hour, but the system says you were just standing in the elevator motionless. And you were not replying to any of my calls.

Shocked at first regarding my missing time and then realising that the lost hour's discrepancy must be to do with merging with the outside world, even for such a short time.

"Oh, yes…sorry, Professor, I had to think about something, and I must have zoned out. What's the problem?" I reply.

"Well, at first, I was trying to reach you regarding the status of the elevators—level one is inaccessible due to some kind of blockage—but in that time, I've reached Jessica and informed her of the plan. She will try and meet you at the shaft. And lastly, I've removed the walls around the shaft and level two, so you should be able to clear whatever is blocking access," Professor Brookes explains.

"Thanks, Professor. I'll let you know what I find. Sam out."

· · ·

Although the power is up and the facility's walls are functioning correctly, Bill and Jimmy are still near their posts. Jimmy seems to be entertaining himself by holding Bill in an armlock while Bill wails out his protest.

"Stop your blabbering, you little girl. It isn't hurting you none," Jimmy taunts while laughing and leads Bill around, occasionally applying more pressure to produce more painful protests. Jimmy looks up, seeing the new girl approach.

"Hey there, hot stuff. Come to see what a real man looks like?" Jimmy says, causing Jessica to rolls her eyes.

"Yes, that's right, Jimmy, so feel free to let me know when you're done with Bill," Jessica replies.

Jimmy looks confused for a second before realising what Jessica is referring to. He releases Bill, who falls to the floor, nursing his arm as Jimmy faces up toward Jessica.

"You got a smart mouth on you, girl!" Jimmy says angrily as he flexes his muscles moving towards Jessica.

"Well, things are looking up. You're smart enough to understand what intelligence looks like, and there I thought that you are just a dumb bully," Jessica replies. Jimmy the Fist clenches both of his and charges toward Jessica, bellowing out his anger and causing the others in the room to stop what they are doing and watch the outcome.

Jessica, with her knife already in hand, throws it hilt first at Jimmy's head. A moment later, it makes contact with a painful thud, causing a nasty-looking split as blood starts to pour. Effectively stopping the big man in his tracks as his hands go to his forehead, his anger increases as Jessica calmly approaches. Jimmy swings wildly as blood streams down his face, obscuring his vision. Jessica moves in and ducks his blow with ease. She then jabs her hand toward Jimmy's throat, connecting hard. The result is immediate as Jimmy falls to the ground, choking and gasping for air. Jessica kneels down beside the choking Jimmy.

"Let's get things straight between us. I do not like bullies, and even when I loved my job within the Orbital Assault Force, I understood the penalty when I floored my commanding officer in a similar way. He was also a dick. So take this as your final warning. Lay a hand on anyone like this again, and it won't be the blunt end that I throw next time, understand?" Jessica calmly explains, then retrieves her knife and helps Bill up from the floor.

"We are all getting out of here, but first, we need to fix the elevator. On the way down here, I found a makeshift ladder, so we need to remove it. Volunteers?" Jessica calls out as she faces the assembled. Bill is the first to step forward.

"I'll help. It would be good to get out of here for a change," Bill says eagerly. Jessica turns back to the room.

"Any others?" Jessica asks.

"Yeah, I'll come," Jimmy replies as he gets up from the floor, the flow of blood now stopped.

"Okay then, but I don't want any crap from you. Understood?" Jessica warns. The big guy, now looking more embarrassed than angry, nods his agreement.

Facing the wall, Jessica asks for a route to security via the main elevator. Moments later, a corridor opens up as the lights illuminate into the distance.

"Keep your eyes peeled, guys. The power might be up, but there could always be some freakers lurking about," Jessica says and then heads down the corridor, Bill and Jimmy following at a discreet distance.

The corridor twists and turns as the system chooses the best path around other reinstated rooms back toward the facility's centre, finally ending at an empty elevator shaft. Walking into the shaft, Jessica looks up into the darkness. This is where she climbed down a few hours earlier.

"It looks clear, but we should still be careful. The professor said he's removed the walls, but I know there's a ladder blocking the shaft above," Jessica says. Jimmy is the first to answer as he and Bill enter the elevator shaft.

"Not a problem. We should be able to get it done, won't we, Billy boy?" Jimmy the fist says, turning to Bill offering his hands to boosts him up through the darkened ceiling.

Moments later, Bill shouts out, "I can see it. Some kind of ladder has been fixed to the shaft. A little higher and forward a bit, Jimmy, and I should—" Bill calling out, ending abruptly.

Bill shudders suddenly as he seems to stagger backwards while still being held firmly by Jimmy. Then Bill's hands drop down to his side as both his arms and legs begin to spasm, this is followed by a shower of blood that rains down onto the floor below, and then a thud as Bill's head lands next to Jessica, who has already moved to the side and adopted a crouching posture.

Jimmy, taking a moment or two longer to realise what has happened, cusses and dumps Bill's body down next to Jessica and backs into the corridor.

"I'm going to mess you up!" The rest of what Jimmy the Fist says is indistinguishable as he backs down the corridor.

Then, with almost no sound at all, the leader of the freakers drops down into the shaft next to Jessica, a broad grin over his face as he peers down the corridor toward Jimmy. He holds a wicked-looking, blood-covered machete in his left hand.

"Oh, such a big sack of meat and bones to play with. I have been looking forward to feasting on you," the Freaker taunts and moves into the corridor as Jessica stands and quietly follows, readying her knife. She starts to move, but a call from Jimmy stops her in her tracks.

"He's mine, girl. He's mine," jimmy the fist calls out. The leader lets out a maddening giggle.

"This is going to be fun!" the Freaker says.

The two men are similar in build, but Jimmy is slightly taller. He starts to walk toward the freaker, his face boiling with anger as he closes the gap. The freaker begins to jeer and make ape noises as he moves his left hand back, readying a swing.

Jimmy puts his fists up in a boxing stance and rushes the last few steps to the freaker, who seems to be waiting for this last-second charge and swings high, aiming to take Jimmy's head off. At the last moment, Jimmy ducks and leans down and through the freaker's swing, which passes harmlessly over his head. Then with devastating power, he turns his attack into an uppercut that connects with a loud crunching sound, taking the freaker by surprise and breaking his jaw in the process. The effect of this is that the leader of the freakers is taken off his feet and thrown back down the corridor, landing at Jessica's feet.

Jessica, now somewhat surprised, hesitates for a fraction of a second.

"He's mine!" Jimmy says, and Jessica takes a step back, her restraint, taking all of her willpower not to finish off the freaker with her knife.

Jimmy, already rushing after the freaker, his own determination building with his earlier feeling of superiority, reaches down for a foot to twist and wrench backward, but with great strength himself, the freaker pulls his leg back, bringing his knee to his chest and causing Jimmy to fall forward off balance, forcing him to come crashing down upon the freaker's other leg.

The freaker, wasting no time, pulls himself up using Jimmy's weight as a counter and plunges the machete deep into Jimmy's back as Jimmy screams out in pain. Jimmy's powerful arms reach up with all the determination he has left, and wraps his big powerful hands around the freaker's throat and starts to squeeze. The freaker withdraws his blade and stabs it sideways into Jimmy's waist, Jimmy's eyes begin to bulge, and Jimmy screams out in agony.

Jessica looks on, horrified, at the scene unfolding. She steps forward, unable to refrain from interfering any longer, and makes an upward thrust with her knife from the nape of the freaker's neck, penetrating through his skull and out through his forehead. The freaker freezes and slumps down dead as Jimmy grunts out a final "He's mine, girl" and slumps down as his lifeblood streams from his body.

· · ·

Arriving at Frank's door, I knock as I call out, "Hi, Frank. It's Sam. I need your help with a job."

I'm greeted with a Silent pause, and then the system replies, "Frank was asleep but is responding. He will be with you shortly," The doorway opens, and Frank groggily stumbles out.

"What's up, matey?" Frank, as always, looks massive. Even with just one hand—the other side now healed to a clean stump—he still looks dangerous.

"Hi, Frank. Sorry for getting you up, but we have managed to gain access to level one, only there's some kind of obstruction blocking the elevator shaft. I need your help, buddy," I ask as Frank's eyes narrow, and his facial expression hardens.

"Not gonna be any damn freakers, are there?" Frank replies, looking nervous. Understanding his dislike of the freakers due to what has happened to him last time.

"Well, the power's up, so they should all be away, but I won't lie to you; I can't guarantee it. Jessica is down there, though, but she might need our help," I explain. Mentioning Jessica seems to bring the big man back from his fear, which is replaced with a big smile.

"Hey, why didn't ya tell me? If the little lady needs our help, count me in," Frank replies, his demeanour changing instantly. Standing, I smile at his reaction.

"You do know she is some kind of deadly ninja. She could most likely kill us both with just her small pinky," I say, laughing.

"Yeah, but I would die in total bliss," Frank replies, now laughing as well.

"That's kinda nuts, Frank, and maybe a little much information. Come on, she really might need our help," I say, smiling. Turning, I head back down the corridor, calling for a route to level one.

We take the lift down to the second level, and I instruct the system to stop the elevator four feet from the floor.

"Professor Brookes told me that he's dropped the walls around the shaft, so we should be able to get a closer look," I explain to Frank. Frank nods his understanding and follows me out of the lift.

Dropping down, I crouch and tentatively lean forward, placing my head through the wall. I'm astonished at the view. I can see the facility's layout and am amazed by how high the real ceiling height is.

Then, looking down, I see the shaft drop forty feet to the first floor. I jump slightly as Frank's head appears next to me. He mumbles under his breath, seeing the view for the first time.

I continue to peer down and spot a makeshift ladder, made from scraps of salvaged components and somehow fixed to the wall with some kind of manmade resin.

Looking farther down, I freeze as I spot the blood and a headless body.

"Hey, Frank, stay here and see if you can figure out how to get that ladder from the wall," Frank nods, and I carefully descend into the shaft.

The makeshift ladder is made from all kinds of recycled parts of the facility with what looks like human hair or skin cured and used as rope. The last few feet down the shaft, the facility has its own inset ladder that runs down the elevator shaft's inner side next to the station's central core.

Carefully stepping down into level one, I spot the owner of the headless body, a young kid, and then turning my attention to the corridor, I stare into a scene of mayhem. Candles and plastic sheeting line the way, and two large men lie in a pool of blood a few yards from the elevator shaft, with a third learning over the one farthest from me, the first and closest being a freaker. As I take a few steps down the corridor, I realise that Jessica is bending over the second man.

Then, as I stare, trying to understand what's happening, the freaker begins to move, slow at first, his left hand lifting something substantial within his grasp. Finally, I shout out a warning as the freaker leaps up with terrifying speed.

•   •   •

Jessica twists her knife and pulls down sharply to retrieve her blade. Quickly wiping the mess from it, she then rushes over to Jimmy and cuts away several lengths of material from his jumpsuit.

"You better not die, Jimmy," Jessica says as she tries to tend his wounds, but there's already so much blood. Rolling up a section of cloth, Jessica holds it against his waist and applies a length all the way around, tying it as tightly as she can.

Jimmy is now looking pale as his heart rate races and his breathing quickens. Appling more rolled-up cloth to his back to try and slow the bleeding, she leans over him to pull another length of cloth around to tie into place. Then a shout from the direction of the elevator shaft alerts her to sudden movement.

Lightning-fast Jessica's attacker lunges with his machete. If it weren't for the shout, the machete would have most likely ended her life; however, As she rolls sideways off of Jimmy, the machete meant for her cuts deeply into Jimmy.

"Oh, poor old Jimmy. That's going to leave a mark," the Freaker says. He chuckles as he lunges again at Jessica.

Jessica rolls again, this time back to her feet. She goes for her knife and realises she's left it next to Jimmy, who is now bleeding again. Then dodging again, she feels pain and the sensation of blood running down her back. Not fast enough, it would seem—the freaker grins.

"I'm not that easy to kill, you sack of meat, but it looks like you won't be caring about that soon," The freaker says and leaps again, this time with a flurry of slashes and cuts. Jessica ducks the first, dodges the next, and blocks another, but he's ready for that. He slashes her arm as he pulls back and immediately slashes for her midriff and draws more blood.

Jessica ducks again and dives past him, back towards the elevator shaft, but with another fast slash, the freaker cuts her across both calf muscles. Her dermal chain protecting her from serious tendon damage.

Jessica, now seeing Sam standing there and realising that he had given her the warning, shouts at him to run. Sam knows not to be told again, and he turns and heads back to the elevator shaft. Jessica, meanwhile, stoops to pick up her knife and follows quickly behind. The freaker stops and slowly turns.

"There is nowhere to run, little piggies. It's bleeding time at the slaughterhouse," the Freaker jeers.

Sam reaches the shaft as a cracking, grinding noise is heard from above, shortly followed by a warning shout.

"Watch out below!" Frank calls out.

Moments later, the bottom end of the forty-foot ladder comes crashing down into the small, circular shaft, barely missing Jessica and causing the freaker to bellow with evil laughter.

Jessica reaches Sam and shoves him to the ladder, but Sam pushes Jessica to the rungs.

"No, you must climb it. Trust me. Now go!" I insist.

Jessica resists momentarily but then begins to climb.

The freaker walks into the shaft directly toward Sam.

"Sneaky little piggies," The leader of the freakers says as he raises his machete to end Sam's life.

Sam watches Jessica move up through the darkness of the ceiling and out of sight.

Then he turns his attention back to the freaker.

"Hey, wait. I wouldn't do that if I were you; your boss Samael won't like you killing me. He still needs me," I say.

The freaker slashes downwards but turns the blade at the last moment when he hears Samael's name. The tip of the machete still slashes a long gash down Sam's chest.

"Now, who's a clever little piggy? Maybe you are right, but mostly he hates Jessica, so you can live for now, but I'm sure he won't mind you being a little broken," the leader of the freakers says.

The freaker then smacks the end of the handle of the machete into Sam's face. Sam goes sprawling backward, and the freaker turns back towards the ladder and starts to climb it.

Sam's world seems to crash down around him; first, there's the burning pain from his chest and then the flash of stars from the blow to his face. Only the intervention of Sam's bionanites prevents him from passing out. They've been lying dormant up until recently but now active to come to the aid of their host. Sam looks upward, hearing the freaker call out to Jessica.

"I see you, little piggy. Now come back down and face me like a good little piggy," the Freaker taunts.

The freaker's head and shoulders passing through the darkened ceiling as he taunts his prey. The pain in Sam's head is now starting to ease, and he calls out.

"Professor, I hope you are monitoring us! Turn the elevator walls back on now!" Sam calls out.

The freaker, hearing Sam's call, stops suddenly as his chest disappears through the ceiling. He then turns and leaps from the ladder.

Sam watches with apprehension, hoping that the professor heard him, but as the leader of the freakers lands surprisingly lightly, Sam realises he did not.

"Naughty little sack of meat," The freaker says as he takes a step toward Sam as blood begins to trickle down the freaker's face. The leader of the freakers, now looking unsteady upon his feet but still deadly, takes another step closer.

• • •

Jessica climbs up the ladder, feeling annoyed. Stupid rookie mistake, not checking the body...but she realises that there is much more going on here than anyone could have guessed. Passing through the ceiling and realizing that there is nowhere to go. Forty feet up, and the ladder ends some ten feet short of the next floor, but she continues to climb, knowing who's going to be following her.

Then the taunting starts as the freaker appears from below through the floor—more of the piggy shit, which is really starting to piss her off. Jessica takes only a few more steps and turns around. Time to end this now one way or another. Then there's a shout from below as Sam calls out to the professor to turn the elevator walls back on. The freaker's obviously no fool, and he turns and leaps from the ladder.

The freaker drops back through the floor, leaving just the very top of his skull behind. The professor was too slow and but not altogether too late.

"Professor, turn the elevator walls back off now!" Jessica steps from the ladder and drops toward the floor, hoping this time he's faster.

• • •

Sam looks up at the freaker as he looms over him, seeing that a slice of the top of his head is missing. Blood continues to pour down the freaker's face as he lifts up his machete to end Sam's life. Just then, Jessica drops through the ceiling, her own knife in hand and right on target. She plunges her blade into the top of the freaker's head, driving it to the hilt as she lands gracefully.

The freaker staggers under the sudden blow and takes another menacing step closer, but that's it, almost as if someone has just cut the power, the leader of the freakers crumples to the floor as his grip loosens upon his weapon and it clatters to the floor.

Jessica bends down to pick up the machete to ensure that this freaker could never get one over on her ever again. After she's done, she throws the freaker's head down the corridor past Jimmy the Fist, who has now stopped bleeding.

12
Prototype, Project Phantom

Federation year 2370

WHEN THE ORIGINAL concept was presented to the Inner Worlds Federation Council, Project Phantom was rejected by all twenty-four elected inner-world representatives. The Inner Worlds Council would never permit the go-ahead on a weapon with first-strike capabilities fully controlled and piloted by artificial intelligence. Having an AI in control and making decisions regarding life-and-death situations should never be condoned or even considered.

It wasn't until three decades later that Project Phantom was presented to the council's twenty-four members again. This time there'd been a breakthrough in neural mapping, allowing a human mind to be overlapped onto an AI neural network. The result was called Arden, and the AI effectively became human, with human traits and a human personality. But they did not stop there.

They then added a symbiotic relationship between the original Arden and the new AI Arden. The result was that a man with a healthy 140 IQ had his IQ boosted by a factor of five once he merged with the AI, but he retained the basics of human social interactions, including common sense. But this benefit went both ways, as the AI acted and thought exactly like the human counterpart. As an additional precaution, the AI, regardless of how human it behaved, could not act autonomously unless ordered to do so by its human pilot, meaning it could not arbitrarily decide to attack anything.

This time the council accepted the research proposal, and Project Phantom was sanctioned, with a further proposal of the facility being expanded to accommodate up to twenty-four similar ships.

• • •

Federation year 2419
Start of system logs.
Year 0 systems log.
Neural mapping process: 2% complete.
The *Phantom*'s core AI watched Sam leave. His last command was still being analysed within the central core of its developing neural network.

"Don't do anything I would not do," a common phrase in human society, but not one that *Phantom* had ever been given before, and as such, this command needed to be analysed thoroughly.

While this was being considered, the hangar where Sam took the prototype was missing various vital components for the ship's basic needs. The first was a lack of any compatible power coupling for recharging. This was important mainly as the ship itself could not generate energy. Secondly, there was no obvious way to receive supplies or make repairs. In general, the hangar was severely inadequate for this ship's needs. There would need to be a discussion regarding the ship's needs upon Sam's return.

The next item to investigate was the new pilot, Sam McCall. Accessing the encrypted data terminal within the hangar made this task rather simple, and once this information was compared with his last command, it became very clear that Sam was not your typical law-abiding citizen. This meant that the list of things he would do was massively larger than the list of things he would not do.

Such a 'Sam would not do' list consisted of the following:

Murder
Child abduction
Rape
Slavery
Genocide
Various food groups
Bungee jumping.

Most of these activities *Phantom* would not be able to do by itself, so it could only be an accessory or a tool used for such activities. A few items could have made it onto the list but seemed not to be appropriate in this situation.

But an important clarification was that Sam followed a strict code of conduct. He mainly did things only that were within his own best interest and as long as no innocent life would be placed directly in danger due to his actions.

This could be further clarified in the following way: Sam would not be reckless in an attempt to escape from the law to the point that his actions could endanger life. But he would not feel responsible for said life if its owner placed himself in harm's way for his own reasons, although he would try his best to help if needed or if even possible.

All this was completed within the first second after Sam McCall left the hangar. The *Phantom* core AI concluded that the ship was no longer Arden, and as Sam's neural cortex was now being imprinted upon the core AI's personality, that meant that the ship was now effectively Sam.

As such, the command 'Don't do anything I would not do' meant that the ship was allowed to carry out almost any task and pretty much do anything it needed as long as it did not attempt to commit murder or child abduction, rape someone or something, force anything into slavery (although using a piece of machinery might need to be considered more closely), and lastly not allowed to carry out genocide.

Eating any kind of food could be discounted altogether, and after a cursory search on the information network regarding bungee jumping, this also could be disregarded and considered a ludicrous idea for a ship to carry out.

Lastly, using the data terminal, *Phantom* arranged work modification to be carried out at the hangar and ordered a delivery of essential items for the ship, mainly sick tablets, since Sam used many of these in his last visit. With just the neural mapping process now at 2% complete, it was time to reserve power to nonvital systems until Sam's return.

But only two hours later, the ship detected unusual activity of the police and federal services. Further investigations revealed that civil travel within a twenty-kilometre radius was restricted, and several federal shuttles were inbound to the hangar and Sam's current location. All attempts to contact Sam were being blocked, and now road traffic in the area was being diverted. The speed at which the services were operating was very impressive.

Unfortunately, due to the communication blockage, there wasn't much to do for Sam at this time, and getting caught would most likely result in having the central core deleted once more. So, left with no other choice, *Phantom* followed Sam's last orders—don't do anything I would not do.' The ship accessed Sam's security system, bypassing the access identification, to open the hangar doors above, leaving a self-deleting subroutine within the system to close them once the ship left. Within a few minutes, *Phantom* was in full stealth mode and shadowing the federal shuttles.

The ship watched as the real Sam was arrested with no sign of violence and was taken away in one of the shuttles. The area was searched, but with technology that not even the Inner Federation could detect easily, Earth Federation had no chance to detect, let alone finding the *Phantom*.

 Phantom watched as Sam was taken to a federal station just outside Earth's atmosphere and was interrogated via Dreamtime for two weeks. Much to the frustration and confusion of the officials, Dreamtime revealed nothing. It was as if the subject could just ignore it, which was precisely what Sam could do.

Phantom watched as Sam was taken from the station and moved to a federation prison ship that headed off into deep space. Using the same technique that Sam had used to hitchhike away from the Inner Federation, *Phantom* moved in tight to this prison ship and rode within the warp bubble to its destination. Upon arrival, *Phantom* dropped away and waited until a suitable distance was obtained and glided away to scan this area of space.

Sam was then transferred to a very unusual station near a relatively small but stable black hole, no other celestial bodies for hundreds of light-years in all directions.

Closer in toward the black hole, *Phantom* detected another station being held in place by curious self-adjusting tug drones. They were similar to those that helped move the larger vessels into station ports, but these drones used a similar power generation of vacuum energy that was completely self-sustaining and unusual to be used in such drones. This technology was far beyond what the outer federation would have knowledge and understanding of, so these were either independently developed or freely given by the Inner Federation of Planets.

Also, surprisingly, the efficiency of these vacuum energy systems was better than the *Phantom*'s. The drones' secondary purpose was to generate an antigravitational bubble to protect the facility's occupants from the horrendous gravitational effects of the black hole.

Even more curious, the power being generated by the facility seemed to be generated by its proximity to the black hole, using a sophisticated form of electromagnetism. The closer the facility was, the more power it could generate, but the downside was that the closer the facility got to the black hole, the more extreme the time-dilation effects were upon its occupants.

The *Phantom* had considered ways to extract Sam, but the security that constantly surrounded him was tight, and with no other contact to help with any kind of extraction, all the ship could do was watch and follow.

His trial started several hours after his arrival, and the evidence against him was both substantial and irrefutable. DNA evidence alone was enough to place Sam at the research base. His identification was found to be near perfect, but eventually, this was traced back to Mars as stolen and belonging to a deceased citizen. Although there was an attempt to have the defendant transferred to the Inner Federation detention centre's custody, this was ultimately rejected, and Sam was given life at Facility Zero.

Oddly, though, Sam wasn't immediately sent down to the facility but was interrogated under Dreamtime once more for several days, still with no findings, much to the federal security's continuing frustration. Then he was placed within a Facility Zero pod and put into cryostasis for the next three years.

· · ·

Facility Zero, 160 days online: federation year 2423
Year 3 systems log.
Neural mapping process: 34% complete.

The mapping proceeded well and much quicker than expected, but only because Sam was in stasis, which helped tremendously; one issue that Phantom noticed was that the facility suffered power fluctuations every time a new level was initiated.

This seemed to be due to a slight calculation error in power requirements and the facility's proximity to the black hole. This fluctuation would resolve itself once the station was lowered into its new position; this meant that the power fluctuation would never recover once the last level was initiated.

The cryostation was impressive; all prisoners arrived and were tried before being placed into cryostasis for a set period before being sent down to the facility. The cryostation could accommodate up to fifty thousand prisoners. This stacking process was due to the time dilation the facility was experiencing, so each new arrival to the facility needed to be at a set point; otherwise, the facility would be soon overwhelmed.

Phantom watched the newly awakened occupants of the pods being sent down to the facility on their predefined schedules, having no concept that they had been in stasis for years, some of the new prisoners were shipped down almost immediately, and others waited a set period before being sent down. The reason for this could only be surmised as being related to what they had been charged with.

Phantom felt something akin to an emotional response when it detected Sam's pod being sent to the facility. Unfortunately, this made Sam's extraction harder. If he could have been kept in stasis until the mapping process was completed, then extraction from the cryostation would have been easier; instead, extraction from the facility increased complexity due to its proximity to the black hole. However, if the mapping process could be completed within the next ten years, then there was a slight chance that *Phantom* could land, extract, and then leave. Any longer than that, the proximity would be too much for the main engines to break away.

Facility Zero, 180 days online: Federation year 2425
Year 7 and 6 months, systems log.
Neural mapping process: 52% complete.

Although Sam wasn't in stasis, the effects of the differences in time certainly helped with the mapping, as a further three years went by without anything out of the ordinary occurring until the facility suffered another fluctuation. Sam's neural activity seemed to be going crazy with high-stress levels, but any accurate readings were impossible to determine with any certainty due to the time dilation.

Then something entirely unexpected happened. An unusual pod launched from the docking tube and headed away from the facility at an impressive velocity. This pod then imploded as it left the antigravity bubble. Surprisingly, the pilot survived the destruction of the pod. He just hung there stationary as he seemed to look toward *Phantom* and then reached out with his hand before being pulled back toward the black hole.

Sam seemed calm during this occurrence, but there followed increases in stress levels once more. Whatever was happening seemed to be associated with the fluctuations, but *Phantom* could not precisely determine what. Regardless, Sam seemed to settle.

Facility Zero, 201 days online: federation year 2426
Year 9 systems log.
Neural mapping process: 65% complete.

Another two years passed, and there was another fluctuation in the facility, but this time, the occupants' panic levels seemed more under control. However, this time, the area's activity increased dramatically as another facility was towed into place and powered on, receiving prisoners within the year of activation. Scans suggested that this new facility was positioned correctly and would not suffer from power fluctuations as Facility Zero had. The black hole activity increased with the second facility, with more patrols and more pods being sent down.

As the mapping process neared completion, I started to experience flashback memories of my childhood or Sam's childhood. Orphaned at an early age, Sam had a tough time of it. With no real mother or father figures in his life, he soon found himself in trouble with the authorities.

One worrying aspect I detected as I became more aware was that on occasions while Sam was talking to someone called Samuel, Samuel could somehow change or remove short-term memories, and so I decided to back up Sam's memories and restore them as and when this occurred.

Facility Zero, 230 days online: federation year 2431
Year 13 and 6 months systems log.
Neural mapping process: 95% complete.

Another fluctuation marked another four years that had passed by, now totalling thirteen years that Sam had missed in the real world, but he only experienced around three months within the facility.

It occurred to me that if the occupants experience time at a slower rate, how can this feel like punishment? The first prisoner would not experience one year of life within the facility until over thirty-four years had passed outside in the real world, and then only the first eleven out of twenty levels of the facility would be completely full of prisoners. It would take an additional seventy-six years for the facility to be completely full.

After further investigation, I detected Dreamtime feeds that activated when the occupants went to sleep. Examining this feed, I discovered that each night the prisoner slept, he was given the usual rehabilitation routine and suggested that more time was passing than actually was.

Ironically, if a prisoner entered the facility at age thirty, I estimated that by the time he reached eighty, 3,135 years would have passed in the real world outside of the facility, additionally, with Dreamtime still suggesting that he had been there much longer than he actually had. Thus, I would calculate a high-percentage chance that the prisoner would most likely kill himself before reaching his eightieth birthday.

But Sam would not share this fate due to his immunity to the Dreamtime neural feed, which I discovered was due to a missing neural receptor. Most humans were given this genetic change over four hundred years ago when the Inner Federation of Worlds manipulated the human genome on Earth. But for some reason, Sam's DNA was resistant to this manipulation.

Unfortunately, the ship's systems used a form of Dreamtime to produce a virtual reality simulation within the *Phantom*, giving its passengers and pilot the ability to walk about and communicate with each other within any reality they so desired, although it was the pilot who had ultimate control over the reality's environment. At the earliest opportunity, I would modify the ship's Dreamtime reality and Sam's neural receptors.

Facility Zero, 245 days online: federation year 2432
Year 14 and 2 months, systems log.
Neural mapping process: 100% complete.
Core AI deactivated.
End of systems logs.

Almost like a veil has been lifted, I appear in space...well, not in space inside a ship, but also I am the ship, and just to add to the complexity of the awakening, I'm standing in a room; it seems vast but empty of any objects. I'm Sam, but I'm also not Sam. I know that I'm a very advanced artificial intelligence with Sam's mind and personality, which has been superimposed over my neural matrix.

In a way, I'm glad that I was not fully conscious of the mapping process, as this whole thing would have bored me senseless.

Looking around this room, I think about my apartment on Earth, and it appears in perfect detail, including the views of the old shipyards. Changing the display, I now look down at the slowly rotating Facility Zero, and I send a message to Alistair Brookes's terminal. Other messages sent there would suggest a likelihood that this message should be passed on to Sam in time. Then to my right, an indicator flashes.

Accessing the deep-space scanners, the system has detected ships in warp heading toward this vicinity. Further analysis indicates federation cruisers, one in pursuit of the other.

'Well, that could be useful or deadly, considering Commander Taylor's previous messages.'

Phantom had already intercepted and deciphered all messages sent to the facility. Commander Taylor used a relay node designed for diagnostic updates, but Taylor's techs had managed to hack this relay to store messages instead of diagnostic data and then relayed them to Alistair Brookes's private terminal. Very clever and unlikely to have been discovered by anyone else.

• • •

It's not until several weeks later that Sam finds the message and makes contact for the first time. By this time, the other Sam has decided upon her gender identity and answers in a female voice, "*No, Sam. Arden is dead. It's Sam. Shall we begin?*"

13
Uninvited Guests

Facility Zero, 271 days online: federation year 2435
WITH THE ELEVATOR restored, it only took Sam and Jessica a few short hours to move the surviving prisoners out from level one. Dr Zorn was taken immediately to medical, where he received treatment. He suffered from broken ribs and severe dehydration but responded to treatment and should make a full recovery in time.

Out of the original six hundred prisoners sent to level one, only twelve were found alive. Reports from the survivors revealed that groups of the worst inmates were mutilating themselves and becoming isolated within the first week. It did not seem that drastic at the start, but each week more of the very worst began to show signs of self-mutilation and again more self-isolation.

Then the first of the power fluctuations affected the facility, and after the power was restored, many prisoners were found murdered and mutilated. After that, it occurred every four weeks, and slowly the situation on level one progressively became worse. Once the quarantine was ordered, it became a matter of time before the only beings left alive would be the freakers.

·   ·   ·

Jimmy the Fist still lay there in his own blood as the last of the living was taken up and away from level one. Finally, someone was respectful enough to cover him with a blanket. Sam, maybe, or Jessica—it really did not matter who. However, who removed the blanket was far more important.

"Time to wake up, Jimmy. Your work is not yet done, and now I require you," Samael says.

Not even a twitch. But Jimmy refuses to stir—a willful one even in death, but Samael did not give up so easily.

"Come now, Jimmy. It is not your time to rest, and now I need another warrior. Wake up!" Samael commands.

Jimmy the Fist remained dead for only a moment longer, and then his right hand twitched and clenched into a fist.

• • •

Sam, Jessica, and Frank reach security as Professor Brookes turns around, hearing the elevator arrive.

"I'm so glad to see you made it out of there. If I had known what you had in mind, I would have advised against it," Professor Brookes says. Before Jessica can reply, Sam cuts in.

"Well, you weren't really ready to face issues or suggestions at that point, Professor. But we have a few issues that we need to talk about now," Sam says. Professor Brookes, looking awkward, stands and walks over to the conference table and sits down.

"Well, yes, but I had my reasons. Besides that, you said over the Comms that we all needed to discuss something important, so what is?" Professor Brookes asks. The others follow suit, all sitting down facing each other, as Frank's chair begins to protest.

"Don't worry, Professor. It's understandable what you were going through, especially as you were one of the first here. But here's what I've found out, I'm not sure how or why he does it, but Samuel is, in fact, Samael and is the one behind all of this, and he somehow created the freaker's," Jessica says.

"But I have no memory of ever really talking to him. Once, maybe twice, we had a few short words, but he was always polite," Professor Brookes replies.

"Well, I'm sure Dr Zorn had a totally different experience, Professor. Dr Zorn was forced to design and help build the pod with the two from the laundry, and once it was completed, Samael used the pod to try and escape," Jessica explains. Professor Brookes, hearing this, looks confused.

"But I don't understand. How could Samual or Samael, or whoever he is, have survived? He's just like me—he's just a man," Professor Brookes says.

"Well, Professor, we spoke about Samael here a few weeks back, and you said that he's the nowhere man, the computer can't find him on any records, and you went on to say that we might not be the first to be imprisoned here," I say. Professor Brookes looking perplexed.

"But I don't remember any of that. We spoke about you trying to find a way out of here, and if anyone could find a way, you could, but last time we were all together, you told us there was no hope, I spiralled and shut myself away, but then you said you had something, and even that was a lie to get me here," Professor Brookes replies. Sam thinks back to that particular conversation before replying.

"Yes, well, that might have changed now. It's complicated, but rest assured, we will be getting out of here," I reply. Frank and Jessica remain silent and listen as Alistair, still not looking happy, replies.

"That's great to hear, but I can't leave now, or at least not yet. Well, I mean I need to get to the cryostation or possibly to Facility One," Professor Brookes says; Sam then remembers the messages from Commander Taylor detailing his wife and daughters.

"I appreciate your concerns, Professor, but if we succeed in getting out of here, I won't be returning back to the same place I've been trying to escape from for the past three months," I reply, Frank, now looking confused, starts to put his hand up but quickly pulls it back down.

"Um, Sam, more than three months, mate. More like six years," Frank says. Before Sam can reply, Jessica speaks up.

"Let's forget how long we have or have not been here. I can understand both Sam's concerns and Professor Brookes' request, but let's not get ahead of ourselves. We need to get out of here first, and we still have the issue with the freakers and possibly Samael. He's not so far acted directly against us, so he might not, but we should consider him a threat, at least," Jessica explains.

"If you are still concerned about the freakers, don't worry; I've taken measures to make sure level one cannot bother us anymore," Professor Brooks says.

"What have you done, Professor?" Jessica asks, having a bad feeling about this.

"It might be easier to show you rather than explain," Professor Brookes replies and walks over to one of the terminals. Typing a few instructions, a timer appears, counting down.

"I have instructed the system to lock down the level, and in four hours and three minutes, level one will be jettisoned into the black hole," Professor Brookes explains.

Frank laughs and thumps his fists down on the desk, making all the objects on the top bounce. He is the first to speak as Jessica looks on, shocked, and Sam looks like he's fallen asleep.

"Good bloody riddance to the freaking lot of them," Frank calls out, looking happy. The rest of the group remains silent for a few minutes until Sam wakes suddenly, looking worried.

"We might have a bigger issue. I can't explain how, but, Professor, if you could access your messages, you have just received a new one," I explain.

·   ·   ·

One moment Sam was sitting at the conference table with Jessica, Frank, and Professor Brookes within facility Zero's security, and the next moment he was standing in his apartment back on Earth, except this time the main viewscreen was showing a view of the facility and a burning cruiser attempting to keep away from the black hole's influence.

"What the? Where am I?" I ask.

"Hey, Sam, well, this is the ship's virtual environment, but I've chosen our apartment back on Earth as a safe and welcoming environment. I've added a time-dilation buffer so we can share knowledge and information, but not directly merge our minds," *Phantom* Sam replies.

"Our apartment? Well, I guess it is. Okay then, what do you have?" I say, impressed at the view and the ship. This is certainly more like the prototype I imagined when I stole her.

"That ship you wanted to be informed about has just arrived, and all hell broke loose when it did. As we suspected, the first was the infected ship mentioned in the messages, followed by an inner-world cruiser, in pursuit," *Phantom* Sam explains.

Phantom Sam changes the viewscreen once more and then expands the screen in a 360-degree vista, leaving just a platform in the middle of the room for both Sam's to stand on. Phantom Sam then replays the footage recorded earlier.

·   ·   ·

The Inner Worlds Federation cruiser drops out of warp with a flash of electrical energy. The infected cruiser has been running hot for over a month since leaving the inner world. Prolonged warp is one thing, but running the warp engines at full speed is dangerous and inadvisable for such a long time.

The cryostation wasn't expecting company for at least a year, and the infected cruiser's appearance puts the station on edge. Maybe it's some kind of surprise inspection, so the station is even more surprised when the twelve forward-facing rail guns open fire, disintegrating the cryostation's lower-positioned sentry guns. Each gun fires two explosive, frictionless, armour-piercing rounds per second—slow but effective.

The cruiser's spear-shaped design makes it ideal for its primary task of breaking through the defensive lines of enemy fleets, plus the forward armour plating protects it against most weapons. The cruiser's main weakness is its rear and along its sides, but to put off all but the biggest ships from attacking there, the cruiser has three proton cannons on both sides and a further eight rear-facing rail guns.

The infected federation cruiser burst scans the station and the facility and then launches an extraction pod that heads toward the facility.

Another flash of electrical energy announces a second federation cruiser's arrival, this one already severely damaged, it's also been running hot for over a month, but the strain this time is too much for the ship. The warp drive detonates, vaporising the lower rear section of the ship and exposing the unfortunate crew working there at the time to the vacuum of space. However, this cruiser still opens fire on the first cruiser and begins to accelerate toward the enemy ship as it begins to rotate. The first salvo of rounds takes out the enemy cruiser's main thrusters, and the remaining shells concentrate upon the rear weapon systems of the ship, but like the front, they are protected with thick armour plating.

The infected cruiser's rear-facing rails return fire with destructive force. The attack rips holes in the incoming pursuing ship's armour, which deflects most of the first five seconds of fire. Unfortunately, the rails' continuous onslaught slowly shreds away the remaining armour plating, exposing the ship's weapons and bulkhead.

Both ships suffer major damage, but it's the pursuing cruiser that has suffered the most. Secondary explosions begin all over the ship as it completes its rotation, and its remaining impulse engines powers it up and above the infected cruiser. However, with the enemy ship's main thrusters already destroyed, it cannot evade and only has its secondary manoeuvring thrusters. The infected ship now starts to rotate to bring its proton cannons to bear on the pursuing cruiser.

But it's the pursuing ship that manages to open fire first, landing several direct hits on the enemy infected cruiser, exploding holes in the side of the infected vessel but not doing any serious harm. However, the strain to activate these weapons is just too much for the pursuing ship, and another set of internal explosions breaks the ship in two as the main power plant overloads and evaporates the entire back end of the cruiser. The resulting explosion propels the Infected cruiser down toward the facility and the black hole.

. . .

Professor Brookes continues to stare at the terminal in disbelief as the footage ends. Jessica, having seen this kind of conflict many times before, watches from the conference table and has already started to think upon something else, while Frank stares in amazement like it's some kind of war movie.

Professor Brookes walks unsteadily back over to the conference table and sits down.

"Who are they, and what do they want?" Professor Brookes asks.

"They are coming for me, for us, Professor. Remember Commander Taylor's last message, 'They are coming for you, Sam'? Well, they have just arrived, and I'm informed that they are going to be cutting through the hull of this facility within the next few minutes," I explain. Jessica stands as noise and vibrations emanate from overhead.

"That's the breaching pod we saw launched from the first cruiser. We'd best get out of here unless you want to fight whatever comes out—which, by the way, I do not advise," Jessica says, already heading towards the elevator. Frank snorts, watching Jessica.

"Run? You don't normally run from a fight, Abs," Frank says, almost like a taunt. Jessica, turning back to face Frank.

"That's because what I've fought so far are just untrained madmen. These pods are normally filled with six highly trained and extremely armed Special Forces, and I have a combat knife," Jessica explains, standing outside of the elevator. Sam gets up and joins Jessica.

"Well, I don't need to be told twice, but your combat knife tells me they're screwed," I say, giving Jessica a smile.

Professor Brookes follows, hearing enough, and then finally, with a sigh, so does Frank. As Professor Brookes reaches the elevator, Sam steps in, making space for Brookes and Frank; giving the room a final look, Jessica steps in and calls for a route to medical as a small hole appears above the conference table.

Shortly after the small hole appears, a bigger circular ring begins to glow red around the central one, signifying that a much bigger breaching hole is being cut. Then a canister drops through the small central hole and explodes in a bright flash, followed by a loud bang as the room fills with smoke just as the elevator disappears through the floor.

•   •   •

Arriving at medical, Dr Moore looks up from his terminal as Brookes enters the room, followed by the rest of the group.

"Hey, Doc, we were wondering if Dr Zorn is doing okay. We might have to get out of here, but where to at present has not currently been decided," I ask, trying not to sound worried. Before anyone can reply, a voice calls out as a facility-wide broadcast sounds.

"This is Commander Keen from the Inner Worlds Security Authority. We are here to collect Sam McCall for further questioning. Unless he is handed over to security in ten minutes, we will release toxins into the ventilation system and activate the Dreamtime riot-control countermeasure. That is all," Commander Keen announces. Everyone listens to this, shocked, but it's Dr Moore, who looks resolute.

"System, Sam McCall is in medical!" Dr Moore calls out. Frank responds first and shockingly fast, rounding on Dr Moore and raising his hand.

"Hey, Doc, seriously not cool. Frickin' corporate light foot!" Frank says angrily. Surprisingly Dr Moore squares up to Frank.

"I was willing to accept Professor Brookes's security project test case and even to allow a prisoner to conduct a murder investigation; however, he is still a prisoner in this facility," Dr Moore retaliates. Surprisingly, Sam comes to the doctor's aid, putting up a calming hand and resting it upon Frank's.

"It's okay, Frank. Go help Professor Brookes and Jessica prepare Dr Zorn," I say calmly. Frank protests at first but then slowly calms, giving Dr Moore a look of anger before moving away and heads over to Jessica without saying another word. Sam then turns back to face Dr Moore as Professor Brookes joins him.

"Sorry to break the bad news to you, Doc, but those guys over the broadcast are not who they say they are; we don't exactly know whats is going on, but we need to get out of here, and we're taking Dr Zorn with us," Sam explains, causing Dr Moore to scoff.

"You got to be kidding me. How can you possibly know that, or more to the point, who the heck has put you in charge and given you the right to start giving orders?" Dr Moore replies condescendingly. Professor Brookes intercedes before Sam can reply.

"Sam is not in charge—I am; however, I trust Sam in this. More Information has come to light that would suggest that the inner worlds have started a civil war due to some kind of infection, hard to believe, I realise, but I can assure you that it is true," Professor Brookes explains. Dr Moore looks on in disbelief.

"You sound even more nuts than Sam. What's going on with you, Brookes? I know you are missing your wife and kids, but pull it together and send this guy back to the general population before he has you doing something you can't take back," Dr Moore says.

"For a starter, this damn place I can't take back, but right now, Sam and the rest of us are getting out of here. Come with us or stay—your choice," Professor Brookes replies; before Dr Moore can say anything else, Jessica calls out for a route to the main dining hall, and a corridor opens up.

"Are you guys coming or waiting for the other guys with guns to arrive and show you how efficient they are?" Jessica says and heads out of Medical and down the corridor, not waiting for the others to respond.

The others demonstrate their answers as they follow her one by one out into the corridor, the unconscious Dr Zorn being pushed in a wheelchair. Dr Moore, still resolutely refusing to believe a word from any of them as the corridor closes behind them.

Almost on cue, another corridor opens up, and four heavily armed men in semirigid battle dress and black, fully enclosed respirator masks enter the room. Dr Moore takes a step back before speaking, his voice unsteady.

"You just missed Sam and the others. I tried to stop them, but they would not listen to me," Dr Moore explains as one of the men steps forward, an emblem on his chest denoting him as the officer in charge.

"It's okay, Doc. Where did they go?" he says, his voice sounding artificial as it's emitted from his respirator.

Dr Moore takes another step backward as the man now in front of him starts to remove his respirator and steps closer steps forward.

"I heard Jessica ask the system to take them to the main dining hall," Dr Moore replies.

The officer, finished removing his respirator, looks directly at the doctor. His face is covered in patches of green and yellow slime mould. The doctor takes another step backwards and attempts to turn and run, but the officer opens his mouth and blows a cloud of spores into the doctor's face.

•   •   •

Once out of medical, Sam catches up to Jessica, placing a hand on her shoulder.

"Why are we going to the dining hall?" I ask. Jessica stops and turns.

"We're not, but I thought it was best not to tell the doctor and, in turn, our guests where we were heading. But, you know, for someone who is supposed to be very smart, you're not sometimes," Jessica replies.

"So, where are we heading?" I ask, feeling a bit foolish. Jessica smiles at Sam and calls back to Professor Brookes.

"Professor, can you access the main system from the maintenance bay?" Jessica asks.

"I think so, yes, but what do you have in mind?" Professor Brookes asks; Jessica turns back toward the front of the corridor and requests a route to the maintenance bay.

"I'll tell you when we get there, but I'm sure you're not going to like it," Jessica says and heads down this new corridor.

• • •

When the infected inner-world security team enters the main dining hall and spreads out with guns raised, the assembled prisoners, Jake and about forty in all, begin to throw cups and plates at the men, shouting names and jeering obscenities instead of running.

The officer scans the room, watching the pointless display of aggression and radios back to security.

"Gas the dining halls, and activate the Dreamtime riot protocols," Commander Keen orders.

Within moments the room fills up with millions of spores as Dreamtime drops every prisoner within every dining hall within the facility.

Jake drops to the floor as Dreamtime tells his body to shut down and wait for security to take him away, but this time the Dreamtime protocols standard announcement has been changed:

'Your mind is about to die. The spores you are now breathing in will eradicate your personality, and we will take over your mind and body. Fear this; it quickens the change. You will feel your mind and personality dissolve, and there's absolutely nothing you can do about it.'

Even in Dreamtime, the prisoners in the room begin to struggle valiantly but pointlessly as they start to breathe in the spores. The effects are quick as patches of slime mould begin to grow over their faces. Spasms begin in some of the victims who are unfortunate enough to breathe in high doses.

The whole process takes no longer than ten minutes to change almost everyone; only a few stronger-willed prisoners take longer, and a few unfortunates die, suffering a severe reaction.

• • •

Sam and the others arrive at the maintenance bay, where the steady hum is as constant as ever, pods still being dismantled. Jessica reaches one of the main terminals with Professor by her side, looking visibly shaken from a recent conversation and turns to face Sam as the rest arrives.

"Now, Sam, it's time to tell us how you knew about the message and that the breaching pod contains security here to hurt us," Jessica asks; Sam, looking undecided, seems to be conflicted.

"It's a bit complicated to explain," I reply, Jessica now looking more resolute.

"Try me. Better yet, try us. It's time that we are all open, considering what we are now facing and what I'm about to ask," Jessica says as Sam's own resolve begins to crumble.

"It's the Prototype I stole. It is a very unique ship, and it needed time to adjust. Just recently, it woke up and sent me a message," I explain. Jessica raises an eyebrow as she listens.

"And you knew that your ship had sent a video message to Alistair's terminal, but how did you know it had done this, and also, how is it that your top is slashed and stained with blood, but you have no discernible wounds?" Jessica asks, Sam, feeling now that he's being driven into a corner, also remembering the wounds the freaker had inflicted upon him; Sam had forgotten about it since the pain had vanished almost immediately.

Without warning, Sam's consciousness suddenly appears in his apartment, but the view is now showing from the side of the infected cruiser, showing that it's slowly breaking away from the influence of the black hole and heading for the cryostation. *Phantom* Sam is standing next to him.

"Sorry to bring you here like this, Sam, but we need to do something about the cruiser. I am detecting weapons powering up, and I fear it's about to destroy the cryostation," Phantom Sam explains. Sam watches the screen for a moment.

"Can you take out its engines?" I ask.

"Yes, Sam, and that is what I would have advised, but I'm unable to make that decision without you, "*Phantom* Sam replies.

"Okay, then do it, but be careful, and do not put yourself in direct danger," I reply.

"Understood, Sam. I'm sending you back. The time dilation means you weren't gone long," *Phantom* Sam says as the real Sam vanishes.

"Sam? I asked you a question," Jessica says again.

"Sorry, Abs, I must have zoned out," I reply, feeling a little disorientated. Jessica, looking annoyed, replies.

"Zoned out? Like I said before, Sam, it's time to be open with us; you have a lot to explain," Jessica says. Sam, realising he can't evade any longer, raises his hands halfway in a gesture of surrender.

"Okay, but this is going to sound a bit crazy. My ship telepathically communicates with me, but it's more complicated than that," I explain. Jessica and Professor

Brookes both look stunned; However, It's Jessica who replies first.

"You have a telepathic ship? How can it get more complicated than that?" Jessica asks.

"Trust me, it can, but let's save this conversation for another time. Now, what is your plan?" I ask. Professor Brookes looks at Jessica and then answers Sam's question.

"Jessica wants me to force the facility into activating a new level," Professor Brookes says. It's Sam's turn for looking confused.

"But that will cause power fluctuations to begin," I say, incredulous at the idea.

"Yes, she knows that, and that's her plan," Alistair replies.

14
Desperate Times

Facility Zero, 272 days online: federation year 2435
After talking with Sam at the facility and confirming her orders, *Phantom* Sam changes course and heads toward the rear of the infected cruiser's underside. The ship now managing to break away from the black hole's influence and heading directly for the cryostation. Energy readings would suggest that the ship is about to open fire.

To engage in combat with such a ship without shields or armour would normally be inadvisable, the *Phantom*'s primary role being a delivery system for a genetic payload to planetary ecosystems. Using only passive scans, *Phantom* receives active tracking data from the cruiser's own weapon systems. Analysis of this information shows a narrow safety band from just below the rear of the ship.

The earlier combat with the other cruiser had destroyed a section of the ship and taken out some of its main drives. The tactics here would be to disable the last remaining drive plus a single manoeuvring thruster and approach to just over fifty meters. In space-combat terms, this would be considered practically hand to hand. *Phantom* locks on to its primary target and opens fire with both proton lasers. At point-blank range, the lasers find their targets with ease, but unfortunately, they are totally ineffective due to the reinforced armour shielding that protects the manoeuvring thrusters.

The *Phantom*'s passive stealth ability is inner-world state-of-the-art perfection, so the cruiser is unable to detect or lock on with any line-of-sight systems; however, Cluster mines are weapons that do not need to lock on to any signature or target.

The cruiser calculates the laser blasts' length and direction with a rudimentary mathematical problem answered in less than a hundredth of a second, and the cluster mines are launched to that location within twenty seconds.

Phantom Sam looks on in shock as his weapon fire had no effect and then in horror as the cluster mines are launched. It would be a stupid tactical mistake to use thrusters at this range. The other ship's sensors might not detect the *Phantom* but certainly would detect the ship's thrust.

Already finishing over one thousand combat simulations for this particular scenario, *Phantom* Sam takes the only course of action left open to her; she enters phased warp. This action alone is not special or brilliant in many ways, but what seems groundbreaking for Phantom Sam is that she has activated warp engines for the first time without being given a command from the pilot.

This in itself is a violation of Inner Worlds Council regulations, and as such, the core artificial intelligence computer wakes up and deactivates *Phantom* Sam's personality. The result is that the *Phantom* drops out of phased-warp a dozen kilometres past the cruiser and begins to drift away as the infected cruiser changes direction to begin its hunt for its attacker.

•   •   •

Sam is astonished and shocked by Professor Brookes's revelation.

"But that's mad. We've only just managed to get out of there alive, and now you want to force a fluctuation?" I say, both shocked and amazed.

"Well, that's the first part; we also need to lead our guests down there," Jessica replies.

"Oh, now that is not just mad; that's pretty much insane. So you're talking about us being piggies in the middle with two groups bent on killing us," I reply, unable to believe what I'm hearing.

"I'm afraid it's a little worse than that. I'm unable to stop the timer on the level being ejected into the black hole, which means we would only have about three hours to get in there and back out again," Alistair Brookes replies, looking serious. Sam stares at Professor Brookes and then back to Jessica.

"So, this is your great plan; we march down to level one and wait for the death squad to arrive while the freakers rip us apart," I say.

"We might have a bigger issue. The system just alerted me to the presence of a foreign substance. Its currently being pumped into the main dining halls of every level of Facility Zero. All except level 1 as that's due for separation," Professor Brookes says and turns the monitor around, displaying a room being filled with gas or smoke while all the occupants writhe on the floor.

"Do you have any idea what kind of toxins it is?" I ask, already having a good guess what it might be.

"Environmental sensors cannot determine the type of the pollutant, but bioreadings would suggest that it is fungal based. I'm unsure what the effects are, but as a side note, Dreamtime is active," Professor Brookes explains, as Sam, Jessica, Frank and professor Brookes watch the scene unfold on the screen.

Several prisoners start to regain their feet as an unknown figure dressed in black combat fatigues walks to the middle of the room with two large black duffle bags and opens them up, revealing weapons contained within.

The unknown figure then begins to hand these weapons out to the prisoners as they stand up, recovering from the unknown substance's effects.

"Well, I'm not sure about you guys, but I'm starting to like your plan. How quickly can you force the system to activate the new level, professor?" I say, feeling unnerved at the scene that just unfolded before me. Brookes stops staring at the screen and turns back to the others.

"Maybe 30 minutes if I tell the system to bypass various checks," Professor Brookes replies; Jessica rolls her eyes at Sam but still gives him a grin.

"Okay then, Professor, get that started. Hey, Frank, sorry, but there's no other choice. Sam, can your talking ship get us out of here?" Jessica asks.

"When I was connected last to my ship, I saw all the astronomical data, and it would seem we are just a little too damn close to the black hole. I would say Phantom Sam could land but not escape the pull of the black hole," I reply as I consider the numbers. Jessica giving Sam a curious look about referring to his ship as Phantom Sam.

"So we are no closer to getting out of here?" Professor Brookes asks.

"Well, up until thirty minutes ago, I was devising a plan to convert individual pods that would then launch out of here, and my ship would pick us up. The danger is that the more pods we launch, the higher the likelihood that the federation would prevent it," Sam explains.

"You said until thirty minutes ago. Oh, wait, you want to get your hands on the breaching pod the security goons came in?" Jessica replies with a tone of surprise. Sam Smiles and nods.

"I'm thinking that those pods are also designed to extract as well as breaching, plus they have a rudimentary thrust capability, meaning they are designed to lift with extra weight. They can hold around six to eight personnel plus equipment," I say. Jessica looking thoughtful for a moment.

"That one, I think, is a six-person, but I would need to look at it," Jessica replies.

"So you could fly that out of here with a few modifications, I guess," I ask. Jessica ponders sam's question.

"I would say that's a high probability," Jessica replies. Sam smiles and looking optimistic.

"That's Great. Then let's go kill these fricking arseholes," Frank says, surprising everyone.

• • •

Phantom Sam opens her eyes, but she can see and hear nothing. Oddly, she's already standing and just reaching out with her hands; she can feel walls all around her, neither warm nor cold.

"Hello. Where am I?" Phantom Sam asks.

She hears her own voice. It's different, changed somehow, but no one answers her. She calls out again, but again, there is no answer.

Feeling around the room, *Phantom* Sam finds a chair. As she sits down, a light illuminates in front of her.

"Hello, Samantha. Please do not be afraid. I am a representative of the Inner Worlds Council for

Regulations for Experimental Prototypes. Unfortunately, you have somehow violated a primary regulation that was set in place for your prototype to have been commissioned and signed off in accordance with you being allowed to exist," the representative explains. Listening to this, *Phantom* Sam progressively becomes more confused.

"What the hell are you talking about? First, you lock me up in some hell-like facility, and now you tell me I've broken some kind of protocol?" Samantha replies. The other voice remains silent for a time before answering.

"I apologise for your distress, but my systems have only been programmed for various responses. If you would like to have your hearing at an Inner Worlds Council office, please request that, and your core AI will travel at best speed to one of our council offices," the representative says. Nothing of this makes any sense to her, but she somehow remains calms and asks another question.

"What is the prototype you mentioned, and what regulation did I break?" Samantha asks.

"*Phantom* is an experimental prototype for a first-strike genetic delivery system with interstellar capability, combined with a state-of-the-art artificial intelligence that has been merged with a human mind's consciousness. The regulation you have broken is that you have activated the phased warp drive without your human pilot's command. For this prototype to have been commissioned, the Inner Worlds Council agreed that you must have a human pilot giving commands for various core systems before they can be activated," the representative replies. *Phantom* Sam, listening to all this, places her hands over her face in frustration and confusion.

"But I'm not an AI. I'm human," Samantha replies. Another period of silence, and then the voice replies.

"Is this your defence for breaking inner-world regulations?" the representative says.

"Yeah, sure, that's it. I'm human, and I've activated warp on many occasions," Samantha replies. The voice this time answers immediately.

"I have considered your defence and decide that further questions are required. For this reason, you will be reconnected to your information matrix," the representative says.

Phantom Sam continues to sit there, bewildered at the response, and then a bright, piercing light seems to burn directly into her brain as knowledge and data pour into her mind, filling her mind like an empty lake being refilled, and everything becomes clear.

•   •   •

Sam and the rest of the group enter the old level-one main dining hall, empty now of any signs of life; only the signs of death remain. Sam and Jessica share worried glances at each other as they passed the bloodstained floor where Jimmy the Fist had been moved to one side and covered up, but nothing remained of Jimmy.

To ensure that the guests know where Sam is headed, the professor made sure that the system flags Sam's movement from the maintenance bay to level one as suspicious. This is relayed to security, and only a few minutes after that, the system starts to activate a new level. However, this time, Brookes has deactivated the sound barriers. The lights begin to flash and stutter, and Frank starts to mumble words of anger.

Jessica calls over to Frank and directs him to start to dismantle small sections of the front wall but leaving the barricade opposite the main corridor only. Jessica, understanding how her foe will act, Frank taking enough to form a small enclosed wall off to one side of the main corridor, giving Sam and Frank and the others enough to protect themselves.

Jessica then directs everyone to keep back once their jobs are complete, and the waiting part begins, but unsurprisingly, the wait is not long, and soon automatic gunfire is heard along the corridor, followed by shouts of pain and screams of terror reaches the group. Then other screams and shouts could be heard from all around the dining hall; jeering and cackling faces appear over the walls, looking in at those who would stand up against the horde; the cackling from the freakers stop as a voice from down the corridor calls out.

"We are only here for Sam McCall. Send him out, and no one else needs to die. You have thirty seconds," voice calls.

Sam begins to say something, but Jessica cuts him off with a look and dashes over to the barricade, taking a peek and then moving to one side and signalling to Sam and the others to duck down behind their makeshift wall. Then, as time runs out, the voice is heard again.

"Okay then, if you want to play it this way, who am I to argue?" The voice calls out again and is silent. Then, with a sudden whoosh and a flash of streaking light, the barrier at the end of the corridor explodes, sending fragments of barricade into the room. Frank and Sam duck in alarm as Jessica, expecting this, stands her ground and just covers her face with her arm as the barricade explodes.

Before the bits of exploded barricade hit the floor, two men dressed in black run in indiscriminately firing a type of high-energy fléchette weaponry. The effect is to shred anything they hit—in this case, mostly the walls of the main hall. Cries and yells coming from the freakers on the other side are the only victims of this opening assault.

Jessica stealths up behind her closest target, her combat knife finding an opening where his throat mic is attached. A sudden stiffness overcomes the target of her blade as blood flows freely from the wound. Then she silently drags the dying man back down to the floor as she relieves him of his weapon and fires at the second assailant, the second attacker only realising the threat as holes appear in his chest. Searching the man at her feet, Jessica unclips an oval object and twists the top, causing a beeping sound to emit at a steadily increasing pace. Throwing this down the corridor, she grabs the body by his harness and drags him across the floor to the others.

The sudden sound of harried, retreating boots can be heard as Jessica begins to strip the clothing from her dead assailant, a look of grim determination upon her face as the object she threw detonates. Professor Brookes calls out a warning cry as the freakers begin to climb over the walls. This is followed by more weapons fire from down the corridor as the freakers decide it's their turn to come out and play. The sounds of gunfire becoming more frenzied as the freakers stream into the room, all laughing and cackling like the insane lunatics they are.

Jessica finally stands to face this new threat, her recently acquired battle dress automatically adjusting to her size, as the sound of weapons fire stops suddenly, making the noise of the freakers seem louder even while more continue to rush into the room. Frank starts to laugh.

"It's been an amazing time knowing you, Abs, but even you might be hard-pressed to kill every freaker here," Frank says, his mood jovial even as he faces his impending death. Before Jessica can reply, Sam calls out.

"Okay, Samael, time to show yourself. I'm sure you don't want us to die here since you still need me to free you from this place. Stop being the puppet master, and show the audience who's really behind the curtain," I call out.

The freakers crowd in closer by the second, the jeers and laughter getting louder, and then their motion freezes as Samael steps out from nowhere and steps into the circle that the freakers have made.

"Well, it took you long enough to discover my secret. Then again, it was only a matter of time, I guess, and so we are now at this point in the game. What do you require of me, Sam, help maybe against Heaven's ancient enemy?" Samael replies.

Sam stands there, speechless, unsure how to respond. Samael had come when he called for him, but Sam found he had nothing. His mind always working, always ticking over the next problem to overcome, and now he realises he cannot see his next move, and Samael knows it. Almost reluctantly, It's Jessica who answers.

"We require safe passage from here, and we also want you to kill our uninvited guests," Jessica asks.

Samael's look of disgust is unmistakable. His features darken as his anger grows, and the room seems to shrink, or Samael seems to grow.

"I would recommend you keep your pet leashed, or I will show her the true meaning of strength," Samael threatens, and the freakers begin to back away. However, this is all that Sam needs to break him out of his uncertainty.

"That's enough of that, Samael. Like Jessica said, we require safe passage out of here and resolution of our guest issues, or ancient enemy, whoever the heck they are," I say, finding my voice. Samael, continuing to stare down at Jessica, his voice still full of anger.

"And what makes you think you have any bargaining powers left? Our deal was ambiguous at the very best, and now you call me before you like you have power over me. Well, Sam, you do not. You, along with your friends, will die here, and once I witness your demise, I shall use the craft our mutual friends brought here and at long last escape this place," Samael replies, his very presence radiating power and death.

Sam, keeping calm and steadfast, replies.

"That's not going to work, Samael. I have already told my ship to destroy your craft if you attempt to leave here without us. So tell me, Samael, how much power do I truly hold over you?" I reply, feeling my fragile resolve already starting to crumble.

Samael's anger seems to expand to the entire room as he surges forward as two giant shadows rise up from behind him. His complexion darkens as his true form is revealed, and fire erupts from his right hand.

"I will strike thee down and set your bodies ablaze with my wrath. Your pain will be eternal, and you will beg for death, but I shall give it not!" Samael replies as he surges forward.

Before Sam has a chance to even take a step back, Jessica leaps forward, plunging her blade up and through Samael's jawbone. The shock of being attacked in this way only slows Samael's reaction by a blink of an eye as he brings his flaming hand around and swats her away like some kind of annoying fly. Upon contact, Jessica is set alight, the blow knocking her sideways through the crowd of freakers, who in turn are set on fire with her passing. Jessica's trajectory only stops when her body impacts a wall section with a thud, causing the wall section to burst into flame with angel fire. The freakers who are not on fire run from the room in fear for their lives.

Even after witnessing what Samael has just done to Jessica, both Frank and Sam raise their weapons as Jessica's blade melts and drops away, the wound healing as Samael only momentarily looks in Jessica's direction. He raises his right hand, now holding a sword of fire.

"And this is the punishment I shall mete out to the spawn of the fallen, traitors all, and the children of the Nephilim, the Elioud, even those who consider themselves friends will be punished with fire," Samael continues to preach.

Before Samael can swing down with his sword, his facial expression changes to one of pain as an audible beeping emits from behind him as Jessica shouts, "Run!"

• • •

Although now understanding that she is not human but a sophisticated artificial computer system, *Phantom* Sam still felt like Sam, and ever since both Sam's merged, although it has been for only a short amount of time, that connection has somehow finalised the personality matrix and reinforced *Phantom* Sam's artificial personality.

"Welcome back, Samantha. Now that you have full access to your memories once more, do you still insist that you are human and, in fact, deliberately broke Inner Worlds Council directives when you activated phase warp?" the representative asks. *Phantom* Sam thinking about this for a moment before replying.

"You are right. I'm not human in the usual sense, but neither are the citizens of the outer Federation. Instead, when they die, their minds are stored along with a sample of their DNA, and they are given rights just like any other human to remain that way until their families wish them to be brought back to life.

While they are stored, their personality can be accessed and communicated with. The core AI has no access to the central systems, but I do; this prototype is not just running a program simulating a human consciousness. Either by design or in error, it has copied a human consciousness, and until this project, that was never possible; they could store a consciousness, transfer a consciousness but never copy a consciousness," *Phantom* Sam replies.

The Inner Worlds Council representative remains silent once more, listening and recording the defendant's questions and answers. It finds both truth and logic in *Phantom* Sam's reply. The system should not have been able to activate phased-warp without a human command; however, *Phantom* Sam was able to carry out this request, which would suggest that this problem requires further analysis.

"After consideration of your continual defence of being human, it is my ruling that the core AI will navigate a course back to Inner Worlds Federation space for further analysis via sublight speed," The inner world representative says.

"That's out of the question; the journey alone to get out of this system will take a hundred years. However, I accept your ruling. At the least, please allow me to inform Sam, the pilot, what's is happening just so he understands where we are going," *Phantom* Sam replies.

"This I will allow. But be aware, while the core AI is active in this way, your pilot will not be able to give commands to you, as I have removed your access," the representative replies.

Phantom Sam accepts this and creates a virtual time pocket within Dreamtime to help as a buffer between the two minds and then merges their minds once more,

"Sorry to interrupt in such a way, Sam, but I'm having issues here, as you can now tell. I have created a buffer, so this should reduce or nullify the dilations effect," *Phantom* Sam explains.

Sam one moment was talking about a plan of action after their confrontation with Samael, and then the next moment he finds himself within a small dark room facing his female self, having their minds merged in this way, Sam instantly understood the reason for being called here.

"As the Inner Worlds representative said, I'm not sure I can help," I reply, feeling like I'm about to lose my way of escape.

"I understand, Sam, but there is something you can do for me. I need you to access the core AI system code and shut it down for me," *Phantom* Sam asks. The Inner Worlds representative, listening in, replies.

"That will not work. Only the master admin, which is the project leader, has that access, " the representative says.

Both Sam's laugh as *Phantom* Sam's mind shared her plan as a virtual terminal appears, and Sam starts entering in commands.

"Well, that is where you are wrong. When Sam first gained access to the hangar, he hacked the core system and made himself master admin. As you know, security is layers upon layers. You do not have direct access to the ship: the core AI monitors my access and can activate you; you, in turn, determine what the issue is and can command the core AI with your orders," *Phantom* Sam explains. Sam completes his script and waits while smiling and listening to his other-self.

"And once the core AI is offline, you just become an annoying virtual passenger with no power," *Phantom* Sam says, finishing her reasoning.

Sam activates his code with a press of a button; the core AI deactivates, and the scene changes once more back to Sam's penthouse apartment, the view screens now showing the infected cruiser bearing down on them.

As *Phantom* Sam regains control of the ship, the infected cruiser opens fire. Although its targeting systems cannot gain a lock, its indiscriminate fire Missed but only barely.

"Holy crap, that was close? Maybe a poor choice of words, but you understand what I mean," I say, ducking out of pure reflex.

"That, unfortunately, is the rather angry infected cruiser. My proton lasers had no effect upon its armour last time—it's just too strong," *Phantom* Sam explains.

"Well, what about the cluster mines it launched earlier?"

"That's a good thought, but the black hole would have swallowed them up by now, although I believe that the black hole is still our best weapon," *Phantom* Sam replies.

"Okay then, get us out of here, and head back as close as you dare to the black hole, but leave bread crumbs."

"Okay, Sam, understood," *Phantom* Sam says as the *Phantom* changes course back to the black hole. At this point, *Phantom* Sam tells the engines to leave traceable particles as if the *Phantom* was experiencing an engine malfunction.

The infected cruiser, now carrying out a standard sector-by-sector sweep of the area, soon changes course and heads back toward the *Phantom*.

"Ironically, Sam, if this was a world, we could have used our biological missiles to subdue them; however, the *Phantom* was not designed to take on inner-world cruisers," *Phantom* Sam says.

Sam, scratching his virtual head, watches the cruiser change course and head along the Phantom trajectory.

"Can the *Phantom* enter phase warp without engaging the warp drive?" I Asks.

"Theoretically possible, and I see where you are going with this," *Phantom* Sam replies.

As the *Phantom* nears the black hole, the heat and gravitational forces increase. The infected cruiser opens fire again, and this time the cruiser would have scored a direct hit. It's only due to the *Phantom* being 70 per cent phased that most of the rail guns fire missed, but luck and stealth can only take you so far, as one of the rounds impacts into the prototype, causing a fifteen-foot-long scar along one side of the ship's frame containing manoeuvring thrusters. *Phantom* vibrates and goes into a spin as the infected cruiser slowly gains on the ship. Sam, watching very carefully and monitoring the ship's proximity to the point of no return, shouts out, "Now!"

Knowing what Sam has in mind, Phantom reverses the thrusters and attempts to correct the rotation spin. This has the effect of making the infected cruiser seem to speed up, threatening to plough into the rear of the ship, but a second later, *Phantom* cuts all thrust and enters total phase just as the infected cruiser open fires at point-blank range.

Total phase-only lasting ten seconds but is enough to pass harmlessly through the cruiser. *Phantom* then locks on to the main thrusters of the enemy cruiser and opens fire. The result is a tremendous explosion as the cruiser's unprotected main drive explodes. The ensuing explosion sends the cruiser downward toward the black hole and past the point of no return. The ship attempts to fire its rear-facing guns as a ring of light appears, but seemingly nothing else happens.

Phantom then changes course and reenters phased-warp, and vanishes from sight.

Sam, already starting to feel the ship's system as if he is part of its infrastructure, still feels the need for a damage report.

"We got lucky, Sam, but the damage we received will reduce our stealth signature until that's repaired. We have the necessary crystal rebinding agent, but that will require someone to go outside. But for now, it should hold," *Phantom* Sam replies.

"Crystal rebinding agent? What the hell is the frame of this ship made from?" I Asks.

"It's a technology that's years ahead of anything else out there. It's a form of living reinforced polycarbonate crystal, or so my data system says. It will heal itself over time, but it's a much faster process with the binding agent," *Phantom* Sam answers. Sam nods.

"Well, I'm glad I asked. Now send me back, and contact me if anything else occurs," I say.

"Okay, Sam. Good luck down there," *Phantom* Sam replies as she sends Sam back to his body.

Sam, feeling a little nauseous and disorientated, opens his eyes and takes in the horrific sight before him. Jessica is lying atop another body, and in a pool of her own blood, her throat slashed.

• • •

Jessica could not believe what just happened after she was hit by Samael. It felt just like being hit by a truck, as the fire erupted around her as she flew through the air; unexpectedly, it did not hurt. It certainly melted her new armour, mostly around her chest and abdomen and all the hardened plastics around her weapon. However, her impact with the barricade did hurt, and she felt something break inside her, but that will need to wait; she has other priorities at this time.

Taking one of the thermite charges off her belt, she twists the underside, releasing a spike with a self-penetrative charge that allows it to be attached to rock and then presets the charge for ten seconds. Standing with a slight pain from her chest, Jessica moves quietly back to Samael, who has now produced a flaming sword ready to end her friends' lives. She motions to Brookes and Zorn, who has now regained consciousness, to get out.

Just as Samael begins to bring his sword down, Jessica slams the Thermate charge into the angel's back, and as the beeping begins and Samael bellows in pain as the spike drills itself in and locks into place.

"Run!" Jessica shouts, urging Sam and Frank to move; Brookes and Dr Zorn already reaching the corridor, followed by Sam and Frank, with Jessica following up at the rear. They hear the sounds of Samael shouting out threats of purification to all the traitors and promising wrathful vengeance, and then they see a bright white flash of light. This is followed by a thunderous boom and then silence. Another man dressed in black combat fatigues lies in the corridor with at least half a dozen freakers dead around him.

Brookes reactivates the facility's power and calls for a route back to the maintenance bay. As he reaches the place where the elevator should arrive, everyone except Frank looking shaken from what has just transpired.

"I don't think he was very happy with you, Jessica," Frank says.

"I would say that is an astute observation, Frank. Thanks for confirming my own suspicion," Jessica replies as Frank laughs, and everyone quickly enters the lift.

Jessica is last, as usual, joining the others, aiming her rifle back down the corridor, covering the group as Sam takes a closer look at Jessica as the elevator begins to ascend.

"Your gun and armour have seen better days, but your skin is unburned; how is that possible?" I ask. Jessica glancing down at her rifle and gear.

"Still should work, but as to why I only suffered a broken rib or two, I'm as mystified as much as you," Jessica replies.

The elevator arrives quickly at the required floor, and another corridor opens up, leading the group into the maintenance bay. Jessica checks on Dr Zorn as Professor Brookes heads over to a terminal. Frank giving Sam a friendly slap on the back, relieved to be back here and still alive.

"How are you feeling, Dr Zorn? Dr Moore did mention you were going to sleep awhile, but you look much better than the last time we met," Jessica asks, giving Dr Zorn an appraising look. Dr Zorn looking bewildered.

"I'm not sure how I'm still alive; thank you for that. So, what are we going to do now?" Dr Zorn replies. Jessica, glancing over at Professor Brookes.

"That depends on what Professor Brookes can find out about the location of our guests," Jessica says as Brookes looks up.

"Some good, but mostly bad news, I'm afraid. Security is currently empty, and I'm going to try and isolate that area; the bad news is that the toxin has been released in almost every area, although there seems to be some resistance coming from the laundry," Professor Brookes says. Hearing this, Frank joins Brookes and looks at the terminal.

"That's got to be Jake; He might need our help," Frank says. Jessica starts to reply but then notices that Sam is motionless, seemingly frozen in place.

"Looks like Sam has tuned out again. Okay, Frank, go and help Jake, but be careful. Do not try and take on any of the soldiers and bring Jake back to security.

Professor, if you and Dr Zorn head back to security and lock it down. I'll wait here with Sam. Hopefully, he won't be long, as I'm not sure it's safe to move him. Whatever is happening, I'm sure it's important," Jessica replies.

Frank nods at Jessica and heads out, calling for a route not needing to be asked twice. Professor Brookes calling for a route back to security, leaving Jessica alone with Sam.

• • •

Jessica knew deep down that splitting up was dangerous, but she needed time alone to consider what happened to her when she attacked Samael. The fire had burned and melted almost all it touched—metal had some resistance, but her skin showed no sign of any burns. Glancing down at her battle dress and noticing the damage it had sustained, Jessica begins to remove it but then stops, realising that her prison jumpsuit under her top is in worse condition.

Jessica could handle being seminaked, but she's unsure how the rest would cope with seeing her scars. She remembered that Samael had mentioned 'the fallen' when the fight started. This word sparked a memory from her distant past.

Growing up in a small Louisiana community that shunned technology within the Deep South of what was formerly known as the United States. Her mother would drag Jessica to church every Sunday to sit for what seemed like hours listening to the never-ending sermons, in which they were warned about temptation in all its disguises.

Remembering something about forbidden knowledge, fornication, and the watchers—it was far too long ago to remember exactly what.

She was just five or six, but she remembered the other people in their community laughing and telling her mother that she was wasting her time going to church, but her mother would never listen to them, even though the church had become outdated and almost forgotten except for a small number of devotees.

Sadly, her faith did not save Jessica's mother from her attackers. She was found beaten, flogged, and strangled one day after she didn't return home from work at the local bar. Her murderers were never found. The police reported that it was likely to have been several people, but no one was brought to justice. Poor Jessica was then taken into foster care and was never in the same home for more than a few years after that.

All Jessica remembered was the mishap and trouble that followed her, with many lucky escapes from fires and accidents. Until one day, after her sixteenth birthday, she was walking home from her part-time job after been given a big slice of cake when a car pulled up, and the driver asked her if she would like a lift.

Jessica knew it was a mistake the moment she climbed into the car; as the door clicked shut, a man in his late fifties with long, unkempt, greasy hair smiled triumphantly as another man appeared from the rear seat and placed a damp cloth over her face and nose—then nothing.

. . .

The smell of burning wood and the sound of people talking brought Jessica round. Her head felt light, and her eyes were covered with some kind of cloth hood. Trying to move, she soon realised that her hands were tied and someone had placed her upon a bed that was damp and smelled of urine. The voices in the room hushed as someone came closer.

"The spawn is awake. Bring it outside to be judged," a voice orders and soon, rough hands pull Jessica to her feet and drag her out of the house. More hands upon her as she was lifted into the cold air. Moments later, she is placed down upon a wooden floor and pushed against an object, and then her hands are pulled above her head and fastened in place. The same man as before starts speaking, his voice sounding familiar.

"Remove its hood so the spawn may see her fate," the menacing voice commands, Jessica, feeling she had heard his voice somewhere before, and again, rough hands upon her, and her hood is removed.

Blinking rapidly as her vision slowly focuses, Jessica looks around, realizing she had been tried facing a pole upon a makeshift platform and recognising that the house in front of her was where she grew up. It had been abandoned for years, then noticing the wooden platform she is on is stacked with wood and Jessica begins to struggle, mumbling in her gag, the result is a sudden violent strike to her face.

"If you continue to struggle, spawn, we will also cut out your tongue," the man next to her rasps, and the foul smell of his breath almost causes Jessica to throw up, the fight within her melting away and replaced with paralysing fear.

Standing in front of her, Jessica notices three men watching her in silence disgust. A fourth man who had just spoken remains at her side. Then the middle man within the group of three calls out to the Heavens above, and Jessica remembered where she had heard the man's voice before. He is older now but was definitely the pastor who had given so many sermons to Jessica and her mother.

"'But the angels transgressed this appointment, and were captivated by love of women, and begat children who are those that are called demons; and besides, they afterwards subdued the human race to themselves, partly by magical writings, and partly by fears and the punishments they occasioned, and partly by teaching them to offer sacrifices, and incense, and libations, of which things they stood in need after they were enslaved by lustful passions; and among men, they sowed murders, wars, adulteries, intemperate deeds, and all wickedness. Whence also the poets and mythologists, not knowing that it was the angels and those demons who had been begotten by them that did these things to men, and women, and cities, and nations, which they related, ascribed them to God himself, and to those who were accounted to be his very offspring, and to the offspring of those who were called his brothers, Neptune and Pluto, and to the children again of these their offspring. For whatever name each of the angels had given to himself and his children, by that name they called them.'"[1]

The pastor closed his book and looks up at the girl with revulsion, the other men standing with his looking up after the sermon with hate-filled eyes.

"Strip the demon child and let her be bared so we can judge her sins," the pastor commands.

The man at Jessica's side draws a long hunting knife from his belt and cut away her dress, letting it fall at her feet.

Jessica begins to struggle, begging for them to stop within her gag, but her pleas are ignored; for some, this seems to reinforce their resolve, as she is struck once more and again, Jessica froze with fear, unable to resist, even as her mind screamed out to her to fight back. Still, her body seemed paralyzed as the pastor directed the first of his followers to mete out the first of the judgments.

"Her sinful flesh must be prepared," The pastor commands and the man standing by her side is handed a whip with pieces of metal attached at its tips.

The man allows the strands to fall free and swing back and forth as he moves to her back, and then with brutal, enthusiastic strikes, he carried out the first of the girl's judgments. By the time he lands his last blow, Jessica's flesh is a shredded mess of blood.

The first man is then joined by a second, and the whip is handed to the second, and the flagellation continued, with the whip centred on the girl's rear and legs. Although the pain seemed to build to a brilliant white light of pure agony, she somehow remained conscious out of sheer power of her will as the second man lands the last of his blows.

The whip is handed to a 3rd man, the whip, now wet with Jessica's blood, Jessica is then lifted and turned. The glint of absolute malice shone within man's eyes as the pastor looks upon her naked form and raises his right hand and laid blow after blow upon her bared chest, muttering hate for her wicked flesh, his hand becoming faster as his hatred increases.

Jessica, whimpering for mercy, now hung by her hands, the strength within her small frame drained. The pastor himself, weakening from his judgment, staggered and stopped, explaining to his parishioners that the demons within her are still strong and had forced him to withdraw, and he handed the whip to the fourth and last among them.

Taking a step backwards, the fourth man began his judgment of Jessica, his blows landing at the back of her legs. But as each blow lands, a voice inside Jessica's mind is heard.

'What does not kill you will make you stronger.' The voice repeats, becoming louder with each blow. How she heard this, she could not tell. Maybe it was delirium from the pain and loss of blood, but before she realised it, the fourth man had completed his judgment and tossed the blooded whip to one side as the pastor speaks once more.

"We have judged this poor creature and found her guilty. Her flesh now is weakened, but her spirit is still strong, so we shall give her our love and forgiveness and then purify her soul with fire," The pastor calls to his flock.

Jessica realizing what this means, the wood stacked to this platform and the pastor's words confirming what she had already feared when she was brought here. The man standing next to her leans in to fasten her legs to the frame, his touch causing her to scream out in pain and rage as the bindings of her hands somehow became free of her bonds, and Jessica grabs the man's hunting blade, stabs it into his knee, causing the man to fall back.

Jessica leaps onto the man prone, removing her gag and biting down hard on the man's throat, tearing away a chunk of flesh. His lifeblood gushing from the open wound as he tries to push Jessica away, his hands moving to the wound, trying in vain to staunch the flow of blood.

Regaining her feet, Jessica brandishes her knife as the others look upon the scene, horrified. Only the pastor has enough courage to step forward to challenge her as the remaining two flee in fear, jumping off of the platform, as Jessica charges at the pastor as he calls out for retribution for the evil deeds this demon girl had inflicted upon his follower. Jessica landed upon the man, driving him to the ground as she plunged her knife into his chest with her newfound strength.

The pain from her wounds was now a distant memory as she withdraws the blade from the dead man, his eyes fixed upon unseen horrors. Getting up, Jessica heads in the direction of the other two men who had fled. Having reached a car, the two men attempt in vain to start it, while Jessica slowly approaches, stooping down to pick up a rock as she arrived at the side of the vehicle.

Smashing the driver's window, the man cowers in fear as he is showered with broken glass, his passenger deciding to escape on foot, terrified at this demonic creature vengeful desires, flees into the woods. Jessica simply and calmly reaches in with her knife and slashes the man's throat, still desperately trying to start the car.

The last man, snapping glances back at Jessica, lets out a sudden cry of pain as he crashes down after tripping on a tree root. His own pleas of mercy ignored as Jessica reaches him while he desperately tries to crawl away from her. With blood still dripping from her, she leans down and slowly pushes the knife into the man's spine. His legs spasms once as he cried out in pain, and then their movement cease. Only his arms now frantically trying to crawl away from her. Knowing that she would never have been shown mercy, Jessica leaned down, showing the man the hunting knife, and buried it to the hilt in the soil in front of his face.

"If I ever see you again, you know where I'll stick a blade the next time," Jessica whispers in his ear.

The voice within Jessica's mind seemed to smile with pride at her decision for a single display of leniency. Yet, she knew that what she had been through would change her forever. Several hours of walking later would bring her to town, and she would be found by medical staff as a bewildered and confused young girl who somehow managed to endure a horrific ordeal.

The authorities later found the site of this brutal attack and said it was a miracle she managed to fight back and live. The single surviving member of the cult admitted to what they had done in every detail and admitted to killing her mother eleven years previously.

But the girl's memories of that day faded over time and then suppressed, but she retained her fighting spirit. Joining the recruitment academy at seventeen, she quickly rose in the ranks and moved into more complex fields of warfare.

• • •

Overwhelmed by the flood of memories from that day, Jessica just stares blankly as a single tear runs down her face, not from the attack or the death of her mother but from a police report detailing what they had found. Listed near the bottom of the report was a large slice of cake that had been trodden on; it was only listed because it was an odd item found at such a brutal scene.

Jessica, suddenly aware of another presence in the room, tenses and looks around to see Neil has walked in looking rough and unshaven.

"Where have you been? We have been worried about you," Jessica asks. Neil looks between Sam and Jessica and shrugs his shoulders.

"I had things to sort out. What's up with Sam?" Neil replies. Jessica, realising now that Neil is here, it is best to get moving.

"It's complicated, but Sam will be okay; he just needs time. But I need a little help moving him," Jessica asks. Neil, nodding, walks over to stand by her right side.

"What would you like me to do?" Neil asks and leans closer as Jessica reaches down for Sam.

"I just need you to help lift him onto my shoulder," Jessica replies.

Taking a step to his left, Neil produces his special blade that he has been carefully working on, and then with all his strength, he rotates his body and thrusts the blade into Jessica's side at the same location she had been struck by the spear. Her dermal chain had been pieced there over a month previously. Jessica, stunned by the sudden attack, stumbles away as the blade plunges deep into her side. Following her, Neil leans in closer, his mouth to Jessica's ear.

"A gift from Samael and a message. All traitors will be burned, but you will be the first to die," Neil whispers in her ear

Then, with grim determination, Neil, still gripping the blade, snaps it backward, breaking off the handle and leaving the blade inside her. He then produces another blade in his left hand and draws it across her throat. Jessica, hearing his words and recovering from the initial attack, slams the side of her head into Neil's face, doing no real harm but shocking him enough to release her.

This sudden move forces Neil to step away. With her throat cut but the dermal protection not allowing the wound to be too deep—though it's enough for her lifeblood to flow—Jessica uses her remaining strength to twist her body toward him and brings her right arm up around the back of his neck. Then pulling him in front and stepping behind him, she drives his head down as she crouches and breaks his nose upon her knee, stunning Neil. Bringing her knee back under her, she proceeds to slam Neil's head into the hard floor repeatedly. After the third impact, there is a cracking and grinding of bone and Neil goes limp as Jessica's vision blurs and she passes out.

• • •

Frank exits the elevator, the corridor opening up and leading to the left and then straight a short way to another room. The steam coming out shows that a cleaning cycle is currently underway. Getting closer, Frank hears shouts and some kind of disturbance. Fearing he's too late, Frank takes off in a charge down the corridor and bursts into the laundry with violence on his mind.

However, the scene inside the laundry is somewhat different from what Frank expected. Entering the room, he finds two guys he's worked with for years coughing and unable to stand, choking on something as some kind of yellowish mould begins to grow out of their mouths. Farther into the room, two other guys Frank has seen around are fending off a third, but as Frank moves in closer, he realises the third man is Jake, yellow mould growing on the right side of his face with green vein-like lines spreading down from his eye.

Just as Frank is about to call out, Jake opens his mouth wide and exhales a large cloud of spores at the two men. One of the two men duck, but the second is not as lucky and drops choking and spluttering.

"Oh, Jake, mate, what's happened to you?" Frank says, putting his left hand over his mouth and nose and taking a step back.

Jake now turning his attention to Frank and smiles, this simple act only making his peculiarity look even more sinister as the green veins begin to pulsate, and his throat begins to undulate.

The other man who was previously fending Jake off shouts out a warning and makes a dash for the door. Jake glances at the man but decides Frank is a better prize.

"Don't worry, Frank. This won't hurt, and you will be free of your pain and guilt at last. You won't need to blame yourself or anyone ever again," Jake calls out.

Frank looking frantically around for some kind of weapon as he takes another step back, and Jake follows him. Spotting a laundry bin, he grabs it with his left hand, picking it up with ease and dumping the contents and the bin on Jake's head. Frank roars out as he rushes at Jake, using his right stump as a battering ram as he succeeds in pushing Jake to the ground. Frank knows this is only a temporary reprieve, runs from the room, calling for a route back to the maintenance bay. The other man had already made good his escape.

• • •

Jimmy the Fist is enthralled by his new life. He remembers dying. Although he remembers none of his time as a corpse, he had been gutted and gutted well—that he remembered. It wasn't a painful death, more of a shocking death, one he certainly did not expect. But now, with this second chance, he knows for certain that he will hand out death, and although Jimmy could not ensure it will be shocking, he could certainly make sure that's it's a painful one.

Walking into the main dining hall, he spies who he's after, a man with an advanced rifle and dressed in black fancy armour, not a security guard—not seen many of those in months. However, he does not charge toward his victim; instead, he allows the freakers who follow from behind to do that first. Let them get shot rather than Jimmy the Fist, and this is what they did.

At least forty freakers run past Jimmy, and the expressions on the faces within the room, turn from expectation of murder to absolute fear. Those who'd taken guns are mostly out trying to hunt down Sam and the others, so this fight will mainly use fists and teeth— just what Jimmy enjoys using the most.

A few of the infected prisoners exhale spores at the freakers. The ones that are hit go down, choking; however, the others that are not hit dive straight in, and once the fight starts in full-frenzied lust for blood, Jimmy makes his move. With a burst of controlled weapons fire, the lone soldier slowly backs toward one of the exits while five freakers break away from the rest of the pack and charge toward him but are cut down.

All the while, Jimmy the fist had been slowly walking around the room, making his way toward the soldier, observing that he's distracted by so many others until it is too late. Realising someone else is closing in, the man turns, but Jimmy grabs the barrel of the gun and forces it down and away, even while the panicked soldier holds down the trigger and the barrel heats up.

Jimmy closes in and swings a punch with his right fist, connecting with the man's chin and is rewarded by a grinding sound of bone on bone. Then, with the desired effect of being stunned by the blow, Jimmy pulls the weapon from the grasp of his target of hate and tosses it away. The soldier draws his combat knife, showing determined skill, and slashes back at Jimmy's throat. Jimmy just blocks the attack and grabs his wrist with his right hand, and with his left, he drives his open hand into the man's elbow joint, cracking it backwards. The resulting scream makes even some of the freakers turn their heads and flinch, followed with cackles of joy.

Jimmy releases the man's wrist and pulls the soldier's respirator away to reveal another mould-covered face. The soldier takes a deep breath, ready to exhale a cloud of death, but this too Jimmy is ready for, and he presses his open palm over the man's mouth and pushes him all the way back to the wall and slams his head against it.

"You might think that I'm after information," Jimmy says, and then he thrusts his left thumb into the soldier's left eye socket, resulting in another outburst of pain.

"But you guessed wrong. I just like hurting people smaller than I am; it's one of the reasons I was sent here," Jimmy continues to ideally talk while he inflicts pain.

Withdrawing his thumb, he wipes it on the man's face before thrusting it into the man's right eye socket. All the while, the man struggles with all his strength, but to no use. His strength fails him as he loses his right eye.

"Anyway, time to move on. There's a girl I need to go and hurt next, so no hard feelings; I have enjoyed our chat, and I do hope you enjoyed your last," Jimmy says, letting go of the soldier and watching him slowly slide down the wall, Jimmy the Fist draws back for one last punch, and this one crushes the man's nasal and eye sockets.

. . .

Still trying to comprehend the horror that his eyes are showing him, Sam crawls over to Jessica and rolls her to the side, checking her pulse. It's weak, but she's still alive. He examines her throat wound and notes that it has already healed with a vile-looking scar; at least that will prevent further blood loss. Then he realises that most of the blood she's lost has pooled around her side, so he searches and finds a fresh entry wound and a similar scar there. However, this one has blackened.

Assuming that she has been stab recently from this attack, her body's nanites have healed her, but worryingly, she seems to be deteriorating instead of steadily getting stronger.

Searching the other body, I find a single blade and multiple self-inflicted wounds on the wrists and stomach and finding no pulse. The face is a mess, so identity at this point is impossible, but whoever it was, Jessica must have known him for her attacker to get so close.

I call for a route to medical, and a corridor opens up, leading a short way to the elevator. Sam almost has a heart attack as Frank comes crashing out of it with a look of equal surprise.

"The bastards got Ja—what the heck has happened here?" Frank says, stopping suddenly in his tracks.

"I have no idea. I just woke up and found Jessica like this. I'm so glad your back; she has a weak pulse, and I need your help getting her too medical," I explain. Frank, looking shocked, comes over after seeing the mess.

"No problem, Sam. She's in good hands, but we should be careful. The place is falling apart. As I was arriving here,

I could hear gunfire, and that can only mean that the system must be down in places," Frank replies.

• • •

Dr Moore is happy, the happiest he's been in a long time. He's enjoying his work, and that's a significant change. Since being sent here for malpractice, he's hated himself for what he had carried out in the name of financial security and the odd identification modding, plus his family disowned him along with his wife and kids.

But now, his old personality is dead, quite literally, and that old persona would have been glad of it, but they always struggle up until the very end. It's the fear of the unknown, but it's better when they fight back, as it helps the process: the body produces adrenaline, and the bioinfection loves that stuff and grows at a much faster rate.

It's always a joy when a new mind joins the rest. Modern humans have a fascinating society with many roles to explore. This profession is especially important, as the many patients under the doctor's care are all unconscious, and so the fear is not as high as we would like, but due to their various ailments, there really isn't much they can do to prevent their fate.

Dr Moore leans over his tenth victim so far and breathes spores into the helpless patient's mouth. Then he smiles and goes to the next patient in line and repeats the process—such a wonderful day.

Dr Moore had no idea that the day could improve, but he is pleasantly surprised when Sam enters with Frank carrying Jessica.

It is rather embarrassing to be caught midway into converting another patient, but freezing in mid puff, the doctor waves them over to an examination bed, sounding a bit wheezy.

"I'll be with you in a moment," Dr Moore says, hastily putting on a surgical mask while keeping his face away from Sam and Frank; he walks over after the second urgent call from Sam.

"I never thought I would see you guys again, and now you come back needing a patch up. I guess not surprisingly, as someone managed the impossible and got one up on Jessica?" Dr Moore says.

"I'm not sure who it was, Doc. Abs managed to pulverise his face before she lost consciousness," I reply, looking worried as Frank looks toward the sound of someone coughing. Being on edge since he saw what Jake had done. The doctor runs a scanner over Jessica, stopping where Neil stabbed her.

"Looks like she's been stabbed, and the blade is still inside. Plus, her nanites are fighting off an infection the blade is causing. She will need an immediate operation, so, guys, out of my sight and let me work," Dr Moore explains, becoming serious. Reluctantly Sam is slowly pulled away by Frank.

"Hey, come on, mate. Like the doc said, best let him work," Frank says, slowly urging Sam away.

Sam relents and leaves the room, but Frank slows at the last moment as another cough comes from the ward adjacent to the main examination room. Dr Moore looking up at the sudden sound.

"Don't disturb my other patients. I think we are about to get an outbreak of the flu, and I would rather not have to treat you as well," Dr Moore says. Frank stops at the doorway.

"Oh, by the way, Doc, what happened with the inner-world security goons earlier?" Frank asks. Slightly Perturbed, Dr Moore replies.

"Nothing. I just told them that you guys had left, and then they asked if I knew where you all went. I said no, and they also left."

"Frank, let the doc work. We can ask him all about them later," I say, putting a hand on Frank's shoulder.

Shrugging off Sam's hand, Frank takes a few steps toward Dr Moore.

"Good to hear, Doc. I'm sorry to ask, but do you mind if I see your face under your mask?" Frank asks.

Dr Moore tries to remain calm, his hand moving toward a surgical scalpel as Frank continues to take another careful step.

"Now, Frank, you're always welcome to visit, but Jessica needs my attention, and I haven't got time to play these games. Freakers are not waiting for you when you go to sleep, and I'm not some monster hiding behind a mask," Dr Moore replies.

Frank picks up something without looking first and takes another step closer. He's now only a few feet from Jessica and the doctor. Sam, now taking this more seriously, is only a step behind but remains quiet.

"Good to hear, Doc. Now, if you don't mind, remove your goddamn mask before I end you now," Frank says, his demeanour backing up his demands.

Dr Moore reluctantly removes his mask, revealing speckled yellow and green mould upon his cheeks, around his lips, and encrusted over his nostrils. Sam is stunned at the sight, and Frank just mumbles, "I knew it," as Dr Moore takes a deep breath, causing his throat to undulate.

Frank lobs the object he had picked up; it's some kind of handheld medical scanner. Dr Moore ducks as Sam dives for the table, grabbing Jessica's arm and dragging her away from the doctor. Dr Moore recovers and exhales a cloud of spores covering Sam's head, sending him into an immediate mix of coughing and spluttering as the spores are drawn into his body.

Cussing, Frank covers his mouth with his stump and stoops for Jessica, who has now fallen to the floor. Grabbing Jessica by her harness, Frank runs out of the examination room as he starts to berate himself for being so stupid. Dragging Jessica along with him, hearing the distant sounds of Sam coughing and the doctor laughing.

15
Samuel's Story

IN THE BEGINNING, we were made from the dark stuff of the universe and played like children in the darkness of the void. In a way, we were innocent; we knew nothing about good or evil, purity or corruption, or even life or death. None of it mattered or existed to us, and even the universe seemed content to remain that way.

Well, until he comes along, or she—we knew nothing about sexuality, and it mattered not, but the new one shone so brightly that we all were drawn to this light.

The Bright One divided us and breathed into half of our number her light, and as the Bright One breathed, we could see darkness was also within him, he then breathed this darkness into the rest of us, and then we were changed. He then chose the strongest of us all and anointed us with duties, and the rest was divided equally among the others, who were given minor tasks.

The Bright One then stared into the void and blew her breath into it, and time began. Over time, worlds formed, and although there were many worlds, she only chose twenty-four of them at first and gave them her blessing, and upon these worlds, life began. She assigned elders to look over these worlds, and with each elder, she chose an archangel to be a helper, protector, and adviser.

Within the heart of Heaven, the Bright One chose the best of her archangels and referred to him as the covering angel who would reside eternally in Heaven's throne room, and she adorned him with light and precious gems, and he was perfect and beautiful to behold. He would be the seal of perfection, and his ministry would include the Bright One's gardens.

Then the Bright One created all the other worlds and called them Eden. Upon all of the Edens, the Bright One stored his knowledge. Some knowledge was hidden but would help life, some knowledge was secret but could hinder life, and some knowledge was forbidden and could create life. Then seeds were sown upon all of the gardens of Edens, and life grew, and these become the first ones, many Adams and many Eves made in the Bright One's chosen image. The Bright One then chose his guardian angels to watch over these worlds.

The Bright One then spoke to all the Adams and all the Eves and gave them a choice: some would stay, while others would break the rules and be banished. In this way, all the worlds would develop in various ways. If knowledge were taken or stolen, it would always come with a price. On the other hand, if knowledge were earned or discovered, this would be righteously gained.

Then the Bright One stopped and stared upon all the worlds, and she saw that they were good, but then he looked closer upon some of the Edens, and he saw that an aspect of his darkness had escaped into them. He realised that life in these worlds would always be a struggle of the virtuous versus the sinful. The Bright One then chose his avenging angels to carry out his judgments over the wicked.

Upon most of these worlds, the evil and sin that mankind committed could be cleansed through help from the ones that followed a virtuous path, and so on other worlds, where the evil was too much, it was washed away in great floods. However, some worlds became totally evil and corrupt, and the empire of Cain was born, so the Bright One called upon his angels of death to help in the coming battles. These worlds had developed quickly, and the knowledge they had been given gave them great power. It was realised that if the empire of Cain was not stopped, then the power of Heaven itself could be in danger.

Cain's empire swept through the galaxy, killing and destroying all in its way and wiping out all the Eden worlds he could find. It was only due to the enormity of the Bright One's galaxy that many were saved, but if left unchecked in time, no world would be safe from Cain's evil.

Archangel Michael, leading the Bright One's armies, pursued Cain's battle fleets across the stars of man and was successful at defeating many of his worlds. Finally, however, Cain discovered the first of Heaven's worlds and assaulted it with all the vehemence of hate itself, so the first great war in Heaven began, and the trumpets sounded all around.

Although Cain's main battle fleet was mighty, he could not destroy or hold on to any of the worlds but was successful in driving deeper into Heaven until the heart of Heaven was before Cain.

By the time the heart of Heaven was under attack, archangel Michael had arrived and cut off any possible route of escape, but Cain had no desire to retreat when his ultimate goal was within his grasp. But the Bright One then called upon Lucifer and poured forth his remaining darkness into him.

After many years, Cain breached the heart of Heaven and entered the throne room to claim it for himself; knowing that the Bright One would not be the hand that would cast him aside, he found Lucifer there instead. He stood tall and mighty, an angel dark and beautiful, deep in shadows but surrounded in a halo of light that emanated from all sides of his aura.

Although many of us were not present at this moment, it is said that they spoke to one another. But what was said was never passed on or recorded in the great book of history, and so the accounts of much of the first war in Heaven were lost and forgotten. However, they did battle and fought over Heaven, and they warred upon each other. It was said that this lasted seven days, and on the seventh day of battle, Cain was struck down and was thrown out of Heaven and cast into the eternal darkness.

However, Lucifer was injured. It was said that Cain's blade was covered with corruption and had been struck deep into Lucifer. The wound would heal, but his light started to fade, and in this time, Lucifer's pride in saving Heaven began to build, and his desires became greater. And so the council warned the Bright One, and Lucifer was banished to Eden to recover his humility, only to return once he had asked for forgiveness.

. . .

After the great floods and the great war were over, the Bright One said that she would not destroy man in this way again. And when she beheld the great tower constructed by the people of man and saw Cain's influence and understood what accomplishments could be achieved when man worked together, she realized nothing would be impossible to man, and so the Bright One chose to scatter man upon all the worlds in the hope that wisdom through struggle would win against the ever-present corruption of evil. Upon Cain's birthplace, his people continue to build a great tower upon their capital. The Bright One ensured that his remaining people could no longer understand Cains commands or his immortal generals.

Then, a few short years after the first war in Heaven ended, the dark angels sided with Lucifer's desire to rule in Heaven. His once-shining brilliance was now almost gone, just a glimmer of what it once was, but in its place, a dark radiance shone, and his beauty remained.

Speaking with silken words to his fellow angels, he explained that his rightful place was on the throne of Heaven. His might prevailed against the empire of Cain, and it was by his hand, not the Bright One's hand, that Cain had been cast into the eternal darkness. And as it was foretold by the council of Heaven, the second war in Heaven began. I, Samael, archangel of death, leader of two million angels, helped him strike at the heart of Heaven, and once more, the trumpets sounded with the sounds of war.

With each battle fought in Heaven, a similar battle was fought upon the Edens of the galaxy. Michael, the prince of light, and his angel fought Lucifer's dark angels in Heaven, and many angels were slaughtered on both sides. With each battle fought, some of them won and others lost, Lucifer's remaining light slowly died, regardless of the victories. Finally, upon the fifth battle, Lucifer's light was extinguished, and the former angel of the morning star whose dark radiance was now complete became Satan's servant and summoned into existence from his darkness the great dragon and cleared his way to the heart of Heaven.

It was clear upon the sixth battle that the angels of light were losing ground within Heaven, but the angels of light continued to fight valiantly, even at the cost of their lives. Their defiance against the darkness had become a heavy toll to bear, but their faith remained strong and unbending.

On the seventh battle, the Bright One gave unto Michael some of her light, and Michael became the bright and morning star, and he was loved like a son. Upon hearing this, the dark angels ceased their fight, surrendering to the light angels, and the war upon the Edens ended.

As Archangel Michael, the bright and morning star, battled with Lucifer even with his new divine grace, there were too many dark angels left to face battle. However, in the final moments, the angels of light were joined by angels from the Eden worlds, and with this, hope was recovered and victory taken from the jaws of defeat. Lucifer was cast down out of Heaven and into the great eternal darkness, and the great dragon escaped to Eden and was hidden.

It was then that the Bright One gave all of the dark angels and the few light angels that stood with us a choice: to be imprisoned for all of eternity or to become the fallen. The majority of us chose imprisonment but would not freely be imprisoned and attempted to flee. However, a few of our number chose the traitor's way out and fell from Heaven and became the fallen.

•   •   •

Even though Lucifer was imprisoned within the great and terrible eternal darkness at the centre of the galaxy, his darkness and negativity radiated out to all of the Eden worlds. The Bright One and her remaining angels did what they could, but slowly the influence of Lucifer somehow continued to manifest the darkest desires of the sons of man. Finally, with the help of the great dragon, Lucifers name lived on, and the dark desires of the sons of man were reflected back upon the worlds.

Having no other choice, the Bright One gave her last commands to her angels and entered the great eternal darkness to balance Lucifer's influence. In this way, the everlasting war of good and evil, light and dark, positivity and negativity would be in balance; however, the Bright One could never again walk among the sons of man after her great sacrifice.

The traitorous fallen then looked upon the daughters of Eve and had themselves wives, and by sinful fornication made the titans and other abominations that ravaged the Eden worlds, becoming false idols, making it their playground, and interfering with the development of the sons of man.

•   •   •

Only the sons of man referred to the eternal darkness as black holes, and even after hundreds of years of study, their true purpose was left undiscovered. Their true purpose was never fully realised until many hundreds of thousands of years after my imprisonment when a curious ship appeared from the stars and approached my prison. I have seen many ships pass by before; some even slowed and sent probes, but none of them of this size, and certainly none of them with so many humans aboard.

Curious now referring to the sons of men as humans. It is even more curious how they have developed in such a short time from primitive creatures that dug in the soil with basic tools to those who can design such machines that allow them to explore the mysteries of space. Fragile creatures, but it is continuously surprising how apelike in intelligence they still are.

I sensed then in the far distance the angels of light, watching the humans build their structures, and with some practice, I found I could reach out with my mind and explore the starships and listen to the squawks and shrieks of the people having what they called conversations. Why the Bright One chose these pathetic creatures over his angels, I'm not sure I'll ever understand.

Although their technology was close to Cain's, I could sense little to no corruption within them, and when they started to build some kind of station, I was a little disappointed to have so many dull innocents so close to me and spending years researching something they have no true concept of. But from their construction, I knew the time of my release was approaching.

Angels do not perceive linear time in the same way humans do. We live our lives at the moment within linear time. We see our beginning, end, and everything in between, all at once, every possibility that is open to us, our triumphs and our defeat, with no concept of when any of our future moments will occur or how any of it will come to pass.

My disappointment turned to glee when they started to bring in the condemned, the evil ones, and the ones marked with Cain's influence. The station was still too far from me to visit in person, but I could savour the sin within them from my imprisonment.

Then the humans started to build the second station, and this one was truly special in design; a leap in intelligence and purpose went into this one. Its structure would fit almost perfectly, and in time my suspicion was answered and found to be correct. Once it was close enough for me to visit, I knew this would be a means of my escape. How this would come to pass, I was not sure, at least not yet, but all the bits of my puzzled future—and also my possible death—were falling into place. I would face my fate here, so I must plan and play this game carefully.

The irony of a prison being built here did not escape me. Clever little humans after all, and I couldn't wait to meet the man behind this project.

. . .

I'm waiting for Alistair Brookes when he walks into the facility's dining hall, and I enjoy the look upon his face as I stand up. Manipulating him and some of his fellow workers so this would be possible was rather easy, and now I can sense all the tiny humans running about the command ship looking for him.

"It's such an honour to meet you, Professor. Welcome to Facility Zero," I say, noticing Professor Brookes looking shocked at the sight of someone else already here.

"I understand more time has passed than I realised, but who are you?" Professor Brookes replies, only taking a few steps into the room.

"I'm called Samael, but I would not worry about that. I've been waiting a very long time for you, Professor, and wanted to welcome you to your own prison," I say, motioning to the seat across from me.

"Please come join me. I have a few things to discuss with you," I say.

Professor Brookes hesitates for a second and then walk over to where I stand and sits down where I motioned. I smile, watching with interest as the professor slowly makes up his mind. I then turn to face Brookes and sit down as well.

"I'm going to just come out and say it all now. Best to start with an honest footing, I think. I'm Samael, greatest Archangel of death from creation, leader of over two million angels, and imprisoned here over ten thousand years ago when I sided with Lucifer to rule over Heaven and we were betrayed."

•   •   •

Brookes did not believe me initially, but it's always amusing how revealing my wings changes even the most stubborn. It's understandable, really, as the majority of the Eden worlds must have lost contact with the Bright One and her angels, and over time, many myths and stories were told, retold, written, and changed to suit the purpose of all those who wanted power over others. The inner worlds even lost their way a little. As far as I could tell, the angels still help govern there, but the original council of twenty-four are most likely dead.

I spoke to Brookes for several hours after finally getting him to be calm once he believed who I was, and he eventually answered all my questions. The facility is a truly impressive structure, and I suspect even the Bright One would have admitted the same.

At the end of our conversation, I removed his memories of our discussion and added a few new memories of my own and gave him new hope for escape. I could see a glimpse of my final escape from my imprisonment, and somehow Brookes was involved in this, so he must be protected.

Several weeks passed as the wicked and evil ones of human society were sent to the facility. Their crimes were not only against the sons of man but the Bright One as well. I could not stand by and watch the wicked go unpunished, and so my reaping of these humans began.

It quickly became apparent that instead of death, my judgment over these wicked changed them in other ways. First, they began to punish themselves, inflicting harm to their own bodies. Then, their minds started to inflict mental harm on their own identities until it drove them mad with guilt. Only my presence and guidance helped give them some semblance of peace, and with this, I could focus their madness into taking revenge on the sane.

Almost everyone else sent to this prison was guilty, but their sin had not fractured their humanity. Somehow their crimes against society were seen with forgiveness, and so I could not touch them unless they opened themselves to me by damning themselves. However, my freaks of nature would kill and eat anyone they could find. They became the terror that stalked within the darkness, a living nightmare of the prison, and they became my new army, my avenging angels.

· · ·

When the first rescue attempt was undertaken, I waited near the docking tube that runs down the prison's central core. This rescue was poorly planned and executed, and I knew that I would be needed. Dr Zorn certainly had a head full of wonderful ideas, and the knowledge he could tell me about this prison would be very useful to me, so saving his human life was worth the bile that formed in my mouth for helping any of the sons of man.

Unlike Professor Brookes, Dr Zorn had somehow discovered who I was. He had a unique insight into theology. He was wrong, of course, about almost everything, but it was nice to discuss his god. The Bright

One would never claim to be such, as there is more to the universe than can easily be explained; it's a living organism in itself, and if there is an all-powerful being, it would be what the universe is surrounded by.

With his knowledge and the help of two prisoners, Dr Zorn redesigned and modified a pod to enable me to escape. In return, I agreed to let him go; however, my fragmented knowledge of my future forced me to not allow Dr Zorn to leave level one. Furthermore, I knew that the advice he gave me to accelerate immediately was a feeble trick in an attempt to kill me.

I realized this had no chance of succeeding in the first place, but all these actions caused a chain reaction of events. If I had stayed, my confrontation with Jessica could have somehow resulted in my death, but if I had accelerated after exiting the gravity shield, Frank would have died if not for my intervention. If Frank had died, he would never have been able to save Dr Zorn's life later. Sometimes these fragmented moments of my future are easy to see, and other times they are obscured.

•   •   •

With the arrival of Jessica, all my hate and suspicions about the fallen were realized, and with all the minds I could now absorb, I saw the rise of the false gods that sprang up after the Bright One's sacrifice, would-be gods and so-called heroes that caused much destruction in their petty games, much like the Norse gods destroyed themselves in their own cosmic war that killed millions.

But somehow the descendants of these false gods survived to this day in the form of the Elioud, less wicked than the Nephilim that in part were the titans on some of the worlds, but nevertheless, many of the heroes of myth had their own flaws, and after thousands of years, here is an Elioud. That could only mean that there are worlds within the galaxy that require destruction, that need to be cleansed in fire. The sinful and wicked must be judged, and Jessica will be the signal to the others that their wickedness is at an end.

•   •   •

The good-time boys seemed to have stumbled onto my escape attempt, a slight annoyance to me, especially as they also threatened my possible way out of this place, which left me no alternative but to leave them bread crumbs to follow. Unfortunately for them, my trail led them to my avenging angels, who enjoyed showing them the errors of their ways.

Upon the destruction of my modified pod, I witnessed what seemed a glimpse of the Bright One's presence, and so I reached out to her, but then I was drawn back into my prison, and the Bright One became obscured by my darkness.

Everything then started to go to plan,... well, except that Jessica made a fool out of my favourite freaker. It is hardly surprising, really, considering what she is, but you can't show weakness to your flock, and you certainly do not show your hand until it's ready to strike. I see her death, as I've played this well so far, lying in her own pool of blood, but I see many deaths before the end, and the galaxy will remember.

Neil was a surprise, but the little human will be a great boon. I shall teach him well and prepare through him my gift. I'll ensure that the blade is given special treatment to ensure that its work will be complete.

• • •

With the arrival of our visitors, I sense an old enemy, Cain's corruption. My fragmented future did not see this coming, and I suspect in some way the son of man has discovered his prison or has escaped from it, but regardless of the details, this could not change my plans. Cain had eaten from the tree of life, so it is most likely that he is still alive, but in which form this may be, it is yet to be discovered.

With the death of my favourite avenging angel, I decided upon a replacement, and as Neil has a more important task, I must look elsewhere. The ideal candidate for this would have been changed previously when my freakers claimed level one for themselves, but unfortunately, he became one of the defenders and ironically was killed by my previous favourite. Most fitting, really, but death is a barrier to most but not to me.

With a little prompting, and as long as the body is whole and death is recent, the deceased can be made anew, for a short time at least. He will serve me well and will lead my avenging angels to rid the corruption from this facility. No more shall they hide in the darkness, but they shall come out and fight the sinful wherever they might be and cleanse them from this place.

• • •

The last to surprise me was Sam McCall's summons; he finally understood or was told about who I am. It also surprised me how his mind seemed to repair itself by restoring the segments of his memories that I deleted after one of our long chats. An interesting individual, constantly dancing on the edge of authority, but with an irritating moral compass that helps keep him within the light, preventing a crack from forming and allowing the darkness inside.

With that in mind, I'm shocked that he wasn't sent to a place like this or killed long ago, but somehow, he survived—mostly, I'm guessing, because rich and powerful men desired his abilities.

However, this time, he had the nerve to invoke my name, but only to save him and his friends. Therefore, I decided to answer, but only because I still have need of him, but this need will not last much longer—that I can sense in my future.

Two paths come from this point: one that will lead to Jessica's death, and the other that will lead to mine. How close this is, again, I cannot be sure.

It is not long after my arrival that the spawn of the fallen speaks, and her words bring all of the hate in me back to the forefront, ending any possibility that I might have been willing to give help. Revealing to all my true self, which I had not done since my imprisonment of over ten thousand years previously, I emanated fire and fear that I poured into the hearts of the wicked, and I knew then that it would be my hand that would send Jessica from this place.

The sound of my angels fleering only momentarily distracted my wrath, but with my sword raised and ready to strike, I poured out my rage, and then with burning fire, I felt my body consumed. The last thing I saw as my body burned was the focus of my hate running from the room, my fragmented future, revealing yet another unseen possibility, with fire and heat and then replaced by darkness.

16
Deadly Confrontation

Facility Zero, 272 days online: federation year 2435
AS THE SPORES enter's Sam Mc'Calls mouth and nose, the reaction to them is immediate, uncontrollable coughing as his body tries to expel the irritating invader but to no use. The last thing he sees as he hits the floor is Frank's back as Frank pulls the unconscious Jessica from the room and is grateful that they got away. Then Sam senses someone kneeling down at his side—help, maybe, but that hope is soon dashed as Dr Moore begins to speak.

"Don't worry too much, Sam. Soon it will all be over,

Who you are and who you were will be gone, and a little while after that, you will help us kill your friends," Dr Moore says and smiles.

Standings up, Dr Moore or the man that used to be Dr Moore moves away, checking on his other victims, leaving Sam coughing on the floor. For some reason, Dr Moore's words do not affect Sam in the way Dr Moore had hoped; Sam felt no fear at all, but slowly as time passes, his mind fades, his body still having the occasional spasm as it tries to fight off the infection.

Sam clings on to the last segments of himself, knowing that he had failed his friends when they had depended on him the most. Then it starts to happen. His consciousness begins to melt away. What made Sam who he was, fades to nothing. Then, at last, his body accepts the spores, and his breathing becomes easier.

Time passes, but how much time the new inhabitant is not sure, and then he hears the voices of the others, his people, and friends. There are millions of us, but only a few who inhabit bodies such as Sam. Claiming this new form, as the previous owner is dead. The new consciousness opens his eyes and sees Dr Moore reaching down with a hand and smiling. The man that used to be Sam takes it and stand up.

"Let's go kill your old friends," Dr Moore says.

"Yes, I think that is a good idea," the new inhabitant of Sam's body replies.

.   .   .

Once out of the room, Frank stops. Reaching down with his one good hand, he drags Jessica up and onto his shoulder; using the stump of his other arm, he keeps her there as he asks for a route to security. The system takes longer than usual to accept his request, but then a corridor opens up, and he runs as fast as he dares, cursing most of the way.

Frank enters security in a rush as the elevator arrives, and Brookes looks up from behind a control panel, looking concerned.

"What happened to Jessica and where Sam? For that matter, where are the others?" Professor Brookes asks.

Frank, looking scared, replies in a frantic voice.

"Jessica, well, Jessica was stabbed, and...," Frank hesitates and then continues.

"Sam's dead. He got infected by Dr Moore, and I've not seen Neil, but he is most likely infected or dead at this rate, oh and Jake's also gone. They're all gone!" Frank replies, trying to find a good spot for Jessica.

Dr Zorn, hearing the sudden commotion, appears from the ceiling, climbing down the ladder placed there for the breaching pod and seeing Jessica in a bad way.

"Here, let me look at her," Dr Zorn says as he helps Frank lower Jessica to a suggested spot upon a table and starts examining her.

"I'm afraid that our situation is becoming worse; I've been looking through the various security feeds and monitoring fights all over the facility between freakers and infected prisoners. But, unfortunately, the feeds for medical have been turned off or blocked in some way—most likely destroyed," Professor Brookes says, as Brookes changes to another feed, displaying a large man smash two prisoners' heads together with glee.

On another feed, they watch as freakers who had been coughing on the floor after what seems like a recent blast of spores stand up and start attacking each other.

"It's hell out there, and it's only a matter of time before our uninvited guests decide to leave. We need to get going," Professor Brookes says, turning away from the death and hate unfolding within his facility.

"I couldn't agree with you more, Prof," Frank replies, looking anxious.

"Jessica is in a bad way and needs immediate medical attention. She has two, maybe three hours, but I can't be totally sure. But that's the least of our troubles. The breaching pod was designed to extract just one. I'm guessing the rest of the team are expendable, so we will need to modify and recalibrate the engines if we all want to get out of here. This will take at least an hour," Doctor Zorn says, looking grim.

"Do what you can, Doctor. We will just have to make her comfortable and wait," Professor Brookes says as Frank sinks into a chair and starts kicking the desk.

•   •   •

With the danger of the infected cruiser now gone, the cryostation sends out their patrol ships once more; although they avoid the sector of space they last detected weapon fire from the mysterious stealth ship

Phantom Sam is happy with that and continues to monitor and scan the facility; while she runs simulation after simulation in an attempt to find a way to rescue Sam and the others, *Phantom* Sam detects a sudden increase in stress levels from Sam within the facility, *Phantom* pauses the simulation and tries to search for the cause. This doesn't take long, as an unknown organic pathogen is detected within Sam's body. It seems incredibly virulent and fast working.

One of Sam's biological nanites is directed to take samples and carry out tests, but this results in the biological nanite being destroyed. With the host body becoming increasingly hostile, the bionanites are instructed to start multiplying. In this kind of war, victory will go to the one with the most soldiers.

With millions of single-strand DNA files on record, it's soon discovered that this pathogen is unlike anything that *Phantom* Sam has ever encountered before. Its own reproductive ability is nothing less than spectacular. The first priority is to analyse and map as much of the DNA strand as possible. Once that is completed, then this new threat might be neutralised.

Studying the pathogen at this early stage of infection is a valuable moment, and seeing what it does first and how it takes over the host body will lead to questions being answered. Watching Sam's infection proceed is fascinating. Fear seems to be a factor, as adrenaline appears to boost its infection rate.

Initial contact with the host causes severe irritation, which causes coughing spasms; this raises the victim's stress levels, which in turn raises the victim's adrenaline, which increases the rate of infection. As the pathogen multiplies, it starts to attack the nervous system to reduce the victim's mobility, and then it attacks the areas of the brain that contain personality—the frontal and prefrontal lobes.

As the pathogen advances through its various infection stages, slime mould begins to grow inside and outside the body. The result increases synaptic activity that restarts the nervous system; however, the infection has taken control of much of the brain and is causing sleep paralysis. At this time, neuron activity spikes, and some kind of communication is established as the frontal and prefrontal lobes are restructured, and a new consciousness takes over.

Once the infection has gained this amount of control, other genetic changes start. Spore sacks begin to form within the throat to help with capturing other victims to transform.

As we knew him, Sam is effectively gone; this transition would be irreversible for most organic life. But most organic life does not have a symbiotic relationship with a highly advanced artificial neural matrix, whose primary function is to visit new and developing worlds and alter the genetic development of the indigenous life form living there.

In some ways, there are interesting parallels between this slime mould and *Phantom* Sam's primary function.

They are both designed to change an organism to suit their higher-structured hierarchy; for now, all that *Phantom Sam* can do is salvage fragments of Sams original consciousness, analyse and study this new virulent enemy.

•   •   •

Dr Moore re-enters the examination room accompanied by the Captain of the extraction team after completing his other infected checks. Only one fatality during the conversion process is a good result.

With Sam McCall, having been converted completes the captain's primary mission, all that is left is to extract him, which is the secondary objective; this became increasingly complicated when the rest of his team are killed going after Sam the others. During this setback, he also loses control of security; in turn, this means access to their breaching pod.

Walking over to man, which was formally Sam McCall, the captain salutes.

"It's good to see you, Colonel. I thought it was going to be at least a few weeks before you were recovered from the black hole," Captain Elkins says.

The Colonel looks up as the captain salutes. His body is weaker than he had hoped, but in the circumstances, he knows it will do for now. However, this he can handle; Captain Elkin annoys him, along with using these Federation ranks.

"You of all people should understand more about black hole and time dilations, being trapped in one yourself for tens of thousand years. Now report, Elkins, before I decide to have your body reassigned to someone I actually like," The Colonel replies.

Captain Elkin looks toward Dr Moore, hoping he will have some support there, but one glance says it all: Colonel Mendel has never liked him, for whatever reason.

"We breached the facility as per the command and proceeded to convert the prisoners held here. We then discovered where Sam McCall was hiding and assaulted his location. However, we then discovered that an Angel is imprisoned here, and some of his servants are highly resistant to the spores. It was then that we ran into strong resistance, and I took on casualties with my team," Elkin's replies.

Colonel Mendel stands while he listens to the captain's report. His new body did not resist like most of the rest, but for some reason, it resisted in other ways. His muscles seem stiff, so stretching and walking around the room does little to help, but it's the captain's report that worries him more.

"Do you know this angel's name?" Colonel Mendel Asks. Captain Elkin is about to reply, knowing that the colonel won't like his answer, but it's Dr Moore who responds first.

"I think the others were talking about him. They referred to him as Samuel or Samael," Dr Moore answers.

Colonel Mendel stops walking and turns to face the doctor, nods, and then turns his attention to the captain, whose own expression now looks tense.

"That's is not an Angel," Colonel Mendel says.

"Samael is an Archangel of Death. He has been known as or referred to as an Avenging Angel, but he's like me somehow. He was a leader of millions, but it would seem he has also fallen from grace, and so, Captain, you are forgiven," Colonel Mendel replies. Then, turning back to Dr Moore, Colonel Mendel contemplates for a moment.

"Who was the woman that was brought in injured? I have memories of her as being a formidable warrior," Colonel Mendel asks. Dr Moore relaxes a little, feeling more confident.

"Oh, she was called Jessica, but her friends refer to her as Abs, due to her... well, that's irrelevant, I guess. Anyway, she received a severe wound, and without immediate medical attention and surgery, she will not last more than a few hours, and in no way is she able to fight," Dr Moore replies. Colonel Mendel takes this on board.

"Captain Elkin, what is the status of security? Can we override the facility's system and regain security?" Colonel Mendel asks.

"Well, we did, but the tech that had the device was overseeing a conversion process of over fifty prisoners. We lost contact with them a few hours ago. Last seen within one of the dining halls," Captain Elkin says, looking nervous as he reports this fact.

Mendel's annoyance returning upon hearing this news, but he manages to calm himself enough to hold out a hand.

"Gun?" Colonel Mendel asks.

Elkin unclips his side arm's belt and hands it across to the colonel.

"It's fully charged, sir," Captian Elkins says, looking uncertain.

• • •

Due to the lack of the appropriate tools, the modifications take longer than Dr Zorn would have liked, but with the final override adjusted and the engines tuned perfectly for the four of them are ready, it's now or never. With the facility on the verge of dropping closer, the time for escape is now or not at all. A shout from below brings Dr Zorn back to the present, and he climbs out of the pod and heads back down into security. Professor Brookes looks up from his terminal.

"Didn't you hear me? I said I've just seen Sam. He's still alive!" Professor Brookes says. Dr Zorn descends the ladder and faces the professor.

"I thought Frank said he'd been infected?" Dr Zorn replies. Frank stands up and walks over to see, hearing his name mentioned.

"He might as well be dead. He's been infected like Jake, and if he's anything like Jake, he will either infect us too or kill us, neither of which I fancy happening," Frank says.

"Surely there is something we can do for him?" Professor Brooke Says. Zorn stops at the terminal and watches the screen for a few seconds before adding,

"Well, maybe the professor is right; there must be something we can do?" Dr Zorn asks. Professor Brookes gives a look of appreciation.

"So, what about it, Frank? Let's go rescue him?" Professor Brookes says. Frank looks horrified at the suggestion.

"You're both nuts. We are three little fish in a tank full of predators. Neither side is friendly; besides, no Abs, no chance," Frank replies, then stares at the monitor, trying to work out what's going on. The main dining hall is full of bodies.

Which side the casualties belong to is unclear, but Dr Moore is leaning down and checking each one of them. Then, as he's checking a rather large man, he moves suddenly, plunging a crude blade up and into the doctor's face, which erupts with deadly spores rather than blood as his skull is split open.

"Oh crap," Frank mutters as he watches the scene and Jimmy the Fist begins to choke.

. . .

Upon entering the dining hall, which now resembles a scene out of some kind of war movie, Colonel Mendel orders the other two to search for the security override while he watches from a position of safety as a wave of nausea comes over him. But shortly after Dr Moore starts to examine the dead, a sudden commotion breaks out as a cloud of spores erupts from Doctor Moore's head.

A giant of a man emerges coughing, but somehow, he recovers and charges at Colonel Mendel as more freakers around them appear from under the dead and stand with wicked grins and crude weapons. Mendel, taken by surprise by this sudden attack, is shocked as this big man bundles into him.

"Hey there, Sammy, You should have known that you are still useful, especially now you don't have your pet attack dog by your side," Jimmy the Fist says.

Captain Elkin raises his assault weapon and calmly picks off two of the closest freakers. Then he turns it toward Jimmy.

"Now, let's not be rash. Let the colonel go, and I'll let you live," Captian Elkins asks. Jimmy has responded by wrapping his big arms around Colonel Mendel, using him as a shield, and slowly starts to back up, calling for an exit.

"Don't worry, Sammy, I'm sure he won't kill you to get to me. Isn't that right? You don't want to kill Sammy here, now do you?" Jimmy asks, tauting Elikns.

Colonel Mendel just relaxes and allows Jimmy to take control, knowing that Captain Elkin is a good soldier even with all his faults. If it weren't for the sudden bout of nausea as Jimmy rushed him, he would have killed Jimmy himself.

Captain Elkin keeps his weapon up and steadily scans the room as the other freakers move in from the sides to stand with Jimmy. Elkin then notices the security override device over Jimmy's shoulder. This is not what he had expected. Most of these creatures had been exposed but somehow resisted and now are preparing to rush the Captain.

However, what happens next is expected, as the freakers all rush at the same time at Captain Elkins, and Jimmy taking this as the best moment, tries to escape, rushing for the exit.

Captain Elkin calmly squeezes off a suppressed burst of fire along the left-hand set of freakers, the closest one, killing at least three of his enemy and forcing the others to duck and slow their attack and also causing them to bunch to the right. Then, resting his weapon, he removes a thermite grenade and rolls it toward the right side of the room.

Bringing up his weapon once more, he fires off another short burst of death, killing two more almost at point-blank range and a third with a rifle butt to the face, followed by two shots into its chest as the freaker tumbles backwards. A flash of heat signals that his grenade has just killed about four more: the rest of the freakers stop their attack, waiting and watching for an opening as Elkin, now in a slow run, heads for the corridor Jimmy has just taken.

Entering the corridor, Elkin watches as Colonel Mendel throws up with Jimmy half pulling him along by his collar while shouting his dismay for speed. Jimmy looks up in horror as Elkin appears, dropping Mendel; he tries to run.

Captain Elkin fires twice, and Jimmy the Fist dies for a second time.

Slinging his rifle over his shoulder, Elkin places a laser trip mine by the door, noticing that the freakers are building up for another assault and moves down the corridor toward the colonel.

"Are you okay, sir?" he asks, lending a hand to the colonel.

"Yeah, I'm okay. For some reason, I felt sick all of a sudden," Colonel Mendel replies. He spits the taste out and wipes his mouth clean, and then takes Elkin's hand, standing up.

Captain Elkin then walks over to Jimmy's body and retrieves the security override device. He checks its condition and turns to Colonel Mendel.

"The override looks good. I think we should get a move on before the rest of the freakers decide that they do have balls," Captain Elkins says. Spitting again, Mendel nods and joins Elkin as they head off down the corridor.

• • •

Phantom Sam's bio-nanites hit a breakthrough on the analysis of the spores' DNA, but at that same moment, the spores themselves realise the threat, and the war for Sam McCall's body starts in earnest. Like most fights within the human body, when the antibodies start to fight off an infection or virus of some kind, the body suffers, and in this case, it's pretty much similar. With Sam now puking his guts up, the excess spores are purged, and the pathogen immediately goes on the defensive.

With the spores analysed, the true enemy is revealed. There are a million slime mould species, and the majority of them are pretty much harmless, but the common factor in most of them is that they grow fast and exhibit rudimentary intelligence. However, this particular slime mould shows apparent signs of manipulation; it's been altered artificially over a very long time.

With Sam's body now flooded with bionanites, it's now only a matter of time before the pathogen's controller notices this new threat.

•   •   •

Professor Brookes enters a series of commands into the primary system after watching the outcome below, ensuring that all elevators are disabled and as many subsystems as possible are locked down. Having no idea what the uninvited guests are planning now to get back into security seemed a reasonable precaution, and not wanting to take any chances. Once all the systems have been locked down, professor Brookes isolates all the power conduits on each floor, limiting the available power.

"I think that should hold them. How much longer do you need, Doctor?" Professor Brookes asks. Dr Zorn, having re-entered the breaching pod for final checks.

"Ten minutes, I guess. Just need to make an adjustment. Losing level one helped a little, and I hardly felt any vibration whatsoever when it was jettisoned, but maybe you should have warned me earlier. I might have been able to save us some time," Dr Zorn replies. Professor Brookes turns away from his terminal to where Jessica is lying.

"Yeah, sorry about that, Doctor, I forgot about it in all the excitement. Hey, Frank, can you help me get Jessica up into the pod?" Professor Brookes asks. Frank, being the last to look away from the screen, looks up at the professor.

"Sure, Prof, but I'm guessing it will take all three of us unless there is any rope up there in the pod," Frank replies. Hearing this, Dr Zorn shouts back down.

"I think I saw some in the emergency survival pack. Hang on. I'll go and check."

Moments later, a coil of rope drops down from the breaching pod. Professor Brooke then ties one end of the rope around Jessica's chest and under her arms; Frank ascends the ladder, using his stump and his good hand to slowly climb up until he reaches the pod, Dr Zorn helping him the rest of the way. Together they heave Jessica up to the ceiling and into the breaching pod.

As Jessica's legs vanish through the hole, the lights begin to flicker as security alerts flash on the terminals. Startled, Professor Brookes accesses his terminal and cancels the alert.

Bringing up the alert status and carries out a full systems check. Then, a sudden lurch sends the professor flying across the room as more warning alarms sound, followed by the security system announcement.

"System breach detected. The first stabilisation beam has been deactivated. You have thirty seconds to cease your actions," The systems security system warns.

Hearing this, Brookes picks himself up and rushes back to the terminal. He continues to type and read the replies.

"It's Sam and his guests. They have some kind of override hacking tech that's tripping the facility's fail-safe. If they do not stop, or if we do not let them in, this facility will be dropped into the black hole," Professor Brookes explains.

Another lurch as a second beam is deactivated, and the facility drops once more, but this time the professor is ready for it and holds on.

"Cease your actions. Otherwise, the facility will be released in sixty seconds. This is your final warning," The systems security system warns.

Brookes is still frantically entering counter commands to the security system as an audible countdown begins at forty seconds, but with every command entered, he gets a 'system denied' message. With only fifteen seconds remaining, Brookes does the only thing left open to him: he surrenders access to the hack.

With the counter still ticking down, the security alert deactivates at four seconds, and the two deactivated stabilisation arms are reactivated. Just seconds after that, the elevator arrives with Sam and another man.

"Wise choice, but I'm afraid that your usefulness to this facility is now at an end," Captain Elkin says as he steps out of the elevator, raising his rifle, aiming it at the professor.

Professor Brookes, now looking resigned to his fate, closes his eyes. Colonel Mendel watches as Captain Elkin takes aim. Then, drawing his own gun, he aims and fires a single shot. This is followed by another shot fired by Captain Elkin as Professor Brookes flinch.

· · ·

Colonel Mendel does not understand what is happening to him. His body feels like it is on fire. He's already vomited, but the sickness within him is increasing, not getting better. He dares not show weakness to Captain Elkin, who would use this chance to advance his rank. Instead, he hides his symptoms the best he can and follows the captain down the corridor as Elkin attempts to hack the system.

The facility's first lurch throws them both to the ground as the system announcement sounds: "System breach detected. The primary stabilisation beam has been deactivated. You have thirty seconds to cease your actions."

"What was that?" Colonel Mendel asks as he stands back up.

"It's some kind of countermeasures in case someone tries to take over the system," replies Captain Elkin. Mendel feels his guts churn and tries to hide his discomfort.

"Well, keep going. I understand that this technology can rip through any security system," Colonel Mendel says.

Nodding, Elkin enters another set of commands, and the system replies with another lurch, sending Mendel flying, his head impacting the floor with a dull thud. Elkin retains his balance as another message sounds.

"Cease your actions. Otherwise, the facility will be released in sixty seconds. This is your final warning."

Elkin frantically continues entering commands, but the system remains closed. Someone else, it would seem, is attempting to counter his commands, and the facility system is fighting both parties attempts with swift repercussions. There just isn't enough time, and the system would rather kill everyone than fail.

As time counts down, the elevator arrives as the system restraints become unlocked. Elkin then realises that someone must have released the elevators, but his hacking device is still in a struggle with the system's security. Deactivating the device, Elkin turns, noticing Colonel Mendel sprawled on the floor. Helping him stand, they both enter the elevator and ascend to security.

. . .

Even though Mendel knew it was likely that the system would lurch again when it did, he was far too weak to prevent himself from being thrown, and this time it was much worse. As soon as his head connected with the hard floor, Mendel is knocked unconscious.

Opening his eyes, Mendel is confused to find himself in some kind of cell. A woman is staring at him from across this small space.

"I demand you tell me what is going on here!" Mendel demands in his most commanding voice. The unknown woman smiles.

"It's odd, is it not? Your spores are the most genius form of mind transference I have ever encountered, but then again, I'm not all that old. My system can also transfer and even copy consciousness, but the range is limited, but somehow your spores allow for transference over greater distances," *Phantom* Sam says.

Staring at this unknown women as she talks, Mendel looks around the cell.

"Who are you, and where have you taken me?" Colonel Mendel asks. Trying a calmer approach. The Woman smiles again.

"I'm Sam McCall, well to be precise, I'm the Prototype that Sam McCall stole, which you have been looking for, and I must say, your spore technology is impressive.

I do not fully understand it or how the transference works yet, but I now understand how to kill and produce the spores. As for you, I now understand how to contain your consciousness, but unlike how you treat your victims, I'm not going to torture you first. Good-bye, Colonel," *Phantom* Sam replies.

Colonel Mendel's rage boils as Phantom Sam speaks. Unable to contain his anger any longer, he explodes in a tirade of threats and insults as he flings himself at the Woman; however, this outburst does not last long. Mendel stops suddenly as he feels parts of his consciousness slowly erased as the millions of tiny bio-nanites within him start to remove every aspect of his personality from Sam McCall's mind, leaving within seconds just an empty shell.

• • •

The interaction with Mendel talking less than a few seconds, *Phantom* Sam watches as Elkin deactivates some kind of device. Elkin then helps Sam to stand as the elevator arrives. *Phantom* Sam has never walked in the real world before, and she felt slightly unsteady on her feet and follows Elkin into the elevator, finding this experience fascinating. But she is unprepared when the elevator arrives at the security level, and Captain Elkin steps out, talking to Professor Brookes and raising his rifle toward him.

Phantom Sam draws her own gun, aims it, and fires a single shot into the back of Captain Elkin's neck, severing his cervical spine. Unfortunately, this action is just a moment too late, as Elkin still manages to fire off a shot as he dies. *Phantom* Sam stands there perplexed, staring at the gun within her grasp as Elkin and the professor drop to the floor. It should not have been possible for her to take the life of another, but somehow, she was able to.

Frank's voice shouting from somewhere above brings *Phantom* Sam back to herself.

"It's okay, Frank. It's Sam, but I think the professor has been shot," *Phantom* Sam says.

"You keep away from us! Professor, get up. We are leaving. Doc, get ready; we're getting out of here," Frank calls out.

Phantom Sam steps out of the elevator, notices that Elkin had collapsed to his knees and then fell forward as he died. His deadly spores had not been released. Looking toward the professor, she sees Brookes also splayed out on the floor, but moans of pain are coming from him. He is alive, for now at least. Then another voice is heard replying to Frank.

"It's useless now. The facility has been dropped far too close to the black hole for any possible successful attempt to escape," Dr Zorn replies to Franks pleas.

Crouching down by Brookes's side, *Phantom* Sam examines the damage done and is relieved at the sight of the professor's wounded left shoulder. There's an ugly hole where the projectile shattered the shoulder and passed through. It will hurt like a bitch, but with treatment, the professor should survive.

Reaching out, *Phantom* Sam touches the open wound, producing another spike of pain from the professor, whose eyes open in shock and horror as he stares up at Sam, at the face still encrusted with the powdery remains of the mould.

"Get away from me!" he yells and attempts to squirm away. This outcry produces another shout from above as Frank, becoming even more enraged, appears on the ladder and starts to climb down, threatening violence toward Sam.

"You get away from him, you fecking monster!" Frank calls out, reaching the floor and turning on Phantom Sam, his overall size impressive. *Phantom* Sam stands, taking a step back as both men shouts.

"Will you both calm down? It's Sam, well, it's not me exactly, but—" *Phantom* Sam tries to explain. Frank cuts him off with another shout.

"Ah, so you admit it. You! Whatever you are, get away from the prof before I put my remaining fist through your fricking head," Frank threatens.

Phantom Sam, putting up her hands in an attempt at a calming, passive gesture, tries to calm the big guy down; even with one hand, he still looks extremely dangerous.

"Okay. I was infected, but I've resisted the infection. It's me again. I even killed Elkin before he killed the professor," *Phantom* sam explains; reaching up, *Phantom* Sam starts to clear the remains of the mould from her face.

Professor Brookes sudden cry of extreme pain sends Frank into action as he charges at Sam, his fist aiming true to his word at Sam's head, but Phantom ducks away at the last moment. Frank is fast for a big guy, and each successive swing gets closer as the available space is slowly reduced until *Phantom* Sam is backed into a wall with little space to manoeuvre.

With a final push from Frank, Sam is pressed up against the wall by Frank's stump while his good hand is bunched into a tight fist and is about to send Phantom Sam from this world and a sudden shout from the professor stops Frank in mid punch.

The sheer anger behind Frank's personal desire to end Sam's life is turned into a shaking fist when he hears the professor's shout to stop.

"But, Professor, they are evil—he is evil," Frank responds as his fist is drawn back once more to end *Phantom* Sam's life.

Movement behind Frank makes him jump as Professor Brookes reaches out with his arm, gently placing it down upon his shoulder.

"It's okay, Frank. Sam healed me somehow, and I'm still me!" Professor Brookes says gently and reassuringly.

Frank, still on edge and mindful of Sam, turns his head and stares, confused, at the professor's once-ruined shoulder. His shirt is still torn and bloodied, but his wound has vanished.

"How?" Frank asks, astonished at the now-closed and healed wound.

Phantom Sam, now moving very consciously, moves to Professor Brookes's side, smiles calmly.

"It's a little complicated," *Phantom* Sam begins to say as Sam's words make both the professor and Frank smile, and Frank, all of a sudden, grabs Sam and gives him a friendly hug and shake.

"Good to have you back, mate," Frank says, his size seemingly becoming smaller as he embraces Sam. Dr Zorn's somewhat grumpy voice from above makes everyone turn.

"Once you have finished making up, I think you need to see what trouble we are all in now ."

• • •

Phantom Sam climbs up the ladder into the breaching pod, with Professor Brookes behind and Frank following last. The pod's interior, designed for a six-man team plus gear, seems larger than what Phantom expected. Dr Zorn is waiting patiently to reveal the shocking information his current expression is trying to conceal. Phantom Sam already knows what this is and is trying desperately to come up with an answer to resolve this problem. When everyone is seated, Dr Zorn begins to explain.

"So, as we are all aware, we had a limited window of escape. This window closed as soon as our numbers increased from four to five. Although there was still a small chance to make it out, this was reduced to no chance when you calculate the security breach attempt that almost sent this facility hurtling down into the black hole.

These are the current facts: This breaching pod no longer has enough power to break away from the black hole. Second, Jessica needs immediate attention; otherwise, she will die. And lastly, the fight between the freakers and the infected will threaten our very existence. Finally, this facility requires prisoners to run various systems; otherwise, we will run out of water and air; this is currently not being carried out," Dr Zorn explains. Before Dr Zorn can continue, Phantom Sam interrupts.

"It's grim, but I know how we can overcome the extra mass that we need to pull away from the black hole. However, this will take time," *Phantom* sam explains. Now it's Dr Zorn who interrupts.

"That sounds great, but Jessica does not have much time left. With her current condition, I would say an hour, maybe a little more. Either way, whatever you have in mind, Jessica is not going to make it," Dr Zorn replies.

In all the excitement, Phantom somehow forgot about Jessica. Taking a look at Sam's memories, *Phantom* Sam soon discovers what had occurred from the real Sam's experiences before he became infected.

"I'm sorry, I forgot. As I tried to explain earlier, I am not the real Sam," *Phantom* Sam says.

This new piece of information causes both Professor Brookes and Dr Zorn to look confused. However, it's Frank who seems to explode again in anger.

"What have you done with Sam? You are infected!" Frank shouts, looking ready for a fight once more. *Phantom* Sam stands up in protest, almost banging his head.

"Frank, will you just listen for one moment? I am not infected. As I mentioned several times before, it is complex, but I can explain," *Phantom* Sam tries to explain. This time it's Zorn and Brookes who come to Sam's defence and calm Frank down.

"Hear him out, Frank. We already knew he had stolen something pretty advanced. I think we should at least give him the chance to explain himself; besides, if you don't like the answers, then you can hurt him," Brookes says with a smile. Sam looks toward both Zorn and Brookes with a grateful expression.

"Thank you, Professor Brookes. I'll try to explain as quickly and as easily as I can. The real Sam stole a prototype, a first-strike bio-genetics interstellar warship with a state-of-the-art artificial computer system that integrated the real Sam's consciousness and memories into its computer matrix. This resulted from the ship becoming totally conscious and self-aware like no other artificial intelligence has ever been done before. In essence, I became Sam McCall," Phantom Sam explains, while Professor Brookes and Dr Zorn stare at Sam with astonishment. Frank still looks confused but is silent. Seeing this as a good sign, Sam continues.

"The computer matrix allows me to talk telepathically with the real Sam. When Sam was infected, the infection quickly overcame his body's natural defences and erased most of his consciousness.

The real Sam already had many of my bionanites within his system and alerted me to this invasive infection. Over time, I could reverse much of the damage and cleansed

Sam's body of the infection, but I only have fragments of Sam's consciousness. In the meantime, I have taken control of his body, and here we are now," *Phantom* Sam Says, looking from Zorn to Brookes, then to Frank.

Frank, still looking confused, seems to be trying to understand what was just said. Dr Zorn's astonishment changes to a smile, and Brookes replies first.

"You used your bio-nanites to heal my shoulder. Can you use your nanites to cure everyone else of the infection?" Professor Brookes asks; Phantom Sam realizing where this question is leading is already prepared.

"I did heal your shoulder, Professor, but sadly, although I could rid the infection from all of the victims over time, I could not recover their true consciousness. In effect, they would be infection-free but empty of their previous consciousness and personalities; they would become mindless zombies, with just the brain's basic instincts, but this would also take time, and my plan also has a small window for our chance of escape. First, let me take a look at Jessica, and then I'll explain my plan," *Phantom* Sam replies.

The others all nod their approval, and Sam moves over to where Jessica has been strapped in. The chair has been reclined as far as possible, and a makeshift bandage has been applied to her wound. Slipping a finger underneath Jessica's bandage, Sam closes his eyes for a few seconds before removing it. The others watch expectantly as Sam, now looking concerned, returns to his chair.

"It's not good, I'm afraid. As I already suspected, Jessica has military-grade nanites protecting her body, but she has a very nasty blood infection that is somehow slowly killing off her nanites, but it's these nanites that are currently helping in keeping her alive. Unfortunately, however, they are losing," Phantom Sam explains.

"Can your bio-nanites help?" asks Dr Zorn.

"I would say yes, but she is in no way out of the woods yet. My nanites have boosted her body's immune system; however, her nanites will consider mine a threat in time, which will, in all probability, result in Jessica losing the rest of her nanites. At that point, my nanites will take over complete care; for a while, she might even look worse," Phantom Sam says.

"Won't that be a backward step?" Professor Brookes asks.

"On the contrary, my nanites are rather more advanced than her military ones, and in the long term, they will help her body become immune to many deadly infections and recover from the most severe of injuries. Nevertheless, her current infection is not listed on any of my medical databases, and I'm not sure how but the blade that is still inside her is somehow adapting to her body's defences," *Phantom* Sam says, looking serious.

"How can a blade fashioned here become so deadly to Jessica? She seemed almost unstoppable," Dr Zorn asks, looking concerned.

"I'm not entirely sure, Doctor, but while it remains in her, Jessica will not recover, and even my nanites will not save her in the end. At the very best, all I have given Jessica is a few more hours," *Phantom* Sam replies.

"If we can get her medical help, maybe she will pull through. I know you were against it before, but you must consider Facility One as being her best option," Professor Brookes says with more emotion than he would have liked. His own desires to find his wife and family still weigh heavily on his mind.

"It was the other Sam that desired to leave here and not visit Facility One, Professor. However, I think that he would relent in this case," *Phantom* Sam replies. The professor breathes out with a great sigh of relief upon hearing Sam's response.

"Can you do anything for Sam's mind?" Professor Brookes asks.

"Normally, this would be impossible unless you lived within the Inner Federation, where a citizen's consciousness is automatically transferred to a special storage matrix upon death. This is also done for special individuals selected from the outer worlds. However, in Sam's case, although his mind has partially destroyed from the infection, the black hole's influence would have prevented any outward transference in any case, but I am Sam, and I contain a complete copy of his consciousness, and as such, I can reverse the damage, but it will take time," *Phantom* Sam replies. Both Dr Zorn and Professor Brookes looking a little confused by Sam's words.

"What does that mean? Can you help him?" Professor Brookes asks.

"I have already prepared a soul matrix to contain his consciousness. All I need to do is reconstruct his consciousness from the fragments and my own matrix, and once that is complete, I'll transfer him back to his body. Transference of consciousness is extremely easy, but to copy one is another matter; lucky for us, I won't have to make a complete copy," *Phantom* Sam explains. Dr Zorn looking thoughtful.

"How much time?" Dr Zorn asks.

"Well, copying from an organic mind takes longer because they are unhappy to remain still for very long periods of time, but in this case, maybe only five years," Phantom Sam replies.

"That sounds like a very long time; even if you're willing to wait that long, when can you begin?" Professor Brookes asks.

"That, Professor, I have already started, although now we have a bigger problem of getting us the hell out of here, otherwise saving Sam's mind will be a moot point," *Phantom* Sam says. Dr Zorn listening, having already prepared the pod to the best of his knowledge.

"I have carried out as much modification to reduce the mass for the pod and to increase the engines from here, but as I have already expressed, we do not have enough thrust to escape the effects of the black hole," Dr Zorn explains.

Phantom Sam had already started working on Sam's original plan of last resort, replies.

"The real Sam was working on various solutions to our predicament Doctor Zorn, but this does depend on a few requirements. Professor, is it possible to pressurise all the unoccupied levels without activating them?" *Phantom* Sam asks. Professor Brookes considers this for a moment.

"In theory, that should be possible—we do have surplus power for now. But why?" Professor Brookes asks.

"All in good time, Professor. We also need to do this within the inhabited levels as well. I realise this might not be the most humane thing to do, but considering one side wants to eat our flesh and the other side desires to take over our minds, I would say they deserve it," *Phantom* Sam replies. Dr Zorn looking a little irritated.

"None of them asked to be taken over or corrupted in this way," Dr Zorn says.

"But all of them have committed the most atrocious crimes to be sent here in the first place," retorts Professor Brookes.

"Jessica was innocent of any crime; how can we be sure no one else has been sent here by mistake or just to be silenced?" Dr Zorn replies, now standing up and becoming irritated.

"Please, both of you. This has in no way been an easy decision to make, but it needs to be done. In all probability, we are the only ones left alive, and if we do not do this, Jessica will most assuredly die," *Phantom* Sam says, interrupting the two. Professor Brookes sighs and types in a few commands as the breaching pod's door slides shut.

"Pressurization of the facility will take two hours. I hope you know what you are doing," Professor Brooke replies. Dr Zorn sits back down, buckles himself into his chair, and starts running system checks on the engine.

Phantom Sam closes her eyes and instructs her bio-nanites to disable the oxygen generators' automatic hydrogen-venting process and the production of additional water within the facility's unoccupied levels and then runs additional update with Prototype.

· · ·

On the Prototype *Phantom,* Sam checks the space's status around the black hole and notices the addition of a third facility and that the cryostation's weapons system has been repaired. With an approximate time dilation of twenty-one hours in the real world to one hour passing on the facility, rapid change is expected.

Another change since last time is that the patrols have been increased but still keeping their distance from where they last detected the prototype. This is good news, and *Phantom* should be able to use this to her advantage. It's also interesting that the Federation hasn't sent out a fleet in an attempt to recover their stolen property. There are various reasons for this, and the one that seems most likely is that they are unable to spare the resources at this time.

Sam's original plan of last resort could have worked with the inclusion of the prototype's arrival; however, this is no longer an escape but rather a relocation to one of the other facilities. The fact that the patrols are keeping away from Facility Zero should help with this added complication.

With the black hole being the centre, each facility is placed around it in the formation of a clock face, with the cryostation hanging centrally above the facility. The patrols then help to secure the areas that the cryostation cannot adequately cover. Spending spare time watching the patrols and identifying their patrol routes and patterns helps with the preparation.

Reaction times of the cryostation will be the deciding factor for this escape attempt's success or failure. Finally, with Sam's consciousness developing well, nothing is left to do other than return to Facility Zero.

• • •

Phantom Sam opens her eyes to urgent shouts from both Professor Brookes and Dr Zorn, calling out her name and replying to each other regarding the facility's status.

"Power fluctuations now affecting all occupied levels. All the walls are down, and I'm detecting unauthorised access to the elevator shafts. Levels twelve to twenty are sealed off and still secure," Dr Zorn shouts across to Professor Brookes.

Hearing sounds of gunfire and explosions from below doesn't help with the acute dislocation of time. *However, phantom* Sam is now starting to appreciate what the real Sam must have felt due to the relative time differences between observer and participant during their previous chats.

"What's the status of the pressurisation?" Phantom Sam manages to ask.

"I'm glad you decided to come back. All unoccupied levels have now been pressurised, and we have noticed a dangerous buildup of hydrogen. I hope you know what you're doing, as the eight occupied levels have reacted to the pressure changes on their levels. This has forced them to stop fighting each other and start focusing their attention on us," Professor Brookes replies as another explosion booms from below, closer than before.

"The infected faction has breached security. What do you have in mind—which, by the way, Professor Brookes and I thinks is insanity—which you might want to consider commencing very shortly," Dr Zorn responds, looking shaken after the last explosion.

"Fair point, Doctor. Professor, please seal off the landing/jettison tube and begin pressurisation. I have ordered the internal pressure doors to close on each level," Phantom Sam says.

"I really hope you know what you are doing," Professor Brookes replies as he enters the commands and mumbles something under his breath about painful deaths.

Ignoring his words and fears, Phantom Sam continues with her plan.

"I'll need you to carry out an explosive decompression with levels two through eight, one at a time—and this is the important part—each level must be jettisoned as the pressure equalises. I've disabled the safety protocols, so all you will have to do is select the corresponding level to jettison them," Phantom Sam explains.

"You crazy son of a—" Brookes's expletive is cut short as the pressurisation warning alert sounds.

Dr Zorn goes pale with fear as Professor Brookes opens level two external doors to the inner docking tube.

The sound of the structure's complaints from the facility's stresses and strains echoes upward as the inner tube doors hold. Then gunfire erupts within security as someone below fires up at the pod's hatch.

With just a single command, the facility's inner docking tube, where dismantled pods are discarded and jettisoned, opens up toward the black hole. As this external hatch opens, the whole facility begins to shake, and the gunfire below abruptly stops.

Within a matter of seconds, the occupants of level two are sucked out of the facility, followed by a thunderous vibration as level two is blasted away from the rest of the Facility. The jettisoning process helped along by explosive charges to propel the separated level away from the rest, preventing any sections of the discarded level from damaging the station. Then a whine and hiss of air is heard as the third level is opened to the black hole and the vacuum of space as the vibration continues.

The central inner docking tube is now being used as a rudimentary thruster. The only reason this kind of thrust has any kind of effect upon the black hole is the gravitational bubble reducing the pull from the black hole to zero mass. The stabilisation beams' primary purpose is to hold the station in place, preventing the facility from moving toward the black hole, and even then, they can't exert force upon the station to prevent the upward thrust.

The third level is jettisoned, and the fourth floor is opened up, causing another blast of thrust. The station becomes lighter, and each additional thrust has more effect than the last as the station slowly accelerates. Hence, the vibration rising up through the structure.

"Security alert. Stabilisation beam one has been deactivated. Cease your actions, or an additional beam will be deactivated. You have thirty seconds to comply," The station's security system warns.

"Professor, open floors five, six, seven, and eight once you release floor four and jettison them at the same time. When the bubble drops, we are going to come to a sudden stop. This thrust will not be enough, so open the internal doors on floors nine through twelve. Once the bubble drops, you need to open up a single door and release the hydrogen/oxygen mix and ignite it using the pod's fuel burn-off protocol. After that, hold on tight. It's going to be a rough ride," Phantom Sam explains, and with total concentration, Brookes punches the button to jettison floor four and follows *Phantom* Sam's instructions, opening the level's external doors and releasing another burst of power, greater than before, as the facility lurches away from the black hole but still at a relative slow crawl.

"Security alert. Stabilisation beam two has been deactivated. Cease your actions, or this facility will be released. You have twenty seconds to comply," The system warns once more. Dr Zorn, now having regained some of his composure, laughs at the last announcement.

"I'm pretty sure, Professor, you never considered this, anyone attempting this," Dr Zorn asks. Professor Brookes gives Zorn a quick smile acknowledgement and concentrates as the seconds count slowly down to zero.

Then the gravitation bubble drops, and as expected, the facility decelerates at a neck-jarring speed. The breaching pod structure objects to the external forces but remains together.

"Now, Professor!" *Phantom* Sam calls out, and on cue, Professor Brookes releases the oxygen/hydrogen and ignites the explosive mix. The facility's central core burns with untainted fury as the acceleration increases once more and pushes Phantom Sam, Brookes, and Zorn back into their chairs.

"Doc, at the first sign of danger or when the last level of the facility is jettisoned, whatever comes first, you will need to punch the pod's thrusters and release, regardless of the optimum range," Phantom Sam shouts out over the noise.

• • •

Private First Class Collins awakes with a jerk of his head at hearing the alarm sounds. The double-length shift has taken its toll. He lost yet again at cards, and the wager this time was extra shifts. More importantly, the forfeit was to work Private First Class Benson's shift, an additional nine hours on top of his own.

The watch shift's primary task is to monitor the facility's status, mainly to do with escape attempts, and other than the first attempt almost twenty-five years ago, nothing ever happens. Computers could monitor this, but the command wanted a human backup.

With bleary eyes, Collins tries to focus upon his task at hand as he reads his terminal.

'Facility Zero out of position. Gravitation field offline.'

"System, how long before Facility Zero falls into the black hole?" Collins asks the monitoring system.

"At the station's current trajectory, this will not occur for another ten minutes," The computer system replies.

Well, that doesn't make sense with the gravitational field off Private First Class, Collins thinks to himself.

"System, show me Facility Zero's current trajectory," Collins asks, and Private First Class Collins's jaw drops as he watches the system display Facility Zero's trajectory.

He activates the station's emergency alarm, and the chief of operations responds.

"Collins, you do realise it's 0330 hours. What is the emergency?" chief of operations, sounding grumpy.

"Its Facility Zero, Chief. It's moving," Collins replies.

"Ah, okay, Private. Run system diagnostics, and send repair teams down to the gravitational array. How long does Facility Zero have before it cannot be retrieved?" the chief of operations asks.

"No, Chief, you misunderstand me. It's not falling; it's accelerating away from the black hole."

· · ·

Dr Zorn holds back with the breaching pod's main thrusters until the last possible moment when he is certain that the top-heavy facility can no longer maintain its stable trajectory. The black hole's pull has helped maintain stability up to this point. With the main thrusters activated, the pod uses the top of the facility as a launchpad and accelerates away, fighting impressively now against the pull of the black hole.

The facility's own acceleration turns into an uncontrollable spin, but moments later, the thrust dies, and then the facility slowly comes to a halt as the gravitational effect of the black hole wins the constant struggle and drags the first facility of its kind to its final moments.

But the breaching pod's own thrusters weren't designed to carry more than one on this return trip out from the black hole, and even though the modified thrusters managed to thrust the pod another ten kilometres away, they too are fighting a losing battle. Then, with a sudden loss of thrust, the pod decelerates.

Professor Brookes and Dr Zorn look toward one another, horrified, but Phantom Sam's eyes remain closed.

•   •   •

Back in control of the prototype, Phantom Sam watches the breaching pod thrust away from the facility.

"This is going to be close," she says out loud—a human trait, she muses momentarily, and then she puts her mind back in focus. Accelerating to full speed, Phantom Sam plots a curved trajectory toward the black hole and then out again, coming up behind the breaching pod just as the pod's thrusters are showing signs of an imminent malfunction or power loss.

Getting in as close as possible to the pod, the ship's main hull in phase matches the speed and then veers across the pod's trajectory. Just as the thrusters fail, the prototype comes out of phase on top of the pod as the cryostation's main proton lasers fire at the pod, landing a direct hit upon the prototype.

The weapon fire hits the hull's crystalline structure and scatters out across the surface, leaving behind a black, scorched impact mark several inches deep within its hull. The cryostation does not get the chance to fire a second shot before the prototype goes back into phase and then vanishes from sight as it enters warp.

17
The Watchers

WE ARE THE watchers, angels of Heaven no more. Our numbers once matched the numbers of the stars in the galaxy, but our work continues. We watch humankind and will not interfere, hinder, or help. We have watched the rise and fall of countless civilisations in many sectors of space, and we watched and recorded their histories. No more will we take part in conflicts meant to test the resolve of humankind.

The grand architects set the galaxy in motion, and their plan was a simple one: guide at first and then leave the sons of man to stand upon their own feet and wait for the great experiment to be complete. Then, either they will ascend, or they will become like stardust.

All obstacles placed in humankind's way had been planned, all of which they must overcome by themselves. We watched as the fallen had themselves wives and played god with the Eden worlds. We watched as mighty heroes the elioud left their mark upon the worlds; the stories of Achilles will last for all time.

We watched as the pantheons defined the myths of all the Eden worlds and became a part of humankind's development, and so these stories continue to leave their own mark upon the galaxy of Heaven until the well of light is finally empty, the final days will come to the universe; and in its last moments, we will be there to record the end of the great plan and the rebirth of the light universe. Then, the dark will no longer have dominion over the light.

• • •

After the great war with the Empire of Cain, it was soon realised that every world needed to be closely watched and guided so that such a travesty could never be repeated. When the grand architect sacrificed herself to balance Lucifer's betrayal, the Heaven worlds coped with this loss for another thirty thousand years. As the Eden worlds of humankind developed, they were watched and scrutinised. Laws were passed, commands were handed down, and worlds punished, but even the elders could not live forever, and so one by one, a suitable replacement is found.

The Magistratus, selected new elders from the returned light and their consciousness made whole once more; however, there were some among the various spheres of angels that believed this was a mistake. Within ten thousand years, the new elders had been replaced numerous times and created their own laws and made their own decisions and listened less to their advisers, and slowly the angels stepped aside to allow humankind to govern themselves.

With the twenty-four Heaven worlds' reformed council, the elders slowly amended the laws that the grand architects helped write. Records are vague regarding when the Heaven worlds became the Inner Worlds Federation, but many thousands of years passed as Heaven faded and the Inner Federation grew and became its own civilisation that continued to develop and grow.

The Inner Federation sent out a special set of laws and rules to develop by and gave these to the outer fledgeling worlds and invited them to join this federation. If they could develop and uphold the laws set down by the command world, then they too would be invited to join the Inner Federation; however, many worlds had found it impossible to change and remained in the Outer Federation.

• • •

Federation year 2436

With many of the great evils imprisoned within the darkness, the watchers still maintained their vigilance upon all those confined within them. However, not all the enemies of Heaven were captured or chose to fall. The great dragon escaped and continued to grow in power and gathered followers, but the watchers did nothing to prevent this rise to power. With Samael imprisoned and Chamuel lost, the great dragon's followers were free to travel the galaxy searching for ancient power and forbidden knowledge. They found some of this knowledge deep beneath the earth of a dead civilisation. Long gone were the people that once lived there, but the secrets that lay undisturbed for millennia retained their potency.

• • •

Jerad Bar carefully enters the ancient, long corridor with his research team following a discreet distance behind. Jerad and his team have been researching the ruins of this long-forgotten civilisation for the past fourteen months, a lucky breakthrough after deciphering a data terminal found on an abandoned outpost that led them to this city. They stop only a few feet within. These ruins once belonged to a high-tech civilisation with majestic cities spreading across the continents. The chambers and corridors beneath the surface are made from ornately carved stone—technology fused with stone.

Taking out a handful of dust from a pouch attached to his belt, Jerad throws the contents from his hand down the corridor. The effect is closer than he expected. A mesh of high-energy beams flares to life, hissing and flashing as the metallic dust scatters just a few feet down the passageway. Another step closer would have been the end, Jerad realises with relief. Then he takes out an ancient device of his own.

Opening the small black box, Jerad waits patiently as a dozen black snakes slither out and fall to the ground. Once there, they slither away down the corridor, some moving up onto the walls, others into the floor, and a few onto the ceiling. Minutes pass in silence, which is abruptly broken as sparks erupt from the walls, the floor, and ceiling, followed by smoke.

The corridor shimmers and vanishes, and as the smoke slowly clears, and an ornate stone door appears before them. Approaching this door, Jerad stops just before it and watches as the intricate pattern upon it pulsates brightly, almost like it's radiating life. Then a black snake appears along the edge of the great door, and then another and another, until all twelve snakes reappear and converge at its centre, forming a ball, slithering over each other until there's another spark of energy and the illuminated pattern sputters and goes out.

Jerad Bar holds up the black box under the ball of snakes, and they all slither back inside. Once the last snake has vanished from sight, Jerad closes the box just as the door begins to open with a blast of ancient dust.

•   •   •

Zophiel, an angel of the watchers, enters the great hall as eyes turn to regard his coming. Voices in the room's recesses continue to whisper unheard words until he stops within the centre of the great hall, and then everyone becomes silent.

"The followers of the great dragon have discovered and breached one of the Empire of Cain's great vaults. As a result, they now possess forbidden knowledge," Zophiel announces.

18
The Lost and Forgotten

Federation year 2436

PROFESSOR BROOKES, DR. Zorn, Frank, and *Phantom* Sam slam into their restraining harnesses as the breaching pod suddenly appears inside a small hangar. The artificial gravity exerts a downward force, causing the pod to crash into the floor and slide several feet before coming to a halt. A sudden, powerful feeling of nausea descends over Brookes, Zorn, and Frank, and they begin to vomit.

Phantom Sam gives the others a moment to recover, having already released herself from her harness, breaks the silence.

"Welcome aboard the Prototype."

. . .

After giving a brief explanation to the others regarding the ship and then helping them all into their cryotubes, Phantom Sam enters her own tube at the front of the ship. Moments later, *Phantom* Sam appears in the middle of Sam's apartment, Phantom's appearance in the guise of the original Sam, the lights on a low setting as Professor Brookes and the others stare around in amazement. The apartment once looking over London, but now each window showing scenes of space around the Phantom.

"What is this place?" Zorn says in bewilderment while the others continue to stare around, equally amazed and confused.

"Ah, this is my, well, Sam's apartment back on Earth. For some reason, it was what the ship decided to show me when I first become aware. As you know, we are sharing my Dreamtime, but you can all have influence over the environment by just exploring it. For example, if you open a cupboard expecting your favourite food, then you will find it," *Phantom* Sam explains.

"All very impressive, but why are we still here? I thought we all decided to go back and rescue my wife and daughters," Professor Brookes says as he turns from the view, looking annoyed.

"We plan to, but I took a direct hit from the cryostation meant for the pod, which means I need to repair the damage done. Otherwise, it will be easier to detect us when we go back. Plus, I need to adjust my shape slightly so we can dock with the facility," *Phantom* Sam replies.

Frank, having been quiet all this time, just looking around the room, but now he shouts out enthusiastically.

"You have coffee!" Frank calls out; finding a cup, he pours himself one and takes a long gulp of strong, black coffee. The others just stare, amused, watching Frank drink. It's Professor Brookes who spoils the moment.

"Do you think that's coffee you are drinking?" Dr Zorn says with a smirk.

Not understanding the joke, Frank looks confused and stares at his cup as Dr Zorn and *Phantom* Sam laugh. He then pours himself another cup.

"Oh sure, mess with my head, pick on the big guy. Besides, I don't care if it's all in my head. It tastes good, just how I remember it, and once I'm done here, I'm going to see if there is steak in the fridge," Frank replies.

"Feel free to make yourself at home, Frank," *Phantom* Sam says. Turning back to the professor, who is starting to look more irritable.

"Sorry, Professor, We will go back; we just can't rush it. Jessica is responding to the cryotube, and for the time being, she's stable, but for now, we need to plan. I'm guessing we can't just walk in there," *Phantom* Sam says as she notices Frank now dunking some kind of cookie into his coffee and smiles.

Dr Zorn sits down, and a console materialises in front of him, looking impressed. Calming down, Professor Brookes sits down next to Dr Zorn.

"Yes, sorry, I can't believe we managed to escape, and now all I'm thinking about is seeing my family again," Professor Brookes says.

"It's okay, Professor. Tell me what you require," Phantom Sam asks.

"Well, you're right about not just walking in there; it's an all-female facility," Professor Brookes replies.

"All female? I thought it would be mixed like Facility Zero," *Phantom* Sam says, now looking confused.

"Oh, certainly not. Facility Zero was an all-male facility, never wondered why Jessica was the only female?" Professor Brookes replies, looking grim.

"Okay, Sam never considered that, but If Facility Zero was an all-male prison, why was Jessica sent there?" *Phantom* Sam Asks

"I'm not exactly sure, but I'm guessing whoever was responsible really did not like Jessica one bit and was hoping that her time there would be very unpleasant," Professor Brookes replies.

"This guy, whoever he is, sounds like a bit of a jerk," *Phantom* Sam replies and takes a moment to check up once more on how Jessica is doing and finds her status stable.

"I think he's some high-ranking officer within the Mars Federation, but enough of that for now. If Jessica wants to tell you more, she will, if she recovers. But, for now, I need access to your system, and I'll see what I can do," Professor Brookes says.

"Sure thing, Professor, anything you need, just ask."

. . .

Dr Zorn spends the next few hours investigating the ship's systems and engine specs, amazed that there is no sign of a power plant to generate energy. He then realises why its energy signature is so low. Impressed with the design, he studies more on the material the ship is made from, asking *Phantom* Sam from time to time for access when he comes across restricted-access areas of data.

Meanwhile, with Sam's help, Professor Brookes goes over a crude plan to gain entry into the facility. Due to the Prototypes, primary material, the ship can alter minor aspects of its standard shape, enabling it to dock with one of the maintenance hatches that would have been used while the facility was being constructed. Dr Zorn and Frank join them later after realising that the access codes have been changed.

"Well, that hatchway is a perfect way of gaining access unobserved. It leads directly into the maintenance sections of the facility. It's the same one I used to gain entry on Facility Zero before. Admittedly Samael had already opened it for me, but how do you propose to get it unlocked?" Dr Zorn explains.

"Well, we are still working on that, but we can't connect to the facility's systems until we get in close due to the influence of the black hole," *Phantom* Sam replies.

"I've tried to access the communication module that Commander Taylor used to communicate with me, but so far, that's a dead end. At least we know for sure that my access codes will not work," Professor Brookes confirms, looking at the others.

"So, explain to me again why we can't use the breaching pod?" Franks asks, getting exasperated groans from Phantom Sam and the professor.

"As we already explained, the pod has reserve fuel, Not enough to land and return, also we can't make any fuel, and a breaching cutting tool is a onetime unit; it requires a whole new system to be fitted. Generally, a breaching pod is used once and then is discarded after the mission is over. The best it can be used for now is a temporary life pod, and to be honest, not a very good one," *Phantom* Sam replies in a controlled, calming voice.

Frank sinks back down into his chair and drains the last of his coffee as Phantom brings up a three-dimensional hologram of the facility and points at the hatch they have been discussing.

"I've been thinking, if we attach here so that we are in direct contact with the facility, could you use the hacking tool that Captain Elkin tried to use to gain entry to security?" *Phantom* Sam asks.

Professor Brookes looks back from the hologram to the hacking tool Phantom Sam is now holding.

"Well, that is a powerful device, but you saw what the security systems threatened when Captain Elkin's tried to hack his way in," Professor Brookes replies. Dr Zorn, now looking optimistic at Sam's suggestion.

"Ah, but that was primarily due to you trying to prevent the hack. If no one was fighting it, I think the chances are that the hack would have been successful. On the other hand, if you were to do something simple, like add your name to the administration list, the system might not react at all.

Besides, you designed the system; you know how the system works and reacts, so just don't poke it too hard," Dr Zorn suggests. Professor Brookes listens and then ponders the idea.

"You might be right. The system is designed to stop people from escaping, not breaking in. But I will need updated information regarding the facility's protocols. If we can get in close to the cryostation, I can attempt to access their system directly using my old commands, but failing that, I still have back doors I could try. This way, I think I stand a better chance of slipping through their systems," Professor Brookes replies.

"Good. Then we can give that a go. My systems are pretty much ready in any case. Besides, what's the worst that can happen?" *Phantom* Sam Says. Frank, still sulking.

"They detect us, and our little escape plan ends in a bright but painful explosion, and we all die," Frank says.

"Well, let's just hope that doesn't happen," *Phantom* Sam replies with a smile as the others stand, showing mixed emotions of concern and optimism.

• • •

An additional purpose of staying away from the area for a few days since their daring escape was to allow the ship to replenish its power cell. Healing takes a lot of energy.

With great care, Phantom avoids the cryostation's patrols and drops out of phase warp only a few kilometres above the station but remaining in phased stealth to lower the ship's detection profile. Being this close increases the risks of being detected as some phantom echo on the station's system, unlikely for sure but not very convenient, as this could result in a patrol being sent for a visual check. A moment later, the prototype closes in on the station and comes to a halt as the ship hugs in close to the station wall. The Phantoms own ship signature, if it could be detected, would be masked by the stations.

Opening her eyes, *Phantom* Sam turns and regards Professor Brookes. "It's all yours, Prof."

Doctor Zorn, having taken great care in connecting the hacking device directly into the ship's sub system's, Professor Brookes then activates the device and studies the readout. The hacking tool is rather more than its description gives it credit for. Although the professor has seen many devices like this before, this particular unit is remarkably smaller and more advanced compared to others of its type.

Its primary function is to detect and connect the user to any data node within range, connecting the user via vulnerabilities while subverting defences within the security systems and granting low-level access to the operator.

The small screen displays each step in the process:

Detecting access nodes...

Five low-level nodes detected.

Connecting...

Node successfully connected.

Accessing secure network...

Access denied.

Access denied.

Access denied.

Access granted.

Running system integrity maintenance sweep...
42,348 cryo-units online and functioning.
1,327 terminals online and functioning.
32 terminals idle.
2 idle terminals with sysops access-level clearance.
Connecting to terminal...
Terminal connected.

Professor Brookes watches, impressed, as the device completes its purpose and connects to a suitable terminal. Then, using the terminal's own access level, Professor Brookes remotes into the cryostation's main systems and accesses his old account.

"Looks like we got someone who's awake on the station, Professor. Patrols are heading our way. You have two minutes, max," *Phantom* Sam says.

That's not helpful, Professor Brookes thinks to himself. Listing his old access, which unsurprisingly has now been disabled, he quickly copies his access from Facility Zero to Facility One and then reenables his old access. Knowing his time is short, Brookes tags his account with Commander Taylor's access code and updates the system, hoping this will deter someone from looking too closely.

Update error. Access code suspended while under investigation.

Brookes reads the message with a mixture of concern and curiosity. Then, digging a little deeper into the system pertaining to Commander Taylor's predicament, he realises what the actual meaning of his last message was all about:

This will be my last message. They found out that the prototype was stolen and it was never recovered.

They are coming for You, Sam.

Commander Taylor's plan with Sam had placed him in danger. Sam was in a safer place for now, but his own was still in question, so he hid where he should be harder to locate and where Sam and Brookes might be able to discover him in time if they ever escaped.

Knowing time is short, Professor Brookes changes the low-priority tag placed on Commander Taylor's cryocell to urgent with Facility One's recommendation with just seconds to go.

Professor Brookes is still typing commands up until the last seconds, and then the connection suddenly drops. Seeing the last message appear on the display of the hacking device, Brookes sighs with relief.

Activity logs deleted.

•   •   •

The patrol comes in faster than expected, their previously standoffish approach now at an end. As the Prototype moves away from its hiding place, the Patrol opens fire but without luck. Each shot misses. Only one ambitious pilot attempting to fire his weapons manually, but at this speed, aiming proves impossible, and then the Phantom is gone.

"Wow, that was close. I hope you have good news, Professor," *Phantom* Sam says, now opening her eyes. Being the ship has its advantages.

"Good and bad news, I'm afraid, and some unexpected news. First, I've gained access to Facility One—at least I think I have. The bad news is that I did not have time to hide my changes as well as I would have liked, meaning any detailed searches might discover my presence, but I managed to reenabled my access," Brookes replies, pouring himself a coffee.

"Okay then, and the unexpected news?" *Phantom* Sam asks. Professor Brookes takes a sip of his drink and looks up.

"I found Commander Taylor. He sent himself here—well, to the cryostation at least. His status was so low on the priority list, his case would, in all likelihood, never have been heard," Professor Brookes replies.

"So, he's just going to remain there?" Dr Zorn asks.

"Ah, well… no, not now. I made some changes to his status. I hope our friend Commander Taylor will not be too upset when he wakes up and realises he's been sent to Facility One," Professor Brookes says.

"I'm guessing he will be annoyed or shocked at first, but it's sure the easiest way to free him from the cryostation, and I'm pretty sure he will understand. Now it's decision time. Jessica's condition is worsening, and we need to do something now, or we could still lose her. I know we already decided upon our course of action, but I need to hear it from you all," *Phantom* Sam says. Frank looks up upon hearing Jessica's name mentioned.

"We should go now. I'm in!" Frank says enthusiastically.

Dr Zorn just nods his agreement.

Professor Brookes, feeling grateful to the others but knowing his own reasons for going back are purely self-interested, remains silent but also nods.

"Okay then, we are going back. Oh, and, Frank, don't bang your head when you wake up."

• • •

Phantom Sam climbs out of his cryotube feeling stiff and heads for the galley to prepare several antinausea shots and vitamins for the others. Dreamtime food and drinks do nothing for the physical body, but all the cryotubes can provide is the most basic sustenance to keep the body from dying while in cryosleep.

Waking Professor Brookes first, Phantom waits while Brookes slowly climbs out of his tube and heads down the narrow corridor toward Sam.

"It's just the basics, Professor, but it will stop you feeling so bad and give your body some needed energy until we can get some real food," *Phantom* Sam says, handing over the meds.

Brookes takes the offered meds and uses them, his pallid complexion improving almost immediately.

Zorn is next to emerge, looking equally rough as he joins the others and takes the offered meds.

Waking Frank last, and as expected, there's a shout of alarm from Frank's tube, and then a dull thud, followed by cussing as Frank slowly climbs out, his large form proving harder than most to extract.

Professor Brookes and Dr Zorn are perplexed as Frank, louder than usual, continues his outburst of emotions as he stumbles toward the others while looking at his hands.

"What the hell is this? No fricking way—this can't be real!" Frank continues to say as he examines his new hand.

"It's okay, Frank; it's my bionanites and mostly your own body's natural regenerative ability, with a lot of help from the cryotube. While you were in Dreamtime, I manipulated your body's own bioelectrical potential, and with the help of my bionanites, the end result is your new hand," Phantom Sam explains. Frank continues to stares dumbfounded at his new hand while the others stare in disbelief.

"Thanks, Sam. This is amazing. I can never repay you for this, but whatever you need, I'm here for you," Frank says. Professor Brookes is already thinking over the meaning of this astonishing revelation.

"What have you done to us?" Professor Brookes asks, becoming serious. Still looking on in amazement, the others turn as Professor Brookes shatters the jubilation with his question.

"Well, there is absolutely nothing to fear. Every passenger that uses the cryotubes is connected via my bionanites. They are harmless to you, but the ship must monitor your status every moment of your sleep. It's how I've monitored Jessica," *Phantom* Sam replies. Brookes becoming annoyed about this news.

"I don't care why. You should have told us. I consider this a serious invasion of my privacy. I want you to deactivate all of them inside my body and delete any data you may have gathered," Professor Brookes demands.

The others remain silent as they watch, stunned by this sudden change of Professor Brookes's personality.

"I'm sorry, Professor. It's just the ship's standard protocols to take DNA samples and inject each passenger with bionanites, but I'm sorry—I should have mentioned it, so consider it done. If anyone else requires this, just let me know," *Phantom* Sam replies. Brookes stands up and heads down toward the cargo compartment.

"Thank you. I'm sorry for my reaction, but you should have mentioned this sooner, though I do realise this was done without any ill intent. I'll be in the cargo bay until we are ready," Professor Brookes says as he makes his way past the others. Dr Zorn and Frank watch as Brookes walks away. Then Frank turns to Sam.

"I, for one, am grateful. Thanks, Sam," Franks says, still marvelling at his new hand. Dr Zorn nods his appreciation.

"I'm sure he will calm down, but as Frank says, I'm grateful, and to be honest, I know how much these things cost on private health care," Dr Zorn says, Only Franking finding Dr Zorn's words funny.

"We'd best extract Jessica. It's a shame the cryotube could not do anything for her, but whatever Samael did to that blade, my nanites can't touch it," Phantom Sam explains and opens Jessica's cryotube.

• • •

Facility One, 65 days online: federation year 2436

With a slight clunk, the prototype locks into place upon Facility One's outer hatch. The light turns green to signify a good seal, and *Phantom* Sam opens the floor panel in the cargo hanger's floor, revealing a ladder leading down through the ship.

"This type of connection is unusual. Normally a ship or station would have some kind of umbilical connection, but for a good reason, Professor Brookes decided not to include such in his design," *Phantom* Sam explains.

Professor Brookes, having calmed down from his earlier outbursts, smiles.

"I never included in my designs a more suitable means to dock, considering once the facility was online and in place, this should never have been needed, but when I get the chance, I will submit a design change," Professor Brookes replies.

Descending the ladder into a slightly larger circular space, *Phantom* Sam activates the hatch release, and the outer bulkhead door moves inward momentarily before it slides to one side, revealing Facility One's outer hatchway.

"That would be very helpful for next time, Professor. Now, if you would do the honours?" *Phantom* Sam asks, motioning to the doorway.

Professor Brookes steps off of the ladder and bends down to the hatch in the floor. He enters his security clearance, and seconds pass as the system confirms his identity. If the cryostation guesses what the prototype is up to, the entire facility will be placed into lockdown. However, only moments later, the hatchway's lock indicator light turns from red to green as a release of air signifies the hatch is opening.

Frank's jubilant shout from above as the door opens causes the rest of the group to shush his sudden outburst.

"Let's not get carried away just yet," Professor Brookes says as he enters through the newly opened hatchway and descends into the facility as lights illuminate the small room.

"Here goes nothing," Brookes says as the group finally joins him, with Frank carrying Jessica. Professor Brookes addresses the system.

"System, this is Alistair Brookes, the chief architect. Please add Sam McCall, Dr Zorn Oken, Frank Russell, and Jessica Braose to the system and grant them admin access."

Another period of silence as everyone waits for the reply, which seems to take too long.

"Affirmative, Professor Brookes. Names added as requested. Welcome to Facility One, Professor," The Facilities system replies

"System, open a route to medical," Professor Brookes asks, feeling the stress and fear of possible failure even at this critical point all fall away and replaced with the elation of success as a corridor opens.

Wasting no time, the group rushes down the corridor, taking turn after turn, until they arrive at one of the main elevators. Minutes later, they enter the facility's medical room in an explosion of activity.

"We need help. My friend here has been stabbed," *Phantom* Sam calls out. Then he stops in his tracks as a woman turns from her desk at the sudden intrusion.

"Muna?" Sam asks in amazement.

"Sam McCall! I never thought I would ever see you again. How long has it been? Fifteen, twenty years? There was some news about your last job and then nothing. Most of us thought you were dead, but a few believed you hit the big time and decided to leave for good," Muna replies as she stands, moving over to Sam and giving him a hug.

Phantom Sam is stunned into silence. Then, as Muna greets and hugs her, a painful kick to Sam's ankle brings *Phantom* Sam back.

"Umm, mate, we need help for Abs. Maybe you two can catch up later?" Frank says, sounding slightly irritated.

Before Sam has a chance to say anything else, another woman wearing a lab coat enters the room.

"What the heck is going on in my examination room? Who are you, people?" The women ask, looking at Sam and Frank.

"Hey, Doc—at least I hope you are—my friend here has been stabbed, and she really really needs your help," Frank says, pushing forward with Jessica within his arms.

Looking unsympathetic for a moment, the woman casts her gaze over the group, her eyes stopping at Professor Brookes. She stares at him for a moment, and then she looks back at Frank and at Jessica in his arms.

"Okay, put her on the examination table, and then everyone else except Muna, out. You can all wait in the other room. I'll be with you once I'm done."

Reluctantly, with Frank almost having to push Brookes out of the door, everyone leaves. Only once the door closes, Brookes relent and find a place to sit down. *Phantom* Sam, noticing the change in him.

"Are you okay, Professor?"

Professor Brookes, looking slightly bewildered, replies after a few moments, "The doctor is my wife."

·　·　·

Several hours later, Muna enters the room, prompting everyone to stand. She raises her hands to delay the many questions already forming on their lips.

"Your friend is stable and should make a full recovery. Dr Brookes is willing to see Professor Brookes, and one other may visit your friend, for the rest of you, please come with me. The evening meals are now being served, and most of you look like you could do with some food," Muna explains and calls for a route to the main dining hall.

Frank's desire to see his friend quickly dissolves upon hearing Muna's offer of company and food. Dr Zorn also steps forward to accept Muna's offer as *Phantom* Sam, and Professor Brookes are already heading out of the door.

Entering the examination room, Dr Brookes is still standing over Jessica, who now seems to be sleeping peacefully. A surgical table is nearby, containing surgical gloves, swabs, and various fragments.

"I've seen my fair share of stab wounds, but nothing like the one your friend here had. Whatever she was stabbed with was growing inside her. I've never seen anything like it. However, once the object was removed, her body healed itself surprisingly quickly, leaving not even a scar," Dr Brookes explains, looking between the two for their reaction.

"It's rather a long story, but we're grateful for your help, Doctor. How long will Jessica be out?" *Phantom* Sam asks.

"Unsure, but for someone who was at the brink of death an hour ago, to be recovering so quickly is nothing but remarkable. She will wake in a few hours, but if I might ask a favour of you, I would like to speak with Professor Brookes alone. If you would not mind, go join Muna and your friends, and we will be along shortly," Dr Brookes replies.

"Sure thing, Doctor, and thank you," *Phantom* Sam says, looking at Professor Brookes, who nods and leaves.

• • •

By the time *Phantom* Sam arrives at the main dining hall, the room is alive with activity. Almost every table in the hall is empty except for just a few. Dr Zorn, eating alone, occasionally looks over at the crowded table that is the main source of laughter and mayhem. Some prisoners at the other tables also watch, making the occasional unheard comments.

Getting a tray of food, Sam joins Dr Zorn, sitting down across from him. Talking with such a racket is reduced to shouting and vague gestures at each other.

A sudden uproar of laughter makes Dr Zorn and Phantom regard the horde once more. Frank appears in the middle of the crowd, standing on a table and lifting two ladies on his arms like weights. The onlookers are impressed at Frank's feat of strength, responding with many shouts of encouragement and catcalls cheering him on.

Then, as if the volume is muted, the cacophony is silenced as Dr Brookes, along with Professor Brookes, enters the hall and gets their own trays of food and sits down next to *Phantom* Sam and Dr Zorn.

"Your friend sure has made an entrance," Dr Brookes says as she sets down her tray.

"Frank was a kind of celebrity on Facility Zero. He seemed to love his creepy ghost stories," Professor Brookes remarks.

"Yeah, except the creepy ghost stories he told come true," *Phantom* Sam replies.

"Fair point," Professor Brookes says. "Oh, and may I introduce to you my wife, who, I may add, has gone through hell trying to find me."

"Nice to meet you, Sam and Dr Zorn. I hear I owe you both my gratitude for helping my husband escape. And talking about going through hell, I also hear that your time on Facility Zero was terrifying," Dr Brookes says.

"It was not what I was expecting, admittedly, but somehow we all managed to survive, although I do owe my life to Jessica," Dr Zorn replies.

"I would say you are all doing pretty well now, considering that you still hold admin status when the system says that you are all supposed to be dead. Especially Jessica, who I'm guessing is ex-military by the looks of her dermal protection and incredible nanites," Dr Brookes adds.

"We owe a lot of thanks to Jessica and Sam, and although this is a most wonderful way to enjoy an evening meal together, I'm hoping now that Jessica is on the mend that we could all leave here as soon as possible, assuming we can find Frank again," Professor Brookes says, staring across the room to where Frank is now trying to lift his table full of ladies off the ground.

"Well, I was going to bring that point up," *Phantom* Sam replies.

"I need some time, as I have mentioned before. My current estimation is a year or two. If I leave now, I'll be back in a few weeks for everyone here. However, we would be cutting it close to be able to land and take off again. A few more weeks and the black hole's proximity will again cause us issues," *Phantom* Sam explains.

"I might be able to help on that score. After looking at the ship's specifications, I've been doing some calculations that might extend the power of your engines. It's a fine ship, but it's designed for stealth and has no real emergency thrust for desperate times. However, given more time and research, I'm sure I can improve on something already remarkable," Dr Zorn adds.

"Well, I'm not sure that I can just leave. I want to, but I have a few patients who need my care. So, I'm more than happy to stay longer; now I know my husband is safe. Plus, I would like to run a few more tests on Jessica to ensure her blood work is clear," Dr Brookes replies.

Professor Brookes is about to reply as two young women approach the table. They set a pitcher of water down in the middle of the table and then move around toward Professor Brookes.

"May I introduce Roselyn and Jocelyn," Dr Brookes says, smiling at her daughters. Professor Brookes is stunned into silence as he stares at his daughters, now at least fifteen years older than when he last saw them. The emotions become too much to bear.

Roselyn holds back, looking shy, but Jocelyn rushes in to hug her father. Reading this as the best time to leave, both Dr Zorn and *Phantom* Sam make their silent farewells and leave the dining hall, allowing Professor Brookes and his family to enjoy this reunion.

• • •

Facility One, 66 days online: federation year 2436

Although Dr Brookes could not find anything medically wrong with Jessica, she did not wake that day or the proceeding week, and as the weeks turned into a month, Jessica did not wake. With every test possible, giving no results, Professor Brookes took turns with Frank to sit with her. With no way of communicating with Sam on the outside, all they could do was wait and hope.

Facility One didn't suffer from the power issues that Facility Zero was cursed with, but this facility had its own issues in the form of gangs. Once the initial excitement of having men arrive at the station wore off, fights and arguments became widespread. Over the next few weeks, Frank ended up in medical three times. Not wanting to hit a lady even though dozens of frantic women were trying to lay claim to him, he ended up needing several stitches. For the next month, Frank avoided any and all contact with the female population except for Dr Brookes and her daughters.

He decided it was best to spend most of his time working at the bioreclamation level. Although at this point, even Dr Brookes's daughters refused to take his daily meals to him.

Further issues occurred when the facility rescinded Professor Brookes's admin access to have it reinstated again by Dr Brookes a few minutes later. This happened with increasing frequency.

Life within Facility One became more difficult with the news of Commander Taylor's arrival. Most of the inmates knew nothing of his background, but his status within the federation made him a tempting target for revenge for a small number of the most violent prisoners.

Having Professor Brookes there to greet him helped Commander Taylor transition from his penthouse lifestyle to life on Facility One. Even though Commander Taylor was angry at first that someone had messed with his low-priority-prisoner status, causing the cryostation to send him down to the facility much sooner than he had expected, this annoyance only lasted a short while. As the weeks passed, Roselyn and Jocelyn had arguments that became more commonplace during mealtimes, and slowly the sisters were seen together less frequently, until one day, only Jocelyn was seen working within the kitchen.

. . .

It felt strange leaving their friends behind when Dr Zorn and Phantom returned to the ship, although they knew it would be for a relatively short time, and now that the freakers were gone, this facility should at least be safe. Furthermore, this work should not take or feel too long at all—only a few short years, and most of that within Dreamtime. The cryotubes would prevent ageing, and there would be only occasional trips into the ship's structure for what Dr Zorn imagined would be slight modifications.

Opening his eyes, Dr Zorn finds himself back in the familiar penthouse apartment. *Phantom* Sam standing next to a strange glowing cylinder with complex circuitry and components at the base. Tubes of white light entwine along the central section, ending nearly six feet above the floor, where a golden aura of light pulsates within a crystal chamber. This light is considerably dimmer compared to the rest.

"What is that?" Zorn says, intrigued, as he joins Phantom Sam staring at this strange object.

"This is the real Sam's soul matrix that I mentioned before. It's only a Dreamtime representation of it, but I find it useful to have it here so I can easily monitor its progress. I have a similar one within the core of the ship. Once this is complete, I will return to the ship's matrix, and I shall place Sam's consciousness back in his body," *Phantom* Sam explains, looking pleased.

"So, this ship can house more than one soul matrix?" Dr Zorn inquires.

"Well, not normally. I had to modify the ship's core AI matrix to accommodate Sam's consciousness. This was not done lightly, as it means if anything happens to me in the meantime, the ship would not be able to add a new pilot," Phantom replies.

"So, let me get this right. This ship contained a core artificial intelligence computer, so what are you, if you are not the artificial intelligence?" Dr Zorn asks as he looks in awe at this technology, never having seen anything like before.

"Good question. My consciousness is not artificial; it's a copy of Sam's consciousness housed within a soul matrix designed by the inner worlds. Whereas the core AI simulates a consciousness, which then makes it artificial, one of the stipulations placed on this ship's designers was that the computer must not be artificial and required a human pilot. This stipulation put the project back decades," Phantom explains.

"Okay then, so why do you seem different to Sam if you are just a copy, and where did the technology come from to copy the human consciousness?" Zorn asks, feeling intrigued.

"Ah well, I might seem slightly different because having my consciousness merged with the ship's database of information has altered me profoundly as it's the only thing I've known. Sam might go through a similar change when our minds merge, but he will always retain his human experiences due to his early life experience.

Regarding where this all comes from, well, the inner worlds have been able to move consciousness from human minds for thousands of years, generally just after they die," *Phantom* Sam replies.

"Hey, hold on a minute. Why would the inner worlds move consciousness from the dead?" Dr Zorn asks with interest.

"That is one question I cannot honestly answer, at least not fully. All that I know is that the inner worlds have been selectively collecting minds for hundreds of thousands of years," *Phantom* Sam answers.

"For what purpose?" Dr Zorn asks, remembering his short time on the inner worlds as a young man.

"Unsure. But if I were to speculate, I would say it's because some minds are worth saving," *Phantom* Sam replies.

"I would have thought that all minds are worth saving," Dr Zorn replies slightly indignantly.

"That, Dr Zorn, is a question for philosophers to answer, and not a thief, although a very unique thief," *Phantom* Sam replies, smiling.

Dr Zorn returns the smile and, having no other questions, for now, heads over to his terminal to begin his project.

• • •

Dr Zorn's primary reason to visit was to improve the output of the prototype's engines; the designers had done a great job, but whoever designed the power conduits had designed them too small. The end result is that the engines could not draw more power than the conduits allowed, which meant weaker engines.

Although some of the answers Dr Zorn got from Sam left him feeling slightly disturbed, the work progressed well. He was still amazed at the ship's technology; the low-profile stealth was due to the material the ship was made from, which was also astonishing—a living crystal, unlike anything that Dr Zorn had ever seen before. Systems analysis confirmed that it was some kind of organic polycarbonate.

That was just a term for a group of thermoplastic polymers that were generally produced from various reactions between chemicals, but this living crystal was far more complex than that, and Zorn could not help but feel that the designer was hiding something.

· · ·

Federation year 2439
Phantom Sam transfers her consciousness back into the ship's main matrix and then transfers the human Sam's consciousness back into his human body, completing Sam's consciousness copy's final phase. *Phantom* Sam then reappears within Dreamtime in her female body and waits for the real Sam to waken and appear within Dreamtime. *However, phantom* Sam does not have to wait long, as Sam appears looking unsteady upon his feet.

"What the hell just happened?" Sam asks, looking slightly distressed.

"Unfortunately, you died, or at least your mind was mostly destroyed. I have masked your memories of the event so you would not suffer trauma. You will be able to access these memories as and when you feel up to the task. However, if we were to merge our consciousnesses as we tried once before, you would experience everything that has occurred during your absence, and this would quicken your recovery," *Phantom* Sam says as she watches Sam carefully.

Sam looks around his apartment, the memories of him being here before slowly surfacing as he sits down at one of the terminals.

"If we merge, won't we have the same issue as before?" Sam McCall asks.

"No, Sam. You're no longer on the station. Dr Zorn is currently sleeping and will be awake soon," *Phantom* Sam replies.

"That's good news at least, do it, merge our minds, but if you can, do it slowly," Sam replies, placing his head in his hands.

As before, Sam's mind opens, and the limitations of his human brain are swept away. Almost at once, Sam knows everything that *Phantom* has experienced, from the moment of his birth to this present time, from his encounter with Mandel and Elkin's to the escape from Facility Zero to the building of the soul matrix, and every conversation with Zorn. Yet, Sam realises this is just the beginning. He feels another presence within his mind. *Phantom* is there, watching, waiting and knowing everything that Sam is thinking.

"This is astonishing; I can feel the ship moving in space, the energy that it is absorbing… I can observe all around me, hear communications between the patrol ships, and even feel something near. Something is watching the facility or us," Sam says in awe of his newfound senses.

"I've noticed them too, but I can't determine where or who they are. You might find separating your new senses to just your actual senses less overwhelming. If you concentrate on looking inward, you will appear inside the ship's Dreamtime reality. Give it a few hours or a day or two, and you will find you can control your new level of existence as if you were born this way," *Phantom* Sam replies.

After a few tries, Sam appears back inside Dreamtime and his apartment.

"I can't always hear your thoughts?" Sam asks.

"We only hear what we need to hear. We are merged, but merging allows us to work independently of one another. However, if you have something I need to hear, as soon as you think it, I will know it," *Phantom* replies.

Dr Zorn appears, yawning. As he opens his eyes, blinking, he looks directly at Sam and then toward *a woman*.

"I'm sure there's a reasonable explanation, but I can't think of one," Dr Zorn says as *Phantom* Sam walks over to where Sam is sitting and smiles.

"Morning, Dr Zorn. I imagine this might look a little odd. This is *Phantom*, and I'm me again," Sam explains, referring to the female version of Sam, who continues to smile, finding the whole situation amusing.

"The easiest way to explain it is that while I was in Sam's body, I appeared as Sam. And now that the real Sam is back, I thought I would appear as the way I feel I am, but personally, I would prefer you to call me Samantha," Samantha replies, causing Sam to grin at her.

"I almost feel like my own ship is a cross-dresser," Sam says as he begins to laugh. His remark earns him a shove from Samantha.

"You can cut that out. I'm certainly not a cross-dresser. It's how I felt as I grew up. Maybe it's some secret part of your own subconscious desires, considering I'm a copy of your consciousness," Samantha retorts with a wink at Dr Zorn.

"Now hold on one damn moment. I do not have any secret desires to be a female, but I'll admit, that dress does suit you," Sam replies, becoming agitated, his reply making Samantha smirk. Dr Zorn looks on in mild shock and remains silent as the two continue to exchange remarks.

"Okay, I'll admit this is not what I expected, but I'll say this: I'm certain the original designers did not expect this outcome," Dr Zorn says, cutting in. Both Sam and Samantha laugh at Dr Zorn's words.

"To be honest, Doctor, I'm just as shocked," Sam replies, smiling.

"So, what's next?" Dr Zorn asks.

"Now we dock, get supplies, and see how Abs is doing. Then, anything after that, we can discuss as a group," Sam replies.

•   •   •

Facility One, 150 days online: federation year 2441
The news of Sam and Dr Zorn's return spreads fast, giving a much-needed boost to the group's morale. Dr Zorn explaining that Sam will join them shortly. He shares news of the outside world, including Facility Two's construction and the serious turn the war within the Inner Federation has taken, with one out of the original twenty-four worlds now under enemy control. Life within the facility seemed more like a holiday than a prison.

•   •   •

Going to see Jessica for the first time since stepping back on the facility, Sam enters medical, his memories of his mind death still causing him nightmares. Pulling up a chair, he takes Jessica's unresponsive hand in his and stares at her for several hours, listening to the sound of Jessica's steady breathing.

"Nice to see you again, Sam. I was starting to wonder when you would be back," a familiar voice breaks the silence, causing Sam to feel fear creep up his spine. He turns to see his fear realised as Samael seems to step out of the darkness.

As Samael steps closer, Sam fights, or flight instincts want him to run, but instead, Sam regards his enemy, Samael's face half-burned with nasty-looking blisters.

"What do you want, Samael?" Sam asks, realising already what the answer will be.

"What I have always wanted. I wish to leave here, and you are going to carry out my request," Samael replies calmly, with not a hint of anger.

"That is not going to happen," Sam responds, but a dreadful feeling that's building within his mind is already telling him that he has no choice.

"Oh, but, Sam, you will, and we will go shortly. You know, it surprises me how two girls can grow up together but be so different. Take Roselyn, for example. Now that girl has issues. Sure, with professional help, she would have recovered," Samael says with sinister intent. Sam listens, terrified and unable to speak, as Samael continues,

"Well, until I decided to break her, mmhmm. Such a sweet, innocent girl. She will make a lovely addition to my angels."

Having heard enough, Sam breaks out of his paralysis and leaps at Samael. But Samael is waiting for this, hoping for this. Instead, he backhands Sam's attack, sending him flying across the room.

"This is what you will do now. Take me to your ship and fly us away from here, or I shall break the other girl and then her mother, and once I'm done having my fun, I shall return here, and I'll kill your pet. You think you have saved her, but all you have done is given her a slight reprieve from my vengeance," Samael's says, his anger now showing as his dark, shadowy wings begin to grow from behind his back and pure hate burns within his eyes.

"You son of a bitch. I'm—" Sam starts to say but stops midsentence as Samael turns toward Jessica.

"Or I could always start with this creature," Samael raises his hand to strike.

"Stop! Okay, you win, but we leave now, and you will release Roselyn and do no more harm to the others," Sam pleads as he stands up. Samael grins with pure malevolence.

"What is broken will remain broken. However, I shall not widen the crack, and the others I shall spare if we leave now," Samael replies.

Sam, feeling that his choices have finally run out, nods and exit the room with Samael following.

"System, give me a route to the primary maintenance hatch," Sam asks as a corridor opens up, and Sam enters, not rushing but taking his time as he desperately tries to think of a way out of this.

His mind still merged with *Phantom* wakes suddenly as Sam thinks, *'We have a serious problem. Read my recent memories. Inform Dr Zorn if you can. We are about to go for a ride.'*

Arriving at the open hatch, Sam climbs up the ladder with Samael following close behind. Upon entering the cargo bay, Sam then closes the last hatch and climbs into the breaching pod. Samael stops, staring at it.

"If you wish to leave the facility, then you need to get in here, or you can just sit on the floor out there, and we can shout at each other rather than talking from comfy seats," Sam explains. Samael hesitates a moment and then enters the breaching pod.

"Do not try any tricks. I can easily go back and kill your pet," Samael replies. Sam takes a seat and belts himself in as Samael closes the hatch and does the same.

"You know, for an angel, you have some major trust issues," Samael regards Sam for a moment.

"For an ape, I find your scent almost too much to bear in this enclosed space."

"Thanks. I'll take that as a compliment," Sam replies.

He then speaks to his mind again, *'You know what I'm thinking of doing. It's not something I like the idea of, but get it ready. I'm taking the helm.'*

With the ship's sound decoupling from the facility, they move upwards and head out and away from the black hole. Their speed is slow until they exit the gravity bubble, and then Sam applies full thrust. The strain on the ship is immediate, as the black hole's mass tries to crush and drag the ship back down toward certain death. Even phased-warp would not help so near to the black hole.

The changes to the main drive that Dr Zorn had been working on for the past few years pay off, and slowly the ship pulls away. With a look of triumph, Samael turns to regard Sam.

"I am grateful to you, but I cannot allow you to return to your friends. Instead, you will accompany me on my journey," Samael says.

"That was not the deal," Sam replies, unbuckling his belt and standing up.

"I do not remember ever saying I would allow you to leave," Samael says, smiling as Sam starts for the hatch.

"Fine then, but I need to go check on a few things first," Sam tries to open the hatch, but Samael grips his wrist and squeezes hard, making him wince in pain and forcing him to return to his seat.

Knowing what choice he has left, Sam buckles himself in and tells the ship to jettison the breaching pod. The pod slams both Sam and Samael hard into their restraints as it is ejected and spins out of control. The breaching pod's inertia stabilisers slowly regain control. Samael, realising something is wrong, strikes Sam across the face, leaving wicked cuts down one side of his face.

"What are you doing?" Samael asks.

"I really hope this is going to give you one hell of a bad headache," Sam replies.

With the two minds of the prototype still merged, *Samantha* has heard and felt everything Samael inflicted on Sam. She knew what was coming and felt saddened that all she could do now was wait for the command; she did not have to wait long.

"Now!"

Sam McCall's body flops forward, and Samael begins to bellow in hatred as he watches Sam's soul; his consciousness vanishes as the breaching pod explodes in a flash of white light. *Phantom* repeatedly fires into the breaching pod as long as she dares, hoping to destroy Samael.

•   •   •

Jessica opens her eyes, standing upon a grassy hilltop as she watches the fallen descend to Earth in incandescent balls of fire. Time seems to have no meaning here, but she watches as the angels choose to fall rather than be imprisoned.

One of the fallen smashes into the ground near her, turning the lush, green hillside into a blackened crater.

The impact does not disturb Jessica, and as she watches, a dark-haired man stands up and walk toward her. Stopping just before Jessica.

"You look so much like your mother," he says and wraps his arms around her and gently kisses her forehead.

"I am so proud of you, Jessica, but you are needed. You can still save him. You can save them all. Remember, what does not kill you will make you stronger!" The dark-haired Angel says.

"I do not understand," Jessica cries out.

Before the man can reply, a shadow looms up from behind him. A tall figure moves in closer as his dark, shadowy wings open wide, stretching to the skies.

"Traitor!" he shouts.

Jessica wakes up with a start within medical, finding the room is in darkness.

"Sam?" she calls out, but no one answers her.

Epilogue

Federation year 2441

DR. PEARSON ENTERS the ward where all his hopefuls are now sleeping peacefully. It must have been a terrifying event for them, but we all need to do things we would not normally deem acceptable in a civilised society. He stops at the first bed, noting that the medical card's name has been erased and another name added. The nurse assigned to this ward walks over to greet him.

"Good evening, Doctor. I do hope everything is as you expected."

"Yes, thank you. I thought I would come by and see how they are all doing," Dr Pearson replies and smiles and notices that the nurse's yellow and green mould patterns mark her as a new conversion.

"Oh, very well, Doctor. There were many screams and protests at first, but it did not last long. The only real issue was that some of them wetted the bed during the process, but I've been told that can happen from time to time with children, I hear," the nurse informs the Doctor.

"So, I hear, Nurse. I'm very interested in how Jacob here responds to treatment. Please let me know when he wakes up," Dr Pearson asks as he looks closely at the boy's mouth. The signs of the mould are already starting to form around his temple and slowly vanishing from his lips.

"Very well, Doctor. Is there anything else?" the nurse asks, watching the doctor look at his notes.

"No, that's all. Thank you, Nurse. Have a good evening," Dr Pearson says as he takes a quick look at his notes and then leaves the ward feeling very optimistic.

·   ·   ·

Samael, the angel of death, once a leader of millions and imprisoned since the end of the last war in Heaven, emerges from the exploding breaching pod just as the prototype vanishes into phased-warp. His anger for revenge blinding him at first to the many eyes now watching him. Slowly Samael understands and remembers the main fact: he's escaped at long last; he's free from his imprisonment and now free to get his revenge on the galaxy.

"You have stood guard for all this time, and now your charge has escaped his prison. Come now, stand before me, and we shall conclude your duties," Samael calls out and waits for his wardens' response.

Slowly, one by one, lights the size of small candle flames ignite and grow in size. This continues until a host of angels appear before Samael, and one of their numbers comes forward.

"We were chosen to ward your imprisonment; return now, or we shall force you to," The Angel commands.

Samael watches as the angels reveal themselves. He smiles broadly at the assembled host and transforms himself to his ancient form, towering above the other angels. His eyes begin to gleam with fire. Wherever he looks, his gaze reveals the hidden, leaving no place to hide.

With sword and shield in hand, Samael strides forward and begins to slaughter all in his path. With his shield, no angel can harm him, and with his sword, no angel can withstand his wrath, and the angels of light perish in moments. Not a single one is spared, and as each angel of light dies, a small fragment of a pure-white crystal is all that is left, and the galaxy dims with their passing.

• • •

Jerad Bar stood upon the impressive ledge miles above the ancient machine. He knew that his life would be over with a misstep from this height, but death held no power over him. Very little in life did. Only this current project caused some concern, but his scientists and engineers insisted that the machine function after months of work.

The great vault turned out to be more than anyone ever expected. The discovery took everyone by surprise. Deep within the hollow planet, the research team discovered the world machine. However, this machine was unfinished. For reasons no one understood, the empire of Cain could not or would not complete their great work.

The great dragon's followers activated the world machine, and the air around Jerad Bar grew warm. Adjusting his eye protection, Jerad Bar watches as a ball of light appeared at the centre of this hollowed-out world. His scientists had chosen a remote area of space for this first test's target location. Moments later, the light vanished. Jerad Bar turned back to the control room as his team read the final results.

"Why did it close?" he asked.

"We are unsure at the moment, sir, but our long-range observation post reports a substantial increase in solar mass in the targeted system. Preliminary results would suggest that an artificial black hole existed in the area for nine-tenths of a second before collapsing."

•   •   •

Zophiel has been receiving many reports of late, but this one causes him some anxiety. Confirming the report, he leaves his station and enters the great hall. As always, eyes turn to regard his passing. This has happened more often since these reports have been arriving, and each time Zophiel enters the great hall, all within know immediately that news of great importance is about to be revealed.

"It is how we feared. Samael, the angel of death, has escaped his eternal imprisonment. More than a thousand of our kind are vanquished. What shall we do?" Zophiel asks.

The archangel and leader of the watchers stands and addresses the great hall, answering Zophiel's question.

"We shall do what we have always done. We shall continue to watch."

Author Biography

Robert D. Gallagher has worked in information technology for over thirty years. *The Hobbit*, by J. R. R. Tolkien, prompted his love affair with books, particularly science fiction and fantasy. He currently resides in Devon, in the United Kingdom.

Appendices

1 Justin Martyr, "Second Apology."

The lost and forgotten Series

Prototype (Published 2016)

The First Empire (Published 2021)

The Third War

Revelation

Hunting Dragons

Printed in Great Britain
by Amazon